INTO THE WILD

Axe Druid Book Six

CHRISTOPHER JOHNS

MOUNTAINDALE
PRESS

CONTENTS

DEDICATION

This book is dedicated to you. But there are so many people who have helped me along the way. The moderators and admins at the GLS, without whom none of this could've been.

The good folks at Mountaindale Press who believed in me and continue to push me to be the best I can be.

My loving wife who supports and believes in me. My pride and joy of a son, who likely doesn't yet know that these books are as much a part of my legacy to him as all I could teach him. I love you both. And to the wee one yet to be born, I cannot wait to read you all the books my friends have made. May you be as creative and wild as you should be.

And finally, my readers. This is only a few of you, but I want to thank each of you personally: Sean, David, Eli, Eric, Nick, Jay, Lucas, Tara, Ezben, DJ, Tyler, Brandon, Doug, John, Nathaniel and your wonderful daughter, Sergio, Victor, Abe the Smith and your lovely wife, Maurice and so many more. I may not say your names—but I want each of you to know how much you mean to me.

Thank you. All of you.

With deepest love and respect,
Aptly and wonderfully dubbed,
Star Fox.

ACKNOWLEDGMENTS

I hereby freely acknowledge that there are authors out there whose work astounds and dumbfounds me. Their worlds are as intricate and vast as the stars in the sky, and yet here you are. You've stuck with my friends and I through all of this, and here we are together for this wonderful journey. Thank you for being who you are and for trusting me to bring you on this adventure with a bunch of jerks just having a good time.

CATCHING UP

So, those of you who've made it this far have seen how far we've come. We, being my friends and I. Let me just reintroduce y'all so everybody is up to speed, yeah?

Yohsuke – My brother from another mother who I served with in the Marines. Fast friends for a while now, he's my best friend and he's a real O.G. gamer. You know what it is. He's our spell blade with a pact to a demon and an abomination elf as well. Half drow, half high elf, all angst. Also happens to have recently contracted vampirism, you know, because that's a thing.

Jaken – A goofy, surfer-like gamer buddy of mine from home who recently had a darling little girl. Proud papa and powerful paladin of Radiance. His Fae-orc avatar is a little wild at times, but he's a super nice dude. Admit it, you like him.

Bokaj – One of my former coworkers at a local gym, guitarist and singer for a band and a lovely musician who finds time to school me in most games. He's a little cold at times, but that's mainly because his avatar is an ice elf and he's distancing himself so he can fling arrows like a little kid flings boogers.

Let's not forget his psychotic, tail-biting asshat Tmont, house cat and panther companion.

Balmur – Our Azer dwarf buddy who is also a friend from the gym who I would sit and talk about the latest and greatest RPGs with when we weren't spotting lunks. Super awesome guy, though he can be a bit quiet at times. Useful trait as a rogue, you would think.

James – Another buddy from the Marine Corps I met through Yoh. He's a New Yorker through and through and he can be a little confrontational at times, but he's working through all that. Meditation helps. He's a little more dragon than half-dragon, half-elven lately due to a bad trip on some black dragon magic. His wings are fucked up and weird, but we love our monk.

Muu – Jesus Christ. This guy is my roommate back home. Lovable, affable, and has *no* idea when to shut up. His antics make his role as a fighter all the more reasonable because his mouth has a tendency to piss people off. Funny as he is, he's a damned fine addition to the team and we're happy to have him as our dragon-kin dragoon. Green-scaled asshole that he can be.

Maebe – Where do I begin? Queen of the Unseelie Fae, Lady Darkest, and ruler of my heart—my beloved wife. Crazy, right? Believe me, I know. She's been stuck in the Fae realm sorting things out and I miss her terribly.

Vrawn – Maebe and my... uh... you know what? Fuck it— Vrawn is my/our girlfriend. We love her in our own ways and while I'm dumb and stupid, she seems to really like us both. This whole relationship is just odd to me, but it works so who cares, right? I've even heard this kind of thing referred to as us being a "throuple?" That's wild, but I digress.

Kayda and Bea – My babies, my lovely, sweet girls. Kayda, my storm roc companion whose very birth I helped with has been with me since almost the beginning. Her wisdom and council saw us all through tough times and I would be lost without her. Bea... well, she was a nuisance for a little while, but through some of my own faults, her awesomeness, and liking to eat things that seriously should be thought about more, she's become a little different. Though she wasn't in the best of shape last we saw her.

Then again, neither was I.

And I couldn't honestly tell you about the others, the people who had sailed here with us aboard the Pussy Willow, or even the great sea dragon who helped us fight the massive kraken possessed by one of the final generals of War on this planet. Five of them, and we had killed two, almost killed the third—the kraken one ate him, I know it was weird—and the final one seemed to be eluding us somewhere on the Continent of Beasts. Those of you keeping count, that's still two alive, feel me? Cool, moving on.

After an almost week-long fight we had managed to catch some Z's thanks to Samu, an angel of Radiance's. With it, we had a fighting chance, but no one but Mother Nature herself had seen the sea dragon coming. And boy, did he come to fuck shit up or what?

Injured in the conflict, his blood poured into the ocean and coated us all. Making the living beings sick, and eating the magic away from everything it touched.

That meant our weapons, armor, gear, and the collar that held Bea had been lost.

In a huge sacrifice of strength, Mother Nature saved my gust raptor partner and gave her back to me but, like me, she was mighty sick. A dire otter called Milktongue rescued us on her behalf and had been tasked to care for us while we recovered.

Only thing is, I don't know if we will. Things have been weird around us lately, massive beasts roaming closer and closer, driven mad from the attack on one of the oceans' four guardians. Without my magic, sickened by the blood of the ancient beast, and alone save for a younger and weaker Bea, I don't know if I'm going to be able to pull it out of my ass to get back to my friends.

I can only hope… I can only hope that my friends and loved ones are okay.

CHAPTER ONE

"Please eat something, Bea-baby, come on," I muttered to her as the little reptile whined and refused to eat the fish I weakly tried to nurse her back to health with.

Milktongue, her giant otter self, watched us matronly from where she rested after fishing for us and trying to get us potable water. Not easy with the ocean and all, but there had been fresh water nearby and she took my water pouch to get it.

You know, since all my magic was gone and all my enchanted items had been reduced to normal bull crap. Not that I could even manage to lift them. I felt like an awkward teenager all over again, only muscular as fuck without the strength.

Suck it up, dude—you're alive and your friends and loved ones need you to pull your head out of the sand to get to them, I growled at myself.

The sickness hadn't been all that bad at first, but the second day I had a fever that had been so bad it dried out the cooling seaweed that Milktongue and her mate brought and laid all over my body to help me.

Her mate... he was something. Larger than she was by more than half, and his body seemed to have natural spiked protrusions that burst from his forearms and back like weapons and defensive growths. He looked like a badass, his dark, tanned fur wet all over his body. Though he looked like an absolute monster, he was super sweet. He had slept curled around me out of the water while I was delirious from my fever, trying to make any noise I could to get help from someone with healing magic.

I swore then and there that once my magic returned, I'd never take it for granted again. I didn't know how Muu and James did it.

Thinking about my brothers had me more than a little worried, but I was sick of being able to do nothing so I did what I could.

Two days after my fever had spiked, I began to feel a little better and had focused on getting Bea to eat.

Grasping her jaws and pulling as hard as I could, I poured water into her mouth so she would at least stay hydrated and pulled her head onto my lap. It was all I could do before feeling like I was going to pass out from fatigue. I panted there against the cool cave wall and watched the ocean waves rise and fall against the white sand. The brackish blood of the ocean guardian Orlow'thes still in the sand.

The blood didn't even seem to stick to their skin, and I was grateful for that too. Luckily, the foul shit had no sort of effect on either of the dire otters and for that I was so grateful, because apparently Milktongue was a hugger.

She would come over and chitter at us happily, lick us like we were her pups, and then smack our sides with her hands before heading away for some her time or to eat.

When I could breathe somewhat normally, I pried open Bea's mouth and shoved a little of the clean raw fish into her. I washed everything they brought us with water so it wouldn't be contaminated. Hopefully. She tried to spit it out but I clamped my arm around her muzzle and held on for dear life.

"How can you have any dessert if you don't eat your meat?" I tried joking tiredly. My body wasn't the only sick thing on me.

You try being funny without being able to function as a human being. Shit's hard.

She fought me hard enough that her fore and rear claws dug weakly at my skin, lines of blood dribbling out of my shallow wounds.

Finally she stilled and I saw her throat bobbing as she swallowed the morsel. Shortly after that, her stomach gurgled noisily and she relaxed and opened her mouth. I found myself smiling at her despite the pain in the ass she could be and fed her some more. She ate excitedly for a moment, then the sickness overtook us both in a wave and we stilled again. Soon after that, I gave her some water and closed my eyes to sleep.

Sometime later, I woke to sniffing coming from the opening of our little hiding spot. Really, it was only a shallow cave in a cliff side that hid us from sight and sun, but not from everything. For a moment I thought it was Spike—yes, that's what I called Milktongue's mate, get off my back.

But the wolf-like head that appeared in the doorway was definitely not Spike.

It snuffed toward us and when its eyes found me, it growled, bluish fur standing on end and crackling with unseen energy. Eyes lighting up like distant thunderclouds.

I had nothing in my inventory that I could possibly throw at it except food that we would need if anything happened to our caretaker, and I wasn't about to try to throw my only available and usable weapon at it in hopes I could get it to go away. I had a small rock I could weakly lob at it, but that might just piss it off.

I swear to whoever is listening right now, I will never take having a big ass axe for granted again, so please help me get this fucker out of here! I smiled and made soft noises at the creature for a second, but it just started to drool.

"He-he-hey there, big fella," I tried to greet him in my best friendly-mid-western way. "Listen, I feel like shit, and so does the squirt here. So unless you're with Mother Nature's posse, it'd be just great if you could fuck off?"

More growling, globules of drool dribbling down its bared fangs to the ground, small jolts of visible electricity arcing from it to the earth below. "That's a neat little trick, man. Show me how to do it?"

I slid Bea off my lap with my good hand and then scooted forward to put the majority of her behind me. Tiring as it was, the threat of immediate danger helped to give me a little more strength. If only to protect her.

To give her the chance I thought she would never have again. I blinked at the wolf, prepared to face it down as I mentally scoured my inventory for something—anything—that might help me in this moment. I had daggers and shit that I could try to use, having not really thought about the piddly weak shit that I had collected from low-level mobs before coming here. They would be kind of heavy with my lack of strength but if I could time it right, I might be able to cut it and make it run. It would be interesting to see if I could beat the hell out of it with my bad arm.

As the wolf inched closer, I steeled myself for the lunging brutality of the attack and whipped out a small dagger that I couldn't even read, because the system messages were blurred for some reason.

As it threatened to crush me, I stabbed forward with the blade, piercing its flesh by the throat, teeth tearing into my right shoulder as I did. Electricity shot through me, but it did little more than make the wound grow numb.

My life, already significantly drained from fever, began to wane. My health bar faded fast until a much larger figure, and then two more, stepped into the shallow cave. The largest of them snatched the wolf away from me. Whatever it was followed the wolf out seconds before Spike and Milktongue clambered over to stand before us protectively.

Roaring ensued, what sounded like great thuds and the tearing of flesh followed by yelps of agonizing pain and then silence before the larger figure returned. Almost too large to fit in the narrow area, this huge creature huffed and growled at

Spike and Milktongue as if it were speaking, sniffed the air, and then growled again.

Both dire otters turned to look at each other before glancing at me then fleeing the cave. The large beast smelled musty, large claws delicately sweeping for something. Could it have been me?

"Damn it, why would Milktongue and Spike leave us here like this?" I wondered to myself, shoulder still bleeding. My life draining slower now, but it still stung like hell and it wasn't stopping on its own.

I reached for the healing magic within me and as soon as I tried, I was met with a wave of nausea that pitched me forward and made me vomit violently in the sand. Then I felt the gigantic claw grasping me and pulling me by my slightly sundered armor.

I tried to wave the creature away, growling fiercely at it, but being covered in my own vomit and blood probably made me seem like much less of a threat than I was.

I made a last-ditch effort to stab my assailant, but the blade was unceremoniously slapped from my hand as I was flipped onto my back in time to see a gigantic bear's beady eyes and open jaws above me. The roar it hit me with was so loud and violent that my fur felt like it was in one of those hand driers in the movie theaters, that feels like it's just making your hands more wet as it blows on you. Yeah, that. Gross.

It sniffed at me and sat in the sand above my head, huffing almost indignantly at me while fiddling with my armor. Much like I had before, it found the straps and snapped them easily, but couldn't seem to figure out how to get it off me without aggravating my wounds, so it just tore the armor apart as best as it could and tossed it off to my right.

"Hey, that's not nice. If you're going to eat me, then just fucking do it, you big furry bastard!" I held up my fist defiantly. "I'll sock you right in your fucking snoot, you better be ready."

It eyed me curiously, scratching its belly thoughtfully before I asked, "You aren't planning to eat me, are you?"

A grumbling grunt, then a fart in my general direction made me chuckle, then gag. "Oh, oh that's rude. Eat me, please."

It leaned down and sniffed at my wound, the bear's long tongue falling out of its mouth to lick some of the crusted blood away. It must have found it distasteful because it grabbed its tongue and retched.

"Oh, now this has got to be the most insulting thing I've ever seen." Then it puked on my stomach. "I'll just shut up."

Five minutes later, Milktongue and Spike returned. Both of them carrying some kind of plants in their mouths. They both chewed the plants quickly, their whiskers bobbing with sour looks on their faces until the bear held out a massive paw. Each of them spat the green, wet goo they had in their mouths into the proffered paw and then sat right next to me and watched.

The bear growled at both of them, grunted, then put a paw on my chest. Milktongue laid across my legs and Spike grabbed my arms before the bear began to smear the green mess onto and into my wound. The pain was enough to make me scream, then the bear shoved the mess into my open mouth. I gagged immediately and went to spit it out, but the other—blessedly clean—paw grabbed my muzzle to keep it shut and it roared angrily at me.

I swallowed out of sheer instinct and began to hallucinate immediately. Voices entering my mind.

"You think he's gonna be alright?" a lighter voice, definitely female, asked from somewhere off to my left. "He's been out for a few hours now, and his wounds don't seem like they've been healing?"

Silence took me for a minute, then the bear's massive head appeared over me. I was suddenly aware of how much I was sweating when a cool draft drifted over me from the sea.

His mouth didn't move, but I could swear I heard, "Don't know. It's worked in the past, but the magic that enters his body seeps away as soon as it hits his blood. I've done what I can. The plants will heal him slowly, animal saliva keeps the wounds clean and activates the herbs. Anything else is in the Mother's hands. I'll be nearby. Do not leave them alone. I'll find some berries or something for 'em..."

The rest of what was said was outside what I could remember since I passed out shortly after that.

CHAPTER TWO

"No seriously, Milktongue, I think he's getting better, look!"

I blinked at the ceiling of our little cave blearily. My vision was spotty and I felt dizzy as I began to sit up. My shoulder was stiff as hell, but I noted that my health was fully restored.

Not only that, but I could actually sit up without as much of an issue. Seemed like a little more of my strength was returning.

And sure enough, at the mouth of the cave sat Milktongue watching curiously as Spike hovered near me, blinking quickly.

A feminine voice came from the cave entrance, "You're right, dear, I think he does look better. See if he's hungry?"

I blinked at that, confused. I hadn't cast any spells to be able to understand them.

I felt the large otter's paw on my right leg, Spike's usual way of getting my attention. He rubbed his belly and pointed to his mouth excitedly. "Are you hungry, little guy?"

I looked at him steadily, then quirked my head and raised an eyebrow. "How long have you been calling me that?"

The otter stared at me, clearly puzzled, before looking to his mate for help. She seemed to be just as shocked as he was.

"Didn't Mother Nature tell you I'm a Druid?" They watched me again, so I asked quietly. "Can you guys even understand me?"

Milktongue answered first. "We can, perfectly, but you aren't speaking our tongue. You're speaking Druidic. It's always surprising to hear from someone so small."

Druidic? The secret language of the Druid that allowed me to speak to nature itself? I could communicate with nature that way?

How much time would that have saved me if I'd known that.

"It's not a common tongue so it kind of got us going there." Spike smiled at me and tapped my leg. "As for the, uh, pet name? Well. Since we first laid eyes on you."

"That's… endearing." I actually smiled at him. "I'm sorry, I know her name is Milktongue, but what's your name?"

"Well, I've heard you calling me something." I said it and his face lit up. "Does that mean 'dad' in your tongue?"

I laughed then, hard enough that I felt a little sick from it and he frowned, which was pretty damned cute to see an otter do. "No, it's a name based off how you look, the spikes on your body?"

"Oh, my spines?" He tapped one and nodded his head. "I'm okay with that name then. This Spike."

"Cool, and what was that bit about 'dad'?" I raised an eyebrow at him and Milktongue joined us, wringing her large otter hands nervously.

"We don't yet have pups and Mother Nature said to care for you as if you were our own…" The silence fell heavily on me after that, her face doing the same disappointed frowny thing as her mate.

"So, you two adopted us?" They nodded at me and I shrugged. "I'm okay with that. I'm really thankful for all that you've done. Honestly, I think I still need your help, but how long has it been?"

"Since you were adopted?" Spike inquired helpfully. He clicked his teeth which seemed to be his thinking thing, and clicked his tongue. "Been about four days now. Mother said you were a quick one to recover, but not to let you be stupid. She said you would be a particularly, uh. Uhm…"

He looked at Milktongue for help and she graciously offered, "Difficult pup to handle once you got your mind set to something. She thought you would push yourself before you were ready. She wasn't wrong. What were you thinking, letting a raiko wolf get so close to you? Didn't your instincts tell you it was bad?"

Her sudden shift into super mommy mode made me flinch. "Well yeah, they did, but that gust raptor over there is like a daughter to me. I'd die before I let anything happen to her."

"That makes us grandparents!" Spike began to make a joyful sort of ululating squeak that he and Milktongue echoed back and forth to one another as they crowded me and pulled me close with their webbed fingers.

Oh, this is going to be a nightmare, I groaned to myself halfheartedly. Truth be told, I was kind of glad they were getting something out of this too. "Who was the bear that came in here?"

"Kuuma?" Milktongue raised her whiskers and sniffed my face and shoulder. "He's one of the nearest elders in good standing with the Mother. She asked us to find him and bring him to you should we be able to. We got lucky that he was scavenging nearby and could sense the raiko before it killed you."

"And what were those plants?"

Spike sniffed my shoulder too, and it made me growl at him when he touched it with his nose. "Oh, sorry, smelling for rot. Anyway, the plants are special herbs that grow in freshwater and in the sun that, when mixed properly with animal spit, have vast healing properties. When you put them on a wound like yours, it'll heal right up. But with the ancient one's blood in your body, it tampered with the healing and you only got a little bit of the benefits."

"Is rot common when using these plants?" I tried to move my shoulder and arm with it, but Milktongue stopped me.

"No, but with your condition, Kuuma couldn't be certain." She motioned for me to join Bea along the side of the cave. "This is a joyous occasion. I will fish for you, and then I will get Kuuma to check on you."

"Thank you, Milktongue." She chattered at all of us as I sat down next to my slumbering gust raptor and then she was off.

"Thank you for being kind to us," Spike began softly, drawing my attention to him. "Druids are very powerful beings. We try not to consort with them here."

"Why?" I frowned at him and he seemed uncomfortable for a moment. "Hey, I'm not going to get mad at you, or think you're not brave. You're taking care of me in my time of great need. That makes us buddies."

"Buddies?" He tilted his head at me and I chuckled. "This seems a good thing."

"Yeah, I have others, maybe you've seen them washed up on the shore?" I was hopeful but also worried, but he just shook his head. "You're sure you haven't?"

He nodded back to me, then himself. "No one else but you. And Druids go mad here. The beasts of this land are powerful, and young Druids who take the trial of the beast typically fail to return."

"Why is that?"

"They cannot contain the fury of the beast." He shook his head sadly. "I have seen it only once, but have heard it spoken of by my father, and his father before him. Even among the elders, the trial is spoken of in hushed tones out of respect for the Mother's lost children."

That's... weird. "What happens to them?"

"Well, like I said, they cannot take the fury of the beasts." He shrugged—or had it been a shiver?—then continued. "A young Druid found the spot in which he was to meditate and find the beast who most meshed with his spirit. It was a great wyvern, three times my size! When an animal is summoned like this, the beast must be conquered somehow. Whether by word, deed, or combat. But this is always done in the Druid's heart of hearts. Inside them."

I was trying to figure out how that could happen when he reared up, raking his body like he was attacking himself, slashing and thrashing about. Then I realized he was still telling the story.

"Then he began to bleed and instead of the animal waking up and devouring him, the Druid *became* one with the beast. Later on, it attacked the city of glass and sharps and died."

"What city is this?"

"The city where the dark ones live." He motioned to me. "Two leggies with pointy ears and many sharps."

"It attacked a drow city?!" I blinked at him, wondering whether it had been purposely trying to die or was just so consumed by a desire to kill anything that it hadn't cared about being in danger.

"Drow pointy eared leggies?" I affirmed the information with a quick nod and he clicked his teeth happily. "Good."

"No, no, drow are bad. Are they nearby? They could kill me."

He shook his whiskered head and cleaned a paw. "Dark leggies stay close to their sharps, don't go too far or close to here."

I breathed a sigh of relief. *Good.* "What do these Druids gain by taking this trial?"

"I don't know." He shrugged, no longer concerned. "Milk-tongue or Kuuma may know. You can ask them if you like. Hey! Let's take a nap."

He excitedly skittered toward me and Bea, who had just begun to stir when the giant otter laid over her and she settled back in.

I had to admit, his body heat was difficult to ignore, like having a living, breathing weighted blanket with hands to pet you nervously as you slept.

It sounded creepier than it really was.

Some time later we woke up to the sound of something being dragged into the area and we all found Kuuma pulling a large doe of some kind in front of the cave.

"I've brought a different type of food, so that their health may benefit." I could hear the wizened age in the bear's voice; elder indeed. He poked his head in and narrowed his eyes. "A nap sounds lovely. Have I woken you?"

I answered tiredly, "Yeah, but that's okay."

He didn't seem surprised whatsoever and merely sat down beside the entrance. "Come then, and let us speak formally."

Spike helped me stand even though I really was feeling a lot better. Bea even joined me, though she could only walk slowly, which had to be galling for her since she was designed for speed.

"Druid." Kuuma greeted me politely with a nod of his head.

"Elder Kuuma." I nodded my head back, but I spoke with a smile. "Thank you for rescuing me and my Bea."

He seemed confused. "Where is the bee?"

I chuckled and pointed to the gust raptor who had taken it upon herself to bite the ever-loving hell out of the carcass on the ground. The blood seemed to do a lot toward reviving her appetite and I was heartened to see some of her spunk returning.

"Ah, an interesting name for a creature so common here." He chuckled and sat back. "Tell me, what brought you to this continent?"

"I was chasing a great evil here, and while we were at sea, we were beset upon by a different beast."

"Yes, and this beast was the one who awoke Orlow'thes." The bear scratched at his thigh and clawed the carcass so Bea could eat a little easier. "His ire isn't something one earns lightly, and all here felt his wrath."

"I can imagine," I sighed and wished for the umpteenth time I could start a decent fire.

"You are well enough now, I imagine that you could handle

a little red meat." The wizened bear leaned forward to sniff at my shoulder. "No rot, good."

"My kind can't eat uncooked meat, or we will get worms or get sick." He looked at me as if I were nuts and then nodded.

"I see, so you require cooked food?" He frowned at me. "How have you been eating fish then?"

"Sushi?" Personally I never cared for it myself back home, but I knew that some fish could be eaten raw. Like the tuna they brought me. Plus, if I got a rock hot enough, I could cook the fish a little.

"Young one." Kuuma turned to Spike who stood up straighter. "Go and find the red-pain flower. Pull it out by the roots and be *very* careful."

The dire otter trotted off and left us alone.

"Spike said you might know something about the trial?"

Kuuma's large head turned back my way and he watched me quietly for a bit. Finally, he answered, "I do. I take it he told you something of it?"

"Everything but why it would be done."

Kuuma took a bit of the meat from the carcass and sniffed it. "I will tell you of it—what I know and can theorize—but I have another question of you. Answer mine, and I will give you my information."

"Go ahead and ask."

His head lowered until he could look me in the eyes. "How does one acquire the title of Friend of Bears?"

I blinked at him and laughed. "Oh, that? I'm friends with the bear queen near where I'm from. Her name is Kyra. I did her people a favor, granted one of her bears an honorable death in combat, and ended a curse in her lands that was driving the local animal populace crazy. We've been close ever since. Well, as close as we can be."

"Then you've done them a great service, and have earned that title," Kuuma grumbled almost to himself. "Then it seems I am to trust you, out of respect for a foreign queen's wisdom. I find this acceptable."

"Thanks?" I quirked a grin up at him and he nodded. "Your turn, it seems. What's the deal with the trial?"

"For centuries, those who called themselves close to nature among the tribes of leggies on this continent contributed to the land in many ways." He took a bite of his meat and grumbled while chewing. "There came a time of great magic and prosperity, when leggies and beast came together—harmonious existence abounded."

He belched and I snorted at him, flecks of spittle and blood bursting from his maw. "Forgive me. In this time of great unity, a powerful beast called Irgdarn had dreams of reigning supreme over his people and coveted the powerful magics of the leggies. Rather than working in unity and becoming one, he kidnapped his caller and tortured his powers from him. With that secret knowledge, he became too powerful to hunt and kill. He tainted the beasts, slowly draining their knowledge and minds from them until they had become little more than monsters to be hunted and killed."

"So why has it become so difficult for the Druids to do the ceremony?" I stopped that thought and added, "At least other than the rage the beasts have."

His silent thinking, pensive and controlled, was long enough that I heard Milktongue join us and put fish near us. "Where is my mate?"

The sound of someone moving across the sand made us all look as the dire otter hustled toward us with a large plant dangling from his jaws.

"Be careful!" Milktongue's voice went straight to worry as she moved to her mate's side, then in front of me. "These things are so dangerous, why would you bring it near our pups?!"

"It's okay, Milktongue." Kuuma comforted her and took the long plant from Spike. He pointed to the plant, red with thorns all over, but the craziest part was the fiery looking leaves. "This is the red-pain flower. If you shake it, or bleed on it, it will burst into flame. Observe."

He held it gently over a grouping of rocks, seemed to

rethink it, and piled the rocks in a circle. "Young ones, find wood for us, please."

Milktongue and Spike both darted off in opposite directions within the wood line and returned with their arms full of small sticks. They did this three times until Kuuma nodded at them to stop. Spike and Milktongue gathered themselves behind us and allowed me to lean against them and relax a little. Bea kept eating and I was worried she would make herself sick if she did, but that was okay for now. I'd rather she overeat for now than starve and be sick. Though if she got sick again…

Worry about that later, Zeke. I sighed tiredly and scratched my ankle.

Once a good amount of sticks had been put inside the makeshift pit, Kuuma shook the flower over it and sure enough a small gout of flame puffed out. This lit the sticks well and soon enough I had meat and fish roasting over the flames.

"Good. Where was I?" Kuuma asked softly over the crackling of flames.

"You were about to explain why the ceremony is so dangerous now." I poked a flank of meat and Bea watched me with her muzzle dripping blood.

"Ah, yes." He stretched his arms out to the side and shook himself out a little. "It's so dangerous because the two minds must compete for supremacy. They cannot become one as they used to because they fear the beast, and the beast cannot understand their intellect. They have been stripped and become opposites of the same rock. Intellect and empathy versus instinct and rage."

The phrasing was off for me, but I supposed that it worked. "And what do they gain?"

"The power of the beast." His teeth flashed for the barest second, and I heard whimpering behind me. I turned in time to see three raiko wolves slinking away from us. "You seem confused."

"I am. I already have many animal forms. Each as varied

and powerful in their own ways as I am." My fingers scraped my skull lightly, then I turned my fish and my meat over.

"If what I understand is correct, the forms you take are only as powerful as you are?" I nodded at his question and he chuckled. "The power of the beast allows the leggies to take on that beast's form and to use *all* of its power. Speed, strength, cunning —it would all be available to the Druid. All of it at any time."

My eyes widened in wonder, that would be amazing! But wait. "What about the beast?! What happens to it?"

Kuuma stared into the fire for a time, then simply shrugged. "I… do not know all of it. And I am not one to give misinformation." He scratched his head and stated, "I think it becomes stronger somehow. More intelligent? Again, just a theory."

"Thank you for telling me what you know." I bowed my head to him respectfully. As I ate, my body began to relax and the pain in my shoulder eased significantly.

"You recover swiftly," Kuuma observed. "Soon, you might be able to fend and hunt for yourself."

"I hope so. I don't care much for being a burden to you all." A shifting behind me saw me landing with an "oohmf" onto my back as both dire otters stared me down, hurt.

"Okay, I get it!" I held my hands up and they seemed to relax. "Never figured I'd be raised by otters."

"I never thought to see them so protective of a leggie, but here we are." Kuuma chuckled to himself and sliced more meat from the carcass. "How has the return of your magic been?"

"It hasn't come back yet." I bit into my meat and sighed. It was bland, but edible. "I'm hoping it'll come back soon."

"It will not," a new voice stated, joining us. All of our heads raised and Kuuma actually stood and turned to stare at a large snake, easily the same size as Lothir, maybe larger. And she had been nearly the size of a football field in length. His wide, triangular head swayed from side to side. "We had wondered where you were hiding, you lazy bear."

"I am not lazy, you worthless worm," Kuuma snarled back, but they seemed to lack the animosity behind their name calling to lend to their not being friendly. "What brings you away from your politicking?"

"It is not only I." The snake slithered closer to the cliff side and began to curl in on itself.

"We have all come." Another animal spoke, this one a black stag with antlers covered in metal of some kind.

Five more animals stepped out of the shadows of the trees to stand arrayed before us. The snake, the stag, a large chipmunk of some kind, a Kirin who looked just like Thor, a mole, and a beaver all staring intently toward us all. All of them much larger and more intimidating than their typical brethren.

"Why have you all come?" Kuuma padded closer on his hind legs, waddling as he did so.

"We come because we need to put something to a vote and it requires all of us." The stag stepped forward, his head lifted high. "The beasts are becoming more and more unreasonable —their rampaging is killing the animals of the continent and demolishing swathes of our environments. If we cannot find a way to calm them soon, then all will be lost and our kind will perish."

"Hold up." I stood slowly, moving cautiously toward the serpent who watched me curiously. "I'm confused about two things. One, are you not all considered beasts? And two, what's this about my magic not returning?"

"Bold for a leggie," observed the Kirin loudly, claws raking the ground. "To stand up and face death like that."

"Pondreth wouldn't eat the Mother's chosen in front of me," Kuuma growled and I could feel the reverberations from where I stood thirty feet away.

"Wouldn't I?" The serpent struck, jaws clamping shut just before actually getting to me. His tongue flicked out and lashed across my still-healing shoulder. My eyes crossed trying to watch the creature and he seemed to take pleasure in that. "We are not beasts, because we are not all gifted elemental affinities in the manner in which the beasts are. Nor are we quite so large and rare."

"But you're huge." I shook my head and motioned to him.

"I am. But I am also *ancient*—*we all are*—and my life is long," he explained as if speaking to a child. "Others of my kind can approach this size if they are cunning enough. As to your question, Orlow'thes' toxin will take roughly one year to flush out of your system naturally."

"I see. Is there a way to flush it out faster?"

The animals regarded me calmly but it was the chipmunk who squeaked angrily this time. "Quiet, leggie!" His cheeks puffed out and his fur stood on end as he hopped toward me. "More than just your life is at stake! Kuuma, we must vote on a course of action!"

"What course can we take?" Kuuma retorted finally. His paws shook as he spread them. "There are none among us who can stand up to the might of the beasts!"

I shook my head. "No, you can't." They all turned to me, the chipmunk ready to jump down my throat again. "Shut it, pipsqueak!"

It flinched and recoiled, but the others seemed to take offense and stepped forward toward me, so I held my hand out to hold them off. "Just listen to me—my brothers and I do this kind of thing *all* the time! We can try to find a way to calm the beasts down."

"As we understand it, it was you who woke Orlow'thes in the first place!" The beaver thumped her tail against the ground. "Your weakness was what allowed that kraken to consume as much as it did and allowed the great guardian serpent to be injured."

"We were surprised and outmatched, but we will find a way!" I insisted—pleaded—as I stepped closer. My body began to tire and it was hard to stay awake. "We made this mess, let us clean it up. All I need to do is get my magic back and find my brothers. From there we can try to find a way to reason with the beasts, and then kill the kraken."

The animals all eyed me dangerously. "He didn't flinch

when I could have struck him down where he stood. He seems brave."

"Or stupid!" The chipmunk squeaked bitterly. "Mice freeze when frightened too!"

Am I going to have to stab a chipmunk? My eyes narrowed at the little shit and he shook slightly.

"Weakened as you are, you stand no chance of making the journey to what could make you strong once more," said the mole, her soothing voice calm and collected. "To what could revive your magic and rid you of the toxin in your veins."

"I'm not alone, though." I motioned to Bea who was as uninterested in all this as she was most things these days. "Bea and I can do this. I will do *anything* to get myself and my loved ones back together. Tell me where to go and when we're well enough, we will be on our way."

"He does have a point." Kuuma nodded. "He is capable, and having witnessed his drive to protect what he cares for, we could stand to use him."

"But he is useless without his magic!" the chipmunk spat and I had to fight my body from moving toward it on its own.

"I'm not useless, but whatever." I shrugged. "Point me in the direction of the thing I need to get to flush this toxin from me, and I'll just leave you all to sort out your own problems."

"Silence!" the stag snapped and all of us quieted, the chipmunk about to say something anyway but the marvelous animal eyed his fellow and the smaller one quieted angrily. "We cannot stand by and wait while you regain your strength, small one. I am sorry for your loss, but you will not be able to assist us in this."

"What can we do? We can't summon Orlow'thes because of what his blood did." Kuuma shook his head and groaned.

"We can go to the cities and summon the other Druids, mayhaps they can be of greater use?" the mole interjected. Some of the other animals actually nodded agreement.

"If you had stated that from the beginning, you would have won the vote, why did you need to bother me?!" Kuuma fumed.

"Because you are part of this council!" the Kirin stated, her voice holding a note of thunder to it. "Your vote matters to us, as does your wisdom."

"Fine, I vote we ask the Druids from the neighboring cities and villages for aid." Kuuma turned and motioned that he was done with this. "For what little good it will do us."

"Kuuma has voted aye." The stag looked to the other animals who all raised their hands except Pondreth who held up a tail. "The ayes take it. Who will venture to the cities first?"

"I will go to the north in my territory and take Hamistea with me." The Kirin pawed the ground beneath her and the chipmunk clambered onto her back. They turned and galloped off.

The stag looked at the rest of the animals. The mole sighed and heaved itself below ground, then the beaver turned and headed down the shoreline, leaving the large snake and Kuuma.

"I am going to take the southern tip of the continent, though my territory is the heart of the wood. Maybe my presence will lend urgency to our plight. Kuuma, Pondreth, will you please take the west? You are both known as legends and they will listen to you."

"I'll go as soon as I can," Kuuma growled and the snake nodded his assent.

The stag turned and bolted away, leaving us all alone in the dying light of the evening sun.

"They should have taken up his offer." Pondreth laid his head on his coils forlornly. "Not many things stare me in the eyes as I strike and don't flinch. Brave."

"I've fought and killed a snake your size before." The snake's head rose from his coils slowly and he eyed me but I didn't back down. "She was eating child sacrifices and trying to make herself out to be stronger and better than Mother Nature."

Pondreth stilled. "You killed Lothir?" I nodded as he laid his head down once more, a small snakey-smile pulling at his scaled lips. "Good. Gives my kind a bad name. I'm assuming you weren't alone?"

I shook my head and recounted the fight against the wannabe goddess and her people. It had been a hell of a brawl.

"Well, that is very much an interesting tale." He scratched his chin on the cliffside, small rocks falling away as he did. "Then we really are in need of you and your friends."

He looked thoughtful and Kuuma seemed to sense where his direction of thought was traveling because he laid on his back and sighed. "It might mean we get kicked off the council for it."

"If it keeps us all safe and protects this continent? Who cares?" Pondreth snorted and turned back to me. "I would like to tell you where to go to have your body freed of the toxins within it. If I tell you this, you will help us. Am I clear?"

"Crystal." I sat down and listened intently. Not because I was getting schooled, mind you. But because I was starting to feel dizzy. "I would have done it anyway—not in the habit of letting others pay for my fuck ups."

"In the heart of the wood, many miles from here, there is an herb that you must consume with the water that flows from the Mother's bosom."

"Say what?" I raised an eyebrow at him, but Milktongue chattered excitedly behind me.

"It's her bosom! The tree shaped like the mother in the center of the wood!" She looked at Spike who had just begun to stir from his nap and smacked him on the rump. "Get up! Things are happening!"

"I'm up!" the otter cried and began to look around in confusion. "Hey, it's dark already?"

Kuuma's stomach bounced with laughter and the ass chewing Milktongue gave him was hysterical. I could imagine he wouldn't sleep tonight.

"You must mix the two, consuming one and not the other will just kill you with the toxin in your system." Pondreth's voice took on a grave tone. "Both are extremely powerful magical substances. Alone, they are potent, together even more so, but they balance each other. It's this balance that will burn the toxin out of you and return your magic."

"Okay, and how am I supposed to help you get the beasts under control?"

Kuuma looked over at me and answered, "Simple. You pass the trial of the beast."

CHAPTER THREE

It took another four days of eating well, drinking plenty of fluid, and sleeping an ungodly amount before my body felt completely normal again.

Well, except for the lack of magic. That, coupled with the fact that I still wasn't really getting my notifications, left me curious. I wasn't sure if that was from the toxin, or if something else was going on. What I did know was that while my magic was gone, I still had my stats.

But I couldn't shift. Like, at all. That had been painful for me. So, what did I do without magic?

"Thanks for getting all those herbs for me, guys." I smiled at Milktongue and Spike as they fidgeted together, watching me pack. "The otter spit too. That'll come in handy."

"Best way to get the herbs to work." Milktongue sniffed and Spike held her hand. "You sure you don't need us to come with you? Kuuma said that the other council members are mad that he and Pondreth helped you; what if they attack you?"

It was the twentieth time she had asked and I was tempted to just let them come along to get her to stop worrying. But they needed to be close to the water.

"They won't attack me because if the other Druids can't get the beasts to calm down, they still have me and my friends as a backup plan." I grunted and winced at the light that grew brighter outside from the cloud cover moving above.

I finished gathering the items that they had brought me and stepped closer to them before pulling them both into a hug. They patted my back no less than fifteen times and I chuckled softly at that.

"Thank you, but we need you here to care for anyone else who might need it." I reached up and pulled Milktongue's head down to give her a kiss on the forehead. "And besides, it's time to try for pups of your own now. You'll be great parents."

Spike grasped my shoulders and then licked me fully on the face, wet otter spit all over me. As I stood there frozen and confused, he squeaked at me and stated loudly, "I'm proud of you!"

I had known my real father on Earth for a little bit, but he was in and around and gone for most of my life, yet here was an otter I had known barely a week telling me he was proud of me? How many times had I thought this same phrase and not gotten to utter it to my son?

I opened my mouth and tried to think of something—anything—to say and drew a blank.

"He means well," Milktongue offered and I just nodded and patted his shoulder under his spikes.

"You guys be safe, okay?" I waved to them and they followed me to the tree line before I was off with Bea at my side. She was still quiet, sulking I could imagine, and since our tie was one that was magical, we no longer had our mental bond. It was just me and this gust raptor who could run off and be free if she so desired it. And I'd be unable to stop her.

"Let's keep our heads on a swivel, okay Bea?" I stroked her head and neck lightly and she ululated softly in return. So she wasn't completely alone and she knew it. Good.

We marched east toward the center of the forest where Pondreth and Kuuma had told me to go, but to keep to a reasonable pace. My body had recovered and I felt great, but that didn't mean I wasn't going to get hurt or sick ever again. Hell, I could fall back into a fever at any second if the toxin flared up.

At least that was how Pondreth had put it.

The animals of the wood stayed well out of my way, my lumbering steps giving them plenty of warning that I was coming.

For the first half of the day, nothing seemed to care that we were coming. *Seems that the animals around here must be pretty cool with people in their forest.*

My optimism was a little short lived though, as I had to hide from more than six of those raiko wolves. I felt confident taking one or two of them. It would be hard, sure, but I could do it. Especially with Bea as a distraction. I had a few things I could do, but with my armor and spells gone I was a little more of a lame duck than I wanted to be.

Hiding from them was hard, but there had been a log that had fallen against a tree that we had been able to climb up and sit in. The wolves could use lightning abilities, sure, but they couldn't reach us so it didn't matter. Watching them try to scrabble up our pathway had been pretty entertaining though.

That first night, Bea and I slept in the large limbs of the tree with the wolves waiting below us.

Night crawled by, dawn rising and giving way to the new day and more wolves below us. As if they had gone and gotten the pack.

"If I could shift, this would be no fucking problem," I muttered to myself. Then I froze. I couldn't shift, sure, but could I use weapon abilities? Except for Ravage and Bladed Storm, they didn't drain my mana at all. It was just for the weapon!

And that meant that I had a means of defending myself after all. But I would need to verify that.

I took out Storm Caller, inert as it was, and activated Devil's Hammer out of sight of the ground below and smacked the tree. A reverberating crack echoing around us made the wolves below begin circling the tree and me grin.

I could do this, it would just be interesting. I could wield the weapon thanks to my strength being so high, but it would still be a little ungainly thanks to the long haft. But I didn't have to worry about that for long.

I explained to Bea what I'd be doing and she just looked at me like I was crazy. "No, seriously, it'll be okay. You can run away and I can let loose."

She stared at me, almost deadpan and I sighed, "Okay, if it gets too bad, I'll run away. Alright?"

She blinked at me and shook her head.

"What do you mean no? This is going to work, watch."

With that, I took a header over the side of the large branch we'd been on and dropped toward the wolves below. Their slavering mouths opened and they began to crowd toward each other—good doggies.

I spun like I was flailing and brought Magus Bane out. I stared at the weapon, glad that it had been in my inventory when I took a dip in the toxin, and activated Charge and Epicenter at the same time. My weapon slammed into a wolf's head so hard that it exploded on impact and sundered the very earth beneath it, the wolves nearby thrown away from us.

Activating Feather Axe, I started my brutal dance of great axe and goofy lightning doggo death.

Magus Bane soared through the air in arcs and slashes, overhead chops and jabs with blade, hammer, and haft that had the wolves fighting to get to me and not get sliced to ribbons. The burn in my left triceps made me smile as the exercise felt great.

In Druidic, I bellowed, "I'm not always this goddamn nice! So who wants out of this fight?"

Two or three of the wolves slinked away, their wounds bleeding and their tails tucked, but that still left another ten behind that seemed to just be more enraged.

"Then come get some!" I still had eight minutes left on Feather Axe and Charge only had a thirty second cool down.

I used Charge, swinging the axe in a near-perfect slice that gutted the wolf closest to me and then used the haft to shove his friend into another attacker. They fell to the ground in a heap of legs and snapping jaws just before Bea landed on the top one and began to bite the throat savagely.

"Yeah! Atta gi—oof!" One of the wolves had sideswiped me and almost bowled me to the ground, but I just rolled with the momentum and came up swinging. I tried to stab it with my metallic fist but I realized it was just like any nubby forearm and all that did was piss me off. So what did I do?

Glad you asked.

I clubbed him with the nub right on his weirdly-shaped wolf head. A spike of electricity shocked me a bit, but other than the measly 3% of my HP that I lost, it just made me growl at it. I kicked it into another wolf, activating Cleave and chopping through both of their bodies as they fought to stand. The few that had survived ran off then, Bea still ravaging their bodies hungrily.

"Good job, baby. I was a little worried you wouldn't be joining me for that one."

She just munched as she was wont to do, and I went about looting the dead. I got a couple fangs out of their mouths, which was cool. Maybe I'd make a cool necklace out of them? I'd have tried to take their fur, but doing a skinning job one handed seemed like an idiotic idea.

I checked my weapon and found it was fine, so I put it away and just got busy walking again with Bea licking her chops noisily beside me.

The rest of the day we spent much the same as the first, we would walk for a while, stop to rest, and then at night find a place to get some rest that was out of the way from anything finding us.

The screeching, roaring, and sounds of general mayhem

being unleashed upon the world weren't at all what I thought they would be.

"What do you suppose that is?" I asked Bea as we rested that evening. She laid next to me and listened as I did. Her heart raced in her chest and I tried to calm her and me. "Yeah, better not get too close to it. That would be an absolute *shit* idea."

Looking up at the night sky, I wondered how Maebe was doing. If she was okay. If Vrawn was alright. Kayda. All of my friends. It was harder to sleep just then. So much harder. But I did it. Under a sky that reminded me of my beautiful wife.

CHAPTER FOUR

Earth shook and I was suddenly awake and aware that we were *not* alone. I glanced around and saw that two creatures were clashing in the center of the clearing we had found. Rather than being the size of normal animals made larger like the ones I had seen with the otters and council, these *were* beasts.

One of them looked like a massive version of a raiko wolf, but had large wings on its back and a spiny tail, and the other looked like a bull, but had horns made of pure gemstone and shaggy fur dense with stones that clung to it like mats.

The two beasts roared and lowed at one another, charging and crashing into each other, biting and attempting to gore the other before separating and doing the same again. They kicked over more than three trees at least as large as the one we had bedded down in and I wasn't going to see if they would do the same to ours.

"Time to go, baby!" I lifted Bea unceremoniously into my arm and took off at a dead sprint, a raucous cracking and shaking coming from the tree as the bull's horn struck it.

Shaken loose, we fell as gracelessly as one might imagine

and landed in a rather thick berry bush that had stinking juices all over it that made me gag.

"Survive first and puke later!" I snarled at myself, diving out of the way just in time to miss a bovine hoof to the body that likely would have crushed me. Bea struggled and I let her down, ensuring that she followed the rising sun as I hightailed it the hell out of Dodge.

Once we could no longer hear their destructive violence, I had to admit, those two were pretty damned beastly alright. "I wonder if that's how all of them are, or if they vary in size."

We rested, eating some of the meat that I had cooked and brought along with us. It was beginning to taste a little gamey, and I didn't feel like it would be a good idea to keep eating it after today.

My stomach gurgled and I found myself reminiscing over Yohsuke's cooking. My mouth watering, I took another bite of my meat and gagged. Oh, I would enjoy his food so much more right now.

Bea seemed to be thinking the same thing and I had to be strong and carry on. At a good clip, we had traveled roughly sixty miles since we started. It was 'many' miles before we would get to the area where the herb I needed to find would begin to grow on the trees, right? Kuuma had said it was about four days' journey from the shoreline where we had been to get to the Mother's bosom shrine. And it would be before then that I found the herb.

Better just to walk it out and see what I could find. Bea stared at me, licking my shoulder where the berries had splattered against my gut, and then wretched, looking at me angrily.

"Okay, okay," I grumbled loudly. "We can hunt down some water and I'll take a bath. Otter baths were too embarrassing to take."

She nodded once and we both began to move, then she stopped and sort of barked at me.

"What?"

She barked again, and touched my nose with her own before sniffing loudly in the air. "You want *me* to hunt for it?"

She stepped back and nodded again.

"Awful talkative today," I grumbled loudly and she just ignored me. Typical.

I closed my eyes and began to sift through the scents in the world around me. Dirt. Trees. Grass. Blood from the fighting beasts far behind us. Droppings and… hm. Water?

"I think I found some. You wanna check for me?"

Bea blinked at me and then quirked her head to the left as if to ask where. I lifted my hand and pointed toward where I had found the watery smell, northeast a way.

She shoved me with her head.

"You know, your life is at stake here too." My complaining just made her shove harder and I just set aside my discomfort and began to work through trying to actively separate the scents around me to try to find what I was hunting.

Half an hour of slow walking later, we found a small brook of water and I fought hard not to jump up and down with joy at my find. It wasn't enough to go into and actually bathe, but I could damp a cloth and wash myself. So that's what I did. I also spent some time washing Bea.

As I wrung out the rag for the third time, her scaled body leaning closer to mine, I hugged her. A scaled muzzle dug into my shoulder and I just held her, suddenly overcome by how I could have lost her and been all alone here. How I could have just lost her after we had finally learned to deal with one another and so that I could atone for neglecting her.

"I'm so glad you're alive, Bea." My voice muffled against her, she didn't seem certain how to comfort me, but I could feel her tail wrap about my lower body slightly.

Ten minutes later, I had finished cleaning her body and set about figuring out how to get us some food as we walked back toward our course.

The sky above us, broken by leaves, boughs of giant trees,

and small birds flying through the spaces between trees and branches.

The ground, littered with leaves, vegetation that seemed only to be growing as we went along, and an aroma of life that was so much nicer than the forests back near Sunrise.

Soon enough, we found a bush of berries that reminded me of blueberries and I sniffed them to make sure they were okay. Bea looked at them and turned away, but I thought it had something to do with her predatory nutritional needs as opposed to them being poisonous.

Before plucking them, I took a minute to check the ground and found multiple tracks to and from the bush and figured that it would be okay to get some of these.

The first one I ate tasted mildly sour, the purple of it not fully ripened I guessed. So I tried a more bluish one. It damn near lit my tongue on fire. I took a handful of them, put them in a small satchel for later, and put them into my inventory before going with the sour ones. Those ones were the safe ones, and I would be eating those and only those, holy shit.

The rest of our journey for the day we spent methodically having me scent things and begin to familiarize myself with my surroundings. It was hard going, but by the end of the day, I'd slaughtered a lone raiko wolf and we ate meat and I had a good sour glaze to put on it. Those flowers had come in handy, and I had a dozen of them squirreled away in my inventory for safe keeping.

As I rested that night, I found myself dreaming of my friends. Their predicaments and how I couldn't help them. I was chained inside my body, all the potential I had and none of the ability.

It was hard. And I woke up more than once with the telltale nausea caused by trying to use magic. The birds around us had quieted and life seemed to still, the air carrying a new scent. One that smelled like rot and death.

Frowning, I leaned over the edge of the large branch I had slept on and found a sort of armadillo-looking creature with fungi and corpses on its back walking beneath us. Animal, humanoid, and other kinds of bones attached to it. It was the size of a tank and moved as slowly as one.

Better avoid that fucking thing. I laid back down and tried to get some more sleep. I needed to be fresh for the next day, as finding those herbs was likely not going to be easy.

————

"Fuck, I hate being right…" Panting, I hid behind a lone tree in the area. This was *so* not turning out the way I had thought it would.

The plan was simple: bypass the flying monkeys, avoid the spores that they seemed to be immune to, and grab the flowers that I needed.

God, don't I wish it had been.

I got three before it seemed, smelled, and sounded like all the primates in a three-mile radius were gunning for me like I'd just stolen the cure for them *ever* needing to peel a banana again. They'd gone completely apeshit.

If I was right, I needed at a minimum one for each of my brothers, Vrawn, Kayda, and Bea. Oh, Tmont's furry ass too. *Maybe one for Odany?* Shit. I wasn't sure if any of them had been hit by Orlow'thes magic-nuking blood, but taking the chance just wasn't in me if I had a way to help them. So that meant at least eleven of the damned things. No telling who had been affected so better to over prepare.

Any attempt at communicating with the damned dirty apes came back with flying poo and indignant screeches. Chest thumping monkeys began to crowd this side of the tree line around me as well, and it was beginning to get a little too hairy for my liking. I inventoried the three flowers in my hand and took a calming breath.

Of course it can't be this damned easy. One tree in this whole place that has these flowers and it's a popular place for monkeys to come and do their… I need to stop monkeying around.

Even I smiled at myself despite the situation and glanced to where Bea growled at our surroundings. "Hey, we need more of them, and if we kill any of these guys, they may keep chasing us. Think you could run a distraction?"

She raised one scaly brow at me as if to say, *really*? "Then hop to it, little momma, we got shit to do!"

With a curt barking growl, she broke right and sped off around the trunk of our hiding place. Screeches filled the air and I cleared my head before breaking right as well. Legs and arms pumping, heart pounding, and my eyes taking in all that I could, I found my quarry. Three more of the blooms, golden leaves with crimson stamens and blue powder, clutched to my chest and went into my inventory swiftly.

Howling and chattering reached my ears, and I went for another section of three. Fuck it, we would go for broke. Three more after that and I would be good.

A furred freight train of furious fun found my left side and flung me away from the fucking tree. I grunted as my back, shoulders, and head cracked against the ground, but I let the momentum carry me into a somersault that put me back on my feet.

"Listen, Magilla, I need these flowers more than I need you alive." The large ape, silver chest and horned head, watched me angrily, beating his chest with fury. "Get out of my way, or I go through you."

Yeah, I was speaking Druidic and since all he did was hunker down, someone had to ring the bell.

Bea called twice and sped through us with four *literal* flying monkeys behind her, and the ape and I sprinted toward each other. I had enough time to put the blooms into my inventory before the bastard's meaty manglers came flying at my face.

I ducked under the right arm and whipped my left fist into his big hairy mug. A dull crack and his head rocked back, one of the horns broken, and it felt like one of my knuckles just disappeared. Trying to keep a fist was absolutely agonizing. And it being my only one made that *so* much worse.

Stepping off his chest, I grabbed two more of the blooms with my mangled left hand, snarling at the pain and then grabbing one with my teeth before legging it the hell out of there.

I could feel the burning in my mouth as my saliva touched the plant and slid back into my mouth.

I spit it into my hand and shoved them all into my inventory before running deeper into the wood.

Bea found me, blood on her muzzle, but several lines clawed down her flank, tail, and ribs.

"Hey, are you okay?" I tried to reach for her, but suddenly it seemed like everything around me was miles away. Through the tunnel vision and swiftly rising adrenal dump, I continued to race forward. "Okay, hun. Daddy's freaking out."

I heard her call to me, distorted echoes of her concerned barking calls reaching me after what could have been an eternity.

"I need you to find the water, baby. It should be about two miles from here, okay?" My fur was so hot. The temperature in this wood had become unbearable. I found myself peeling my shirt off as I moved, slowing slightly to get it over my head.

"Oof." Landing on my back did not feel so good. Finally free of that damned shirt, I glanced up at a green and black tree that swam in my vision. Then a weird-looking dog with sharper teeth than normal popped into my vision.

"No!" I screeched, my hands flying toward the creature's face. "No, bad dogula!"

Then I noticed my hand was gone. "What the fu—"

Suddenly I lay on my back with the world moving above me. My back itched like crazy, but I couldn't tear my eyes from my forearm where my hand and wrist used to be.

Tugging on my leg made me look down to see a long serpent waving above my head, gray and pink and swirling with other psychedelic colors.

"Pretty..." Drool pooled at the back of my throat and gurgled out of my mouth, sliding down the side of my cheek and neck. I closed my eyes for a few seconds and then was *surrounded* by cold.

I opened my eyes and fought to get out of the freezing water when something grasped me by the back of my neck and tugged viciously. I could breathe again, spluttering and splashing in the water, I looked up and saw what looked like a young Momma Nature in her fully nude glory.

More tugging and I could see the Dino-mutt looking me over like I was to be cared for. She tried to mimic eating something and I pulled the flower out. "Eat the plant and drink the water. Okie dokie…"

A snort of suspicious disgust came from the creature and I pulled out one of the blooms and put it in my mouth with some of the water and chewed it. *Gross.* I grunted and went to spit it out but a powerful set of jaws clamped down over mine with a bass growl. In fear, I swallowed and blinked as it let me go.

"That wasn't nice…" I began when I belched and smacked my lips together. "Ew."

The bitterness of the plant and the cool sweet tones of the water seemed to snap at one another inside my body, then my stomach began rioting. No matter how bad I felt, my body couldn't expel what was in me, even though I tried so hard.

Then the burning came. Flames so hot that they should have melted me and the grass I writhed on, and the layers of earth beneath me, roiled through me to the point that all I wanted was the sweet release of death, but all that came were swelling bursts of suffering punctuated by the sound of something in the distance echoing into the sky.

CHAPTER FIVE

Gray fog laid low all around me, the world softly creaking, croaking, and chirruping as though nothing were wrong. I tried to sit up, but suddenly Bea was there with her muzzle on top of me. I couldn't understand why she was so insistent that I stay where I was until I saw the shadows above us moving.

Had it been the monkeys? No, the shadow that moved across the area was much larger than them. Was it a beast? "What is it, girl?"

"Reeeaaaaaaaaaaaargggggh!" A long bellowing cry from above us rent the air, and the sound of wings whipping at the air spiked my adrenaline and heart rate fiercely. I reached out with my mind carefully and gave a small tug at the shadows, hoping beyond hope that whatever I had done had paid off.

I felt the cool familiarity of the void's embrace as they came to my call. I could have wept with joy in that moment, but figured I'd wait until we were safe. The shadows crashed toward us in a wave that covered both Bea and I as seamlessly as I could make them. A large, monstrous-looking bird with fiery wings and crimson eyes swooped down into the clearing and stared hard for fifteen minutes, then grew irritated and flew off.

I made sure the shadows would cut off sound, then uttered, "Thanks, baby."

She nodded once, then looked me over. She sniffed and tasted my hands and forehead carefully, but judged that I seemed to be fine and passed out immediately.

I covered her with a blanket, the wetness making me worry about her scales, and then began the trek through my notifications. I rolled my eyes as I did so; the main ones were for all the times that I had tried using magic only to throw up and pass out. I got one for giving my word. Another for a quest from Kuuma and Pondreth. It even looked like my notifications had changed slightly, which was weird.

Quest Received — Toxic Boogaloo — Kuuma and Pondreth told you in good faith about the secret herb and water combination that would rid your body of the toxin taking your magic. This was in hopes that you would help them with their beastly problem. Reward: Already gained, ???. Failure: Loss of aid and assistance from the wood's protectors and circle of elders.

I had given my word on this one already so I had no choice but to help. Didn't mean I had to do it on my own though. I sat up and touched Bea, making sure she was alright. My magic had returned, but it seemed to be recovering a little more sluggishly than I would have liked. I was only at half my full amount of MP and that wasn't much. But it was enough.

"Milnolian." I called to the Fae creature and hoped he was okay. "Tan'rbleth."

Both Servant and Yve erupted into the area from shadow and the water behind me, they prowled for a moment before turning their gazes on me. They seemed a little more feral than normal, not speaking to me but recognizing me somehow.

Worried, I decided it was more than time to contact Maebe and cast Shadow Speak. My mana drained and it made the bile in my stomach churn a little but it was bearable.

Shadows pooled in the area then formed a gateway of sorts and instead of her shadow form stepping through, Maebe herself joined me. I didn't even have time to look at her before she collided with me and the two large, cat-formed Fae yowled wildly.

"Zeke, my love, why have you been hidden from me?" Her sudden ferociousness was gone, leaving her there to sob against my chest.

"I was sick, and there has been a lot that happened, but we need to find the others." She looked up at me and I looked down at her. "I have missed you so much, my love."

I held up her ring and she touched it frowning. "What happened?"

I sat there and we spoke of events that had occurred while we were on our own. She gasped in horror at the attack we'd endured, but bit back her questions and comments. Finally, I told her of Orlow'thes and his toxic blood.

"So that is why I could not sense you when I returned to this world." She muttered to herself quietly. "This will not do. I cannot stand being away from you like this."

She stood and placed a barrier over her head, then it disappeared and suddenly I knew Xiphyre was coming. Once more, the little Ragalfr stood in the air with his legs spread wide, naked and angry. "This had better be good!"

I reached out and stopped Maebe from lashing out at him, then I noted the look of shocked awe on his face as he stared at Maebe. I blinked at him and then joined and found myself similarly shocked.

She was no longer as short as she had been, and now she was broader through the shoulders and her musculature had gone from lithe to bulky. She looked herself, but like she lifted weights all the time now.

"My queen..." Xiphyre began, but she held up a hand and he closed his mouth, then followed her gaze to me. "He does not yet know?"

"He will know when I tell him, and I alone. I have a question for you." She motioned to my ring and the little man fluttered over to it, touching it in horror. "Can you fix it?"

"How did this happen?!" he cried, and looked from the item to me, his sudden distress becoming rage. "What did you *do*?"

"One of the ocean guardians' blood took his magic and the enchantments of all his gear and likely all the others' gear on contact. He almost lost his life, Xiphyre, and you abusing him will *not* be tolerated.

"Ocean guardian blood is that toxic?" He raised an eyebrow and frowned deeply. "Might wanna get my hands on some."

"Trust me, you don't." I shook my head at his shrugged nonchalance and handed him the ring.

"It seems to have been cleansed somehow, the repair will be... irksome, but simple." He flew over to Maebe. "Your ring, my queen."

She pulled it off her finger and handed it to him with a look of profound loss. Xiphyre held them, one in each hand, then slammed them together. A glow of light flooded from his grasp and sweat poured from his brow. He muttered a few words and then the light, golden at first, flickered several different colors— red, green, black, yellow, white, blue—and stopped all together.

He sighed in relief and handed the rings back to both of us. We went to put them on when he hissed, "Stop! You're unbound. You must ring each other first."

I blinked at him, then at Maebe and just stepped forward with her ring in my hand. I got down on one knee, looking up at her in her surprise. "This is how we ask where I come from. Maebe, will you marry me?"

She smiled, her teeth shining against the black night around us. "I would only ever marry you, my love."

I stood and kissed her as we slid each other's rings onto where they belonged.

"If that is all you need?" Xiphyre looked around and I stopped him. "What, my king?"

I reached into my inventory and pulled out my metallic arm, his eyes widening. "Can you repair this as well?"

"Not without you having to sacrifice more experience to it to get it to work," he grumbled, pulling the item from my hand.

"Seems it hasn't been cleansed either, so it's more likely to take an enchantment than I am a pretty dwarven wife. This is just a useless hunk of metal now. But it would serve as a decent blueprint for another arm. I could do it if…"

Xiphyre glanced over at Maebe who watched him carefully, but I interjected, "Xiphyre, my friends could be in danger. This planet is in danger right now, and we have a lot of shit to do coming up. I need an arm. Are you really going to be so petty over this?"

"That last favor keeps me from being *free*, Zeke," Xiphyre snarled with sudden fervor. "It binds my wings! I cannot fly as I once did! But no, I do not seek my last favor repaid. I seek to make a new deal. One that I cannot make in your presence yet."

I blinked at him, then at Maebe. "What aren't you telling me? Does this have something to do with what Samir gave you?"

Shadows flared around her and I thought that they would spear straight toward the Ragalfr, but all they did was cover us as another shadow passed overhead. This one made the bird that had been here earlier look like a baby; we watched as it circled, then flew off.

"Yes." She nodded once and folded her hands before her as she lifted her head. "This does have something to do with that."

"Then can you tell me?" She frowned at my request, and I stepped forward. "Whatever it is, I know there's a lot on my plate, but you don't have to worry about that. I'm your husband. This is us. I dig the new look too, by the way. I like how strong you look and are. I know you're strong. It doesn't bother me."

"Shut up, my king," Xiphyre whispered kindly into my ear and fluttered away before Maebe or I could reach him.

"Zeke, this is something that was given to me, in a way—but not from Samir." She looked at me pointedly, her beautiful green eyes finding mine and staying there. "You did this to me."

"What?" I shook my head, desperately trying to recall

whether or not I had the ability to do that. I'd like to do it to myself if I did, shit.

"Zeke, this is something that happens to my kind when they are with child." I blinked at her stupidly for a moment, not yet fully comprehending what was going on, until she stepped closer to me and whispered, "I am pregnant. You are going to have another child."

The joy and wonder in my heart in that moment was so intense that all I could do was lift her into my arms and hug her to me. Hard at first, then realizing I was squeezing too much, I relaxed my grip.

Then I remembered something. Something that gripped my heart with cold dread and understanding that brought me to my knees. Maebe lifted my face to hers and kissed my forehead, whispering, "It is okay. It is okay."

"So now you understand," Xiphyre muttered, and I turned to look at him.

The rage his interruption in this moment of absolute turmoil brought to my heart tore through the control I had gained and threatened to burst loose as I left Maebe's side and stalked toward the little man. He just stood there and when I reached him, his face was so calm and understanding that I was more confused that enraged. "I know how you feel, my king. I am torn too."

Maebe joined us and the little enchanter turned to her. "I know that you are loath to use the last favor you have against me, Majesty. I resent you for that and that alone. I only wish to return to my home, and I know that I cannot do that. All I ask in return for this wish of your husband's is one of my own."

"What would you have of us?" Maebe asked coolly, her eyes narrowed at the little man.

"I would see my family." He stopped Maebe from interjecting with a raised hand. "I know that I cannot return home and am bound to you. All I seek is to have my family come to me, at least my boys. It is time to enter into their apprenticeships and I miss them more than you can ever understand."

Maebe turned to look at me, then grasped her stomach, what little of one there was, and looked to Xiphyre. "No, I think that I finally do understand, Xiphyre. Your family and your family alone are welcome in my lands and among my people so that you may train them. This you will do in exchange for getting Zeke a newer, better arm, and swiftly."

Xiphyre smiled so hard I thought his head was going to split in two, a tear streaming down his face. "Thank you, Majesty. Thank you."

"And Xiphyre?" Maebe raised an eyebrow at the little man, his face turned up toward her. "I am loath to use my last favor, but seeing as though events have played out as they have and I may be preparing for something that will affect all the Fae, I will make it now."

Xiphyre looked shocked and I was pretty sure I did too.

"Xiphyre, I ask this of you as a queen and as a favor owed. When your family comes, I would like to discuss a mutually beneficial arrangement. When we discuss this, I ask that you keep an open mind and advise your children well. I will need enchanters and have known no others as strong as you. If they will work with the Unseelie, I will see them equipped and given the best that we can manage and their opportunities to become Unseelie will be boundless. Will you agree to this?"

Xiphyre's mouth was agape, for once. Seeing him speechless was almost unnerving. He seemed to have a quip or rant for everything, but now he just stood there.

"I, yes, Majesty, I would be honored." Xiphyre bowed his head and knelt where he stood. "I thank you for this opportunity for them."

"I extend this offer to you first, Xiphyre," Maebe stated and the man looked up at her. "I cannot have a novice enchanter without someone I trust to deliver to me. And you need to have skin in this as well if you are to convince them of our need."

"You mean that?" Xiphyre asked with wonder and disbelief plastered all over his face. "I can be an Unseelie?"

"If you want to be, yes." She looked over to me. "Do you see this as any issue?"

"I won't lie and say that I have any idea what's going on at all." I shrugged and Xiphyre stared at me intently, some of the disbelief leaving his features. "But I know I like Xiphyre and his work. If he's going to be good for our people, then I want him to be there for us. And us for him."

"Then Xiphyre, exiled and alone, I ask you this—do you have what it takes to serve the Fae from the shadows?" Xiphyre went back to staring at the ground as Maebe spoke. "To watch, protect, and support the Queen of your court and to never lie to her?"

"I, Xiphyre, leader of none and exiled Fae, do humbly state that I do and I will. I so bind myself with my word given to the King and Queen of the Unseelie that I will work for their ends and their means for all time as my life permits."

"Then rise, Xiphyre of the Unseelie." Maebe lifted her hands and with them the little man rose and the shadows flared around us all. The light from his wings, barely a trickle before, burst to life in a new way and his wings grew significantly. No longer small and frail-looking, they were easily double the size of his body. Tears of relief and joy streamed down his face as they flickered behind him.

"Thank you, my Queen." He looked to me and I held out my fist. He grinned before bumping it and pointed straight at me. "You wait! We have better materials now, so we can make an even better one! I'll have Rowland and Thogan on it right as soon as I get back to them! You won't regret this!"

He flapped his wings, wind whooshing around, lifting into the air, and then he was gone from sight.

"Wow." I blinked after the light was gone. "So he's one of ours now? How cool is that?"

"Very cool." Maebe smiled, but it seemed off somehow. Not what one would expect after having secured some of the best possible enchanting for her people to date. "Something's wrong? What's wrong, hon?"

"Yes," Maebe said simply and then I felt her hand grasp mine. "I want you to return home still, to your son."

"But what about you? What about the baby?" My heart dipped into my stomach, lurching as she shook her head. "And Vrawn, I can't just leave you all."

"I know that your son's mother treats him as a prince and he wants for nothing—that is as it should be." I couldn't lie if I wanted to, this hurt. A lot. "While I will miss you terribly and will long for you in every way, I cannot help but wonder if it would not be safer for you to return home. To see that your work here has not been in vain, and that War does what the gods seem to think and his reign of terror ends when he is thwarted here. What if your people need you? What if your son needs you? I can protect our child. I will protect our child, as will the whole of the Unseelie Court. But you need to be there for your people too."

"What about our people?" The hurt in my voice drained away as I tried to work through what she was telling me. "You and Vrawn?"

"We will be together, and have each other. I will not be alone and she will not either." She lifted a hand and put it against my cheek. "I know that you will decide what is best for you, and I will support you in everything, but I could not live with myself knowing that you wondered and longed for your son as you held our child. I couldn't imagine what it would do to you."

"What about our child when I get home?" My anger returned, amplified by the hurt in my heart.

"You will know of them. They will live in your heart, and you can rest easily knowing that they will have everything and that I will tell them of their father, my king, until they have the chance to learn for themselves."

"I'll think about it more," was all that I said in that moment and sighed. "I love you, Maebe. Thank you for trying to be so thoughtful."

The growling and yowls had stopped, and I turned to see

the two Fae watching us, laying together with tails thrown over each other.

"What's going on with them?"

"They have reverted to their feral forms." She frowned at me, then remembered what had happened. "They died on that ship, fighting with you. They returned to the Fae realm and were reborn, as will happen until Samir lays them to rest. They have yet to recover their intellect, however. Send them home, and let them rest for a time before summoning them again. They will likely be back to themselves or some semblance of it by then."

I waved a hand and spoke, "Go home." They faded away.

"What must we do now?" Maebe looked around and found Bea. "You did not lie; she is very small now. Is she affected by the toxin as well?"

I nodded and she sat next to her prone body. "We need to give her the herb and water as well, but I'm worried with how tired she is, she might be harmed by it. It's not an easy process."

"Then we will let her rest and do it as soon as she wakes." Maebe patted the ground next to her and we laid on the ground together for a bit before she finally sighed and spoke. "The Seelie spy I told you of had grave news."

"What was it?"

"They mean to try to start another war." I leaned up and turned to look at her. "They cannot. Not for another thousand years, because of Samir's influence. That does not mean that they might not try to start one here."

She paused for a moment longer and I reached out and took her hand. "You had another thought, didn't you?"

"Yes, and it is just as grave as the last." She looked around and frowned, then looked to me in worry. "They could mean to try to remove the limiter of their activities altogether."

"You mean try to get rid of Samir?" My gaze shot over to meet hers and she nodded once. "Have you warned him?"

"I did. It was one of the things he rewarded me for, other than making you King." She smiled coyly at me and I kissed her hand. "We should rest. If her experience will be as terrible as your own, we will need our strength to watch over and protect her."

"Yes, dear." I smiled at her and pulled her close, then remembered that there was no bedroll to sleep on like a teenager, and scrambled to get it out and ready for my pregnant wife. Wow. This was so wild.

That night I slept better than I ever had since coming to this world. But there was still the nagging thought of my friends being in danger to contend with.

———

"Come on, baby, you'll be okay." I coaxed Bea again to take her medicine and she tried to bite me. "I know that you're scared, but I'm right here and Maebe isn't going to let anything happen to you without someone being mortally wounded, so you need to take your—*now!*"

Maebe clamped Bea's mouth shut around the plant and water that I threw in and we forced Bea to swallow even as the anger and betrayal warred across her gaze.

Soon she began to writhe and screech on the ground, her clawed limbs spreading wide and slashing at the air.

I did my best to comfort her, worrying that any healing I did on her might stunt the process. She writhed and cried out so long I worried that she wasn't recovering.

Crash, boom! Maebe and I turned to find the same large raiko wolf-like creature with wings bursting into the area.

"Maebe, you watch over Bea," I ordered and cracked my neck. "This is gonna be my way of getting back into things."

"If you think I will not step in, you are mistaken." She smiled and stood closer to Bea but readied herself by standing low over her.

"I figured." I grinned and took out Magus Bane. The muscles in my legs tensed and I launched myself forward between the beast's forelegs and leaped straight up at its chest and cast Aspect of the Dragon.

Aspect of the Dragon – The primal warrior's body becomes scaled, stronger, and grows wings like that of the dragon.

+15 defense, +15 strength, +10 dexterity and wings give a flight and movement speed increase.

A familiar voice rang out through my mind, *Finally, I thought you had been hiding from us.*

How is it that the instincts of the dragon bleed through into my aspected form? I growled back mentally.

We are stronger than those other creatures you steal forms from. Allow us to show you.

A burning, acidic wave of thoughts seared my mind and I found myself watching in horror and fascination as my body moved as expertly as if under my own command. My wings flaring wide to assist my movements. The great axe falling from my grasp and flames bursting to life in my hand as my claws dug into the beast's stomach.

It roared and electricity burst from around it, electrocuting my body, but I couldn't gauge the damage because my view was skewed.

This is what it is like to fight with you at the helm, the dragons seethed. I could feel their anger at me. *You move like a dragonling and you refuse to use all of the abilities at your disposal!*

"Then give me my body back and I'll do it my-fucking-self!" I raged at them, my fists clenched. I blinked, looking down at my mental self to see that I still had two hands. Weird. "You don't even have any idea how to use my abilities!"

We understand more than you know. Eyes as green and unearthly as anything I had ever witnessed peered out of the darkness at me next to the image of my fight against the beast wolf.

A lumbering dragon of indeterminate age edged its way out of the shadows toward me, the antler-like horns he had on his head looking more like that of a moose than the deer-like ones that Ampharia had. His eyes watched me, the light voice I heard in my green dragon form came to me, *We tire of the games. We tire of your weakness. We wish to do our part in saving the world as it is, and we will use your body to do it.*

"The hell you will!" I roared and bolted toward it. I called the shadows around us, and they swirled toward me. I smirked; this would be too easy.

A tail snaked out of the darkness and slapped me down, same as the beast outside slamming a paw into my body's chest, pinning me to the ground.

A light surrounded my struggling form and I felt my connection with Bea and Maebe both open wide for the first time since Orlow'thes bled into those waters.

The weight on my chest shifted and I could finally see out of my own eyes. I dropped the aspect and roared mightily up into the creature's face, using Predator's Call.

It stared at me in confusion long enough for me to pull the shadows to me, Magus Bane with it. Once it was in my left hand, I slammed the axe head into the beast's paw and it howled in pain as a toe sagged.

I flipped backward onto my feet and readied myself to charge. "Thanks, guys!"

"You are welcome, my love. Bea is in no state to fight, but I can assist if you need me?" Maebe's question stung, but I knew it came from a good place.

"Not yet," I whispered, knowing she would hear me.

Gritting my teeth, I activated Feather Axe, Cleave, and Charge all at once, sliding forward toward the wolf, his leg wide open to me and swung for all I was worth. My axe sank in deeply, 87 MP returning to me instantly.

I cast Stone Skin in time to help absorb some of the damage that the snarling beast did by biting me, more electricity surging over my body. It seemed to tickle and awaken something within me the more electrical energy surged through me.

I spun and slashed again, my left arm arcing with the angle and then the blade catching the ground for me to pivot off of and kick its chest. Its health seemed to be dropping bit by bit, but there was still a good amount of it to go.

Time to cast some spells! I ground my teeth and decided against using lightning for this. My breathing steadied and my vision sharpened as I listened and opened my senses as Bea had been encouraging me to do.

Chipping away at its health would be difficult, but I had big hitters, and I could cast them and do big damage if I planned it well.

Which made me wonder, hoping this would work, "Hubris?"

Finally, you return! The scepter sounded elated at this news and appeared before me. *I am hungry.*

"I'll give you mana as soon as I can. I'll need some help for this one. You ready?" Without waiting to see if it was ready or not, I grabbed the weapon with my left hand and let Magus Bane fall to the ground.

Taking a deep breath as the raiko wolf turned back toward me and charged forward. I cast Solar Flare in front of its face. I could see the burst of light behind my eyelids and smiled to myself as I opened my eyes and immediately cast Falfyre.

The weapon burst from the end of Hubris just as I started forward toward the stunned and pained beast. Falfyre slid into the raiko wolf's jaw, then throat, then into his chest.

The yelping beast reared up and away from me, but I followed behind with a leap and a shift of my grip. The weapon shifted like I was stirring something inside the beast and it cried out even louder, its health bar dropping wildly.

Finally, I shoved the weapon up as hard as I could and willed the spell to burst inside the raiko wolf. The damage was insane and the beast shuddered before falling to its side, dead.

Rather than the body staying where it was, the body began to fade from view. Where it faded, a small chest stayed behind. "That's weird, that's never happened before."

"It seems there is much we do not know of these beasts," Maebe stated from behind me, her hand resting on my shoulder. "We must collect water from this spring to give to whomever needs it. Check the spoils of your victory and we will go."

I looked to Bea; she stared at me from where she laid. *Hold on, baby. I'll come get you in a moment, okay?*

Okay, she wearily replied with a soft exhalation and closed her eyes.

Fuck it. I sprinted to the chest, tried to lift it and fell on my face. I blinked at it, and found that it was stuck where it was. "Damn it."

So much for opening it later and taking care of Bea now.

I pressed the latch to open it, the dark wood shimmering and fading away as it opened, leaving behind several items. Feathers sharper than the ones I had received from Kayda's mom. Bottled lightning essence that looked like some sort of crafting material, three of those. A wing bone, several bits of its skin and teeth. It was crazy. I'd never gotten loot like this before, at least, not in this kind of manner.

Into the inventory with all of it, and then on our way we would go. Maebe and I grabbed more of the water from the Mother's Bosom fountain and then tried to figure out what to do from there.

"Your next goal is to find our friends, correct?" I nodded at her question and she motioned skyward. "You have the ability to shift once more. Why don't you take your largest flying form and see about finding a city?"

"There are beasts that can fly. They're massive—like way bigger than the one I just fought—and I'm pretty sure if they find us, it's going to be an absolute shit show up there. I can't put you guys at risk like that, and with the way the dragons just took over my body, I don't want to risk that again."

"They *took over?*" She put a hand on my shoulder and pulled me toward her. "How is this possible?"

"Immense magical power and there are two of their minds melded into the form." I shrugged, uncertain of it myself. "They keep telling me that they can do it better and they want to, but they aren't willing to train me. They just assume control. I can fight them with Bea and you, but that was merely something that surprised them enough to shock them out of control. Chances are, they'll be ready for that next time."

"Then we will manage without." She raised her chin, something darker behind her gaze, "There *is* a way for us to find out where a city might be. Have you tried speaking to the animals here?"

"I can sure try." I cast Nature's Voice and called out, "Any birds willing to help a Druid in need?"

Several called out, mimicking my words and whistling teasingly but nothing helpful. West of here was probably a city, right? Near the ocean?

Maybe I could risk flying myself?

"I know that look, Zekiel Erebos—you will not be doing something stupid on your own." The feigned baleful look I gave her rolled right over her skin and she raised a brow at me in challenge. "I swear, if you say 'pie,' I will beat you."

"Yes, dear." I huffed. "There are supposed to be cities everywhere, there was one in the west, but I'm not too sure about going back that way. It's got monkeys everywhere, and what am I talking about? I have magic now. I could kick their asses."

She smiled at me and then looked toward my hand. "You are woefully 'undergeared,' as our beloved friends would call it. Is it not a good idea for you to do something about that?"

"It would be, but the materials I have are subpar for my level and I want to try some new things." I frowned and checked again. Mainly just gold and the like, nothing really all that great, even with the enchantments I could dole out. Not to mention, I was sorely missing that ring for my mental protection. That likely would have given me the mental fortitude to take on the dragons.

"I have things that I can give to you, though some of them are cursed?" She saw my distaste and smiled. "If only you had been born a Fae, you would have gone through the royal challenge with me and we would have looted the place together."

"What's that?" I asked her excitedly.

"Come, we must move for now, and I will speak on the way."

I grinned at her excitedly and collected Bea from where she lay snoozing, and off we went toward the western shoreline.

"The challenge is to prove that you are fit to be royal," Maebe explained quietly so that we might not garner any more attention than normal. "It is a hereditary dungeon within the Unseelie domain that we oversee. The royal in question, typically the prince or princess, goes in to complete however much of the dungeon that they can without dying. If anyone wishes to challenge them for their right to rule, they can pay to go into the dungeon and try to surpass them."

"If they do, they become the heir?" I raised a brow at her and she nodded. "Has that happened before?"

"It is how my family took the throne from the current king of the Seelie." If we hadn't been so pressed for time and travel that day, I would have stopped to pick up my jaw. "Impressed?"

"And slightly perturbed," I amended for her. She chuckled and I had to collect my thoughts before continuing. "How could Samir allow him to take the throne of the Seelie when he was Unseelie?"

"They were banished from our lands as a sign of good faith to Samir." Her voice was controlled but she held a note of something I couldn't place in her voice. "If we killed them, it would have been poorly done on our part, but we would have been safe. That was Samir's way of keeping the courts in check. We have enemies everywhere. Ours is not an easy life, and he did take the throne by action rather than birth, so I cannot call foul."

"So that's why the Seelie had this sudden hard-on for you guys?" She turned to look at me oddly and I explained, "It means that they have something against you, usually. That explains a lot."

"You think?" She snorted and shook her head. "This is a thing that is done in our realm. But enough talk of things that can wait. You have little in the way of protection right now. So I will be teaching you new shadow spells. If you are amenable to them?"

"I am." I smiled at her, then thought of something. "I have all these different types of magic though; I think I want to try something later too. I need to think a little more about the practical application of this spell, so let's practice."

"Do you recall my lesson concerning bringing small objects and creatures through the shadows to you?" I nodded at her and a smile split her face that looked almost sinister. "It is time for you to learn how to maneuver through shadows yourself. Hand Bea to me."

"Seems a little ambitious during the daytime," I muttered evilly and she just motioned for the raptor again.

"It is the perfect time to practice as there is not too much shadow to work with." She stopped me from arguing with a look. "Balmur is adept at stepping through shadows, as that is an ability of his class specialty. Yohsuke is likely well along his way to learning a similar skill. If you have the ability to move in shadows—*through* shadows—you will be that much more fearsome of an opponent. Now, concentrate on the shadows, imagine them as a doorway to where you want to step out of, and do it."

"Just like that?"

"There is significantly more to it than just that, but you have an annoying habit of learning things meant to be difficult and for learning easy things as if they were the most challenging spells in the universe." Her sweet smile after that made it less of an insult and more teasing and I was okay with that. "You have seen Balmur do this in a way. Try it."

I focused my will and intent, reached for the shadows under the closest tree and ordered them to create a doorway through themselves into the shadows of the next tree. Calming breaths entered my lungs and I stepped through into the shadows as they rose like a monolith of ebon design.

And walked right into the damn tree. "Shit!"

I rubbed my nose, tears in my eyes despite being able to handle my shit. Hey—the nose is sensitive, man!

"That was excellently done, Zeke!" Maebe clapped softly and I looked to where she was and noted that she was further away than she should have been. "Yes, you did it!"

I clenched my fist and pumped it in the air excitedly, then she added, "You telegraphed your movement and came out the wrong way—but you did it!"

I rolled my eyes and checked to see how much mana it had put me back. Only ten? Nice!

"So the mana cost isn't all that bad!" I grinned at her and she nodded.

"It will be in times where you go longer distances. This time, you will practice going farther, and coming out the right way." She pointed to a tree more than one hundred feet away. "This time, do not telegraph where you will come out. While that monolith of a door has a place to intimidate foes and those you wish to, it will give them time to prepare for you."

I frowned at her, then glared at the shadows. *Little help here, shadows? Think I could get you to let me out like I'm walking through an invisible doorway? Or like a transporting mirror in old fantasy games and stories?*

I felt nothing in return from them but their excitement at my attention and found myself smiling. This time I walked into the shadows that had pooled under the tree like I was on some serious David Bowie shit. They pulled and tugged me for what could only have been seconds but it felt like so long in the darkness, the void moving around me in a wash of needy movement. Clinging to me, pushing and pulling all at once. Then I felt myself lift and standing where I had envisioned looking at the tree once more.

Maebe was there next to me almost instantly. "That took quite some time, my love. But you seem to be getting the hang of the distance thing. The mana cost?"

I checked and saw that it had cost 153 MP that time and

told her as much. "I see. We will keep working on this until you can do it without needing to think about it."

We practiced as we moved, almost like we played a game of hide and seek in the shadows. Finally I had the spell to the point that it allowed me to actually call it something.

Hollow Step – Caster steps into the void and out into an area they have seen. Range: Sight. Cost: Range dependent (1 MP per foot). Cool down: 5 seconds.

Finally, we stopped to eat some food that she had brought with her for Yoh to prepare and try.

"You've been here for how long?" I asked again, not believing it.

"More than a week, trying to find you," she insisted as she watched the sky and helped Bea eat with a motherly smile. "I swear, you can be so dense sometimes, my love."

"I know you're teasing, but what did you do?"

"When I could no longer feel you, I panicked and came right away, fearing the worst. I appeared near the shoreline of the city that you had sailed from, and couldn't feel you whatsoever, but the people there remembered seeing you after I made a few... terse threats."

"Maebe?" I looked at her and she carefully returned my stare. "Did you kill anyone?"

She blinked once, then frowned almost sullenly. "Only a few people in a rather spectacular fashion..."

"Babe, you can't do that!" I was careful not to raise my voice over more than a reproachful hiss lest we have another beastly visitor but the look on her face made me wish a stampede of them had come through the area.

"When it comes to the matters of my court, my king, my child, and our friends, Zeke—" She leaned dangerously close to me, her face creased in rage. "—I will do what I must. The people of that rotten city learned this and swore to me that they had been good to you. And you them. Then you had left on a ship and hadn't returned, but the fish in the ocean had begun to act strangely. I searched for you for days, calling for you until my voice was gone, and I scoured the countryside and ocean through the shadows for you. I killed anyone who stood in my way. As I know you would do for me."

She put her hands on both sides of my face, tears beginning to fall from the corners of her eyes. "I could stand losing you to your home, knowing that you would be there doing your best and thinking of me. But if you had died, there would have been a hole in my heart that would have driven me to destroy this realm however I could. The Unseelie would become the monsters they are so readily condemned to be, and we would relish our vengeance for our king. You would have razed the world to find me; so you do not get to lecture me upon my methods of finding you. Am I clear?"

Rather than just answering her, I pulled her close and held her for a time. She clung to me and I thanked whoever it was out there that I had found her and she me. We would be okay somehow. We would make this work.

As she ate and spoke softly with Bea, I focused on trying to create a new spell. I brought light into focus in my mind, mentally drawing it over my body then carefully making it so that it would refract the light from the sun and whatever else hit it to return as if there were nothing there at all. Not really invisibility, but a cloak of light that would make it harder to see an area around me.

Radial Refraction – Caster spins the light into a mobile dome of refractive rays that will keep anything in the dome hidden from all but the most perceptive gazes for 30 feet centered on the caster. Cost: 120 MP. Duration: 20 minutes. Cool down: 10 minutes.

I smiled to myself and opted to use that the following day to help us. This was the area close to the monkeys so I could imagine it would help us out a little to have it.

Resting went easily that night; we awoke the following morning and I cast Radial Refraction. Maebe frowned, walked out as Bea stood with me and then walked back in. "Very clever.

If I did not know that you were already there, I may have over-looked you."

"Thank you!" I clapped my hands softly and patted Bea. She looked so much healthier and having her voice back in my mind was lovely.

Want find sister! She snapped her jaws, the audible clicking making me grin.

"We will find her, baby. Yes, Vrawn too." Maebe took my hand and we were off in that instant. We walked through the monkey's territory. I frowned as they all looked our way, then seemed to collectively sniff and their hackles raised, but they couldn't actively see us. Their alertness and constant roving through the trees made us all a little more wary, especially since I didn't necessarily want to kill any of them. Sure, the experience would be nice, but I had gotten a pretty big chunk from the beast, about 400 EXP, so if I only killed them, then I'd be set.

But other things had to take priority. I needed to figure out where my friends could be and then do this damned trial of the beast so that I could keep my word to the animals.

Maebe and I traveled through the forest like this for two more days when we came upon another set of beasts, levels 80 and 81 respectively, clashing and snarling at each other in our way, that made us move out of their way.

Finally, on the third morning, we came to a small village that had maybe sixteen huts and a pier with a set of boats and rafts that looked to have been beset upon by something massive. Claw marks and scrapes in the earth and beach marred the land and we found no one there. But Bea and I found a familiar scent.

Uncle goblin! Bea cried and I almost laughed at her calling him that. Seems Kayda had been teaching her sister more than I thought.

We scoured the village a little more and still found nothing of interest, then moved up the shoreline toward a cliff. Still nothing in sight. No tracks, nothing.

"I'm going to take eagle form and fly out over the water to see if I can see anything that will give us a direction to travel." She looked at me warily, and I sighed. "We're near the ocean; if anything comes at us from the sky, we can fuck off into it and or into the trees to hide, but we need to check. I can polymorph you into a bird if you want to try to come with me. I know you can levitate; can you fly?"

She shook her head. "I will go with you. You will turn me into a bird so that I might keep up with you."

I polymorphed her into an eagle and then shifted into my own eagle form and mimicked flying to her. She fell flat on her face for a minute straight, then finally seemed to get the gist of it and we took off. Maebe had a little trouble keeping up, the waves over the water were difficult for even me to navigate at times, but it wasn't long before we found what we were looking for. I sent a mental tug to Bea and then flew northward along the coast line with Maebe following until I saw the timer on my spell for her beginning to count too low to fly on.

We landed and she turned back, her hair frazzled and eyes wild. She turned her gaze to me and pointed at me accusingly. "You never said that flying was so exhilarating!" She ran a hand through her hair and shook her head. "How do you even stay out of animal form?"

I winked at her and growled low, "I have my reasons."

She actually blushed and touched her stomach. "I can feel them."

I laughed and hugged her. Bea was curious and came over to smell Maebe. *Had you not been paying attention when she and I were talking?*

She turned and looked back at me. *Respect you and mate's privacy. I was tired.*

Images and memories of her unable to keep her eyes open as she looked over at me, Mae, and Xiphyre.

Maebe is pregnant, Bea. She's going to have our child.

The raptor froze, her head whipping from me to the woman in confusion, then her elation hit me like a physical wave. She growled and put her clawed forearms on Maebe's stomach and barked wildly in joy.

Maebe seemed slightly confused until I looked her in the eyes and grinned. "She's happy and welcoming the baby."

Maebe rested a hand on Bea's head and patted her gently. "You okay to run with us while we fly together, baby?"

Wait.

"Is the baby okay while I polymorph you?" Panic gripped my chest as I stepped toward Maebe in concern.

She laughed. "Yes. That was one of the gifts from Samir. It is immune to magic other than healing and non-malicious transformative magic. So as long as you aren't intending to use polymorph to get rid of me, then I will change and the baby will too."

I sighed in relief and almost dropped to my knees then. How could I have been so stupid? I silently thanked Samir and could almost hear his chuckling before standing and turning Maebe into an eagle once more so that we could fly together to the city while Bea ran below us on foot.

She followed his scent as best she could but it faded from her nose and she tried to find it again. Finally, we decided to move toward the city in hopes someone there had news or word of him. It took a good few hours to do it, having to stop and polymorph Maebe to get there, but by the time we were within easy walking distance of the massive settlement, she was almost as good at flying as I was.

As we approached, several birds of varying sizes and breeds lifted from the city to approach us and I figured being in the air when they got to us would likely be a bad idea. Maebe and I stood waiting as the birds circled from above, then came down to land one by one where they shifted into humanoid forms.

Several humans, a couple of elves, and a Kitsune approached us. The humans took the lead here, their features all similar to each other. Black hair, dark-colored eyes and almost Asian features with tanned skin and severe-looking expressions.

Quintuplets? Weird.

The man in the middle of the humans spoke first in a language I didn't understand, then switched to Druidic. "Can you understand me now?"

I nodded to him and he frowned even more deeply than before. "What is a Druid from somewhere else doing here? And why did you risk flying and summoning Crimson and his flock?"

"We needed to be certain we were heading in the right direction," I stated simply. "Who are you to control the skies here? And who is Crimson?"

"We are the Mother's emissaries to the city of Xolia, and we are the keepers of her will here." The man raised his chin and it made me want to punch it for some reason. "Who is the woman with you? Why does she not speak for herself?"

"This is my wife Maebe, and the Queen of the Unseelie Fae." All of them looked her over a little more closely, but none of them went to bow or kneel. I observed Maebe out of the corner of my eye and saw that she was content to bide her time. "She is not a Druid."

"Then how was she in animal form?" one of the other Druids asked.

"I used Polymorph on her, so she could fly with me."

They all gasped audibly, the leader looking murderous. "We do not turn people into animals unless it is for the good and safety of all! It is a crime against the Mother's majesty!"

"Clearly she never told me that." I shrugged; I didn't want to be too stand-offish with them because I might need help. "Look, all we want is to find our friends from the shipwreck, I'll take the trial, and then we will kill what we came here to kill and be on our way."

"Of course she would never tell the likes of you, you are beneath her notice." He raised his chin even higher and all of the human Druids lifted their chins too. The others just looked uncomfortable, especially the Kitsune. "You do not rate the trial of the beasts. I'm surprised you even know of it. How did you find out about it?"

"You guys don't know me well enough then, but I don't care about that," I sighed and just shrugged. "The animals who took care of me told me about it. Some of them even seemed pretty high up on the food chain here. Kuuma and Pondreth sound familiar? Yeah. They told me."

"He lies. He cannot have spoken to the Wooded Council," one of the women hissed and strode forward with violence in her stride.

I stepped forward just as quickly. "Did you just accuse the king of the Unseelie Fae of lying?" She stumbled at my sudden animosity. "How about this? I swear to you all here and now that I have a personal blessing from Mother Nature as her Primal Warrior, and that Kuuma and Pondreth of this whatever council told me what they knew of the trial in hopes that I would take it and help them quell the beasts running rampant on your lands, destroying the Mother's work. Do you believe me now?"

Maebe's hand found my shoulder and she whispered into my ear in Celestial, "I felt you invoke your word, be careful who you do that with. While I do not know the meaning, I know that these people seem ready to hate you. Be prepared."

"What did she just say?" The same woman pointed at her and I felt my heart rate spike as she did, my ire turning on her. "Rude of her to use a language none of us understand in our presence."

"Nothing that concerns any of you." I rolled my eyes at that and she seemed to take enough offense that she invaded my personal space to point a finger directly into my chest.

"You don't seem to understand that we don't recognize the Fae here." Her grimace was such that I actually felt bad for what I was about to do. These guys must not get visitors often. "And when we are addressed, or those around us are addressed, we expect to understand and be understood."

I sighed and cast Aspect of the Lion, my body growing and shifting as the spell took hold. My muzzle and muscles thickened and the fur around my head grew longer to make a mane.

The growling bass that filled my voice rang out loudly as I sneered at her. "What point is there to being understood and to understanding if you won't try it yourself? Ever heard of the pot calling the kettle black?"

"This is *our land!*" She spat at me, her spittle actually hitting my chest. "You are on our land and it is our trial and area to protect."

"Maybe you don't understand that the Fae do not recognize your rule?" I pointed to myself. "The Mother gave me this ability herself as a reward for serving her. If you want to have some kind of power or rule over your lands and you're so afraid of outsiders, then so be it. I don't need your permission to assist Mother Nature in her work. Help us, or don't, but you will not stand in our way."

"And what will you do if we stand against you?" the man challenged with his chest puffed out.

"The same thing all other creatures in nature do—find a way around you." I stepped past the woman faster than she must have thought possible, because she tried and failed to grab my left arm. I stopped when I stood in front of the man and bent down to look him in the eyes. "Or find a way through you."

"You cannot hope to take all of us." One of the formerly silent elves seemed to be stating it and asking a question all at the same time.

"You can't know what I'm capable of while you constrain yourselves with needless rules that you claim are for Mother Nature's benefit." The elves and Kitsune once again seemed to find some nugget of truth in what I said, their eyes raising to meet mine.

"She offers power that cannot be rivaled!" one of the human men almost seemed to whine. "The elements have hidden themselves away so that the Mother is the most powerful being aside from the gods!"

"She is powerful, with that I can agree." I spread my palms low in agreement and even smiled as I let my aspect go and reverted to my Kitsune form. "But the elements no longer hide."

"I suppose you'll claim to be blessed by the elements next?" The woman snorted behind me.

"Maybe, but I've lost the interest in showing off." I winked at the Kitsune cheekily and his eyes widened considerably.

"You waste our time." The woman waved a dismissive hand that came dangerously close to being a slap as she sulked by me. I fought the urge to grasp her arm and fight them all then. "You and your 'unsightly' Queen may come into our city, but you will be under surveillance and you will be escorted. Greer, Kyr, and Sendak—you three will accompany this person and his wife throughout the city and ensure they do not break our laws, and you are to keep them away from anything they should not be involved in. We grow bored of this."

The three non-humans shapeshifted in unison, their albatross forms lifting into the sky and turning toward the city.

I raised an eyebrow to the Druids who stood left behind and tutted carefully. "So I see they left the most capable among them to watch over the threats?"

The three of them flinched and turned to look at each other before finally, the elf farthest from me actually laughed before speaking in Sylvan, "You speak funny, but I feel bad that we leave out the Queen."

The three of them dropped to a knee and bowed their heads respectfully.

"Rise, and speak freely with us," Maebe responded generously in Sylvan. "The Kitsune is Unseelie by birthright, but the two of you I cannot sense. Are you Seelie?"

"Unaligned, my Lady," replied the closest elf. They both had dyed black hair and hazel eyes. It was odd to see against their fair complexions. The Kitsune watched with brown eyes and russet colored fur.

"Why would you challenge them?" the Kitsune finally asked. "They're the strongest Druids in the city, probably the whole of the continent, and they would sooner see you die than take the trial. Why?"

"Probably because they can't pass it themselves and I will?" I stared at him and he seemed to be aware I hadn't answered his original question, at least not in a satisfactory way. "Because I'm really not here to do anything other than help you all. We were the reason that freakish kraken attacked, and we were trying to kill it. This is our fault—at least I feel that way—and we try to clean up our messes when we can."

"That is honorable." The closest elf pointed to himself. "I am Sendak, this is my brother Greer, and our friend Kyr."

"The ones they treat like shit," I said calmly and they all dropped their heads. "Is it because you aren't human? Is that it?"

"Humanity is what the city and its leadership pride themselves on. It is what allows them to open their doors to the less fortunate races and take them in," Greer stated as if he had heard that his entire life.

"That makes you sound subservient." I almost spat and he flinched. *It's no wonder they can't pass the trial, they're too timid to tame the beasts.* "No wonder no one has taken the trial and passed in so long. You tout serving nature but you separate yourselves from it. You talk the talk when it's convenient, but forgot how to walk the walk."

"We cannot take the trial, it is not our place." Kyr crossed his arms and looked away.

"They're afraid that you'll be more powerful than them and they'll lose whatever little leverage they have against you." Maebe's sage wisdom echoed my own thoughts precisely. "If you were to aid us, my husband could likely help you all pass the trial. He can show you many things. He is a powerful Druid."

"I do not think it works like that." The elves shook their head as Kyr spoke dejectedly.

"Defining yourself by what someone else forces you to accept as the only way seems to be a theme among you," I growled at them all and they seemed taken aback. "You just saw some of what I can do and it's never been done before. Why can't you learn from me? If not something like what I do, then at the very least you can undergo the trial of the beast and claim the power that is your right."

"We wouldn't dare—" I cast a baleful look at Greer and he quieted.

"They would banish us from the city if we did!" Sendak barked angrily, his features twisting in fear.

"They wouldn't be enough to stop all of you, and even if they did—so what?" I stepped closer to all of them and motioned to the ocean beside us. "There's a whole world out there that needs you. There are multiple realms aside from this one to explore and use as a place to grow. Grow for yourselves instead of being treated like dirt for your birth!"

"They're right," Kyr said at last. "They only allow us to have servile jobs. If we have a knack for magic, they make us serve long terms under their laws and rulings, in houses that cast us aside when we are done! We should do this."

The elves seemed uncertain, so I sweetened the deal a little. "Help me find my friends, and to this trial, and I will teach you everything I can. You do not have to be what they make of you. You can be who you are and who you desire to be."

"We can do this." Kyr turned to the elves and they both frowned before holding out their hands.

"Greer and I will join you in this, but if you need anything, we would ask that you go to our respective peoples so that we can assist you better." Sendak looked like I might strike him but I just smiled.

"Take me to your people, then." I opened my arms and hugged my wife. "You have made powerful friends today, and I mean to make your friends work for me to prove to themselves that they are better than this."

They smiled and we all turned toward the city. Bea trudged along, happy but a little tired from sprinting so long.

Over the course of our hour-long walk to the city gate, we

got an idea of where we would be going and who we would need to see.

The guards at the gate had to let us through due to the three Druids with us, but they made damn sure to search me thoroughly. When they tried to touch Maebe, their hands seemed to go numb instantly, her smile genuine as they complained loudly about the cold.

Once we were inside the city, the myriad colored ribbons and flags waving inside playing against the gray stone and white mortar made me smile despite my initial impression of the place. There was life here and—in what some might have referred to as the dumpy part of the city that we walked into now—we had found the best of it.

Homes and houses made of a stucco-like material interwoven with wooden strips and grasses. They looked cool, honestly. Cooler than the castle-like structures I assumed the humans lived in.

"This is the section of the city that was given to us by the human rulers." Greer confirmed my suspicions and I rolled with it. I liked this place better. "They are humble, but we do our best to make it clean and presentable should anyone come through. Ours is a tightly knit community."

They all smiled and nodded to the people in the streets who seemed to be either cleaning or hanging their washed laundry to dry. The sunlight made for a good mark.

A few of the people ventured closer to us, their non-human features twitching excitedly as they watched us moving through. Maebe had adopted a physically less daunting form thanks to her glamour and I just stayed myself, but the sight of new faces looked like it was invigorating these folks and that excitement bled into me.

"This place is beautiful," Maebe whispered quietly and Sendak grinned at her.

"Thank you, Majesty." The elvish man motioned to the colors above us. "If you would like, we can send some of these colorful makings home with you?"

"I would be more than delighted to see you paid for the privilege," Maebe answered in the affirmative with a smile splitting her face.

Kyr joined us and startled me, I hadn't seen him step away, but he turned to me. "The friend you said that you had scented is here, and he is in bad condition. We had to cover his scent in case something else hunted him. Come with me."

He led us through the street for another hundred feet, made a right, followed that side street down until the stone wall, made a left, and burst through the door of the house on the left of the street.

Someone cried out and Kyr shot from the room like a bad guy caught in an old action movie explosion. He hit the wall with a crack and I had to cast Heal on him before his health plummeted too far.

Muu limped out of the house with his spear in his hand for support like a crutch, red bandages wrapped around his torso and chest. Red with blood. He looked tired but ready for a fight until he saw me and Mae.

"This is the weirdest fever dream..." He swayed where he was and I blasted him with healing spells until he fell unconscious.

Kyr rose from the ground with a hacking cough that made him spit up blood. I made sure he was okay and then we moved Muu back into the house.

The old woman inside was a tiny elven woman who looked like she was meant to be Yoda's mom. She tittered over him almost angrily until Maebe joined us, then she shrieked and fell to her face.

"Rise," Maebe ordered with no delay. "Tend to him and ensure that my friend is well, and if he is, I will reward you for his treatment."

The woman stood, her back cracking dangerously loud and grunted as she checked his bandages. She pulled them away and raised an eyebrow at me, then began to cut them away and pull them aside. She would moisten some of them with warm water before tugging them off him and then stopped when they were all cleared from his chest.

Four long gashes crossed his chest and stomach diagonally, and they seemed to be healing okay thanks to my magic, but they weren't fully closing. They were wide, like something large had struck him.

"It has to be the toxin still in his system," I reasoned and pulled out a bloom of the plant and a vial of the water needed to get rid of it. "This isn't going to be easy on him. He should be able to take it and be okay, right?"

"If those are the two items I think they are, he will need constant monitoring and healing," the tiny elf stated shakily. She looked him over, poking at the wounds softly to check for something. "The wound took much from him and he almost died. If it had not been for the villagers bringing him to me, he would have."

"We can make that happen." She sighed and nodded before taking the plant and water to bring them together and grind them into a paste in a mortar with a pestle. Pouring the paste into his open snoring mouth, she poured the rest of the water in and clamped his jaws shut.

Maebe and I both had to hold him down and he almost sent me flying too, but luckily he swallowed and settled down.

Then the earth shattering screaming began. He thrashed and fought, body breaking into a sweat that poured from his body and flung everywhere.

"Heal him!" the elven woman called. From then on, the other Druids and I took turns casting whatever healing magics we had to throw at him. It took hours and the other Druids were beginning to flag, the mana headaches making them weak. I was holding up decently, but it was difficult even for me. I definitely needed to get better gear to replace what I'd lost.

Finally, he seemed either too weak to struggle, or the toxin had finally been destroyed. Either way, he slept peacefully and we could all rest.

We were ushered outside by the little old elven woman, who stayed inside to talk to Maebe.

Kyr rubbed his ribs absently and chuckled. "Your friend kicks like a beast."

"He's strong, that's for sure." I grinned back at him. "Sorry for the pain he caused you."

"It's okay." Kyr flashed his teeth and the others looked uncomfortable. "Before you ask, I'm the weakest of the Druid council apprentices. They practice new spells on me. I can take it."

"That's not going to work for me." I sighed. "I see another one of those guys, I'm going to beat them silly."

They all stayed awkwardly quiet to the point where I needed to ask a question and I wasn't sure if asking it or not would be appreciated, so I asked anyway. "What do you guys do with the loot that drops from the beasts when they die?"

They all looked at me in shock. "What?"

"Please tell me you did not kill a beast!" Sendak rushed toward me and pressed a hand over my mouth to quiet me swiftly. "Killing a beast is punishable by death!"

I raised an eyebrow and pushed his hand aside. "It was going to kill me, what was I supposed to do? Let it?"

"Run from it!" The others nodded nervously as Sendak spoke. "They're too powerful to kill. They return with vendettas! They will hunt you and try to kill you."

"What's so bad about that?" I smirked despite their caution. "I killed it once already, I can do it again easily with you guys and my friends."

They shook their heads and seemed highly stressed out. Kyr explained, "They come back stronger. It is why Crimson is so strong. He picks fights with the strongest creatures and forces them to kill him so he can return stronger. It's how he keeps the other beasts under his control."

"So he's the one who coveted the Druids' power?" They shook their heads. "If not him, then who?"

"Jinx, the One Who Sleeps, is the one who controls Crimson." They shivered as they said the name. "He's intelligent and powerful in his own way, but he has Crimson working for him, keeping the other beasts under control by killing them and keeping them dumb."

"I see. So then every time they die, they make a return and destroy their killer?" I grinned. "Cool, and where does Irgdarn come into this?"

"He is Jinx's master," Greer explained quietly, a haunted look falling over his face. "He is the one who allows Jinx to control the others so that he can experiment and do as he wishes with his stolen magic. How do you know of him?"

"Kuuma told me a little of the story." They frowned and sighed knowingly. "Look, I know you guys are worried, but it'll be okay. Once we find all my friends, you'll see why I'm not too worried. And I'll be helping you all too, so you're in good hands. But seriously, is there somewhere I can go to get some better gear? And get this stuff made into something?"

Sendak and Kyr turned away, somehow more exhausted, and Greer motioned me over to him. "When they kill each other, their leavings are free game. We find them at times and there is a Kitsune I know who works with them. If you're willing to pay, she will make you something. I can take you to her tonight, if you like?"

"That would be great. Thank you."

Greer nodded at me once and I turned to find Maebe and the old woman walking out.

"Your health is impeccable, Majesty, and thank you for your patronage." The old elven woman bowed her head before turning to me. "My king, your friend will sleep through the night. From there, his healing should be complete if two of you will stay and help him?"

"Greer and I have something to do. Kyr and Sendak, would you mind staying to help Muu recover?" They nodded and walked into the house, I thought happier to be away from me. "Thank you!"

I could hear them chuckling inside and Maebe joined the two of us. "What is it that you must do?"

"Time to find a way to use this loot, maybe get some better gear for us?" I looked her over. "You want to come?"

"Yes, I do." Her grim expression made me pause and my unspoken question made her grimace. "I find the disrespect these people endure... vexing. They have not earned this."

"I know how you feel." I clutched her hand in mine and she squeezed back, relaxing slightly with it. "Come on. Let's see what else we can do for ourselves and our friends."

"Let us be on our way." Maebe's soft smile graced us and I stepped off behind Greer and walked with him.

The stone street had little sand in this area, the walls protecting it from the beaches nearby casting a shadow over parts of the city and with it cool breezes and shade.

The shadows beckoned to me at times, almost like the lightning had and it was a little difficult to track how far we had gone. Eventually I slammed into Greer's back and he stumbled forward.

"Greer, forgive me, I was a little distracted." I blinked at the air and glanced around us. This area looked like it was the poorer portion of the outer city, closest to the wall but very unkempt and hot.

A large Kitsune stood in front of a metallic table working with something small. The broad-shouldered man tinkered for a moment before turning and smiling at Greer. "Friend Greer! How fare you?"

"I fare well, Dir'ish. I have come bearing gifts." The way he said that last bit was like he was alluding to something.

"Ah, I see. Come inside, I will bring the tea." He motioned for us to follow him inside the hut to the left of his table.

The hut was plain, with two cots and a simple table with a tea set in the middle. I went to sit at one of the small cushions and Greer stopped me. "Wait."

The tea set was set aside and the table lifted to reveal a

panel beneath that Dir'ish heaved to the side with a wink and a nod. "Tea is served."

We hopped down into the hole in the ground and the scent of smoke reached me from the other end of the humanoid-sized tunnel. It was taller than I was, and broader too—likely had to be able to fit Dir'ish in there.

We followed it for a few minutes before coming into a large, cavernous room with several implements hanging along the walls, a chained table above our heads hanging about twenty feet up. We had to climb a ladder to get down out of the tunnel and after that a young Kitsune woman with black fur and silver eyes stepped out from behind a curtain at the other side of the room.

"Greer!" she called cheerfully. She looked young, like she might be a teenager, but as soon as Maebe saw her, she stiffened and looked confused.

"Anisamara?" Maebe sounded like she had seen a ghost with the way her voice wavered. She let go of my hand and walked toward the Kitsune woman as if she were in shock. She touched her shoulders and her lip quivered. "Ani, is that really you?"

"Yes, Princess Maebe, it's me." The woman pulled her into a hug and they held each other for what felt like an eternity before she pressed herself away from Maebe and looked her over. "Congratulations, Majesty, on your joyous news. You've grown so much."

"I am queen, now, Anisamara." She turned back and held a hand out to me in a beckoning manner. As soon as my hand touched hers, Maebe's joy and confusion swept over me. "This is my husband and King of the Unseelie Fae, Zekiel."

"Hello, Your Highness." Anisamara dipped into a curtsy.

"It's a pleasure to meet someone of my beloved's past." I turned to Maebe and asked, "You know each other, how?"

"I was her lady in waiting for hundreds of years, and I was with her when she went into the dungeon during her challenge." She turned from me to Maebe and touched the queen's face. "Forgive me. I touched something I should not have and it transported me here. Though, it seems my presence was not needed for you to make something of yourself."

Ah. So she watched over little Maebe and made sure she was okay. Like a nanny?

"How are you so young then?" Both women turned their heads toward me, and I wished I hadn't been so stupid.

"Beast blood. It drops rarely, but it does come. It allows me to be reborn as a child to grow old again. So long as I find some before I die again, I will return." Her head turned toward Greer. "I take it you brought them to me not knowing, I thank you. What is it that you needed of me?"

"We came here to see about having items made from acquired beast components." I began to pull them out and place them on the table that she motioned to. She lifted them and inspected their quality. "Can you make something from these?"

"I could. I have other components that I can use too." She eyed them, then me, and finally Maebe. "Since this is for my beloved queen, I will do so at a discount. The typical fare for my help is to remain quiet about how you got this item, plus the gold to replace components. Is this acceptable?"

"Yes, it is. Is there anything more you need from me?" I asked politely.

"I cannot enchant them, so you will need to worry about that on your own. Other than that, I have all the ingredients I need to make an interesting weapon for you. What do you prefer to use?"

"Could you make me a one-handed great axe?"

"Could probably manage that." She eyed me strangely for a moment then handed me one of the lightning essence vials. "This will not be needed, only one can go into the weapon."

I slipped the other vial back into my inventory and peered about. Pieces of various types sat displayed on various counters and benches in varying degrees of complexity and completion.

"Do you have anything for sale? Such as high-quality rings, armor, or other kinds of accessories?"

She frowned and looked up, motioning to the side of the room farthest from her and me. "Accessories are over there, Highness, though you'll be hard pressed to find higher quality on this continent made from illegally-procured materials such as these. Beast materials are some of the highest quality there is in the world, I would wager."

Maebe followed me over to that side of the room to assist me and speak. I could feel her unease and worry through our connection and rings.

"What's on your heart?" I asked softly, knowing that Anisamara could likely hear us.

"I do not know what to do in this circumstance." I saw her frown as she picked up and necklace made of metal that shimmered like gold but looked white. "I want to ask her how she has been, and to spend time with her, but isn't that weird?"

"It can be." I smiled despite the feelings roiling through my mind. "I had some friends like that back home. Go long lengths of time without seeing them and then you want to catch up, but you realize how different you both are from what you used to be. It can make you self-conscious, sure. But if there's a deep connection, that awkwardness can be forgotten and you can still care about that person, wanting the best for them. If you want to talk to her, see if she's comfortable with it. I can make do on my own for a little bit."

Her hand grabbed my right arm and she wheeled me around to stare into her eyes, so large and green as they beheld me with surprise. "I often find myself wondering how it is someone so young can be so wise. And I remember how fleeting your lifespan used to be in comparison to my own, forcing you to obtain this morbid wisdom sooner. I love you and thank you for indulging my weakness."

"It isn't weak not to know something, Mae." I held her face and motioned for her to go to Anisamara. "Weakness is finding what you don't know and doing nothing about it."

She chuckled low in her throat and went to the Kitsune at the other side of the room, joining her at the table amidst her work.

I went back to my shopping, looking over the work available. Figured I'd splurge and get a whole mess of new gear if I could.

A metallic earring made of a red feather, a small bony ring wrapped around something metallic, two metal rings with what looked like gold and platinum running through them, another ring that looked to be made from a tooth. Bracelets covered in thick fur that had metal underneath for protection. Leather armor with bands of fur attached to it with light, metallic chain-mail connecting the arm pieces to bone-covered chest pieces. Honestly, this was pretty on brand for what I thought a Druid should wear. That or a shaman, but I hadn't really run across any of them here since that lizardman tribe back when we first got to Brindolla.

Man, that takes you back, right? Good times. We almost got eaten—but hey, what good story doesn't have a little snack mishap, am I right?

If I was going to embrace everything this place had to offer and really stand a chance, I was gonna have to buck up and put the money out there to not just look the part but stand a chance. We needed gear, we needed weapons, and we needed to get stronger to kill that fucking general and get on our way.

I picked up the bone, leather, and chain mail armor, matching leggings, a helmet that looked to be made of a skull that sported horns on the sides of it and all the accessories I could grab. Plus the shiny necklace.

I laid them out on the counter and began to meditate for a little while with Greer who seemed excited at my prospective gear.

He was a little timid at first, but when I told him what I had in mind for him, he seemed content. Soon enough, I'd talked him through breathing patterns and visualizations for what could happen out there.

"You can't be nervous fighting these things, you have to go

in with the intent to kill them every time, because they won't let you or your friends run away." He nodded as if he understood. "You have to be ready to unleash your own rage and aggression, I know that it's in you somewhere. Being downtrodden and abused. Given a lesser station because you're different from what people define as normal, that's bullshit. I know you're better than that. So we're going to put that to use, and you're going to destroy the shit out of anything and anyone standing in your way. Those beasts, and those other Druids are obstacles in your way. Meant to be broken down and gotten over."

His scent changed, his heartbeat quickening, and I could see there was something different in him. As if all the signs were there, just waiting for a catalyst—something to break him through to the next level of his thoughts.

Of who he could be.

"You are primal fury," I goaded him, my voice dropping to a growl. "You are wrath. You are animal rage. You are cunning and clever. You are the Mother's instrument of change and protection for her world—and she needs you to fulfill your calling as her warrior. Greer—who are you?"

His chest rose and fell, his panting breaths coming faster as something inside him fought for dominance.

"Answer me!"

Sweat beaded on his brow and he strained against himself, biting his lip hard enough that blood trickled down his chin and he seemed to be losing against whatever his fears and doubts were, so I snarled in his ear. *"Tell me who you are, Greer!"*

He shot to his feet, fists at his side and his eyes open, a purple and gold hue to them as he shouted, "I am Mother Nature's fury! I am her protector and her caretaker! I am her primal warrior!"

"Yes!" I howled excitedly, then yelped as something hard and heavy hit the back of my head.

My head whipped around as I rubbed the sore spot behind my ear that throbbed mercilessly.

Anisamara raised an eyebrow in my direction and made a

shushing motion with her hand. "Can you not see that I'm working here?"

"Just tell me next time, man." It was hard to feel justified when even my wife snorted and rolled her eyes at me. I silently swore to myself that if another, elven version of Shellica had arisen from Maebe's past I would probably die.

Greer grabbed my arm and looked at me excitedly. "I did it. I have a subclass."

"Oh, cool!" I grinned at him. "What is it?"

"Primal warrior." He smiled.

My stomach bottomed out. *How?*

CHAPTER SIX

He didn't show me his screen, but when he cast his own aspect spell, his body thickening and growing more wolf-like in front of me, there was no denying it.

But how can a pep talk like that make someone gain a whole new class?

Mother Nature, do you want to weigh in on this? I asked, hoping for a response and saddened when none came.

"Congratulations, Greer, you're the second that I'm aware of to have ever been a primal warrior." I tried to smile at him, because I was happy, but I wasn't sure it worked too well. "You'll have your work cut out for you, and I don't know if the others will have as easy of a time as you did doing it, but you'll be able to fight a little differently now."

"Will I be able to use weapons?" His question made me pause and while I stared at him, he opted to explain rather than waiting for me to ask. "The human Druids don't allow us to carry weapons. They say that our talents are best suited to support and fighting in animal form or with magic."

"Do they use weapons?" My tone had a bit of a growl trickling into it despite my best attempt to sound curious over angry.

"Swords. Typically their house weapons, which could be anything from spirit swords to beast slayer swords." He pulled out a sheet of parchment and chalk, drawing what looked like a katana and then a huge buster sword. "These and anything between."

"Oh, yeah, I can't wait to see what you guys can do," I swore under my breath. "You know how to use any weapons?"

"Not particularly, though I do okay with a bow? Or maybe a club?" He shrugged and scratched his head.

"We'll work it out and see what works best for you, Greer, don't fret about it." I patted his shoulder kindly, and he grinned at me with his newfound wolfish features.

I sighed and looked at all the gear on the table. It would likely cost a lot. And I would probably need some for my friends... maybe we could trade some too?

Heat washed over the room in waves—sudden dull light flooded the room and then was gone in a flash. A jolting zapping sound sundered the air, knocking me to the floor with Greer joining me, almost landing on me but I was able to roll clear of him. I turned to see both Anisamara and Maebe grinning at us over the table.

"I do believe that the weapon is finished."

I blinked at Anisamara questioningly. "What?!" Having to call out over the ringing in my ears made both women laugh wildly. "What happened?!"

I cast Regrowth on myself and it helped me recover my hearing enough to stand and not fall over. "How did you make it so quickly?"

"I've been doing this for almost three hundred years?" She quirked her head to the side as she seemed to decide that was the truth because she nodded and looked at me. "You brought me enough parts to actually make this weapon, and I had the other components to make them all adhere as a single unit. Not to mention I do have my own talents."

She offered the weapon to me and I had to admit that this was an awe-inspiring weapon. It reminded me of a more primeval version of Storm Caller. The bone portion except for the end as the pommel was covered by a tanned leather wrap, that led to metal. The metallic portion of the head had protrusions that had to be the teeth of the beast sticking out of the side and pointed toward the serrated feather blade. The back of the head had a sickle-like crescent blade with three small nicks in it. The weight of it was nice, a little too heavy but with my badass strength as high as it was, it wouldn't be too much of an issue to wield.

The stats weren't bad, but I wasn't going to let it go without being enchanted.

"I take it you like it?" Anisamara raised a brow at me, her gaze steady.

"I certainly do." I set it down, the weight of it making me grin. It would need a name and I was excited to try my hand at it. "So let's talk business. I picked out the accessories I liked, some armor too. Weapon included, how much am I looking at paying?"

She stepped around me, bringing the weapon with her and set it next to the armor. "Decent armor, lightweight and mobility oriented. High quality accessories with difficult to find materials. Weapon wasn't terribly difficult to make. All said? I'd say this will put you in the neighborhood of about five thousand gold."

Greer damn near fainted, his knees buckling slightly, but I shrugged at that.

"I'm interested in bringing more business to you, and more materials to boot." I motioned to myself with a slight smile. "I'm no slouch as an enchanter either, so I can offer you my services if you need them, maybe in exchange for continued services and discounts?"

"There are enchanters in this city already, what makes you so special?" She regained her composure after a second and a glance behind me where Maebe had wandered. "Forgive me, Majesty. It is difficult to think of you being married and seeing a Sylphy like myself as king."

"King Zeke is the understanding sort, though as a favor to me, please remember your manners." Maebe looked almost pained to say that and I took her hand.

"While it's great to be all prim and proper, I'm not used to kingship either." I shrugged at her and I could almost feel Maebe rolling her eyes. "Let's dispense with the worries about propriety and get down to brass tacks here. I can do things other enchanters have no fucking clue about. I have connections to the elements that they will never have. I can make powerful enchantments for you. If you want an example, give me an item to enchant for you and I'll show you."

Anisamara didn't even so much as hesitate before pulling a ring off her finger to hand to me. "That ring."

I looked down at the miserable bronze thing and shook my head. "You want me to strut, you have to give me room to walk. I need something of decent quality first, the higher the better."

She crossed her arms, glancing around, and then picked up the metallic feather earring I had picked. "Impress me and I'll let you have this for seventy gold."

"What do you want to see?" I held my hand out for it and grinned back at her as it fell into my hand.

"I don't care, but it better impress."

I heaved a sigh and laid the item on the table and called Hubris to me with a thought. Anisamara raised an eyebrow at me and I ignored her and everyone else in the room. I could feel the warmth of the feather and gather this must have been taken from Crimson, some sort of fire bird. A fire enchantment would work well for it, but I wanted something that would make it easier for me to be what I could. To give me an edge over the beasts that prowled the continent and to help me find my friends.

I needed to be more animal for this to work and to be able to rely on my senses better.

I have an idea of how to do this, but are there any runes you know that may assist me? Hubris thought about my question and various images floated through my mind until I chose one. *That one. I think I'll need a couple components for this though.*

"Do you have any fur or feathers from beasts that are considered excellent hunters?" Her already hard gaze narrowed toward me before she moved away and grabbed a patch of fur from a shelf and searched several other places before finally growling and exclaiming as she grabbed something.

She returned with a patch of fur, several red feathers, and a large eye.

Master, the feather itself is a good catalyst already. Hubris assured me. *Use the eye and the fur.*

"Thank you, Anisamara." I grabbed the items required and took the earring in hand. Focusing my mana into my left arm, down the limb, into the scepter, and out of it into the feather was as familiar to me as breathing now, and it was so good to be back at it.

The symbols I used were simple, a wolf inhaling a scent, an eagle's eyes, and large ears, all in a triangle that didn't touch each other. In the center of the triangle, I carved what Hubris called a simple enhancer rune. It looked to me like a diamond with a plus inside it that touched each corner, then a circle that touched each of the other symbols. I was careful not to break the lines of the others.

It took a lot more mana than I thought it should have, and then realized that Hubris had been siphoning some from me for himself, his contentment relaxing my unease. Once I recovered fully a moment later, I brought my will and focus to the fore and filled the engravings with mana. *Sharpen the senses, hone the skill to discern.*

I dropped the eye and fur in and they disappeared altogether. 936 MP filled the item and finally it was ready.

Earring of the Hunter
Hearing, sight, and smell greatly improved.
Here among the brush in the wood, a predator lies in wait, watching and waiting for their prey to make their final mistake.

Earring made by grandmaster bonecrafter Anisamara and enchanted by master enchanter Zekiel Erebos.

I handed the item to Anisamara and she pierced her ear with it. It took a second for her to open her eyes but once she did, she gasped.

"This is incredible!" She looked at her hands, then closed her eyes and let her ears twitch. "There are hunters above us who have been drawn by the sound but are too afraid to enter the cave system here."

She took the earring off and gave it back to me with a smile. "I think we can make an arrangement for things like this. If you'll bring me materials and work, I'll give you a discount and put you to work. How's that?"

"I like the sound of that." I motioned to the gear on the table. "How much for this?"

"For that earring? Seventy gold." She quirked her head to the table and crossed her arms. "The rest? Three thousand."

I could live with that. "Hey, works for me."

I dipped into my own personal funds, more than enough money flowed through my pockets for this, but we needed to keep liquid if we wanted to be good, right?

"I'll have a few products you can work on tomorrow morning, if you are available?" Anisamara looked hopefully at me and I nodded. "Excellent. Then you can take these items and do what you please. If you bring me materials and orders, I would work with you on it."

"Sounds wonderful, Anisamara." Maebe grinned and looked from her to me, my apparent shock at the deference Maebe seemed to so easily give Anisamara overlooked. "Do you wish to return to Muu? I have some things I wish to discuss with my former lady in waiting."

"Yeah, I can go check on him." I watched the two women huddle close, smiling and giggling as they walked away. I gathered my gear and turned to find Greer waiting for me.

"We can check on your friend, and then you may join me at

my home." He motioned to the area above us. "It is not so grand as what you are likely used to, but there is space and a place to lay your head."

I smiled at him in genuine gratitude. "Maebe and I would be delighted to stay with you, Greer. Though, we would hate to impose too much. All we need is a floor to sleep on."

"We will manage something, King Zeke." Greer bowed his head and we were back on our way through the tunnel and up into the small hut.

Dir'ish bowed to us on our way out. "Thank you for coming for tea. We look forward to another visit."

"As do we, the tea was delicious." Greer bowed and I followed suit. The darkening sky above us cast red and purple hues of light over the streets as we headed back towards Muu.

Back at the healer's home, she told us that Muu still slept, I could hear his snoring coming from about a hundred yards away thanks to the earring and I just shook my head. "Thank you for tending to him, ma'am."

"You're welcome, Majesty." She bowed low. "The other two Druids finished their ministrations to the slumbering one and left on their own not long ago." After that, she returned to her home.

It made me feel weird being here, where people treated non-humans like second-rate citizens, and having those same down-trodden people calling me king. What good was my title and crown if I couldn't help them? I mean, they were my people too, weren't they?

I wanted to find the humans in charge and put them in their place, but the wild and monstrous roars coming from outside the city wall stilled me.

We are helping them, I growled at myself mentally. *The sooner we take care of these beasts, the better off they will be and can take care of themselves.*

Further along the outer ring of the city, toward the front near the more human-populated area, Greer motioned me into a simple apartment of his own. It was three rooms, one he used for his privacy to go to the restroom and the other two were living spaces. His room had a bed and nightstand as well as a cushion for him to meditate and read on. The other room he used to entertain guests.

"This area will be fine for us, thank you."

He smiled at me and excused himself to go and get something to make for dinner. "I plan on making one of my favorite stews for you this evening!" He grinned happily and left me there alone in his home. Bea, not to be forgotten, nosed me and sat with her head in my lap for a little bit as I thought about what I wanted to do with my gear. The kind of enchantments I wanted to have on my armor and weapon. A new lightning weapon would be awesome and would help with fighting Baranzil. The bastard kraken, whenever we went to hunt him down, would pay dearly for what he had done.

Before I was consumed by my desire to find and kill him, I turned my attention to prepping for the next step of my journey. First, the armor.

I wanted higher defense, something that would remain light and breathable, but be able to withstand a beating, tearing claws, and elemental buffeting. Seemed that the beasts had ties to the elements in an almost primordial way, like they were elementals themselves, but not.

Before I got too far into things, I turned to Hubris. "Would you be able to help me create a ring to store mana in?"

Just one? The question made me frown at the scepter as it appeared standing next to my right knee. *Display the rings you have before us.*

I put them all out on the floor in front of us and I could feel the scepter's perusal passing over all of the rings.

There are two among them that are fitting for mana storage.

I glanced at the two metallic rings with the gold and platinum shooting through them and felt Hubris give his approval.

Two of them? Out loud, "How much could they hold?"

With my assistance, possibly six hundred apiece. Though with your level as an enchanter, it could be less.

"I'll take it." We set them together and gave them the same engravings of a container filling and holding, then runes for sharing and combining. That way they would share and funnel mana to me as equals or one by one without me having to focus on an individual one.

This will be a delicate process; we must give them equal mana simultaneously. I will guide you, but you may want to have your lady wife assist you in this as it will require more mana than you have.

"Very well." I turned my sights to the other rings and thought about what I could do for them. One for mental fortitude would help, and I decided that was a good enough idea for this one.

Thick Skull
73% resistance to all charisma-based charm spells and mental attacks.

Like the beasts of old, you pay little mind to the thoughts of others, be they loud or in your own mind.

I ignored the information for who made the item because it was just the same as last time.

I put it on immediately and immediately felt a little better. I turned to the next ring and opted to leave it alone for now. There would be something that occurred to me on how to use it.

My armor I turned inside out and began to carve the desired engraving into it, a large shield with the six elements carved into it with lines feeding in a circle to each one. Then inspiration took me and I engraved lines feeding to the elements that opposed and strengthened each other. It was one weird-looking array of points, leading to a symbol in the middle that reminded me of a flower with four petals and a circle through them.

This is very complex, even for me—though I know that this was made in a fit of inspiration. You will need a large supply of mana for this as well.

"I understand." I shrugged, sighing and setting it aside as

well. The least I could do was just try to get everything to where I could on my own.

The helmet I engraved with a feather, surrounded by a diamond to give it strength on the inside.

A bull's horns I carved into the bracelets to give me a little more stopping power and defense, and the necklace I wondered if I could make into another item like my former collar.

I'd have to find the right kind of gems to put onto it. The other had been obsidian and decently sized, but that didn't mean it had to be obsidian did it?

It would work best, Hubris corrected me politely. *Obsidian is a link to another realm where one can rest and wait. It is why some cultures use obsidian weapons as a means of sacrificing victims—to give them their final rest.*

"But my babies don't go to their final rest in there." I scratched my head. "Unless you mean that the obsidian acts as a way for them to cross realms?"

That is the answer I had hoped you would gather. The purer that the obsidian is, the easier it is to send something to another realm for stasis.

"Huh." Sighing, I looked around. "Wonder if I could get my mitts on some? Maybe being able to put my familiars into stasis isn't a priority right now?"

"On some what?" Greer asked as he stepped through the door with a basket in hand.

"Oh! Welcome back." I smiled at him and the aroma of warm bread made my stomach growl. He tossed me a small loaf with a knowing smile and I bit into it before answering, "Obsidian."

He laughed as I spoke with my mouth full and poured water from a jug into a large metal pot over a fire pit in his small hearth. "I know where to get my hands on some, but you may find better out in the wilderness, because they reserve the good stuff for humans."

"You know, the more I hear about the people here, the more I want to march into the city and make them feel like shit." He gave me a sad, knowing smile of understanding and went about trying to start a fire. Rather than wait, I simply snapped my fingers and a spark took and a flame stoked to life.

He flinched and looked back at me while I raised an eyebrow at him. "I wasn't lying when I said that I could show off."

"How can you do that?" He looked alarmed and like he was about to bolt.

"I have a lot of friends in high places, some of them elemental primordials." His mouth moved but only a slight whine came as a means of communication. "Greer, you're freaking me out. You gotta use your words."

"How is that possible?! The elements hid themselves away from the world when the humans broke their rules and tried to enslave them."

I looked around, relying on my new earring to listen for anyone trying to overhear us when I said, "There are things happening in this world that make no sense, but the elements admit that their assistance is needed and necessary in this case. That they've hidden away for too long. So, my friends and I have been trying to help them out too. Let's keep this under wraps, right?"

He nodded and did his best to get back to what he was doing before finally looking back at me. "I'm sorry, but I have to know—what can you do?"

"Let's leave it at 'a lot' for now," I replied coyly with a small smile, almost daring him to question me again.

"Alright, keep your secrets." Greer shook his head and chuckled before turning back to his cooking.

He chopped meat to add to the skewers beneath the pot. This looked to be so that the water would boil while cooking the meat. After he finished, we sat in companionable silence for a bit.

Eventually he broke the silence. "You keep speaking of your friends, how many of them are there?"

"The one you met, James, Jaken, Bokaj, Balmur, Yohsuke,

Vrawn, Odany, and Kayda." So eight. "Eight. Really, Kayda is another of my familiars. Don't you have a familiar?"

"I do not." He frowned and I sighed. "What is wrong?"

"Don't tell me that the other Druids forbid you?"

He shook his head. "They believe we would be foolish to think we could partner with animals designed to be here solely for Mother Nature's glory."

"It's no wonder no one has been able to pass the trial, you've sequestered yourselves from nature by living outside its balance!" I shook my head and thumped my knee emphatically. "I have two of them, and they've helped me so much. Their bond shows you how to be better. We need to find you guys at least one each."

"That's something they could throw us in prison for!" he stressed but I gave him a funny look.

"So then why didn't you toss me in there for Bea?"

"She is a gust raptor, they are difficult to control and if she follows you, she's not harassing the animals in the woods." He glanced toward her and gave her an apologetic shrug.

"So I was the lesser evil. I see." That provoked... surprisingly less ire than I thought it would. But it still made me wonder what kind of creatures the raptors were. "Are they that much of a menace?"

"Around these parts? Yes." He stirred the pot and added some vegetables into the mix. "They pick at supply trains to other cities, hunt in packs, and kill things larger than them. Their alphas are insanely strong and their elemental affinities give them interesting abilities that make them difficult to fight en masse. That you have one and she hasn't tried to devour you is interesting."

I could feel Bea's mind brush up against mine and how hungry she was. "Doesn't mean she won't try if she doesn't eat soon. One of those skewers may help, or you can point me to a butcher and I can get her something."

A large hunk of meat fell onto the floor next to her head

and I turned to see Kyr standing there with Sendak behind him. "We figured we should check in on you."

They looked toward my gear and visibly flinched. "You have to do what you have to do, guys. I'm going to get this done and help you. You have to trust me and my ways. Okay?"

"He means to get us familiars!" Greer clapped excitedly and both Kyr and Sendak stared at me with open shock.

"I'll need to know what kind of creatures are in the area to help you get them." I looked around but saw little in the way of what I needed. "Do any of you have a physical map of the continent?"

"I can bring one here." Sendak turned and fled the room immediately and left the three of us there.

"You want to help me with my enchanting, Kyr?" I asked suddenly. His eyes widened in surprise and he looked stunned. "I want to make some mana storage rings and it'll help me to have the extra mana to throw at it. Will that work, Hubris?"

It should suffice, should this one have enough mana.

"I suppose I could offer my hand in this, yes." He sat next to me and I summoned Hubris and motioned to it with my nub.

He grabbed hold and I spoke softly, "Alright, all I need you to do is slowly funnel your mana into the scepter, and I will take care of the enchantment. Okay?"

"Yes, sir." Kyr frowned and grabbed Hubris as I chuckled at him.

I pulled out the components I'd like to add, which was a bit of powdered mana that I had left over from fucking up and taking off my arm. Then as I looked about, I saw the lightning essence, and something occurred to me.

Hubris, is it possible for me to take raw elemental energy and convert it to mana?

If you would like to try it, I do not see why we couldn't make something akin to your Magus Bane. Though doing so with these rings would be foolish, as they are meant to store magic.

I nodded and began to funnel my and Kyr's mana into the

items before me, maintaining focus and willing them to store mana for use as needed by me.

It took a lot of concentration, even with Hubris assisting me, and I felt a headache beginning to creep up the back of my neck as sweat beaded on my forehead.

Sprinkling the powdered mana over it helped the strain a little, but I also threw in a little extra of the water from the Mother's Bosom spring. Two seconds later I felt a ripple in the items I wasn't familiar with.

Stop! Stop now! Hubris cried loudly in my mind and I did exactly as he said.

The rings vibrated, the air around them rippling and humming with energy. I shoved Bea and Kyr behind me, then grabbed Greer by the back of the neck violently and lifted him bodily to me before summoning all the shadows I could muster and forming them into the beefiest version of my Void Shield that I'd ever made.

The two rings lifted into the air and spun not only by themselves but around each other in a wavering circle.

Add mana to them.

"I don't know if that's a good ide—" I began but the scepter struck my shoulder.

Do not question me, boy—do it now!

I snarled and stuck a hand out over the ebony shadows and poured mana into the two rings. A nova of bright colors swam into my view and then a zapping crash before the room went a dull gray and the lights stopped coming.

My mana was gone and so was my shield. Laying on the ground in front of all of us was a ring that looked like the two rings had fused together, making a thicker ring.

I picked it up, still warm and vibrating, and found myself grinning like an idiot and saying a little prayer of thanks to whoever was watching during this.

Nature's Bounty
Stores up to 800 mana. 0/800 available.

Mutated by Mother Nature's influence, the marrow of two beasts joined to give new life to the wearer.

That meant they had become one ring! I slid it onto my finger and felt my natural mana recovery kick in and begin to feed mana into the ring. It would be full within a few minutes and I'd be able to work on other projects with almost double my mana pool.

"Thank you, Kyr." I turned and clapped the man on the shoulder, his vulpine features worried and uncertain. "What's wrong?"

"I've never seen magic like that, and you control the shadows. What kind of person are you?" He and Greer watched me carefully, though Greer seemed more curious than cautious.

"The kind you want in your corner, Kyr." I winked at him and smiled. "You know, I'm more than happy to enchant items for you all too. If you'll bring me weapons and gear you want to have done up for you—provided it's worthy material—I'd be delighted to do it as an exchange of sorts."

"Thank you." Kyr looked thoughtfully at me, then hopeful. "If you don't mind waiting, I have something that I wouldn't mind having enchanted at my house. I live just down the street, if you're willing to wait?"

"I'll take a look at it as soon as you get back."

With my affirmation, he hurried out the door and almost collided with Sendak who carried a large rolled bit of parchment that I assumed to be a map.

They exchanged brief apologies and the Kitsune bolted off to collect his item.

Sendak cleared the table in the living room with Greer's assistance and laid the map out for me to look over.

The continent was massive, about two Africas could fit here and still have wiggle room. The western side of the continent was far from a straight line, the ocean digging into it more than half way up and meeting what looked like a mountain.

A finger jutted into my view as I started to look further north and tapped a location that was marked in a language I didn't understand. Closer to the southwestern border of the continent near a large patch of green that spanned the majority of the middle and southern sections of the map.

"This is where we are," Sendak explained excitedly from across the table. "This large section of green here is the wood, as I'm sure you can guess. Looking at this map makes me a little giddy, so if I annoy you let me know and I will be quiet so you can study."

"Nah, that's okay." I motioned at the map in general. "So this is the whole continent, where is it that the drow live?"

The east side of the map got a double tap. "Maybe a day to two journey north of us, and all the way on the other side of the wood, but you will likely never see one unless you come upon them near their cities."

"And all of the beasts are where, just in the wood?" I asked wearily. If we had to spend all our time in there it would be dangerous working around the trees. I could burn the whole damned thing down with an errant spell.

"They are everywhere, and not all of them are the same size as the ones that attacked you, or your friend." I stared at Greer and he continued. "The raiko wolves are beasts, even the gust raptors, they are just a smaller category of them. The kind that multiply too fast to be reborn so they mate to replenish their numbers."

"Okay, enough of this piecemeal information stuff," I growled and looked them both in the eyes. "I need to know everything you know about the beasts and this continent if I'm to help you, take this trial, and get my friends back. And all of that before I take the beasts and your asshole druid masters down a peg to save your peoples' collective bacon. Got me?"

"I do not know what you mean," Sendak started cautiously with his hands splayed out in front of him like he was trying to calm down a mad man. "But I can teach you our geography and Greer and Kyr can tell you about the beasts. At least what they have been permitted to know. Is this agreeable?"

I made a dismissive motion with my left hand to let him know to go ahead and he started.

"The southern end of the continent, further south than we are now, is all desert once the wood stops. There are marked oases and wild dungeons where beasts roam freely and live in relative peace. Greer will explain that when he speaks." His finger went from the tan portion of the map with a symbol for what I thought was the sun to the eastern side. "This is where the drow claim, this eastern side of the continent has their cities all over it in the swamps and marshlands inland near the outer eastern edge of the wood and beyond. They are unmapped because it is nearly impossible for us to get a cartographer there and their own mages and Druids kill everything that does not belong. Again, they stick close to their cities, so it is not like we will run into them unless they are out and investigating things on their own."

He took a draft of a cup that Greer handed him and then offered me some but I shook my head. It smelled like pee. He shrugged and drained it before his finger moved to the center of the wood. "The heartwood. This is the place where the leader of the beasts, Irgdarn, is believed to reside. Though we are not sure if these rumors are true or not."

"So if the big bad is in the middle of the wood, where does his right hand operate?" I motioned to the map near the center.

"Irgdarn is too smart to keep the only other intelligent beast near himself like that," Greer interjected in a matter-of-fact tone. "Jinx has been banished to the floating isles."

As he said that, Sendak's finger moved to the far north of the continent where several islands dotted the water. "Makes sense. So we don't have to even go there then?"

"That is the one place we must actually go." Kyr snorted and I glanced questioningly his way. "The other Druids will not allow you to go to their sacred trial grounds in the center of the wood unscathed and they command a great many others who will try to stop you. There are three sacred sites where you can undergo the trial. The other is in the far west in the swamps of the southern peninsula where the giguan hunts. The drow are there as well and they view outsiders… unfavorably. The only other option is to go to the floating isles where the other Druids dare not follow."

"And why is that?" I almost dreaded having to ask.

"Aside from the location being all but lost to the annals of time, the creatures there are powerful and travel there is… too interesting for any sort of ease." Kyr grimaced at the words as if they somehow felt off as he said them. "Would it not be easier to find all of your friends?"

"It might be, but I don't know of any way to find them, and if I'm strong enough to compete with the beasts here, finding them could be easier. Is there any reason you're being intentionally vague?" I raised an eyebrow at him and they all nodded. "Why?"

"A geas." Sendak sighed tiredly.

"A what now?" I sat back and eyed them all and they looked like they were about to be physically ill.

"Magical orders given by one person or several people in order to compel a person or people to do something they may not otherwise want to do." Maebe's voice explained from the doorway as she strode inside, looking almost gleeful. "Think of it as a magical compulsory order that can have serious ramifications if disobeyed. Do you see how uncomfortable they are? As if they were close to becoming violently ill? Signs of a geas. Gentlemen? You may feel free to stop conversing about things that you are not meant to."

Kyr, Sendak and Greer all gasped and looked to be attempting to calm themselves visually from what had been close to happening.

"My apologies, guys." I sighed and ran my hand through my fur, just between my ears. "If there are things you can't tell me, just let me know. I hate that those asshats do these things to you."

"To be honest, this was placed on all the apprentice Druids by the city's circle," Kyr piped up with a slight smile. "They don't want their secrets given to anyone—not just outsiders, but other Druids especially."

"I can understand, and I won't press so long as I know." I bowed my head respectfully and then motioned for Maebe to join us. Her nose twitched and she looked pointedly at the pot on the fire with the meat beneath it dripping juices deliciously. "Food done soon, Greer?"

"Almost!" He jumped up and went to stir the pot as Maebe sat next to me, her eyes still on the food. I smiled at her and went back to the map.

"Getting to the floating isles will be interesting if we have to worry about Crimson, but I'm hoping that we can get there easily enough if we plan the route ahead of time." Frowning at the map, I saw several locations that seemed to stick out, possibly other cities.

"I've been as far north as here." Sendak pointed to a settlement on the outskirts of the wood that stopped probably a week away from the coast of the floating isles. "I can teleport us there, but if that will harm the search for your friends, we can travel by more mundane means?"

"I can think on that tomorrow; I'll need to be sure that my friend is okay and will be traveling with us." I patted Sendak on his shoulder and nodded his way. "Thanks Sendak, you're a real lifesaver for this. This helps a lot."

"Always delighted to share his maps." Kyr chuckled and Greer joined him, much to Sendak's feigned displeasure. Now that they were relaxing around us, it was a good dynamic they seemed to have. I liked that.

"Now, Greer—and Kyr, if you'll help—what's the deal with the beasts?" They frowned and Greer looked up from his stirring and seasoning. "How do you categorize them? What's important to know?"

"There are multiple kinds of beasts, the Aelders are those like Jinx, Crimson, and the giguan," Greer began and flipped a little powder in his hand into the pot that gave his stew an earthier aroma. "They are the strongest and hardest to kill. City destroyers if tempted, so we try to steer clear of them and refrain from entering their hunting grounds whenever possible. After that are the Bettae, who are numerous, large, and strong, but will return when killed. Some rate names, others do not. Then the Chimor, those who acquired enough strength on their own to mutate and will return if killed, but as a normal kind of creature. An example of this is the winged raiko wolf you killed; we believe that to be an older Chimor. It would typically have a pack that hunted with it, we do not know why it did not."

"Bea and I did kind of kill a pack previously." Bea's head rose at her name but she merely looked around and then returned to her bone.

"It may have been hunting you for revenge, it seems." Kyr rubbed his furry chin and shrugged. "Seems it paid, so no need to worry about it. After the Chimor are the Gametta, who have elemental affinities, but do not return when killed. Normal raiko wolves, the various raptor species, and other smaller beasts fall into this listing of creatures."

"The higher up on the food chain, the harder to kill and the less numerous they are?" Kyr nodded and Greer mirrored the motion. "I assume the loot is better too?"

"It is likely," Greer replied carefully. "What is found is typically taken into the cities' dungeons for safekeeping and out of the prying eyes of others."

I blinked at him in surprise, and it seemed that both Kyr and Greer were surprised as well. Greer's teeth flashed in an almost evil grin. "I was out sick the day they made the rest of you take the geas not to speak of that part and they never made me take it."

Both of the other men seemed slightly out of sorts, but otherwise grinned as well.

"They aren't expecting anyone to know of it. How quaint." Maebe turned from me to Greer, then back. "I think I just figured out a safer way for you to acquire gear and not have to risk yourself until you need to."

"Are we about to be planning a heist?" I whispered the question to her in awe.

Kyr gagged and Sendak joined him. Maebe turned to them and threw up a wall of dense shadow before turning to Greer and me. "Yes, I do believe we are."

"I fucking love you so much."

CHAPTER SEVEN

The food was good and the company was entertaining enough. Turned out that the item Kyr wanted me to enchant was a sword that had been passed down from his father's father to his father and then him. It was pretty great quality, so I didn't feel like it was a waste for me to do so.

I enchanted it to be sharper and more durable with some diamond powder added to it as a component. He almost wept when he held it and looked at the stats, and I had to almost kick his ass to get him to stop thanking me.

After that, we all wished each other good night and went our separate ways. While Maebe and I laid together in our bedroll, I couldn't help but smile. The plan would work well if it all went accordingly. Would it?

Probably fucking not—but hey, at least I'd get to beat some of those stuck-up Druids' asses, right?

"You seem eager to beat someone," Maebe observed almost expertly.

"Do you live in my head?" I turned to look at her and she snorted at me.

"Hardly any room left in there for anyone, with the way you

make it seem." She laughed against my chest, her lips finding my human skin since I'd shifted into my human form.

"You aren't wrong, dearest." Her scent lulled me closer to sleep.

"I have tried to contact Vrawn; she is not responding. I have sent Fae creatures like Servant and Yve into the continent in an effort to find her and the others." She looked up at me and I stiffened. "Do not tell me that you forgot about her."

"No, I didn't," I assured her. Which was true. "I'd have tried to contact her myself, but the raven was in my pocket and I can't duplicate the message enchantment on it because it needs to be cleansed somehow. I've tried sending Message spells nightly just to see if she's in the area, but nothing. I'm worried about her, but I know she's capable and will defend herself."

"Thank you." Her fingers kneaded the back of my neck and skull slowly.

"You don't have to thank me, Mae. I know I fucked up with her, but I'm trying. I want to find them all. But I can only hope for the best until they either find us or each other. Or I find them. We can only move forward. I trust them to be too damned stubborn to die."

"Your faith is well placed." She giggled. "Seems we found Muu in time. I just hope the others have fared better than he."

"Well, with the Fae searching for them, I'm sure we will have them all together in no time." I held her close and closed my eyes as her sweet scent flooded my nose. "How was Anisamara?"

"She was well," Maebe whispered against my neck, her voice soft and light with a tinge of remorse. "I missed her so much more than I ever realized and though she has refused to return to my service, I find I am not as angry as I ought to be. She deserves her freedom, though in this place I do not know. It is a rather odd train of thought I had never expected."

My palm ran over her back, between her shoulder blades, the knitted muscles there new, but no less her. "She practically oversaw your childhood, Mae. She's like a secondary mother,

I'm sure it is hard to think of her and not feel some sort of long-ing. But she seems to have carved out a place here for herself and her craft. Though I'm not fond of the placement or citi-zenry either."

"Thank you for being who you are, my king." Her sigh of relief was enough.

She was likely grateful I explained away what she thought of as a weakness in a logical way. "Let's get some rest."

"Yes. Sleep well, my king."

———

I woke up to someone pounding on the door and reached for the shadows and light as a reaction.

Greer, bleary-eyed and frazzled looking rushed to the door in a thick robe, throwing it open. "What is the meaning of this?!"

"We have no time." Kyr shoved past Greer into the home and cast his gaze about. "Zeke and the queen—where are they?"

I let my wards fall and presented myself to them as Maebe covered herself in shadows to dress. "What's going on?"

"We think we found another of your friends, and he has been thrown into the dungeon." Kyr peered back behind him and shut the door quickly before lowering his voice. "I cannot tell if I was followed or not, but there was a man found with your other friend Muu. One that had wings?"

"James, a dragon elf?" Kyr growled and punched the wall softly. "What the fuck did they throw him in the dungeon for?"

"Killing a beast that attacked Muu and that village." Kyr spat and a knock on the door only added to the tension.

Greer opened the door. Sendak stepped into the house with Muu following closely behind. As soon as we saw each other he was across the room and we grasped each other in a tight hug.

"Glad they didn't get you, bud," he whispered against my shoulder.

"Same here, man. But I think they got James." I turned my attention back to Kyr as Muu greeted Maebe with a hug. "What's the big deal?"

"The deal is that he is slated for trial and execution for slaying a Bettae." Maebe, Muu, and I stilled. "The trial is a few hours after dawn. We have roughly three hours until dawn now."

"Then there's no time for a detailed plan." I looked over at Muu, his features a mask of concern and anger. "You wanna say something?"

"Not presently, but I'm going to save him. What do you need from me?"

"Get our brother back, there's loot that they're going to be keeping in the dungeon with him somewhere and I have someone who can lead me to it." I grabbed Greer and pulled him closer to me, the surprised man gave a startled cry and seemed to correct himself after I raised a brow at him.

"I will go with them to ensure nothing goes too wrong." Maebe stepped closer to Muu and nodded. "You are to be safe, and use sound judgement to get yourself out safely while you hunt for the loot."

"Where will we rendezvous?" Muu looked between the two of us.

"Anisamara's workshop." Maebe decided for us and I nodded that I could do it.

"What loot is this?" Muu snarled. "Did they take something from us? Why aren't you coming with us?"

"They have materials we can use to gear up and find our friends, and if I go with you, we risk losing out on it." I stepped closer to him and grabbed his shoulder. "Between you and Maebe you'll have brain and brawn."

"And what of beauty?" Maebe asked so suddenly it took me aback for long enough that Muu snickered. "Who is the beauty here, Muu?"

The dragon-kin chuckled and pointed to himself. "Me. Now let's go get our friend."

We split into our two groups, Greer taking me and Sendak and Kyr leading Maebe and Muu to their objective.

"If we're going to the same place, why are we going a different way?" I whispered as we moved along the side streets of the non-human section of the city as discreetly as possible.

"This is the way to the section of the city that dungeon runs concurrent to. You and I are going to skip any guards that we can by doing this." He looked around swiftly between the houses and up and down roads before stepping into a small alley by the wall and lifting a sewer grate up.

It took a huge amount of effort on his part and I had to reach out and save it from falling noisily to the side before he dropped it. "Thank you."

I nodded at him and motioned inside and he pointed toward the wall. "That was merely a lever of sorts. Put it back?"

I did as he said, carefully putting the grate back into its place and heard a small clicking sound for my efforts. The wall behind him opened up and he whirled and bolted in with me closing the distance easily.

The room we entered was small, roughly five feet long and three wide and twelve high. Greer stilled and I almost bowled into him, but caught myself swiftly on the wall.

"Tricky part is the magic in this room." Greer grunted and shuffled a little further away toward the back. "If anyone it doesn't know comes in, it will spray fire at us, then dump the ashes into the bottom of the next chamber. It's an incinerator of sorts."

"And you want me to try to keep the flames off us?"

"Not try—do." He pointed up at three glyphs that pulsed green, then red, and flames burst from them down toward us.

I shoved my left hand up and willed the flames away, then fed water-aspected mana into the air. The room filled with hot steam for a few seconds before the floor dropped beneath us, dumping us toward some unknown room.

"Stay left!" Greer instructed. I looked at him as if he were crazy. As soon as my feet touched the ground after his, we slid to the left together as the ground in the middle and right of the room opened up and swallowed the air. "See?"

"Granted, let's go." His whispered smugness irritated me, but what truly got to me was the fact that this next room had several 'stone' walls that were illusionary. Behind each stood a single humanoid figure that I could just barely make out.

Thinking I was betrayed, I grabbed Greer and dragged him back into the small hall from the room we had been dumped into and growled, "Are you trying to kill my friends too? What do you want?"

"Nothing, I swear!" he spat quickly, his word coming up in a notification. "I promise I have no idea what you are talking about."

I pointed with my right forearm. "There are seven walls in that room and six of those walls are illusions with people behind them. Swear to me you don't know what I'm talking about again."

"I swear I don't know what you're talking about!" His whisper confirmed it—he didn't. I cast Life Sense and sure enough, seven blips on my radar popped up. They were gray though, which meant they posed no harm to us.

I let him go, and he rubbed his neck where I had grabbed him. "What do you see?"

"Six people just standing there, not moving, with their arms down to their sides."

"This used to be the old portion of the dungeon where the insane, murderous, or magically dangerous people were kept away from the general population of prisoners." He frowned and walked into the center of the room and there was no indication of movement from any of them.

I joined him slowly, scanning for any motion and found none to be bothered by so I took a steadying breath and we pressed on. Eventually, we came to an empty room with nothing in it. He shifted some boxes around and finally nothing stood in our way other than a wall of brick.

I frowned at him and he looked pointedly toward the wall,

and then made a gushing motion with his finger up, pursing his lips and pressed a finger toward his ear.

Must be guards close by on the other side of the wall, I reasoned. I sighed and shut my eyes to come up with a suitable way to get around this. The bricks were larger than my head, about a foot tall, and a foot and two inches wide. They were stacked twelve feet high and six feet long. There was no telling how old they all were, so damned near anything I did to the wall would draw attention or ruin the structural integrity of the floor above us. *If I move the whole wall, there could be a fight, and with us trying to get to James, that could be bad so soon. Better to be sneaky.*

I chose a brick at eye level and took the nails of my left hand and slowly dug out the mortar on this side of the wall. I waited until I was sure there was a good amount of space without mortar before taking my shadows and passing them through slowly, until I could feel cool air on the other side with my consciousness.

I pulled the brick to me and then out before looking through. Four sconces held torches that lit the room in dim light, a chest in the center of the floor, and some kind of table against the wall. It was roughly as large as this chamber but with a metal reinforced wooden door that had a slit in it for guards to look through but it was closed from what I could see. The flames flickered over the metal and shone back at me. But the shadows were what I wanted.

I pooled the shadows onto the wall before me and used the sighting hole to pick the shadows I wanted to emerge from. Casting Hollow Step, I walked through the shadows and into the room just behind and to the rear of the door near the hinges.

Greer stared out of the hole in wonder and I heard steps outside the door. I filled the hole where I stood with shadows and waited, controlling my breathing until I heard the metal rasp against the wooden slatting and held my breath.

"Nothing as I thought, Shogi," the voice tiredly droned. "Likely a rat coming in and getting into things. It's fine."

Another voice echoed down the hall as the metal slider returned to its original place. "We check it regardless. Every hour. Besides, that new prisoner seems to be a lot of fun. They're trying to get what they can out of him now, but all he does is stick up a finger and sneer. I can't wait to see that damn non-human die."

Shit, so they aren't going to walk into an empty length of cells after all? We gotta go help them.

I took a deep breath and sent Maebe a message. "Be on your guard, that room is likely full up with Druids. Be safe, we'll be on our way."

"Be safe, my beloved, and be brutal if you must." Her reply made me smile, but I had to get to her to tell her I appreciated it.

I glanced about the room. The chest in the center was massive and locked, not to mention it likely had magical traps on it too. So I just used the shadows to lift it and put it into my inventory. The weight was something else, but I dealt with it once it was inventoried. After that, I cleared what was on the table into my inventory as well before I stuck my arm through the hole and grabbed Greer by the neck as gently as I could. Then turned him into a rat with Polymorph so that I could pull him through.

He bit me and I just dropped the spell and clamped my hand over his mouth before he could launch into an angry tirade. "We need to go rescue the others. They're walking into a full cell area with people who are trying to get James to talk."

"What about the guards?" Greer looked like he was going to be sick.

"I'll take care of them, you just watch my back and if you can fight, fight." I turned and strode toward the door, looking back toward Greer before cautiously trying the knob of the door. It wasn't locked.

These Druids were cocky sons of bitches, I'd give them that. As soon as the door was open, I barreled down the hallway and planted both feet into the guards' chests and they went down hard. I was worried I'd killed them, but when my fingers found pulses, I was off with Greer sprinting to catch up.

One guard I got the drop on at the end of the hallway on the right, my right arm snaking over his shoulder to pull him into a blood choke against my chest. I had to hold my nub to complete the technique and other than his weapon clattering to the ground, it was as quiet as I could make it.

"What in the Mother's world are you?" Greer huffed as he began to panic slightly. I turned to see his eyes widen as he watched the man falling unconscious to the ground.

"Dangerous when my friends need me. Get me to the cells."

He wordlessly pointed to the right of the next hall and made a motion and I just moved on. He would either keep up or not. He was in for a rude awakening when he met the gang.

I peeked around the corner to the next hallway, thinner than the one we were in presently, but wide enough that I could move forward and fight close quarters, but both the guards chatting there had some small clubbed weapons on their hips. I plucked a stone from the wall that had mixed into the mortar and tossed it against the wall, hoping the noise would reach them while they chatted calmly. It didn't.

I heaved a sigh and pulled out a copper coin and stepped a few paces back before launching it into the stones on the other side of the hall. The echoing of the collision scared the guards enough that they only cautiously approached the corner and I had to hope that they wouldn't see me thanks to Radial Refraction. Did it go beyond the hall? Yeah. Did I give a shit?

Come on. You guys know me by now. Say it with me.

Nope.

As soon as they poked their heads around the corner, quite intelligently if I say so myself, they didn't look immediately next to the wall closest to me but leaned toward the middle of the turn where I would have to expose myself to get to them and attack. Clever. Didn't mean shit, but, clever. Just as they decided it was nothing and turned to go back to their posts, the closest one stooped and picked up the copper piece.

"Hey, look what I found all bent on the floor." He showed it to the other guard and I rolled my eyes as I approached softly on my tiptoes and clobbered their heads together with a thud. Both bodies fell and I kept the spell up as I moved toward the end of the hall with Greer behind me, finally silent.

The other side of the hall around the corner to the right had a door that led out into a courtyard. The lightening sky let me know that time was running out despite my best efforts to keep things quick. We still had time though.

"Beyond this place is a set of double doors on both the top and bottom floor. They lead to the same place," Greer explained cautiously in a muttered tone. I could hear him easily. I lifted my nose and began to sift through the scents as swiftly as I could handle, all of them nearly flooding me until I found familiar ones. Muu, Maebe, Kyr, and Sendak had come this way. Then I caught the scent of blood and James' scent. Shit.

Keeping a low profile, we moved toward where the scent was strongest but were forced to clamber up onto the second floor to get there.

"Through here is where they hold the prisoners." Greer touched my shoulder and then nodded to the doors not ten feet from where we huddled in the shadows. "I can go through here with you, but will need to do so in animal form so that the other apprentices do not know that I am aiding you."

"I understand, thank you." Holding my arm out, a small rodent Greer skittered up my arm. He looked like some sort of sugar glider, squirrel thing. Brown fur and a head mostly home to eyes stared up at me. Weird that his animal form wasn't the same color as his skin, though. How did they do that?

I resolved to ask later and turned my sights on getting into those doors.

Inhale, exhale and move. My boots barely made a noise on the wooden planks that made the deck for the second floor. I opened the door cautiously and slipped inside to find more than twenty people standing on this floor with their backs turned.

The shadows off to my left darkened and I knew instantly

that was where my friends were hiding from prying eyes. I shifted that way slowly, ensuring that I took human form so that no one would question me too much. I only wore my normal clothes for this, the need for stealth of paramount import.

The shadows opened for me and Maebe pointed back toward the rail wordlessly; the bond on our ring had its uses for her in finding me and feeling my proximity like that.

I nodded and motioned for all of them to follow me and we stepped off slowly. Someone spoke on the floor below and the words made me want to wring their neck.

"Tell us why you killed the beast and we will make your public execution one that teaches *swiftly*," the sickly-sweet voice implored. "We simply cannot let the rabble think they're better than us, and you needn't suffer needlessly for that, right?"

The rail stood waist high so I had a perfect view of the scene below. A single woman stood in the open-topped cage with James strapped to a table, struggling fiercely. His wings fluttered oddly, and it took me a moment to realize why—they had been nailed through the membrane to the damned wooden table.

A thin, skeletal-looking man swaggered into the cage, pushing a cart with silvery instruments of pain placed lovingly on it.

His fingers drumming the handle thoughtlessly to a rhythm that likely only he heard.

"Speak quickly, so that my associate can forgo his trade." She placed a delicate hand on James' chest but he just stared at her mutely for a moment.

She waited three heartbeats before finally shaking her head. "Vival, see if your methods will loosen his tongue."

"At least have the balls to do it yourself, you sick bitch!" James seethed, his face twisted in pain and fury. "What, too afraid to get your *human* hands dirty?"

"You are beneath me and you know it, and we will learn of why you have come one way or another." She wheeled around and slapped him as hard as she could but James just laughed at her. "What's so funny, filthy animal?"

"Not only are you too fucked up to do the dirty shit yourself…" He laughed louder, but winced and coughed up a little blood. "But you're just plain fucked."

She turned and waved her hand to show the onlookers to him. "*You* are the one tied to a table and on display for peoples' learning pleasure. I think not."

Now, I could almost hear Muu say before a tap on my shoulder let me know it was time.

I looked back and nodded to him, seeing that both Kyr and Sendak had taken animal form and hid in Maebe's pockets while she watched us.

I held up three fingers and counted down, only making it to two before Muu hopped over the railing twelve feet from us easily and landed with a crunch of concrete on the floor.

"Go," Maebe hissed and both of us moved forward, over the rail and into the cage easily.

"Who do you think you are, you *disgusting creature?*" the woman screeched before the man lunged forward with a small blade angled at Muu's back. It bounced off his scales and flew from his grasp.

I held out my hand and the shadows at his feet slithered up his legs and grasped him by his throat, lifting him bodily from the ground. I tossed him away, his back hitting his table and sending his instruments flying.

"Someone who wants their friend back." Muu's snarled response was enough to send the people above us into a frenzy of outrage and a few of them decided that it would be a good time to send lightning coursing down toward us. I laughed and moved as it struck the ground, Muu using their attacks as a distraction to break the table from its setting and lift it with ease.

I stepped from the shadows behind the human woman and lifted her with ease, the others freezing where they were. "Is this one of your leaders?" Several muttered responses failed to reach me and the man behind me started to move toward me.

I flexed my will and a globe of flames engulfed his head, his screams echoed around the chamber and the people above balked, trying to flee. "Mae, keep them here, please."

"With pleasure," she growled in return and the shadows above us and below thickened like iron bars, keeping the observers where they were.

"For far too long you've built on the backs of good people, treated them like lesser beings and playthings to be tossed aside as if they were no better than the gravel beneath your feet." I stared all of them in the eyes, some of them beginning to cast spells that Maebe blocked with ice or shadow. "No more."

"Let go of me, you filthy peasant creature!" I gripped her neck harder, her breath catching as the people watching us stared on in shock and horror.

Growling, "I said no more." I clenched harder and shook the woman hard enough to break her neck before tossing her body on the floor. "You all will pay for your part in this farce of justice."

I reached out and took control of the shadows Maebe held and shaped them into swords, swinging with abandon. No one stood after I was done. No one spoke. All I could smell was blood and the residual fear.

I grabbed Maebe, then tapped Muu with my nub and cast Teleport with a sneer of distaste at the mess I'd left, hoping that whoever found it was as horrified as I was at their treatment of others.

CHAPTER EIGHT

"Any later and National Geographic would've had a show about me." James could barely keep his eyes open now that the danger had passed, but somehow found the energy to be persnickety.

"Yeah, yeah—you're welcome and it's good to see you too." Muu patted him on the stomach and the monk howled with pain. Something slammed in the distance and footsteps echoed down the corridor from Anisamara and Dir'ish's home. The massive Kitsune burst through the entry to the shop and eyed us all.

"We came for tea, dear Dir'ish." Greer looked shaken but seeing the other man looked to have put him a little more at ease.

"Very well, I will fetch some." He frowned at all of us before turning on his heel and stalking out of the room.

"Get me out of this fucking thing, and heal me." James struggled against his bonds and Muu just took a nail and slashed through them carefully.

"Why didn't you snap them, or just get the hell out of there?" My question went unanswered for a few minutes until he was clear from the table and I had to clear my voice point-edly to get his attention.

Finally he looked over at me and shook his head. "They surprised me. Came out of nowhere after I killed that thing for hurting Muu. I had enough time to get the loot it dropped into my inventory before they cast some kind of spell on me that dulled my senses and made me drowsy. I'm still fighting it. The only thing that's keeping me awake is channeling my ki."

"You have access to your ki even with the toxin in your system?" He frowned at me, but nodded. I reached out and cast Heal on him and his health replenished a quarter of what it should have. "Seems you have access to your stuff, but we still need to treat you if we want to be at full power."

"Treat me?" His body glowed a dull yellow and his health recovered a bit more. "Maybe I should sleep, and then heal?"

"May be a good idea." Muu gingerly laid a hand on James' shoulder. "Thanks for saving my bacon back there. I'm sorry that you were the one who got caught over my dumb mistake. I'll make it up to you."

"Dude, don't worry about it." James grinned tiredly and patted Muu's face. "That's what family does."

He passed out right then and Muu just stared at him oddly for a moment before making him more comfortable while we all settled in to wait.

Maebe turned to look at me and smiled. "That was very different of you, my love." I raised an eyebrow at her and she continued. "Bold. Decisive and brutal. Deadly."

"Yeah, is that okay?" I was still a little angry over what had happened. What had almost happened.

"Oh yes, there are times as a ruler when we must decide on the spot if a life must be taken. Those ones were all forfeit the second you stepped in the room. I am just stating this because I know that your morality takes the ability to be at ease with these sorts of things from time to time." I stared at her, still a bit confused and finally she stated simply, "I support you, and think you did the right thing."

"Oh." I blinked and she smiled. "Thank you."

Anisamara joined us five minutes later, her fur and clothes slightly mussed, and more than a little miffed. "What in the Mother's Brindolla are you all doing here before dawn? And unannounced as well?"

"We came bearing many gifts." My tone was full of levity that I didn't quite feel based on what we had witnessed before coming here. I dropped the chest out of my inventory and it crashed onto the ground noisily. All of the other Druids flinched, Muu just frowned around the haul.

Anisamara perked up quite a bit and rushed toward the chest before I stopped her. "Greer, is this thing trapped?"

"Not at all." The elf stepped forward though a little cautiously as he came close to me, and grabbed the impressive-looking lock in his hand and just opened it. "They never lock it because they had everyone geased as far as they knew."

"Wow, how fucking original," Muu muttered darkly, rolling his eyes and stepping forward. He glared at me. "This was for the new gear, right?"

I nodded soundlessly to him. He threw the lid open and then looked to Anisamara. "I'm Muu. I need armor and a spear that will help me fuck shit up. Swiftly, please."

"And provided you pay, you shall have it!" Anisamara clapped her hands in visible delight before kneeling in front of the box and began digging around, pulling long bones out.

I rolled my eyes. *Of course it was a spatial storage container.*

"While you work on his gear, whatever he wants he can likely foot the bill, I'm going to enchant the rest of mine." Anisamara just waved me aside and hurried to her table like a kid about to open Christmas presents.

I shook my head and motioned for the Druids and Maebe to join me. "I'll need some extra mana and you guys are going to assist me a little bit."

"Seems a bit rude to just expect someone to be your personal mana reserve," Kyr huffed as I stared at him. "They do it to us too."

"There's a difference between me and them. I'm going to do some of my own gear, and then whatever it is you've brought me to enchant for you. And then some." I looked him in the eyes, then did the same for the others. "So if you don't want anything enchanted, feel free to back out."

No one moved from where I stood next to a smaller workbench and Maebe's approval thrummed through our rings so heavily that I almost blushed. "Then let's get started."

First, we did my armor; I added some powdered metal ingots that I purchased from Anisamara for eighty-seven gold a pop. Luckily, I only bought two to begin with as getting shavings from it was easily done since I had diamond claws.

Master, you must focus on permeating the different elemental markings with their designated type of mana.

I blinked. That sounded rough. And now he was back to calling me master?

I apologize for my outburst, I thought you were in danger and acted accordingly. I will assist you, feed you mana, and keep your mana from mixing overly much, but you must trust me.

"Let's do this." I had Maebe hold off on touching the scepter just because her magic was so heavily tainted with water and shadow that I wasn't certain it would be a good idea.

Not to mention with the baby... I didn't want to risk it.

Allow her to assist us, her mana is the least of her worries right now. If anything, she has more mana than when first we met.

"Okay." My gaze slid to Maebe who stood by curiously waiting, her eyebrows raising. "Can you help?"

"I was wondering why you had suddenly decided to coddle me." Her chin raised imperiously and she nodded once before grasping Hubris.

It took some ingenuity and drained me and the three other Druids dry, but we did it. Maebe looked no worse for wear whatsoever but she was delighted with the final product and so was I.

Bone Cuirass of the Elements

+21 defense, +13 elemental resistances (all), +3 elemental control

Blessed is he who covers himself in the bones of the elements, for those who attack him attack the elements —and their justice is swift.

Woah. I took a deep breath and moved on to the bone leggings that had the same sort of materials throughout them as the cuirass.

The mana required for this was significantly less than the chest piece because it was a smaller design to engrave. For these ones, I focused less on defense and more on controlling the elements.

I pooled my intent, will, and all of the focus I had in me for this. I even had Bea and Maebe focus on the same things I did. Bending the elements to my will. I wasn't sure how well it would work, but it was something I wanted to try.

Funneling all of the mana I had at my fingertips thanks to the other Druids and Maebe into the leggings hurt something fierce, my nose bleeding from the sheer concentration of it all.

The room spun. *Do not give up, master! If you can do this, you can do anything! Power through!*

Maebe and Bea pressed themselves closer to my body, their presence helping to steady my hands. I sprinkled in the materials I thought necessary, the metal shavings and some extra bone. Just noticing the small dot of red on the bone as it disappeared into nothingness.

A magical pull on my health called to the blood dribbling down my nose and siphoned the crimson life energy into the ether above it. I cut off my mana and my health bar drained faster.

Do not stop! It will kill you.

"My mana is low anyway!" Healing magic warmed me and my health rose before draining and Maebe's hand covered mine on the scepter.

"I will assist you." She stared over at Kyr, Greer, and

Sendak before they put their hands on the staff. "Kyr, you take your hand off. Heal Zeke as we work."

"Yes, Queen Maebe." The Kitsune took his hand off the scepter and cast another healing spell on me.

Focus, master. Push the mana you've been given into the item faster. I will separate it.

I grit my teeth and resumed focusing on my task, funneling the mana into a sieve that Hubris used to keep the elemental energies from touching and polluting each other.

After five minutes and several more healing spells, the draw stopped, the item sated. I almost folded in on myself, but I had to see what we had made.

Elemental Blooded Leggings

+16 defense, +8 elemental resistance (all), +10 elemental control

By blood blessed of elemental favor, these leggings have changed, allowing the wearer a certain degree of comfort, safety, and control with their bonds.

Armor that allowed me to help shape my elemental spells better? I liked it.

"Please rest, everyone." I found the wall behind where I stood and fell against it, exhausted. The room wasn't spinning anymore, so I had that going for me which was nice, but the fatigue was just unreal.

Someone shook me awake, bleary eyes taking in a little bit of dim light before watering. "Hm?"

"It's time to get back to work, my love." Maebe's soothing tone calmed my irritation. I yawned widely and nodded my head. "You only took ten minutes, but it is no longer safe to be here. The Druids search for us. They sent for the apprentices to help hunt us all down."

That woke me up. I glanced around for the three other Druids and they weren't in sight.

"They left to keep up appearances, said they'd be back with us as soon as they could." Muu offered me a hand up. I took it and let him lift me with little visible strain. Damn eighty-plus strength. "Left requests with me and Maebe to get done while they were away."

Arching my back and allowing it to adjust noisily helped get a little more blood to my legs. I felt much better after my micro nap and I'd put my new armor on to celebrate and hopefully ease the strain of controlling my elemental energies.

The armor was naturally light, and moved with little noise other than a slight rasp against my clothes but that was fine.

I moved about, hopped, and stretched this way and that, finding no flaws or drawbacks in mobility.

Three weapons lay on the table for me to look over and I smiled. Each as different as their prospective owners. One, a simple-looking scepter with a large swell on the top of it, not unlike Hubris. The middle, a sword with a bone handle and serrated edge that reminded me of my new axe.

The last one was a hammer. Normal-looking enough with a broad head and a tooth affixed to the back, likely to puncture.

I looked back at Muu and he smiled knowingly. "I gave him the same incredulous look you're giving me. I suppose we could start with that. I want it to be able to grow larger, like to your great axe size, and then shrink back to its original size."

I cracked my neck and shook my shoulders. *I can do that.*

"And also elemental damage if you can swing it—pun intended." I could tell he was trying to be funny, but he just didn't look it with his arms crossed over his chest and a contemplative look about him.

"Yeah, likely." I stepped closer to him. "You okay?"

"No." His simple reply caught me off guard and as I blinked at him, he nodded to the items. "We have bigger fish to fry. Not feeling too wordy, we'll talk later."

"We do, and that's why I worry." I gave his arm a squeeze and he just shook his head at me before I turned back to my work, since I would get nothing else out of him.

Making the hammer grow and shrink wasn't that big of an issue at all. Simple intent, engraving, and enchantment. Deciding on the elemental damage was another thing entirely.

Greer wanted to be able to do a fair bit of elemental damage, so I had to up the ante on that. Figuring things would be interesting this way, I gave it ice damage. To the point where it could freeze someone solid if they got hit too many times or took too much damage from a single strike.

The sword was easier than that; all he wanted was higher durability, sharpness, and lightning damage. I thought about using the lightning essence I had, but I wanted to hang onto that for some reason. Like this nagging thought in the back of my head said to keep it and use it for myself.

What was I supposed to do, drink it?

...Maybe I could? Would it hurt me? I'd think about that later.

The sword finished, I turned my sights on the scepter.

Hubris, you have any ideas on how I can make this thing a weapon like you?

There was no immediate answer from the entity in my weapon, so I called it to my hand and shook it.

Hubris snorted derisively. *There will never be a weapon like me!*

"Can you help me make this thing or fuckin' not?"

I can, but this time, I will require a price of my own. When I didn't say anything, I felt my bond with the weapon loosening slightly.

"Okay. Okay." The bond returned slowly. "What do you want?"

I desire what I always have—knowledge. Answer my questions, and show me something that I can use, and I will assist you in this as I would wish to continue to do.

"Fine." Then I thought about it and made an addendum, "One of each."

Bartering? The voice chuckled. *Fine. One of each. First: what is your home called?*

...Odd question. *Maybe I should make the scepter myself.*

You forget that I can read your thoughts.

"Then you know the answer." I crossed my arms and eyed the scepter in my grip.

Surface ones. That one is buried somewhere deep and I cannot—dare not—try to probe for it.

"Why do you want to know?" I didn't attempt to hide the edge of skepticism and distrust in my tone.

Knowledge for the sake of knowledge itself. I desire to know the bounds and realms of all life. All worlds. I desire to know.

I rolled my eyes and replied, *Earth.*

Excellent. Earth. I have yet to hear of this planet. Now, teach me something that only you, or a few people, would know.

Thinking about it, I decided to default to my Marine Corps knowledge and smiled before replying, *Opha May Johnson was the first female United States Marine, and was the first of three hundred female Marines to enlist during our First World War.*

The scepter stayed quiet for a few moments, then finally, *First, we will need to inscribe several runes on the base of a crystal or gem to serve as an amplifier.*

I smiled smugly. *Good to have you back on board.*

I carved the runes Hubris showed me into the base of a large, uncut sapphire—mirroring that same act in the hole I had to carve into the scepter's bole—with my claws. Magic would interfere with this sort of weapon.

You must simultaneously add the gem to the scepter as you enchant it, Hubris explained politely. *You cannot have anyone else touch the scepter or gem, but you can have them add the components. For this, I suggest the metal shavings from the magical ore you and your friends might have collected from before, and bone from a beast.*

I looked over at Muu. "Hey, the ore we got from the dungeon, you have any of that? The magic kind?"

He frowned and opened his inventory, then shook his head. "Nope, just copper and the common stuff."

"I have some," Maebe offered, stepping closer to me with her hand disappearing into her inventory to pull out a small chunk. "Fainnir thought it pretty, so he gave it to me."

I raised an eyebrow at her and she just smiled. "It was a sweet gift and, to me, he is very much a child."

"I know, sweetheart. I was teasing." I kissed her forehead

and then her cheek before getting back to my work. I swiped a small, but thick, bone from the chest of materials and sat down on a small stool with the staff between my knees for stability. "Muu, I need your help, can you come here?"

He came over and collected the components from me before standing by a foot away.

Now, think of nothing but amplification and control, do you understand? I nodded an affirmation and it continued. *Ensure that the runes match up, all three of them, and do not cross them. Begin charging the items now.*

I focused on amplifying magic and controlling it to the point that I wasn't sure how long it had been, but my mana drained swiftly.

The components need to be added as you press the two items together, begin decreasing the distance between them slowly.

I did as ordered, beginning to move the gem closer slowly, and whispered, "As they touch, drop 'em on, Muu."

I heard a grunt and Muu's shadow moved over my hand.

A steadying breath just before the gem and wood met, then two objects dropped into view and flashed away in a brilliant light that made me cry out in surprise.

The scepter looked fantastic, the wood now sporting a casing of bone and metal stripping that wove in and out of it.

Is there a way to add runes to this? I wanted to try to make it stronger, wondering if I could do it for myself someday.

Not by you, only the owner can do so.

I sighed and set it on the table to let the owner come and get it.

I was happy to see that I had grown in enchanting too, up to level 51. Not bad at all, all things considered, and it wasn't over.

I enchanted my helmet to be lighter, invisible when worn, and to warn me when someone was behind me. After the heavy lifting—all the considerable amounts of mana I had been throwing around—this thing was a cakewalk to enchant. Honestly, I could have added elemental control of some sort to it, but if I was in a fight and it got knocked off, I'd be hurting for more power and it was the most likely thing to happen.

The bracers I would be modifying from the simple horns for stopping power and defense to add more elemental control. If I was going to lean into this thing, I would lean all the way in.

I'd save that for now. I still had a necklace and two rings to enchant. Not to mention my new weapon.

Thinking some more, I opted to make a ring that would not only help with my defense, but to actually give me a shield to use in moments of high stress or need. Kind of like the item I made for Yoh.

Thinking of him made me wish I knew where he was, or how he was doing. Wondering if he was safe.

I shook my head; he wouldn't want me to dwell, and then he'd call me a bitch for doing it in the first place.

I focused wholly on the ring, engraving shields into it and to pull from a store of mana outside my actual mana pool.

If the damage the shield took exceeded its mana pool, the ring would either break, or there would be a concussive shock-wave that would liquify something nearby. Likely the former, though.

I enchanted that with Hubris' aid and turned my sights toward a final ring. I'd have to purchase another from Anisamara.

Maebe's hand pressed into my view and deposited a ring onto the table. I glanced up at her and she smiled. "I explained what happened with the other rings to Anisamara and she gave me this for you. Use it wisely."

"Thank you, and please thank her for me." Maebe left me to my work and I focused on what I wanted this ring to do.

We will use a similar, pool-type concept for this that turns elemental energy into mana that you can then use for spells, Hubris explained swiftly, having me put the ring onto the table. *But first, we will be making a table to enchant it.*

"This isn't going to come cheaply, is it?" I rolled my eyes, suspecting another exchange of knowledge.

Not this time. I colored myself surprised and my eyebrows shot up at the response. *But in the future, I may ask again.*

"Okay then, let's get cracking." He laid out a mental image over the bench in front of me and had me carve with my claws. It took a little more than an hour, but by the time I finished the image, it looked like a seven-pointed star. A septagram? The circle bisected the points about halfway up each one, and on the other side I carved a symbol for the mana type. Inside the circle, I carved a rune for conversion, and in the center, I put the runes for a mana pool.

Those were complicated and honestly, I don't think I could explain them to you if I even tried, so just trust me and let's move along, shall we?

"Zeke, you about done?" Muu grunted to me, looking irritated.

"No, and if you want decent gear, don't rush me." He looked piqued, so I added, "I get that we're in a bit of a hurry, but this needs to happen where the draw on my strength won't leave us fucked out there."

He looked to be thinking on it before he nodded once and turned to walk away.

Now, in the center of the carving is where you will put this ring. I picked the ring up, the metal of it cool against my fur, but the fangs that decorated it were warm. And there were six of them. *Try to match the fangs to the elements.*

"What about the last point of the star?" My curiosity stuck me and I found how little of my craft that I still had to learn vexing.

That will be for pure magic itself, and we will put that there last. You have placed it correctly. Take your mana and cover the carvings exactly as they are with unaspected mana.

I closed my eyes and focused on following what Hubris ordered, letting the mana flow from me into the table. A dull glow filled my immediate vicinity.

Good. Do not fill the elemental symbols yet, I will assist you in that.

A moment later, I had the majority of the carving traced

and filled with my mana. I kept that under control and still as I slowly trickled elemental mana to Hubris, where he used it to fill the symbols, then half of the conversion rune on the opposite side of the circle as well.

Hold it steady, master, Hubris encouraged. *Now I will add the rune for magic, power it and the other half of the conversion runes.*

He did as he said he would and I watched the blue mana flow into all the runes separately. The one for magic rune looked almost like a valknut from Norse mythology, but it opened in the middle oddly.

As soon as that was complete, the magic in the air made my skin crawl, and I had to fight the urge to stop what I was doing.

Shrink it, I will help you.

I grit my teeth and began the task of pulling the image closer together while Hubris assisted me in keeping the line work true and to scale. Turned out that shrinking the symbols and whatnot made me burn through my mana faster. Sweat dribbled down my face and arms, my breathing growing more and more rapid and shallow.

Hold it, hooold it, Hubris encouraged softly as I worked. A growl of annoyance reverberated in my throat and I pulled the mana tighter faster. *Now fold it up onto the ring, carefully covering the corresponding fangs with the points of the star.*

I grunted, willing the image of pure mana to fold up without changing the dimensions of the symbols or runes. Panting now, my vision tunneled and all I knew was this one thing—nothing else mattered.

That is enough, master, you may drop the connection with the mana.

I let the connection fall away and closed my eyes. The strain had been so much worse than anything I had ever felt when enchanting.

Now we can enchant it.

I rolled my eyes and almost fell over when the scepter chuckled at my inward groan.

CHAPTER NINE

The enchantment for the ring wasn't all that hard, to be honest. The engraving fed the intent and focus for the magical effect that was required. All I had to do was introduce the elements that it would be taking in to convert to raw mana for me to use.

That was actually the hard part. That meant that I had to have several spells tossed at me in the span of a few seconds, the different types needing to go in a specific order.

Fire, water, wind, earth, shadow, light, and a random non-elemental spell should suffice, Hubris explained carefully. *Oh, and you cannot cast the spells yourself. It would likely not go well for you to eat your own mana.*

Even if I don't cast a spell? I thought about calling the shadows to the ring and letting it soak them up.

It needs to be a spell of some sort that is cast on you. There has to be intent behind it.

Well, there went that idea. Maybe it would work if other circumstances were met? Who knew? We would have to see about that later.

I stood up and stretched, then looked to the others, all of

them resting or conversing amongst themselves quietly. "Y'all wanna help me finish enchanting this?"

"More of us acting as a mana pool for you?" Kyr raised his eyebrow and looked as if he found the whole thing distasteful.

"No." I glared at him and he took it in stride. Good for him, looked like he was done cowering. "I need you all to cast elemental spells at me in a specific order."

I explained the order and they frowned, Greer looking significantly more worried than his friends. Maebe watched quietly, but the elven man stepped forward and looked at me as if I had said that unicorns would be flying into the room in onesies. "Are you certain there isn't another way for this? The elemental spells we know are quite powerful as we have to use them to chase off beasts."

"What's the harm?" I had all my armor on anyway, and could heal myself if needed.

"You could die?" Kyr rolled his eyes and shook his head. "You really are the strangest man I have ever met."

"That he is," Maebe purred and smiled. "Let us get this over with. One of you be ready to heal him at all times."

Sendak shook himself out and took a ready stance with his hands upraised. A flick of his wrist and a barked word that I couldn't grasp, then a flaming whip shot out of his hand. "Let me know when it is that you are ready."

I cracked my neck and tried to relax but my adrenaline spiked. I snarled and barked, "Bring it!"

The whip arced through the air toward me and I raised my left hand with the ring on it and willed it to absorb the element that came near it. As soon as the whip cracked against my wrist, stinging me fiercely and dropping my health by a measly 5%, the flames dimmed and Sendak frowned.

"Don't stop, water!" A spray of ice shards flung from nowhere in front of me, Maebe having cast from where she stood several feet back. Some of the shards blasted into my arm, the cold numbing the limb considerably. I shook off the pain, still willing the ring to take from the spells and it did. The ice melted slowly.

A gust of wind slammed into me and knocked me onto my back, small slices opening on my arms, the torrent of it lessening only slightly before the cave roof above me looked to have split to drop a large portion of stone toward my head. I rolled to the side, my left hand touching the spell as it slammed into the ground where I had been. It began to crumble slowly, but then the shadows came to life.

They whipped at me from all directions, my life sapping slowly but surely away. I stood at 71% and falling, but a ray of warm, golden energy hit me and still my ring ate at all of it. The attempt to heal me did nothing and finally another weird magic tried to invade my mind. I willed the ring to eat fast, more, but the magic persisted.

Just as quickly as it came, it was gone and the ring on my finger glowed a myriad of flashing colors along the teeth before growing larger and smaller. The fluctuation didn't feel wrong, but settled it against my skin like it was satisfied.

Devourer's Gorging Pool

This ring converts a portion of the magics cast at the wearer into raw mana to be stored for later use when the wearer so wishes, but for everything there is a price. 250/500 MP.

Activation and use of the mana pool will cost 1 HP per 5 MP taken whenever used.

His avarice knows no end but that of the devoured, and he will devour all that he can. Beware that he does not devour you, dear wearer.

"What in the actual fuck is this thing?" I whispered in wonder, glancing at it then looking up at the others. "Who cast the mental magic?"

The others looked at each other, then me, and all of them shrugged. Greer answered, "None of the Druids we know have any sort of mental magic available to them."

Maebe shook her head and Anisamara merely glared at us. "Stop being so loud!"

I ducked my head and just shrugged it off. It could have been an already present spell, perhaps?

"James is doing well enough that we should be able to administer the meds." Muu broke me out of my reverie and I nodded.

We took the time to mix the plant and water together, then forced him to swallow all of it.

Maebe's shadows whipped over him, Sendak going in to make sure that he stayed alive.

I shook myself off and checked my notifications. Nothing. Not having leveled up from that one item was disappointing, but oh well.

I turned my sights on my weapon, the axe almost calling to me. If I could make something so awesome... maybe I could do it again?

Two of the elements I usually leaned toward called to me almost wishfully to be combined into something badass, and who was I to deny them?

I waited until my mana and my ring were full, Maebe attacking me with shadow magic halfheartedly to help me fill the Devourer's Gorging Pool. A painful process, but it turned out that it was good practice at dodging and maintaining contact with the ring.

"If you two keep this up, I *will* kick you out!" Anisamara barked angrily, her glare in our direction giving us pause. We stopped at 457 MP in the thing and I turned back to my crafting.

I engraved the axe with lightning bolts along the side of the head, along the teeth of the axe.

Before I got started, I turned to Anisamara. "Has anyone ever consumed the elemental essence of the beasts?"

"Are you insane?" She balked at the idea and shook her head.

"Usually? No." I frowned, I looked into my left hand and

the essence was just there. "I just feel like this thing is calling to me. Like it *wants* to be consumed, become a part of me."

I shook my own head, growling in frustration. "I know that I have a special bond through the element with Kayda, and it was a special bond that formed with us. Plus, it was the first element that I had ever used to truly enchant something."

Maebe watched me steadily. "Are you certain that you feel this?"

I blinked at her, then at my hand with the small tube of contained liquid lightning. "Yeah."

"There is no telling what that will do to you." Anisamara asserted, stepping closer to us, away from her work bench.

"Hubris, come to me." I held my nub up and motioned to the air.

I am here at your will, master. The scepter swayed in the air beside me.

"I'm going to do something that makes everyone here uncomfortable." They watched me carefully. "I need you to take care to watch over me and them while I do it. If there are any spikes of something that could kill me, I want you to drain my mana and use it to heal me."

"I swear that if you die, I will kill you." Kyr harrumphed. "But I'll have to bring you back to do it."

"You can raise the dead?" I looked at him and he nodded. "Seriously?"

"Yes!" He spat on the ground. "I hate doing it though, so don't make me."

"Is it a Druid thing?" He shook his head and I frowned. "Are you more than that though?"

He nodded once and I frowned before walking closer to him. "If you want to talk about it, we can. But if you would help me out if I need it like that, I'd appreciate it."

He looked away, his scowling face brooding and thoughtful before he smacked my chest lightly. "You seem worldly in a weird way. Maybe I'll take you up on it some time."

I turned back to the bench and the essence, before popping

the top and throwing it into the back of my throat like a tingling shot of booze.

My mind sang and every muscle in my body went rigid, then the voice I heard every now and then when I dealt with lightning burst forth.

Hello, beloved.

My vision grayed, my body no longer a part of that mortal plane of existence, and instead I floated on the clouds in the sky. Deep, dark, and roiling. The scent of static and ozone all around me.

Arcs of azure, yellow, and deep gold lightning spun around me, like children playing tag with an adult until finally they joined a larger cloud. A man sat there, his dark skin reminding me of Thor, the Kirin, the deep gold of his lightning markings scattered across his bare chest. A fine goatee of storm-cloud gray hung from his chin and his eyes sparked with the azure lightning.

The one who answers the call, the one who answered my summons at long last. And the one who rescued my beloved child. Who calls to my children for aid?

"Who are you?"

He lifted his eyes to me, his staff living lightning that danced against the clouds at his feet. His mouth quirked up at the sides. *You know who I am. Though I am significantly weakened, we lesser elements still adhere to the call of nature and her children. It is why your kind can manipulate my power.*

"So that would make you the Primordial Lightning Elemental?" He ducked his head once. "Forgive me, Lord of the Storm, I didn't mean to be so forward."

Do not fear, beloved. The others may claim you, but you were mine first. Ever since you saved that chick from the same fate as her mother, I have called to you. Blessed you with what little aid I could give you.

"Is there something that I can do for you?" My voice was almost too quiet, but he seemed to understand me.

Yes. He stood from his throne and walked toward me. Just before he reached me, he stopped and parted the clouds to my left with a raised hand. I saw a wild landscape of snowy mountains. We drifted closer and I saw something that made my heart soar.

"Kayda!" Looking again, I could see that she was nested somehow, sleeping, and below her lay several slumbering figures. Kirin. This must have been Thor's herd! Where were Vrawn and Odany? "Where is this?"

This is in the northern reaches of the continent you currently reside upon. He waved the image away and we floated back. *I guided her to my other children so that they might protect her and her guests until she recovers. But they are not wholly safe, and I require something of you before I can gift you more of my love.*

"If it's for her—anything." I stepped closer to him and he laid a hand on my shoulder.

I knew I could count on you. I wish you to gift my blessing to one of your Druid friends. My ability is great and with someone else whom I love working to grow my influence, I will be able to protect my children. He paused, his gaze flicking to the plane around him. *My realm and the realm of the prime are close to each other, but even we lesser elements desire representation. Will you do this for me?*

No hesitation. "Yes."

Thank you, beloved. I will gift you a part of my power for this weapon you intend to wield. But before that, I want you to touch your chosen so that I might anoint them.

He leaned down and kissed my forehead. A crackling *pop* sent me flying back into my body, lightning sparkling all around me. The others watched me in fascination, Kyr standing closer to make sure I was okay.

"Kyr, my new friend—welcome to the fold, brother." I reached out and clapped him on his shoulder and lightning struck from me to him, gold, black, and azure sparks electrocuting him and making his fur stand on end.

I felt the blessing coming to me and pulled the shadows in the room around us, so thick and viscous, to me. Raising my nub into the air with my left hand on my axe, lightning slammed into my right arm like a lightning rod and passed into the axe at the same time as the shadows did. My intent and will bathing it and mixing the two magics together as one.

Once the enchantment stuck, I lifted my hand and basked in the warmth of the energy racing through my body.

Abilities Unlocked!

Lightning Elemental Form – Caster takes the form of a lightning elemental. Cost: 100 MP. Cool down: 7 minutes.

Aspect of the Storm – + 12 Lightning damage, +20 Dexterity. Movement speed, attack speed, and reflexes greatly improved. Beware the storm's fury, for it is swift and unyielding to all.

I cannot give you more without harming your connection to the elements, the Lightning Prime whispered to me. *But this much I can do, and know that my children and I love you.*

"Thank you," I whispered to the ether around me and smiled. Looking over at Kyr, I knew that he was reading his notifications when he saw me glance at him.

"What did you do to me?" I smiled at him and he grew even angrier. "What do I even do with this?"

I knew without even needing to have a quest. "Reach out and call for a friend. Someone to help you understand your new gifts. Reach out and say, 'Come to me.' Someone will come."

"What even am I, now?" Kyr huffed loudly, throwing his hands up, but I said nothing. "Will someone else help me understand since he will not?"

A small thunderous boom and a flash of lightning blinded me for a second, then a small electrical voice stated, "You asked, and I am here, master."

Kyr blinked at it, then me, then back at it. "And what in the Hells are you?"

"I am a lightning elemental sent to help guide you and help you understand your new powers and role in the world." The elemental turned to me reproachfully. "You weren't very nice for leaving him in the dark like that, beloved."

"I know." I smiled at the little creature and it sent a small bolt of lightning crackling my way, but it was easily dodged. "Kyr, you have to name him to seal the contract and bind him to you."

"What do I even call an elemental?" Kyr clapped his hands to his face and groaned. "Why are you so much trouble, Zeke?"

"Trouble is the most fun." I winked at him and Maebe laughed loudly. Anisamara had moved closer to the scene and watched dumbfounded.

"How about Cloudy?" Kyr tried.

"No." The elemental shook its head. "You better not call me 'Storm,' either. It's cliché."

"Then I will call you Rai." Kyr sighed and crossed his arms. "And also rude."

Rai crossed his arms the same way and mirrored his master. "Never have been the nicest, but I am the smartest, and I'll help you."

"Did the little one call you 'beloved'?" Maebe's voice whispered into my ear, I flinched and found her floating next to me.

"Yes." I reached for her hand and she allowed me to take it. "The lightning elementals like me for saving Kayda."

"I like you too." She narrowed her eyes at me and kissed my shoulder. "I shall allow this, as I am beloved by shadows."

As if in answer, the void crept up her body and covered her legs. I smiled and reached for my newly-enchanted weapon.

Nether Bolt

+23 Lightning Damage, +20 Shadow Damage, +18 to attack.

Void Spark – Attacks with this weapon have a 20% chance to stun or lock someone within their own shadow.

At times when the black lightning strikes the barren grounds and the world beneath it screams, watch for the sparks in the shadows, for it is they who will haunt thy dreams.

My God! I smiled and moved the weapon about, the dark lightning in it flickering as if alive. I was almost itching to try it out when I remembered something. "Hey Mae, do we know how much longer it will take Xiphyre to make my arm?"

She looked to me, then looked away sheepishly. "It seems I have forgotten to ask him. Forgive me."

I laughed, rubbing her shoulder affectionately as she looked at me aghast. "It's pregnancy brain, it's a common thing for some pregnant women to be a little forgetful."

"I wonder how much I will forget if you refer to a lapse in judgement in such a way again, Zekiel Erebus." She looked at me steadily before nodding once. "I will ask him. Please wait."

I watched as she walked off to a secluded space, then turned to Greer and Kyr. "The two of you need anything else? Have special items you want me to enchant? Clothing? You want to put in for some gear from Anisamara?"

"Do not forget that you owe me enchanted pieces," the woman warned me, then raised an eyebrow at me. "You seem like you are in a better mood. What happened?"

"My baby is alive." I grinned at her and she looked to Maebe. I didn't correct her and went about my business.

I had the time to enchant both Greer and Kyr's battle robes for them, adding some metal and magic to make them a little more durable and protective, then a couple random items for Anisamara. She was delighted to see that I was capable and had me wait while she went to go get what she called 'the good stuff.'

Wasn't good enough that I was literally making miracles and shit happen, *nooo*, I had to enchant random bullshit and make things for her.

I rolled my eyes at her, then the sound of fluttering wings grabbed my attention. I turned toward Maebe to find Xiphyre standing there with a huge grin on his face and his large wings spread wide.

"Hey Xiphyre," I greeted him warmly as he fell to a knee. "I take it you're ready with the order?"

"Not at all." He cackled to himself. "Neither will you be, but this shall be the *grandest* unveiling of a piece that I have had in some time! Come."

He fluttered to a workbench and laid out a large metal plate that had runes, symbols and circles all over it. Next, he pulled a covered object and set it on the plate gently. "Come here, King Zeke, and witness history as I make my first ever not-cursed masterpiece!"

I rolled my eyes and he just rubbed his hands together. He threw the clothes over the item aside and motioned to a perfectly-formed metallic arm in a shimmering gray-cast metal. "New material that is highly conducive to magic, durable and powerful. We've been calling it Thoganite."

A barking laugh escaped my throat and the Ragalfr snorted at me. "I can imagine it would be very powerful."

"It will be indeed." Xiphyre took a deep breath and frowned. "I need components. Have you come across anything you wish to add to this? Anything of high quality, possibly rare in nature?"

Anisamara walked back in, saw Xiphyre, yelped and everything she carried clattered to the ground. "Who let this little cretin into my home?!"

"You!" Xiphyre howled and moved so swiftly I couldn't follow his movements. The two of them collided and wrestled mightily. Smack, punching, kicking—hell, at one point I swear I saw Xiphyre bite the Kitsune.

"Would you two knock it the fuck *off?*!" My snarl of outrage brought them both back to themselves. "He's here because we had business with him. What's wrong with that?"

"This little bastard is the reason why I ended up in this hellish place in the first place!" Anisamara scowled at Xiphyre. "I was trying to rescue him from the dungeon and ended up touching the thing that brought me here."

"I didn't need your help!" Xiphyre roared, his hands on his hips. "I had it under control."

"Oh?" Maebe interjected sweetly. "And I suppose that my

saving your life and gaining three favors from you in recompense was just a fluke?"

The Ragalfr spat and fluttered toward the table, landing on it and sitting there. "Can we just do this? I would rather not have to deal with this insufferable woman any longer than I need to."

"You're just mad that you can't handle yourself in the dungeon." Anisamara rolled her eyes and I had to bite back laughter.

"Can we focus here?" I stared at both of them. "Please? Anisamara, you said you were going to find the good stuff? This limb is for me. If I get it, I can use it to help more. Can I buy anything from you for it?"

Her scowl turned to me and, with a huff, said, "If you want components, I can sell them to you. But they will be full price since it is for his work. No haggling, no negotiations."

I threw my hand up. "Fine! Deal!"

Xiphyre walked to the pile on the floor and dug into it until he found something he seemed to like, then another piece. He pulled them both out and allowed Anisamara to look them over and I just threw her a small pouch with a thousand gold. "If it's more than a thousand just let me know."

She stayed quiet and resigned herself to watch from a distance, crossing her arms after hopping up to sit on a different work bench.

"I will have you drop these into the item when I say so." Xiphyre handed me a long bone and some black fur and leather scraps. "Pay attention."

He rubbed his hands together wildly then clapped three times before slamming them onto the metal plate inside two circles. Magic flared from those circles, into a triangle that touched them, then led to several other runes and symbols. Xiphyre smiled as he worked, muttering words that didn't quite stick in my mind, seeming to melt away from it as soon as I tried to understand them. More runes flared to life beneath the piece. The magic continued to race along the trace work and symbols like fire following gasoline to an explosive barrel.

Once the whole plate lit up, runes and figures shimmered into being on the metallic limb, dancing and swaying as the little man's voice raised in pitch and fervor. His fingers began to tap small runes on the circle, the runes on the piece stilling when he did.

He blinked once, then barked, "Bone!"

I dropped the bone over the item and the object burst into a thousand pieces and funneled down into the limb on the table. He continued to sway and mutter, his eyes half-lidded, the room around us growing cold enough that we could suddenly see our breath. "Fur!"

I dropped the fur scraps onto the limb and they froze as they hit it, wrapping around the piece as if claiming it for itself. Three barked phrases from Xiphyre and his wings flickered out of existence for a moment. Once. Twice. Again they flickered until they were gone. The temperature dropped and ice covered the table around us, the Ragalfr shivering but working on, his nose bleeding profusely into his shirt.

Finally, he howled a single word and the magic was powerful enough that a concussive blast sent most of the people in the room except for Maebe flying back. Luckily, Anisamara's body broke my fall.

I clambered back up to my feet before making sure that both the two Druids and the Kitsune crafter were alright. Xiphyre groaned weakly, sitting up holding his head.

"What the fuck was that?" Muu cried, stepping clear of the shadow barrier around James.

"That was me bypassing the curse that comes with perfect creations," Xiphyre explained tiredly. "Theoretically, it is always different. I'm not sure what this curse would have been, but the negative effect on the environment couldn't have been a good sign. But it is yours now, King Zeke. Put it on."

"Fuck that, are you okay?" I stepped closer to him but all he did was wave me aside.

"Powerful magic like that costs much, but I'll be fine after a little bit." He blinked and scowled. "And my wings are gone. That was a lot of magic I used then. Phew."

"So they will come back?" Greer's quiet question cued an angry glare from the Ragalfr. "Sorry."

"Yes, they'll return. They always do, they're a part of me." He focused and his wings, a little beaten and worse for wear, reappeared on his back. "Now, put that arm on, King Zeke!"

I rolled my eyes and turned back to the bench. I lifted the arm with my left and slid my right forearm into it. It fit well, and as soon as it was there, I could see the notifications for the stats and a prompt.

Fae King's Grasp

Much like the fickle nature of the Fae themselves, this limb is as shifting and everchanging as they are. This prosthetic limb will act as if it were the natural limb of the wearer, and is highly conducive to magic and magical manipulation.

+10 to all spells cast with this limb, +11 to all magical manipulation with this limb.

While worn, this limb can change shape at will, even to the point of becoming a weapon.

Who needs a scepter, stave, or sword of office when you could just punch the life from anything that displeases his royal highness?

Would you like to attune with this item? Yes / No?

"You've really outdone yourself, Xiphyre." I affirmed the connection and the limb drove itself onto my arm, the fur that covered it haphazardly morphing to cover it fully then my arm until it blended in. I flexed the fingers that I had missed for so long while I hadn't had my other arm. It felt good.

Really good.

Maebe stepped closer and meshed her fingers with mine. "Warm like you." She moved her hand and stabbed at my hand with a blade of ice. The makeshift weapon ricocheted off to the side. "With all the benefits."

"You totally just took my fun away, I'll have you know," I growled at her softly.

She looked completely unapologetic.

"As much as I desire to watch these warm, tender moments," Anisamara droned dryly, "I have items I need enchanted and work to do. Do you know when you plan to leave?"

"As soon as James is feeling up to it," I assured her. "I'll work for the next couple hours for you and then we will see how he's doing, how's that?"

"Let's get to work then." She motioned to her stock pile of items next to her hip and grinned. "Hope that arm does well."

Xiphyre laughed once, harshly. "It will."

———

I almost wished that he had been lying, but the arm worked like a dream and, true to his word, it did help with my enchanting.

I enchanted for roughly two hours straight. Complex ones, simple ones, slow and fast. By the end of that, I had gotten to level 53 enchanting and my brain wanted to melt.

I had to rest and recover, the throbbing brain matter in my skull shrieking at me to stop being an imbecile with my mana and just relax already. Being perfectly honest, I was starting to slip and almost make mistakes. The only reason I hadn't so far was due to Hubris and his constant biting commentary.

The shadows around James fell and all three of them walked out, James looking much better than I felt. His wounds healed, and his easy smile in place.

"You look whipped." He raised an eyebrow at me.

"You shouldn't even be able to stand," I observed lamely. "What's going on?"

"The toxin cleared my system faster thanks to my use of ki." He shrugged and his ki glowed within him, brighter than before. "If I used mana, it likely would've taken longer if I had a large amount of MP like you, Yoh, and the others."

"That's likely a fair assumption." I glanced over at Muu who still looked to be chewing on whatever was consuming him. "I found Kayda and the others with some help. We need to get to them."

"Do we still need to go to the north where the isles are?" Kyr still stood with Rai, the two of them having been speaking quietly. He had relaxed greatly since being made a champion.

"They looked to be in a snowy area; Kirin were there." Kyr and Greer looked at each other, then back at me. "What?"

"That snowy area is one of the first places we will need to traverse to get to where we need to go in order to find the old trial site." Greer scratched his head and looked uncomfortable due to the geas placed on them all.

"We need to find a way to break the geas on you all," I grumbled to myself quietly.

"It is incredibly likely that once you discover what they cannot say to you, they will be freed from the geas." Maebe spoke quietly so as not to let them overhear.

"Good." I pulled out the gear that I'd had made for Muu and James. I'd enchanted it all for defense and mobility for Muu, and for James I had gone for pure elemental resistance and magic destruction.

We would be dealing with monsters who could dish out heavy elemental damage and serious physical punishment. We would need the edge.

They changed into their gear; Muu's hard leather armor had a bone chest and a nominal piece and some bone on the back. The rest was hard leather that was almost like metal. His leggings and boots looked much the same. A helm took some finagling. Finally Anisamara just howled in outrage and made him one from a creature's skull. The jaw came down past his ear holes and fit him snugly. It had small, rhinoceros-type horns that protruded from the tip of the bone-like nose area that looked awesome.

Both of the men wore leather and bone arm guards and greaves to help them deal with the damage we would likely experience. Unfortunately, there was no way to give them more accessories because the ones that Anisamara had were promised out.

"You can, however, come back with more items and I will make you more." She lifted some of the newly-enchanted gear before her. "This is all great quality and will fetch a hefty sum on the black market. Thank you."

I nodded my head and went back to the others. They all discussed what they could do, and when I joined them, Sendak smiled. "So, we're heading to the village up north?"

"That would be great, if you could swing it." His return smile was brighter than it had ever been. He held his staff up and winked at me.

"Wait, what about the others?" James frowned at me and stepped away from the circle. "Yohsuke, Jaken, Balmur, and Bokaj are still out there somewhere. If we teleport, we could miss them somewhere. What if they need us?"

I wanted to berate him for not thinking that was on all our minds, but I couldn't. "We'll find them. Kayda, Vrawn, and Odany are out there alone and they will likely need us. Hell, we even have some of the Fae out there looking for them." His concern only deepened and I grabbed him by his shoulder and shook him. "Hey, if we can get to them, and get them the help they need, we will be that much more prepared to find the others and get the fuck even with that asshole Baranzil. Okay?"

James and Muu both peeked up at hearing the General's name, scowled anger seething from both of them. James finally nodded. "Okay, we can do it. Even if we have to split the party to do it properly. Whatever means necessary, can you promise me that?"

He held out his hand and I slapped it away, pulling him into a great bear hug. "Of course, man. We will find our family."

Sendak chose that moment to touch all of us and nod to the other Druids. All hands came in, and the floor lurched away from our feet.

A heartbeat later, we stood on the outskirts of a small

village. The wooden houses well-made and spaced evenly almost like a cul de sac in a nice neighborhood. Docks jutted into the ocean, their stone materials lending them the strength they needed to withstand the tumultuous waters. A large man with long black hair stood on the docks, so broad that I almost thought it was Jaken.

But his skin was pale like that of a human. "What is this place?" Muu stood next to me, his gaze on the village.

"This is Vulpan Village, a small fishing village that we come to from time to time to when they call for aid." Sendak smiled as the wind from the water whipped at his dark hair. "This is the village where I was born."

I followed his cheerful gaze northward and found a vast mist in the air obscuring everything.

"That is the way that we need to be heading." Sendak dry heaved and doubled over in pain. "We will be able to follow you, but we cannot go directly with you. Once you see what is to be found, ugh, you'll know and we will be released."

We nodded and began to move toward the veil of fog and mist. Bea and I scented the air for familiar tracks, hoping beyond hope that one of the boys would be here, but we found nothing but the stink of fish.

We walked north for three hours, careful to avoid making too much noise due to the cries of beasts in the distance. Could we probably take them? Yeah. Did we want to blow our cover just for that?

No one else did, but those materials were nice as fuck, and I honestly wanted to make some accessories for the guys. Maybe even the Druids and Maebe. I don't know what I would make her, but it would be for her and I was certain she would appreciate it.

Eventually night claimed the sky and we made camp in the density of the foggy grounds. Camp was sparse; we didn't dare use an actual fire for fear of signaling someone or some*thing* we were here. We all took an hour of watch, Maebe sitting up with me while I stared into the nether of the fog around us.

"What would you call our child?" Her curious question caught me off guard and I simply stared at her for a second. "A boy or a girl, what would you call them?"

I grinned, unable to contain my joy at her wanting my opinion. "I'm not sure. What's a good traditional name for someone of the Fae royalty? What about their true name?"

"They won't earn their true name until they're born, and even then, they will need a moniker to be called until such a time as they are ready to take the throne." She leaned against me. "That is the way of it, unfortunately, and their true name will only reveal itself to the mother."

"I suppose that's fair. You know your child best."

"*Our* child," she corrected me gently, her hand on my thigh. "Come, what would you call them?"

I thought about it. What would I call our child? Nadïr? Maybe for a girl. Seemed a strong name. Unique. "Maybe for a girl, we could call her Nadïr?"

"I do like the sound of that, *Nadïr.*" She weighed the name on her tongue with a small contented grin. "And for a boy?"

"What are your thoughts on that?" I turned and kissed her head, wrapping an arm around her shoulder.

"I like many names, but one that I have found to be enticing is Azlo." She saw my surprise and frowned at me. "What?"

"Why that one?" I frowned at her, curious.

"I heard it once when I was a child, and ever since then it has stuck with me." I could understand that. "What do you think?"

"I like it."

She grinned at me after I spoke and touched her stomach. I wove my arm through hers and did the same.

"I like you." I winked at her and held her as the clouds of mist and fog swirled on. We rested shortly after that. I dozed while she ran her nails through my furred scalp. The other elves took their turns on watch.

We woke in the morning, Greer having made some food for all of us with a low fire. The gruel that he made was just this side of palatable, to say the least. Compared to what Yoh could make, it was like eating dog food, but it filled our bellies and fueled our being able to move along.

Finally, two hours after breaking camp and moving north steadily, we grew more than a little irked and tired of the damnable fog.

I took a moment to still my mind and circulated wind around us, pressing the fog away from where we stood. Pressure built within me, then I forced it outward and the fog cleared for fifty yards around us.

And clearing our sight to two things, the first being the landscape above the fog that rose high into the sky and past the clouds. Large distances of open air between them.

And standing there watching us curiously was a beast like something straight out of a prehistoric nightmare.

It reared up out of the mist, wings spread wide with a large, streamlined head closing the distance between us. Two glowing blue orbs watched us from within circular eyes above the snout. Then I realized that they were two gems attached to circular growths that looked like horns. Slitted eyes narrowed at us as it hissed violently.

"Fuck!" Muu shouted as the mist-like fog around us began swirling, hitting us like freezing pins and needles before it disappeared once more.

I shook my head, having only lost a bit of health in the attack, then cast Life Sense.

The others popped up as green blips on my radar and the red one was behind us. "Behind us!"

I whipped around and slashed with my new axe, the weapon slicing the air as the creature moved effortlessly away.

"We need a way to mark it so we can find it!" James growled as he swatted at nothing.

"The mist moves with it," Greer explained in a terse whisper. "Watch carefully and we can get it!"

We did as he said but I was just as eager to try out one of my new Aspects that I had just gotten.

Maybe that was the way to get it to come out, disrupt the area around it? I cast Aspect of the Storm, my fur standing on end as static built through me.

Arcs of lightning shed from my body as I stepped forward and willed the lightning in me to seek life as I scented the air. Careful not to hit my friends, the electricity jumped to the water, my MP dropping as it fought further along until a loud screech echoed off to my right. I recognized a musty scent and grinned as I turned toward it.

Muu and James were on it in an instant, their attacks clearing some of the mist away so that we could see it clearly. It had four legs and a set of arms that it used to slash at my brothers. Greer, Kyr, and Sendak hurled spells at it as I rushed forward. The step I took seemed like it propelled me forward so much faster than I should have been.

In three short strides, I leapt at it, Nether Bolt in my fist, and struck. It stiffened and listed to the side for a heartbeat too long and Muu got under its jaws and thrust straight up into the bottom of its throat, shoving his spear up into the skull with a hop. "Grargh!"

The body fell and a moment later it faded, leaving a chest behind that Muu opened and pulled out a short spear that he danced around with.

"Dude." James clapped to get his attention as the rest of the mist began to clear the beach. "The materials and shit? We need those."

"Oh, sorry." He turned back and began pulling out scales, teeth, three vials of water essence, and bones of various assortments and sizes.

"That's a big bone," Muu joked crudely as we rolled our eyes.

CHAPTER TEN

"And now that we know about it, getting up there is going to be a cake walk!" I grinned over at the three Druids who looked at each other with uncertainty. "What's wrong? Is there a geas on you for this shit too?"

"No, but do you remember how we said that travel between the isles was interesting?" Kyr broached and I nodded. "You can't just go from one to the other. You have to make your way to the travel stones."

"The huh?" Muu raised one of his scaly eyebrow ridges at the other man.

"Monuments that allow one to pass through the barriers keeping the various isles floating," Sendak explained, pulling out his map to motion to the different land masses.

"So these aren't natural?" James peeked up and pulled out his journal. "What happened here?"

"This was the home of some ancient society of wizards and sorcerers," Greer whispered reverently, which made me frown at him. "They wanted somewhere to be away from the persecution and misunderstandings of normal people, so they split the earth in twain and raised it. Forcing the very fabric of reality to bend to their whim. They stayed separate from each other, changing and developing different environments on their various properties until they suited their wishes."

We looked up to the floating isles, their majesty and humongous size contained in something clear, but each looked different from where I stood. Like each had its own biology and environment.

"And what happened to these magical beings?" Maebe's voice was low as she squinted up at the various isles.

"The rumors hidden in old texts that were… borrowed from the library of the inner circle stated that a disagreement had broken out between these beings." Greer scratched his head and thought as he stared up at the sky. "One of their ilk had been encouraging the various races to openly defy their gods and the bonds of their mortality, and this did not sit well with all of them."

"Who does that in a place where the gods make themselves known to their followers?" Muu growled and threw his hands up. "That just seems like they're asking for a smiting."

"Wasn't there something that the dwarves had gone through that was similar?" Maebe looked to me and snapped her fingers. "Yes! They had been attempting to create life of their own and Fainne destroyed a portion of their city."

Thinking back, I remembered Thogan explaining that, and it made me wonder, *Just what kind of place are we about to walk into here?*

"What did they do to this person?" James' excited scrawling in his notebook paused and he watched Greer in rapt awe.

"During a meeting to decide what should be done with this individual, they were attacked by Orlow'thes." Chills spread through my body as he explained. "He bled himself on purpose and spewed his magic-killing lifeblood over them. Powerless to fight back, they perished along with the largest land mass in the sky at the time. The great sea dragon dragged the isle into the waves and below into the depths."

"Could you imagine facing something so terribly powerful?"

Sendak shivered and all three members of Storm Company present just glanced at each other.

Finally I smiled reassuringly. "Sounds terrifying." I motioned to the others. "And there's no sort of tundra-like place here on the continent?"

Sendak shook his head, then Greer confirmed it and pointed up.

Sighing, I closed my eyes and willed myself to be calm. I would find Kayda and the others. "We should get moving if we want to get up there then."

"Let us see what we can find." Kyr rubbed his hands together and smiled. "Greer, you seem to be the resident expert on this matter, where is it that these stones are?"

"The first one should be just north of us." The elf pointed a finger at Sendak's map and we moved on cautiously so as not to be forced to fight another one of those beasts.

It took half an hour walking to get to our destination, which turned out to be a cliff, with nothing around it.

"That makes no sense, it should have been here." Greer snatched the map from Sendak and scowled at the parchment. "It is the only place that makes sense, it has to be here!"

"Could that thing be it?" James' voice drifted to us and I looked up to try to find him. He stood next to the cliffside and pointed over the edge, down toward the sound of crashing waves and spraying water.

We joined him, and looked down toward the surf below us. Sure enough, an obelisk-like stone stood against the tides.

"How will we get down there?" James looked to all of us and I shook my head.

"See you down there." Muu stepped over the side and plummeted toward the soft sand on the outcropping around the large stone.

He landed easily and stood waiting for us with his arms crossed over his chest.

Maebe turned to me, winked, then stepped over the side of the cliff and fell. Bea clambered over the side after her. Leaning over the side, I could see that Maebe had slowed, her laughter at my initial worry lifting the corners of my mouth. Bea stomped down the air with ease and I rolled my eyes.

I loved this woman and my raptor was more of a badass than I would likely ever give her credit for.

I glanced over at James. "You have a way down?"

He spread his malformed wings and shrugged. "I could try gliding down."

"If it looks like he will fall, we could always Polymorph him," Kyr suggested.

My wry smirk grew to a full-on grin. "That's the kind of growth I'm fucking talking about!"

They smiled back and hopped over the side of the cliff a second before I did. I shifted into my eagle form and rode the cool winds down. The turbulent currents over the water battered my wings a bit, but I could still control my fall and landed next to the others.

James glided down, his wings spread as far as they would go, though he wobbled and the wind tossed him to and fro.

After two minutes fighting the rising winds from the base of the cliff nearest the water, he folded his wings and plummeted to land near us on the side of the cliff. His claws dug into the stone, covered in his ki, he scraped down the side falling slowly and finally landed near us.

"Shouldn't you be on the Kung Fu, hidden dragon shit?" I raised a brow at him and he shook his head. "What, did they never teach you how to slow your fall?"

"I might learn soon." He shrugged and looked pained, his uncertainty likely a source of shame.

"So, Greer, how do we do this?" I looked over to him and he just shrugged. "Do we touch it?"

"I can imagine that's what we have to do." Muu harrumphed. He reached out and slapped his hand onto it, my breath leaving me so quickly at his mistake.

But nothing happened. "Is it defective?"

"It is ancient, it seems." Maebe stepped closer to it and

observed the stone cautiously. "It seems like a receptacle. Maybe if we were to touch it with mana?"

I thought about it for a minute. "Could be, these people were supposed to be strong spell casters, so mana would be something they all had in common. Everyone grab onto each other. Then touch my shoulder and let's give it a shot."

I passed mana along my new arm and felt a jolt run through me. A profound sense of vertigo made my stomach flip and it was all I could do not to groan at the discomfort. I blinked and looked at the others who all looked to share my discomfort, but the crash of waves had been replaced by the overwhelming volume of a waterfall. The sunlight was gone; it took us a moment to grow accustomed to the darkness, a slight bit of dimly glowing lichen around us being all that lit our immediate surroundings.

"What is this place?" Muu whispered quietly.

"This would likely be the first isle." Sendak's voice held notes of awe and fear. "Somewhere that no one we know of has returned from in centuries."

I blinked at him, then Greer, and growled, "Way to bury the fucking lead, guys." They stared back at me bashfully and I just shook my head. "That would have been nice to know at the time."

"This place haunted or something?" James' query made all of us still. Could it be?

"Not that we are aware of," Greer comforted us, pulling out a book of his own to hand to James. "This is all we have on these isles. We don't know too terribly much other than legends, but there may be people here. Beasts we have never laid eyes on."

"So we need to be cautious and not be caught with our pants down again," Muu observed dryly, a sigh making him sound tired. "Let's get moving."

The others moved on and I grabbed Muu for a moment. He patiently waited until the others were a little way ahead before we began to pace slowly after them. "Yeah?"

"I'm just wondering what's going on with you, man." I kept my voice down and my tone neutral as best as I could.

"I'm just... I'm just not sure what I can do sometimes." He shook his head slowly. "I have all this brute strength, and I was useless without the rest of you. James got taken because of me —almost tortured and killed. If you hadn't found me, he would have been in a really rough spot on his own."

"He would have, but we're a team and you know that." I smacked his arm lightly to get his attention. "You can do shit that makes me look like a weak little bitch on a good day. I used to be able to fight circles around you at home, and now if you and I were to get into a knock-down-drag-out, I'd have to use magic to fight you. You are the muscle and humor in the group, man. Your levity and life are what keep us all sane. Without you to lighten the mood... who knows how grimdark we would have gotten?"

"I can't just keep it on all the time, Zeke." Muu's hand grabbed my shoulder. "We are almost hilariously out of our depth in a lot of this and the pressure is crushing. People coming out of the woodwork to get at us for traipsing all over their way of life, standing in the way of their motives? Fuck all that, man."

"I get it." I pulled him into a side hug and kissed his cheek like I would a brother. "It's hard. But we're all here doing our best. You were sick and couldn't fight—we all were. I got lucky and had two dire otters who took care of me."

He stopped and stared at me long and hard. "You serious?"

"Milktongue and Spike, mates." He snorted at me and I raised a brow. "What?"

"What the hell kind of name is Spike?" I huffed at him and he punched my shoulder lightly. "You named him, didn't you?"

"They thought of me as if I was a pup!" That only made him laugh harder. "I swear to God if you tell anyone, I will turn you into a chicken and throw you into a beast."

"Get that spell ready, pup, 'cause everyone is going to know." We both chuckled and walked around a bend in the cavernous room ahead of us and found the others standing on this side of the waterfall. The water was crystalline, but still bent the light and refracted the other side of the wall it created.

"How do we want to get out?" Kyr turned to us and frowned thoughtfully as he waited for a response.

"I'm not sure, but we could just part the water or look for a way to get out on the sides?" I glanced at Maebe; she just shrugged. "Okay, shadows it is."

I lifted my new arm and willed the shadows in the room to create a roof for us and divert the water above us away. It was hard, but my gear and the arm itself gave me better control than I had ever had on my own and I peeked outside the cave. Water still roared by us, but there was a pathway along the right side of the cave.

I stepped out with Bea joining me and then passing me when she caught an interesting scent. "Bea!"

She'd made it more than halfway down the path before she stopped to look back at me and bark once as if to tell me to fucking hurry. The others in the group sidled by me and out onto the path. I made sure that they were clear before allowing the water to fall as it would have normally.

The area before the falls was gorgeous. A large lake with a river that left it and fled southward over the side of the isle toward who knew what. I wasn't going to check it out. The temperature here was muggy and humid, the kind you might feel in a jungle in South America, and it made my fur feel weird.

"So this is what the isles look like," Greer muttered to himself and I was about to reply when Bea grabbed my arm in her tiny little clawed hands and tugged me away.

"What's going on with you?" I tried to connect with her mind, but all I got was a jumble of thoughts and feelings that made absolutely no sense. "Bea, talk to me."

Come! She whipped herself and her tail around to slap me on the ass and pushed me north before she took off again, this time not stopping.

"She's got a scent of something, let's go." I didn't wait to see if the others would follow or not. I needed to be sure Bea was okay. I had failed her enough, and I wouldn't do so again.

Birdsong above us stopped and a cacophonous bellowing and screeching filled the air. Bea's rage spiked and my adrenaline with it. Another fight was about to be on, and she was going to lead the charge whether she had backup or not.

Her body disappeared over the side of a hill and I stopped just in time to avoid going tails over tits into a ravine that fell fifty feet straight down into a multilayered nesting area. Several small nests fanned out along the different tiers made of sticks and shrubs with familiar eggs. Gust raptor eggs.

A massive iguana-looking creature, long tentacle-like hair waving behind its great head, swayed back and forth wildly making it look even bigger, hissing loudly. It whipped its head left and snatched a couple of eggs into its mouth as gust raptors screeched at it and harried its sides uselessly.

"We're behind you!" Muu called loudly, his new spear pulled out and at the ready. "They're gonna need a cleanup on Isle One!"

I smirked and he launched himself into the air and over the side of the ravine wall.

"We will provide support," Kyr growled and his fur stood on end as he readied himself.

"No, you and Greer will be coming with me." I glanced over to Maebe and Sendak. "Will you both provide cover and support?"

"I would be delighted to cover for you." Maebe smiled savagely and grabbed Sendak. "You will be with me, Sendak. Do try to keep up."

"But I wanted to fight too!" Sendak whined almost comically.

"You obviously don't know that cover means you kill it first." Maebe snorted at the man and I turned to move out myself.

Gust raptors screamed and some of the larger ones buffeted

the side of the creature with wind from their mouths. It didn't seem to mind as it scuttled forward toward another nest twenty feet in front of it.

I leapt over the side toward it just as Muu sped down past me with a roar of rage so violent that it sent a thrill of adrenaline through me once more. His spear slammed into the iguana's back, piercing the skin easily, making the creature rear up. Muu kicked twice with his leg, then flipped off the creature's back onto the ground and rushed forward toward the legs.

"Kyr, call Rai out and get ready to fight using your magic and sword together." Electricity built in the air and I glanced over to see Greer had already cast a wolf-like aspect spell. "Greer, good work. Let's kill this thing and don't hurt the raptors."

Muu struck the iguana's left leg and sent the creature toppling onto its back. We all savaged it, my axe rising and falling as I hacked into it. Greer's hammer walloped the head, and Rai hopped up onto the creature's exposed stomach where the scales looked thinnest with Kyr. They sliced and stabbed as much as they could and the creature lashed out at us with its tail. It slammed into my side, my shield popping up just in time to avoid the majority of the damage, but the small spikes in it left ridges in the mana barrier that singed my fur, taking 10% of my HP.

It was up and onto its feet again in seconds and sucked in so much air that it doubled in size. A wash of primal fear worked through me and I shrugged it off. Greer stilled and Rai stopped moving completely as Kyr went in to slash.

"He's got some sort of fear ability!" I called out just before a blast of cold chilled the air around us and a large spire of ice slammed into the beast. A blast of wind burst from its mouth and shattered the stones along the eastern side of the ravine. Bea sprinted forward out of nowhere and slammed into the side of a much older gust raptor, tossing it out of the way before scrambling away herself. She lined herself up with me and whistled past me. Her back claws scrambled up the beast's chest and she bit into its shoulder. Muu and I attacked simultaneously.

His spear slit the creature's stomach open, then I grinned and cast Fireball inside the opening and watched as the flaming spell burst inside the creature. Its health dove until it was on its last legs and finally Kyr drove his sword into the base of its skull and heaved to the side with a sickening crunch before it freed itself.

The beast stilled and faded from view, leaving behind a chest. Kyr opened it and took out all the raw materials before putting them into his inventory.

Growling erupted around us and I turned to find that all the gust raptors in the area that had been focused on the iguana beast now turned their sights on us.

Bea stood in front of me and barked at them happily, but I cast Nature's Voice and called out myself. "Hey, how are you all doing?"

Bea turned her head to me and growled vehemently before turning her head back to the others who began to close around us in an ever-tightening circle.

"Stop!" barked a singular voice in the crowd and that larger raptor that Bea had saved stepped forward.

He towered over all of the others, even Bea, standing ten feet tall with broad hips and muscular legs. His shoulders and neck had long feathers of gray cast and greenish tinge to them that looked almost like a reptilian version of a mane.

"You save many egg." The raptor clicked loudly for a moment then dipped his head. "But you bring drood. Why bring droods?"

"They help." Bea returned and stepped closer. "They save. They click."

"No click. Droods," the lead raptor asserted with a raise of his head. "Droods take and no give."

"Drood give all." I felt her mental tug that pulled me forward to stand by her. "Love drood. Drood mama."

What is it with animals calling me mama?

"You thieved egg?" The raptor turned his head and several of the others stepped forward to begin smelling Bea as she stood there. One of the venturing even closer than the rest.

"Mine!" This one barked and rushed forward. Bea swept out in front of me and growled fiercely. The other raptor hissed and ducked its head to look at her closer. "Mine egg."

"Drood mama!" Bea growled again, but I put a calming hand on her side.

"Baby, I think she means that you were stolen from her." I looked at the other gust raptor, but they all looked very similar. "I think she might be your real mother."

Bea's heart pounded in her chest as the other raptor continued to stare at her in interest. "I know I hatched you, but she gave birth to you."

"You return to click," the leader decided. "Droods leave."

"No." Bea raised her head and backed toward me. "I leave. Droods click now. Safe eggs. No stay here. Protect mama."

"We kill droods. No leave. No fear." The raptors collectively dipped their heads and eyed us all. "No wind inside. Only meat. Food."

I lifted my hand and willed my mana to form with wind and slashed my hand in a knife-like motion at the side of the ravine away from any eggs. A line of sharp wind slashed into the stone, leaving a sliced score against it.

"Wind love mama," Bea answered for me almost smugly. "We leave. Clicks safe."

"It would have been nice to work together." I shrugged, then sighed. "It would have been nice to give one of them a gust raptor egg, but that won't fly here."

"You no take egg." Bea looked at me and I calmed her with my thoughts. "No one take egg. We leave. Now."

She stepped forward and we all followed behind her. I looked to the ridge up top and saw Maebe and Sendak following along beside us.

Some of the raptors sniffed at the air around us, Bea holding her head high as she passed.

Bea, you know that you could stay with them for a little bit, right? We could leave and camp nearby so you could learn about your people and self. My mind reeled with hers as her desire to protect me and learn about herself warred inside her. *We won't leave you, and we can make camp sooner if you need to stay.*

No want stay. She growled at me. *I stay with click and you. Protect. Love. Live. That leader kill others and eat. Coward.*

I frowned at her. "How do you know?"

Fear. Images of the other raptor's reactions to him moving among them while trying to defend them from the iguana. Bea had seen the scars on their flanks and watched him bite at another one in his way.

"Then why did you save him?" I had to admit I was confused and I think she was too. "It's okay not to know. We do things that are hard to explain."

I patted her back lovingly and she kept us moving. We left the ravine and continued on for a few minutes before stones clattered next to us. Maebe and Sendak slid down the side to join us. Stomping from our rear made me turn as a single raptor, roughly the same size as Bea, rushed toward us. Bea surged forward past me and leaped onto him.

She rolled him onto his back and bit close to his neck before stopping as I stepped closer. Sendak joined me. "Don't do that! That's hardly proper!"

I glared over at him and watched as Bea pulled her teeth a little further from the other raptor's throat.

"Nestmate," the raptor rasped as it struggled to stand. "Egg mate."

"Bea, back off." I lowered my voice to a growl and she followed my instructions. The raptor stood and shook his head before sniffing at Bea carefully. "Are you saying that you're her brother?"

"Brother? No." He clicked his tongue for a second while thinking. "Nestmate."

Brother, I corrected in my head.

Bea looked at me, then to the raptor. "What want?"

"Want leave." The raptor ducked his head and growled. "Alpha mean. Try kill last alpha eggs. Other nestmates gone. Only me. Only you. Want be with you. You click."

Bea looked back at me, and I shrugged. "He can come if he wants to, but we can't just bring him everywhere with us. He will have to behave and someone will have to be responsible for him."

Sendak stepped closer to the raptor and offered his hand slowly. "I am Sendak, would you like to be with me?"

My eyebrows raised in surprise. I hadn't expected someone to be so forward, especially when these guys had been so whipped before. Good to see some more growth.

"Drood smell," the raptor growled and Bea growled with him. "Sendak. Smell."

"I'm sorry?" He lifted his arm and smelled under his armpit. I rolled my eyes and grabbed his other arm. "I do smell. Terrible, actually."

Pulling him close, I whispered, "You could use this as an opportunity to grow. See if you can convince him to bond with you. Offer him food."

"Food?" Sendak opened his inventory and pulled out several cloth napkins full of something that immediately drew Bea and her brother's attention. He pulled out a thinly sliced piece of meat and held it up. "Would you like some? Since I smell bad, as a gift?"

Sendak moved his hand out and tossed the meat to the new raptor and Bea snarled, trying to grab it but missed and gnashed her teeth futilely.

The raptor rolled his eyes in relish and stepped closer to Sendak. "More tiny meat."

"Only if you promise to behave." Sendak held up another piece of meat but pulled it close to his chest when the raptor came forward for it.

"What mean?" He looked over at Bea who merely drooled as she eyed the meat.

"It means be good." I offered. "He needs someone to

protect him, and he has food to do it. Will you be his partner the way that Bea is mine?"

"Partner?" He tilted his head and regarded me oddly. "No eat partner? Protect? Nestmate?"

"Yes, like a nestmate." I had a little bit of a migraine from trying to negotiate in such a way, deciphering their thoughts and speech patterns.

"I do." The raptor's tail wagged back and forth as it eyed the meat. "Look weak. Protect nestmate. Nestmate feed. Partner."

"Oh my." Sendak grinned and held the meat out to the new raptor, then took pity on Bea and tossed her some too. Her pleasure was immediate and overwhelming. To the point that my mouth watered now. What the fuck was in that meat?

"What do I do?" He looked at me and then blinked in surprise. "Do I accept this notification?"

"Yep!" I smiled at him and he did so. "You'll have to name him too."

"Name him?" Sendak looked at the animal and frowned. "What would you like to be named?"

"No need name."

"I have to call you something." Sendak frowned and tried, "Bitey? Swiftfoot?"

The raptor perked up and barked loudly, "I bite!" He chomped and clacked his teeth. One of them was slightly longer in the top row.

"How about Fang?" I offered the name and Sendak looked at me at the same time as the raptor did.

"Are you teasing him?" Sendak looked appalled at me. "He cannot help how his teeth grow. That's highly insensitive, master Zeke."

I opened my mouth, then closed it, speechless. I threw up my hands and walked away then and there.

"I will call you Kaius." The raptor looked happy at that and Kyr just snorted, making Sendak look at him. "What?"

"Kaius?" Kyr looked at him as if he should know what he was saying, but finally just shook his head and walked away.

Muu stepped closer to the Kitsune and asked in a low tone, "What does it mean?"

"Of the long tooth," Kyr explained and I snorted loudly.

We moved on for an hour, the two raptors chatting quickly, and found a good spot to set up camp in a slightly less rocky area with trees sprouting just ahead of us.

Once camp was set, I turned to Sendak. "So as you've seen, both of your friends have grown exponentially in the short time we've been together. Kyr can use lightning magic in a new way, and Greer can use aspects as a primal warrior." I watched him nod carefully as I spoke. "What is it that you feel you want to do?"

"Well, as I am certain you have guessed, I have an affinity for animals." He glanced over at Kaius, and smiled. "I think I would like to continue to work with them."

"So you want to work more with animal companions?" He nodded at me and I frowned. "Do you have any more animal companion slots available? I only have two."

He tinkered with his settings and frowned. "I have three?"

"How?" I blinked at him and he shrugged. "Are you just naturally good with animals or something?"

"Do not let him lie to you." Kyr smirked and pointed accusingly at Sendak. "He can call a bird to his finger almost anywhere with a whistle and a raised finger."

"Animals trust me." He shrugged and sighed. "They have since I was a child. I was basically raised by the neighborhood dogs."

"That could mean something." I frowned at him some more, then asked, "What about beasts? Can you make them companions?"

"I should hope not," the elf growled. "We can barely handle the weakest of them, such as the raptors. Could you imagine me being the partner of something so big as that creature in the mist? Or that iguana? No thank you."

"If animals will be your source of power, you'll want the strongest and most versatile team you can manage." I pointed to Bea. "She is my baby, sure, but she's capable and powerful and can use wind magic. My other companion, Kayda, can use ice and lightning to great effect. Granted, I use all other types so I have a lot more power behind my attacks and will."

"So a varied group of companions creates a dynamic that will allow them to cover for each other's weaknesses as well," Muu explained quietly. I shot him a nod in gratitude and he smiled back. Progress.

"I see." He frowned and looked to Kaius. "What else could I possibly use other than a gust raptor?"

"I don't know, but we're going to try to find you something." James grinned at him and we all retired after eating Greer's food.

CHAPTER ELEVEN

"Again!" Kyr called as Greer stood across the distance from where the Kitsune stood. They clashed together, Greer in his favorite aspect form and Kyr using lightning magic to attack and defend himself. Rai sparked and suddenly stood in Greer's path.

The little elemental reached out and tried to grasp at the lupine elf's arm, but Greer hopped over his head and rounded on Kyr. A shield of lightning burst into existence and caught Greer's fist just in time.

"Great work!" I clapped, Maebe nodding beside me. "Excellent reaction times, all of you. Sendak, you need to let Kaius use his instincts to fight a little more. Remember, he's a beast and can handle himself. You focus on supporting him and him supporting you. Use the connection you have and issue commands that way so that your opponent doesn't know what's going on."

"Yes, master Zeke!" Sendak grunted and sat up from where he lay in the dirt. We had been walking all morning and the Druids had gotten a little restless and began asking me questions about what they should do in a fight.

So, my response that the best way to learn was to do, had led to this impromptu sparring session. They'd done well and took criticism in stride, had to love that.

"Let's get going!" Muu called restlessly, then grit his teeth. "We need to get this taken care of then find the others. I got a bad feeling."

"Bad body odor and bad feelings are entirely different, my friend," James teased as he stretched himself out, grinning.

"Ha-ha, very funny, wings." Muu rolled his eyes dramatically.

"Why do you have a bad feeling?" I asked him quietly and he just frowned. "Seriously, man, what's going on?"

"Remember when I was asking about the gods and what-not?" He stared at me for a moment before I nodded. "It was because one of them took an interest in me and has been invading my dreams, trying to give me advice."

"Who? Why?" James asked quickly, pulling his notebook out.

"Uk'beth, and because he's an asshole mainly." Muu shook his head and sneered. "Fucker spent the first few months I was here telling me what a worthless fighter I was."

"Sounds like a dickhead." Muu just nodded at me. "Is he telling you something's going on?"

"No." He frowned and turned to look at all of us. "Another god came to me last night. She told me we needed to hurry to get stronger because time was running out. I don't know what she meant, but we need to get moving."

"Why'd you keep this to yourself for so long?" I frowned at him again and this time he seemed perfectly calm.

"Because I thought I was crazy, at first." He shrugged and looked me straight in the eyes. "Would you have believed me after my first night if I'd told you I had gods talking to me?"

"Probably not…" I sighed and rubbed my head in frustration. "Nothing else to add?"

"Uk'beth is a dickhead." His normal grin was back but I could tell he was serious. "Let's go."

We got up and began once again to look for our way to Kayda and the girls.

It took us four hours that morning to find something resembling a ruin with a large obelisk in the middle of it that made me grin. *That has to be it.*

"Looks like there's something in there with it," Greer pointed out nervously from where he stood in a tree looking over the wall. "Could be another one of those large iguanas."

"That thing was so easy to beat last time!" James looked so excited for the fight that he began to inch toward the building. "We can take it, let's go!"

I felt a tug on my left hand and glanced over to see Bea tugging me toward the ruin as well.

"Fine. Let's go kill it and move on." I sighed and turned toward the ruins. "Everyone be on your guard."

Weapons came out, the raptors flanking their masters before we made our way forward cautiously.

The ruins were smaller than the majority of the ruins we had seen in our time here in Brindolla. Really no larger than seventy feet wide and possibly eighty back, but the walls were low and shot through.

We entered the doorway to it and found a large iguana laying still there. This one was almost the same size as the one we had fought before but it wasn't moving at all. Not even to breathe.

"This is the shell—we need to leave," Kyr hissed, moving toward the large, gray monolith. He didn't hesitate at all and touched it, shifting away from where we were. One second there, blink, gone.

"What's that mean?" Muu looked to the rest of us before a deep base growl and the crashing of stone nearby made us all jump.

I snarled, "It means get the fuck going!" I shoved him and Maebe toward the transport stone and threw a Fireball toward the noise. Bea and her brother went next and after that I made sure that my Druid students were gone before I allowed James to throw my back against the stone.

One blink and the subarctic temperature hit me like an angry bear with frozen paws. I immediately channeled some flame-aspected mana through my body to help negate some of the cold, but it wasn't working the best.

"Looks like a snowstorm!" Muu bellowed over the gale force winds. He put a ring onto his hand and I saw James do the same and their bodies looked much less cold compared to ours.

The other Druids pulled large furred coats out of their inventories to put on and I just rolled my eyes and dealt with the hand I had been given. Both the raptors whined and I ended up having to make a barrier of shadows with Maebe's help to filter out some of the cold for them. It wasn't much, but it helped us move out of the open area we had appeared in and into a more mountainous area that sheltered us from the blustering winds.

"We need to figure out what we will do." Maebe frowned. "I cannot do this for us and allow us to see clearly. Not unless we mean to bed down here for the night?"

"We should find shelter," Muu insisted after a moment. "We sleep in this, we will get buried and freeze to death. Press on."

We all agreed that was best and huddled closer for warmth. Even if I took my ursolon form, I would have been frozen within the storm. If I had tried to take my fire elemental form, I would likely have melted the snow a little and made ice. Or an avalanche. Better to suffer through it.

We walked for an hour, my feet beginning to numb with the cold of the snow on the ground, before a light shimmered into view.

There looked to be a sturdy, well-built tower in the side of the mountain. A lone figure covered in copious furs strapped together waved for us to come toward the warmth.

"Do we trust it?" I called to the others; they merely shrugged. "They do anything weird, we nuke 'em. No questions, no opportunities."

"Got it!" Kyr snarled and the other Druids looked grim but

understanding. We could die from exposure out here in the elements. And if that guy had to die from exposure to us for our survival—so be it.

We moved forward cautiously, the person waving us through the door hurriedly as the wind pushed large snowflakes through the entry into the warm interior.

Finally, we were all inside, shivering and waiting for the person to come in. They did, eventually. Hauling a large cauldron filled with snow that they placed over a bunch of logs in a low pit in the center of the room, the handle attached to a long pike-like holder to keep it over the fire and not on it.

A muffled voice rasped, "Welcome strangers."

He pulled off his hat to reveal a draconic head much like Muu's, but it was black scaled, the nostrils sort of sunken in and the mouth pressed out. Not too different though. His horns rolled from the top of his head, back behind it slightly, then down to the bottom of his chin on either side of his face and he watched us with gray-brown eyes. "I'm Dendrolaus. Most who know me call me Denny. Not often I get visitors other than my mate here, why have you come? What do you seek?"

He stilled for a moment as Muu stepped forward and the two of them stepped even closer to each other. Denny grasped the other man's shoulders and pulled him into a tight hug. "Forgive them, brother, they were wrong but you are not at fault."

"What are you talking about?" Muu seemed more confused and stricken than anything else.

"The human mages who created you," Denny explained kindly, bumping the bottom of his massive fist on Muu's shoulder in solidarity. "They paid for their crimes against us already, do not hold this against them all."

"Oh." Muu frowned and looked at the rest of us. "All humans who cross my path die painful deaths by my hand."

I raised a brow at him and Denny floundered for a response when Muu just chuckled and winked. "I'm just fucking with you; I have no problem with humans. Some of my best friends are human."

The other dragon-kin looked so relieved that he pulled my friend into another hug. "Good, this is good." He clapped and laughed as he pulled out a flint and steel, striking it and sending a spark into the wood with ease. "Then tonight we celebrate the good nature of we dragons."

We all sort of shrugged it off, happily adding things to the pot to make dinner as Denny grilled Muu. "Tell me, where do you hail from? Are there others of our kind there?"

"I'm from a small village another continent away, and no, there aren't." Muu scratched his scales for a moment. "Why are you here? Why are you begging forgiveness for men you can't have possibly known?"

"But I do—did—know them." He raised his hands to the stones around us in a wide display. "This mountain was given to me so that I might guard the human wizards who lived in the northern lands and their herds. Guarding their experiments and my brothers and sisters."

"So there were more?" James asked, his notebook appearing in hand.

"Many, yes." Denny grinned as he recalled some. "They made us in waves, the dragons last, only because our kind was much too powerful to pollute our blood with normal people."

"What?" Muu asked incredulously. "You wanna run that by me again?"

"We needed stronger beings to merge with us." He pointed to himself. "We dragon-kin are true dragons melded with higher breeds of humanity. The half elementals became our bodies, but the process was... less than ideal. We came out of it with no magic of our own as we should have had. As was our right."

So that was what happened to make the elements fuck off, I growled to myself.

"If they fucked up, why are you defending them?" I asked at last as Muu attempted to process.

"I defend *us*," Denny exclaimed, his hands moving from him to Muu. "Too many of my brothers fell to their wicked magic to count and there are already so few of us. I worry that we will die out and be gone like so many before us."

"You said you knew them." James pointed out with his quill. "How old would that make you?"

"I believe I am somewhere in the realm of a thousand years? Give or take a century or two." He shrugged and grinned as he stirred the pot. The rest of us were flabbergasted and I looked to Maebe who seemed not to care at all.

"So why stay if all of them are dead?" Muu wondered aloud. "You could leave almost any time, right?"

"I met my mate here." Denny shrugged again. "There are beasts to fight and test my arm against, the area is rife with magic, and I can see the prettiest creatures."

"Like what?" James perked up again.

"Horses that live in the clouds like lightning and neigh like thunder." He smiled to himself. "Great wyverns that rival dragons—though we know they are not so majestic as we, brother. And my love, of course."

"Where is she?" Maebe's quiet interjection made me flinch.

"She is upstairs, caring for our nest." Denny winked at us. "We are expecting."

"Congratulations!" Maebe smiled warmly and eyed the stairs behind Denny. "Will she be joining us for dinner?"

"She might if she feels so inclined." His smile was firmly in place but I could see a wariness tightening the wrinkles by his eyes.

We continued to cook and speak for a little bit, nothing of any great import when Denny's eyes went blank for a second. He came back for a moment, then stood and turned to the wall. "I'll be right back."

"What's going on?" Kyr stood and moved himself closer to the door as Denny grabbed a spear from the wall next to it. It looked a simple weapon but the way he handled it was as if he had grabbed something he had used every day for centuries.

"A beast has wandered close for the last time," he snarled, his animosity surprising us. He turned and looked back at us. "I will not require your help, but you may learn something, brother. Would you care to come?"

"I think I would." Muu looked at me and James. "You both coming as well?"

"Not letting you go out there alone." I nodded and rolled my shoulders, before a soft thing smacked into my back. I turned to see Kyr standing coatless and had him nod at me. "You want me to borrow it?"

"I want you to *return it* but after you return yourself." He waved us off and motioned to Maebe and the upstairs. "We will stay and protect the queen and Denny's mate."

"You vouch for them, brother?" Denny eyed Muu steadily, the green dragon-kin nodded then grinned as Maebe raised an eyebrow. "What about her?"

"Oh, she could kill us all." Muu grinned wider as she chuckled. "She just hasn't had a good enough reason to yet."

Denny's look of concern passed as his eyes dulled once more. "Come then, let us go and defend my mountain."

Out into the blistering cold and swirling white we traipsed, fighting to keep up with the sturdy and stalwart defender of the peaks as he rushed west and down the mountain.

"How did you know it was out here?!" Muu called over the whipping winds wailing by our heads and Denny stopped and threw an arm out.

"I have senses thrown over the mountainside." His calm explanation made no sense whatsoever, but suddenly the ice and snow in front of him burst upward as a massive mole with icy claws emerged. "Don't engage with him, just follow me!"

He slashed with his spear and the mole screeched as it reared back from the blow.

We moved on, all of us cautiously following Denny's advice on the matter and moved behind the eldest dragon-kin.

He took us around a mountain peak and down a thin slope where he slid down steadily. We stayed as close as we could, but I lost control halfway down and veered toward the side of the mountain where the snow banked loosely. I was going to fall over the edge unless I pulled something out of my ass. A crashing above us on the slope drew my attention away from my fall and toward the icy mole that careened down the slope toward us. Stone and ice slammed into the slick ice and down toward us. I cried out in alarm when I felt a solid crash into my stomach.

"Don't fall off!" Denny barked at me and slung me bodily into the cave where he pointed the others.

I rocketed past them and into something bony and hard that cracked and clattered to the ground around me.

"You broke it?!" Denny laughed. "So you know how to kill them permanently. Good!"

"I don't know what the fuck is going on, but ow!" I bellowed and the mole clattered into the large cave with us.

"You'll see soon!" Denny chuckled and leapt up into the air, slamming the butt of his spear into a stalactite above the mole that fell with Denny next to it with his weapon ready to pierce the animal. Muu lunged forward with his own spear leveled at the creature's throat while James and I rushed forward as well. My shadows and flames roiled over it in concise arcs that burned it where they touched.

Blood flowed to the point that the creature fell and our breathing was all that we could hear for a moment in the stillness of the cave.

I looked and saw that I was close to leveling up for the first time since we had come to this forsaken place. Good.

"Now that his totem is gone, this beast will not return from the grave stronger." Denny smiled as the animal faded and left a larger chest than last time. "My new friends, as a courtesy, I allow you to take from this chest all of its contents. A gift and token of friendship."

"Thank you." James smiled and opened the chest himself. He dug out several large bones, some pieces of fur and ice. Ice essence. And then he pulled out two long, shovel-like claws that he put over his fists. "Oh, these are going to be perfect. Zeke, you want to enchant these for me?"

"Yeah, man, once we get back to Denny's place, sure." I tried to look them over from where I stood but there was nothing to do in this darkness, even with the dim light refracting off the snow on the ground.

"By the way, the totem can be looted as well," Denny explained as he pulled scraps of fur and elongated teeth from the pile of bone and other things.

"How does a totem keep them coming back?" James wondered aloud as he examined the thing.

"It stores their power and gives them something of theirs to return to. A scrap of fur, a bone—it is bound to them and they are to it." I crushed a few more parts that still stood before a satisfied look fell over his face. Relieved, almost was how it could have been described. "The mages made the beasts as experiments at first, but some grew to love the art more than most of their original studies. They wanted to create perfect animal protectors, so while the others moved toward more *humanoid* pursuits, there were those who created these huge, monstrous beings."

"I thought Mother Nature had a hand in that." I couldn't keep the edge of confusion out of my voice. Worrying that I had been lied to.

"Once the mages had been dealt with, the Mother did step in." He motioned for us to follow him as he spoke on. "She created the smaller beasts in their image, allowing them their wild splendor and their territories in hopes that they would find purpose in her grand design. Some did. I used to have more people visiting in times long past to become one with the beasts, but that stopped. Either because they could not find their own sacred places, or the beasts won their fight. I do not know, but the point is that she tried to do something for them. Now, I can put them to rest when they make themselves a true threat."

"So you don't just go around killing them?" Muu's concern made Denny pause.

"I kill what I must to ensure my mountain and my duties are seen to." He frowned at the snow around him. "I do not enjoy taking life as I once did. Now that I have created it, I find bringing the ultimate end to be... less satisfying than it was. I will protect and serve, hunt for my food, but I will not kill for sport."

"Very well." Muu nodded contemplatively. "I can respect that."

"Good." Denny smiled at us and we crested the hill back toward his home for the evening.

Later on, as we ate, I enchanted James' newfound weapons with higher ice damage and even some added piercing to boot. He was happy with them and I was able to just relax with Maebe after the meal.

"I saw her." Her voice made me turn and look at her. She smiled and pointed upstairs where Denny had slunk away with food for his mate. "She is beautiful. And like him, she is a dragon. But a true dragon."

"What kind?" I found my heartbeat speeding up.

"White dragon." She turned and nodded to the stairs.

I turned my head and spied a tall figure watching us from the stairs, Denny sitting behind her with his mouth moving slowly as he pointed to each of us.

She had scaled skin, but not like that of the dragon-kin. More like that of a dragon elf, and her alabaster scales looked more like ice forking over her pale skin, nothing like what I had seen of Winterheart in his draconic form. She wore a white fur dress that came down to her knees and her hands curled along the wood of the stairs as she watched us with a furrowed brow.

I waved as he pointed to me and her already large eyes widened further before she ducked back out of the way. Denny chuckled and tugged her back down so that she was further into view.

"Do not mind my husband," Maebe called softly, her reproachful glare my way only making me chuckle. "He does not understand what it is to be shy."

"I am cautious because there is no snow here to blend in with." Her voice was nowhere near as timid as she looked. It held just a hint of a feral growl that made my fur stand up on end.

"Allow me." Maebe held out a hand toward the doorway of the room and intense cold flared around us all. Ice and snow built up in a huge mound that built into a sort of protected seat.

The woman narrowed her eyes at the offering, then stepped toward it to look it over. Denny hovered behind her, but once she sat down, her sigh of relief was massive. "Thank you, elven one."

"You may call me Maebe," Maebe offered as she stood and stepped toward the other woman. "I know how you feel as well."

The woman eyed her for a moment, then her eyes fell on her stomach and she smiled, sharp teeth flashing in the light. "I see. Come and sit with me."

Maebe got up and left my side to join her newfound friend and all it did was make me laugh. She was so good at putting herself out there now.

They discussed the babies and how the cold was good for them. I shook my head and watched, content for now.

"Denny, do you know where the horses are?" Muu lowered his voice so as not to disturb the women's conversation.

"They're up the mountain a way." He offered us all another bowl of soup which I took gratefully. "I can lead you there in the morning, and with the mole gone, the storm should die down significantly by then."

"Thank you, Denny. We may forgo your help just to keep you safe, but we appreciate you all the same." I glanced at the tired faces around me. "Then I suppose we should all get some sleep."

I yawned at the others and they nodded. We would do a little more together in the morning and then I would call to Thor and see if he could take us to the Kirin. Didn't seem right to impose on Denny and his hospitality with a little one on the way.

CHAPTER TWELVE

Denny and his mate, Magrean, stood outside and waved us off together as we turned our sights up the slopes of the mountain.

Once we'd made it a good mile or two from Denny's, I pulled my whistle from my inventory and called to my mount Thor.

A crackling of thunder and a bright flash brought the confused Kirin before me. He tossed his head and whinnied at me, his massive head slamming joyfully into my side.

"Hey Thor, how you doing?" I patted his warm hide and he tossed his head again.

"Druid! I am so glad to see that you are alright." He sounded relieved to boot. "Kayda, She of the Frosty Winds, worries herself sick over you. Tell me where you are and I will tell her for you when I return."

"I was hoping you might be able to take us to her." I smiled at him but his confusion only mounted. He stamped his clawed foreleg and stared at me. "We're on your mountain, Thor. We're here where the Kirin call home."

He stilled and looked around, his eyes widening. "You are,

are you? I do not recognize this place. Are you sure you are here?"

"Yes, I am." I smiled at him and hoped that I hadn't brought us on a wild goose chase.

"Then here is what I wish you to do." He sounded excited now, his mane flapping in the wind. "I will return to my people and you will shoot lightning into the sky, as much of it as you can. We will watch for you, and when we see it, we will come and collect you for her. Can you do this?"

"I think that we can," I assured him. I glanced over at Kyr who listened closely and he grinned. "You have fifteen minutes, Thor. We'll see you soon."

He faded from sight and I turned to Kyr, "You wanna help me out here?"

"I would be honored." He stepped closer to me and called Rai out to stand with us. We waited the fifteen minutes before I called Hubris to me and had both Kyr and Rai grab the scepter.

All three of us channeled mana into the weapon and I cast Lightning Storm with it. Lightning pierced the sky, going straight up for more than three hundred feet.

"Well, everything in the area and beyond knows that something is going on up here," Sendak groused petulantly with his hair standing on end.

"You that freaked out?" Muu raised a scaled eyebrow at him and chuckled. "Who's going to come looking for us?"

"Why do you needlessly say such things?" Greer looked like he was about to shit his pants when I heard large wings flapping toward us.

For a second, my heart called with joy at thinking it was my Kayda, but that stopped when a massive scaled head with hateful red eyes crested the side of the mountain nearest us.

"Nice flying lizard!" James tried to call to it, but all it did was growl and stare at us like it was sizing us up to kill and eat.

It took a deep breath in, several spells having been

unleashed on it at once, and roared so loud that the snow beneath our feet began to quake violently.

Ice formed around our ankles and held us in place as Maebe howled, "Muu! I will kick your ass for this!"

He just shrieked delightedly and burst from where he was on the ground into the air above the gigantic wyvern. The thing dwarfed Kayda, it was so large and powerful looking. I was low on mana, seeing as I had dumped everything into that spell.

I hoped that the ring on my finger would allow me the chance to fight and shifted into my eagle form to get above him. Once I was there, I shifted into my fox-man form and dropped onto him with Muu. The dragoon slammed into the scaled and spiked back like a ton of bricks and the creature cried out in pain and confusion.

I could almost feel its mind trying to process what could possibly have dared to attack it in its domain. Muu's spear stabbed down into the meat of the back and he sliced savagely.

I lashed out with Magus Bane, restoring more than a hundred points of my mana and grinned before the world shifted and up was suddenly down. Muu and I fell, his footing lost as the wyvern reared and rolled to get above us. The only chance I had to get him back up to be of use was to be a platform for him.

I kissed Thick Skull and hoped for the best as I shifted into my dragon form under Muu.

Finally! The dragons roared through my mind, Bea and I struggling under their fury and need for control. I wrested my senses back with my companion's help and winged it up after my prey.

"You guys can be assholes later; I need to kill this thing." My deep voice echoed off the mountain faces and snow around us as I tried to claw the wyvern toward me. "So either pitch in or piss off!"

The instincts buffeted me with their desires, what I should do then I felt a firm kick off and knew I couldn't risk this being overrun bullshit so I shifted out of my dragon form and into my eagle form as the dragon's instincts howled.

Wind buffeted my wings and it was all I could do just to keep up with the beast above me. *Dip out of the area of his wings, then use the thermals to rise and get above him.*

The eagle's raspy voice cooled my mind and stilled me for what I had to do. The Druids beneath us hurled spell after spell at the beast and I had to dodge those on top of trying to rise from where I was.

We will definitely be discussing friendly fire! I panted mentally and drove myself on. The cold of the air did terrible things to my feathers and soon enough it was all I could do to just stay aloft. I had no choice.

It was dragon or let this thing control the air with Muu fighting on his own.

I didn't like it, but I shifted to a fox, then dragon, and the instincts came back in a rush. *Crack!*

My neck snapped painfully to the side as the wyvern bore down on me. We wrestled in the air, the massive spiked tail behind it battering my wings.

Finally, the green took over in my distraction. *Watch how a master does this.*

Our head snaked out and a small blast of venomous breath clouded the wyvern's mouth, forcing it to close its jaws and eyes for a second. Our wings wrapped around its body and our jaw clenched as we drove our teeth into the beast's neck. It cried out and plummeted with us.

Muu landed near our jaws and called, "You good?"

Our eyes rolled to him and a snarl emanated from our lips as we shook our head. "Guess not. *Maebe! Zeke did a pie!*"

A rumble of displeasure roiled through my mind, cold shadows pressing closer to me as Maebe's attention flexed and turned to me. *He did what?*

Shit, I groaned to myself and the dragons' instincts began to cool to the point of lethargy and I could take over once more.

I used my tail to maneuver us like a rudder in the air and

slammed the wyvern into the ground, shifting into my whale form to do it.

What? Of course I had to return to my normal form first. We're fighting here. Get your head in the game!

Ice burst from the beast's leathery wings heartbeats before lightning and fire beat at them. Muu slammed into its throat, and James came in swinging for the hills with his fists. I rolled off the beast into the snow and shifted into my fox-man form so that I could swing my axe at it angrily. I was hurting, the fall onto the ground and ice having brought me down to about a quarter of my health bar.

Healing magic surged into me as Rai leapt over my head and into the wyvern's eye, Kaius and Bea sprinting after him. The wyvern's health bar plummeted; roaring in agony, it lifted its head and a plume of putrid flame burst from its mouth that struck me and the others.

I activated my conversion ring as the flames engulfed me, siphoning some of the elemental damage into mana that I could use for myself and cast Aspect of the Storm.

Time slowed down as my perception raised significantly. The world blurred around me as I burst forward over the flames and down onto the wyvern's skull next to Rai. He regarded me oddly for a second before my clawed hands whipped into the beast's head like I was digging for gold. Scales scattered and moved out of the way as the others moved as if dosed in molasses. Eventually I found what I was looking for near the base of the skull and yanked it out. The struggling beast stilled, all of it except the eyes.

"Stop!" My voice sounded like I was being electrocuted.

The others halted their assault, Bea and Kaius growling low but listening—barely.

I dropped the aspect and hopped off the wyvern's back so that I could look it in the eyes. It growled and tried to breathe, its painful attempts all for naught because of my snapping its brain stem.

"This is my family, and I will not see them harmed." It

stared at me with open hatred and rage, struggling inwardly to move, and I could almost see it in its eyes. "You come for me, and you leave them alone. If you attack them again, I'll find your totem and crush it gleefully. We're going to end you now. I hope you can find your prey and live a nice life. Do not fuck with us. Or I swear I will go all kinds of Chaos on your ass."

I brought Nether Bolt up in my right hand and activated Cleave and Execution at the same time, the wyvern's spine separating like a block of wood being chopped in half. The beast expired and we rested while the body faded.

"What in the *Hells* were you thinking?" Maebe rounded on me, her hands on her hips. "No warning, no safe word —nothing?"

"Muu needed me to help him." I motioned to my friend, whose easy smile made its way forward. "If I hadn't given him a platform to jump on, he would have fallen."

"He is quite ingenious in how he will make it out of things, Zeke," she hissed at me insistently. "He would have been fine. You took a massive risk in choosing your dragon form and not telling me first. I can help you through our rings, but I cannot if I do not feel what is happening. And no, I cannot tell when they shut me out."

Crestfallen, I sighed. "I'm sorry. I was so caught up in protecting all of you that I lost my cool. No one is hurt, right?"

"James suffered some minor burns that Kyr and Greer are seeing to, but that is beside the point." She gripped my jaw and pulled my face back to her as I tried to look the others over. "I need you to warn me next time. No buts, no ifs. Do you understand? This is a request from your wife."

"Yes dear."

She sighed in relief and stood, her anger returning as she turned to Muu. "And *you.*"

Muu's eyes widened as she stomped toward him. "Oh God, mercy! *Please?!*"

She was behind him so fast with her foot cocked back to kick that I hadn't seen her move and the snow on the ground fountained upward almost as if it had been a cartoon. She kicked him right in his ass and he crumpled to the ground twenty feet down the slope and coughed. "My ass! She broke my ass!"

She clapped her hands together as if dusting them off, a slight smile gracing her lips as she moved away before Muu looked up at her with a lopsided grin. "You aren't the first one to have done it, either."

"I am certain I will not be the last." She raised an eyebrow and turned to face him fully. "Unless you wish to raise my ire again? I doubt you will live through it once more."

"You got it, mama bear." Muu grunted and tried to sit up. "Message received... now I'm going to go shit out my spine, if you don't mind."

"I will allow it." Maebe blinked at him sweetly. I cast Heal on him from where I stood. He sighed in relief and began to move a little easier after that.

A sense of awareness came over me—we weren't alone anymore.

Ten Kirin stood among us, their manes flowing in the wind. One of them, Thor, stepped forward and bowed his head, "Druid, we have come to take you to the Storm."

"Is that how you refer to Kayda?" I raised my eyebrows at him and he just whickered and tossed his head.

"You will ride on our backs." Another of the Kirin spoke politely. "We will take you."

A little bit repetitive, but okay. So long as I can get to my baby. "Very well then."

I turned to the others and spoke slowly, "These are the Kirin. Messengers of the Storm. Lightning horses and the rulers of their lands. You *will* pay them the respect they're due. Or they will shock you and I will laugh. Am I clear?"

Maebe was the first to step forward and curtsy to the Kirin closest to her, a massive male with growths like lightning along his shoulders. He watched her closely for a moment before returning her bow in kind with a sort of bow of his own.

He laid in the snow so that she could more easily climb onto his back, both of her legs on one side so as to remain the regal figure we all knew she was.

The Druids spoke in low tones to their various mounts while James stared at the one before him with crossed arms.

"You gonna get on her, or what?" They both looked at me, James and the Kirin he stood before, and both shrugged before the dragon elf hopped onto her back with ease.

The fact that not a single one of them had needed to prove themselves worthy was irritating, but so be it. Hell, even Muu sat on the back of his mount and grinned readily. Though he was still rubbing his ass.

"Well, Thor, we ready to ride?" I looked at the Kirin and he shook his head.

"You must collect your prize from killing Mistyr." I turned and looked over at the chest waiting to be plundered and walked toward it.

Inside, I found several large bones that I fantasized about making into huge swords, but I would have to hold off on that. Because I pulled out an actual sword. I almost giggled at how shockingly amazing the weapon looked. The blade was made entirely of bone with serrated edges that had veins of metal woven through it and stuck out on the sides. It was thin, and long, almost long enough to be a great sword but much too slim to be one. I knew instantly that Jaken would be able to use this.

Thinking about him hurt, but I had to hold out hope that they would be okay until they either found each other or we found them.

I finished looting the goods, skins, scales, fangs and even some flame essence that all went into my inventory before hopping onto Thor's back to ride.

Bea and Kaius kept up with the horses easily, needing to air walk for some distances but they looked to be having almost as much fun as we were having.

Kirin in lore had always been agile and could generally kick ass when it came to being in motion, but here in real life? Thor had moves I couldn't even imagine. He could *fly*. And the best part was that his was a form I could now take as my own.

We flew for the portions where we needed to, never longer than the gust raptors could keep up with us, but the bounding and gliding across chasms and over clouds was a heady thing.

Their world was stellar, the sky above the clouds bright and lovely and the snow-capped mountaintops breathtaking in their beauty. Snow-capped tops that shimmered and glowed with light in different hues. Some fiery and orange, others nearly purple with some unseen radiance from elsewhere.

Finally, after a solid two hours of riding up and over the mountains to another set nearby, we came to a halt on a large plateau where a huge nest had been constructed from ice and frozen lightning bolts.

In that nest rested Kayda, surrounded by more than twenty Kirin who stared at us with open curiosity.

"Kayda!" I called loudly, ignoring the Kirin who tried to cross my path. She lifted her head groggily and cried out softly as she tried to stand. "Stay still, baby. Stay still!"

She settled as I came to stand with her inside the nest. Touching her, I could feel that she was ill and I knew we would need to give her the mix of the plant and water.

"She's going to need to take something to rid her body of the toxins inside her." I turned to the Kirin around us and spoke loudly. "This is not going to be pleasant for anyone involved but we will try to keep her calm while it happens. I need you all to stay calm and keep away from her while she's recovering."

Several of them stood closer, stomping and treading the ground as if daring me to try to keep them away when an older, gray and gold Kirin slowly cantered over to stand between us all.

"We will respect his wishes as the beloved of our lord." The wizened creature turned to me and bowed his head. "Do as you must, Druid. We will guard her as we can."

I nodded to him in return and turned to go about my business. It was hard to get the massive bird to swallow the mixture, me having to literally hold her beak shut while Muu massaged her throat with his hands to make her swallow. She whined and groaned afterward, Maebe constructing a thick shell of ice around the bird to keep her cool and quieter for all of our safety.

Once that was taken care of, I turned to the eldest Kirin, "There were two people, an orc and a little girl, with her. What happened to them?"

"They are inside with the youngest Kirin and the elderly, training." He turned without another word and trod through the snow toward a small gap in the rock face no more than forty yards from Kayda's nest.

I looked over at Kayda, then Maebe and she nodded once. "I will watch her so that you can go and continue to mend your bond with her. Give her my love and tell her to come to me, if you do not bring her yourself. Be safe."

I nodded and mouthed, *Thank you.* She smiled and closed the distance between her and Kayda, throwing out her hands and petting the massive bird as the magics duking it out within her caused her immense distress.

Walking through here, the temperature changed significantly, almost taking on a summertime heat that made my nose run a bit.

"What is this place?"

"This is the inner sanctum," the Kirin explained softly, his voice echoing slightly off the stones around us. "This is where the people who used to live among us stayed. They had homes here, but they left one day and never returned."

So it seems that Orlow'thes got them all? Why the need for so many people to attend a trial?

I shook the thought from my mind as I heard Vrawn shout, "No, Odany, you must keep your rear foot planted when you swing your weapon. Otherwise your balance will be thrown off."

I patted the Kirin as he moved deftly aside and sprinted full tilt toward Vrawn's voice. There she stood, twenty feet from

Odany in a small arena that looked freshly made. She had her training weapon in hand, the banded blade of it resting against her broad, muscled shoulder with her back toward us.

Closing the distance, I shifted into my human form and called to her, "Vrawn!"

She turned and dropped her weapon when she saw me, Odany bouncing where she stood. Vrawn took two steps then sprinted toward me with wild abandon of her own. We plowed into each other and fell to the ground with grunts of pain and worry as we checked each other over.

The relief I felt in seeing her was astronomical but it wasn't anything like the dump I felt when she pulled me close, whispering, "Yohsuke is here in one of the buildings. He is recovering but is very sick."

"Thank the gods you all are okay," I whispered against her cheek. "Mae and I were so worried about you."

"She's here?" Vrawn whispered with a slow grin spreading over her face. "Where is she?"

"Seeing to Kayda. Are you okay? How did you all get here?"

"Both Odany and I are fine." She smiled to herself and caressed my cheek. "Kayda seemed driven to get us here, not stopping to rest at all. The only thing she did do was swoop down to collect Yohsuke in the middle of the night when she spotted him fighting something within the shadows and he was not doing well."

She motioned to the large, green field we stood in. "From there, she brought us all here. I have been training young Odany in the way of the sword since then."

"You both aren't affected by the toxin from Orlow'thes?" I frowned at her and she shrugged.

"I was sick for a while, but I am better now." She frowned contemplatively and then nodded toward Odany. "She was brilliant and blasted the bloody waters away from us as long as she could. Kayda was struck by it but she managed."

"I'm so glad she did." I hugged Vrawn once more and

kissed her fully on the lips, my joy and relief mixing heavily. She kissed me back, but when I leaned back, her cheeks were more flushed than normal. "You sure that you're alright?"

She grinned at me, her tusks flashing in the dim light around us. "Yes. I've missed you. Let us find Maebe. I miss her too."

A cool breeze drifted toward us and suddenly Maebe stood next to us within our shadows. "Hello, my loves." She glanced at me. "Forgive me, I heard my name and came here. Kayda is sleeping fitfully, but she is asleep."

I nodded and stepped back as the two collected each other in hugs, Maebe reaching up to grab Vrawn's face before she kissed Vrawn fully on her lips with a smile and soft tears of relief.

"Maebe, you look so different, what has happened?" Vrawn's concern was touching and it made me smile.

"I am with child," she stated with a radiant smile as she motioned to her more muscular physique. "This is how the Fae women compensate to protect their unborn children—we become more powerful and formidable."

"We do not." Vrawn looked at her pointedly and I blinked three times in rapid fire at her. "We start that way and stay that way."

I sighed in relief. *Oh man, for a second there I thought... Well, let's not pull a Muu here.*

"Vrawn." Maebe reached out and caressed the larger woman's stomach. "Is this a way of telling us something?"

Once more, my senses went into overdrive and I took in everything I could. Sure enough, Vrawn nodded proudly and the world slowed down. "I am pregnant."

"Whah—how?" My mouth moved dumbly after that but all I could do was mouth the word 'how,' over and over.

"Zeke." Maebe frowned at me and smacked my leg. "You know very well as to *how* it happened."

"I think he means more along the lines of how it could

happen to him?" Vrawn's concern was touching, but at the same time, her slightly dejected eyes hurt.

"Yes and no." Both women turned to look at me oddly, Vrawn grasping Maebe's hand almost absently. "I just wonder how an idiot like me ends up so blessed and fortunate when there are so many people out there suffering."

Maebe snorted, making me lower my eyebrows at her and she just rolled her eyes. "I have known you for a short time, Zekiel, and though you portray stupidity well, you are far from it. You can be cunning, ruthless, and brilliant all in a matter of seconds when you put your mind and heart to something. When it comes to others, you will give all of yourself until there is nothing left to give. It is that person that you choose to hide in the veil of uncertainty and self-doubt until you need to portray it better."

"Come again?" I blinked at her slowly, hoping beyond hope I wasn't about to be chewed out.

"She is telling you that the persona you tend to allow others to see is not who you are truly capable of being." Vrawn reached out and touched my cheek. "You choose to hide and allow yourself to be seen a certain way for some reason. We see the real you. And that real you is as much deserving of these blessings as you think anyone else is."

"What do I do know, though?" I frowned at both of them. "Two children on Brindolla, two lives that will have to bear my choices. My actions. How is this fair to either of you? To them?"

"Life is not fair," Vrawn cooed at me softly, strangely soothing my nerves. "Life is hard here for some. But we know what you do is important, and our paths crossing was meant to happen."

My heart skipped a beat. "Did you have another vision?"

She shook her head. "No. I believe this to be because I love you." She looked from me to Maebe. "I love you both. I am proud to rear this child."

"You will not be alone, and I fear neither shall I." Maebe's soft smile at Vrawn gave me an inkling of a clue as to what was going on in her head before she voiced it. "Vrawn, will you come to the Fae realm with me to raise our children?"

Vrawn blinked at Maebe, startled, then uncertain. "Is that okay?" Maebe just raised an eyebrow demurely and Vrawn chuckled. "Right, you are the queen. Yes, I will come with you once this is all done."

"Samir barely liked us being there, what will he think of Vrawn being there?" I asked, trying to cling to something that got my mind off of *I have multiple children, what the fuck am I going to do?*

"He will be fine with it, as she is from Brindolla," Maebe replied readily enough.

"But what about the babies?" I touched both of their stomachs lightly. "I know that the two of you are better fighters than me, but if I have to worry about you both being near the fighting, I don't know that I can do it. At least, not in good conscience."

"I will allow you your worry, if for nothing more than I find it endearing." Maebe sniffed and raised her chin regally. "Vrawn and I are capable, and if all else fails—I will protect our children. You have my word."

I received the binding notification from her and nodded, slightly relieved.

"Okay." I shook my head and came back to the other issue at hand. "Again, I ask what I can do. What I *should* do. I don't know what's right."

"From what you have said of him, your son at home has a very loving mother who dotes in him and ensures he has everything," Vrawn began cautiously, my attention coming to her and I confirmed what she said with a nod. "Our children will have the same, but they will have the added benefit of magic and an entire kingdom to help raise them. To ensure they grow up strong and healthy."

"Sounds pretty great, I'll admit, but what about not having a father?" I stared them both in the eyes, both of them trying to maintain that pure contact but failing. Their eyes fell. "Not having that person in your life hurts a lot of kids. I should know. I don't want to pass my daddy issues onto them, or you."

"You think we would let you run?" Vrawn surprised me with her sudden vehemence, her scowl deepening. "If I could keep you here for me, I would. I would be that selfish, and I would think nothing of it."

My hand squeezed hers softly; I knew she wasn't trying to be cruel. She took a deep breath and sighed. "All I wish for you to know is that our children will have two parental figures to care for them. Your son will have only his mother. That is not fair to him, or you. You knew him first."

My skin went cold, though internally I was hotter than I had ever been. Trapped between two damning situations, what was I to do? Either way, someone went without me. And I without my children.

"You are saving a world," Maebe offered quietly, her voice firm, yet gentle. "Millions of lives, possibly more if this stops War for good. You and your friends have sacrificed much more than anyone has ever asked of you, and now you have yet more that can be taken from you."

I needed to stand and move. I needed to lash out and find something to work my frustrations out on. I needed something to turn the self-loathing and rage against and just go until I couldn't move anymore. The confusion and hurt too much for anyone to bear alone.

You are not alone. I opened my eyes and caught sight of a single tear fleeing from Maebe's eyes.

They would suffer too. But they knew it had to happen how it had to. I could die today and they would still be stuck raising those kids alone. Well. With each other, which was still pretty damned good.

"We know you did not ask for this," Vrawn began but I held up a hand.

"I didn't." My voice sounded tired, even to me. "But it's still what happened, and I have no regrets. Not one."

I pulled them both to me and hugged them tightly. "I love you both. I will cherish you both always. I don't know what I will do, but I know that I love you and I will do what I think best."

"It is all I ask," Maebe offered sweetly with a sad smile. "I will support you no matter what, my king."

"As will I." Vrawn thumped my shoulder and suddenly I was acutely aware of eyes on us all.

More than a dozen small Kirin watched us carefully to which Vrawn lowered her voice and muttered, "Mind them well, they will shock you without a thought and treat it like a game."

"That's going to be fun." I rolled my eyes. "How long do we have before both babies come?"

Maebe thought for a moment then stated, "Several more months. At least seven for me. Vrawn?"

"I am uncertain." Her cheeks reddened wildly. "I am new to this and do not know of many orc women carrying non-human or orc children. I don't know if that changes how long my gestation period will be."

My mouth opened and closed, before I said, "I wasn't sure that had anything to do with it, but it seems we have time. Okay. Good. Let's get to work then. I'll go get Yoh started on his medicine and healed up."

"Good idea, my love." Maebe patted my leg affectionately. "I will stay with Vrawn and speak with her of matters that we must contend with."

I nodded to them both and leaned down to kiss their foreheads before turning and stalking toward some of the buildings north of our position. Scenting the air, I knew Yohsuke was this way, his vampiric death smell making me wish I wasn't as good at sniffing things out as I was, or that my earring amplified.

Between a handful of houses, one of the smaller ones in the center that reminded me more of a shed than an actual home was where his scent was densest.

"Yohsuke!" I called softly, knowing his hearing rivaled my own.

A slam in the shed made me jump where I stood. I sighed heavily then steeled myself. I opened the door quickly and stepped inside to find the coffin I had enchanted was the only thing inside the room.

A muffled voice rumbled, "Close the door, asshole."

I shut the door and crossed my arms. As soon as the latch caught, the coffin door opened and Yohsuke stepped out into the darkness. He looked gaunt and sickly. More than he had last time.

"You okay, man?" He shook his head. "You still have the toxin in you?"

"Yeah." He coughed once, twice, and hacked up something wet and gross that he hocked onto the wooden floor unceremoniously. "It's killing me slowly."

"It sucks but it's not deadly that I was told of."

"You don't get it, Zeke." He touched his shirt and pulled it aside. The gray cast of his skin was blackened and mottled with red and yellow. "I'm a magical creature now. I'm undead. I cannot exist without magic, and the toxin is burning it out of me faster than I can replenish."

I shrugged and pulled out the plant and water I had gotten from the forest. "This should fix you right up, man."

He pulled the plant toward him and sniffed at it with a grimace but set it on a small, boarded up windowsill. He popped the cork on the vial of water and hissed violently. "This is holy water, bro. If I drink that directly, it'll fry me from the inside out."

"Dude, there has to be a way to get the toxin out of you." I ran a hand over my bald head, my stress levels rising a bit more with each breath.

"Blood helps, but it has to be powerful magic blood." He spat again. "Odany's blood helps a lot, but I would have to drain her completely to feel normal at all and I can't kill her, man. She's starting to grow on me."

"And my blood would kill you since I'm a werewolf." An idea occurred to me. "What if we were to lure a beast here and have it eat this stuff? Then, you can drink its blood to heal yourself?"

"That doesn't really sound like too bad of an idea, though the holy water will still burn like a motherfucker." I just chuckled to myself. "What?"

"It's treated everybody like shit, why should you be any different?" I closed the distance between us both and pulled him into a massive hug. "It's good to see you alive, brother."

"Good to be alive, bitch." He grinned at me and pulled back. "Congratulations on the kid. You happy?"

I snorted and corrected him, "*Kids.*" His eyes narrowed and I pointed toward the door. "Maebe too."

"Dude, no fuckin' way!" He grimaced and spat another globule of brackish grossness onto the ground by his feet. "Let's take care of this shit and we can celebrate right, okay?"

I grinned and turned to head outside when Yoh snapped his fingers, I turned and he pointed at the dimly-lit window. "The light, man. I can't be in the light. It'll kill me with as weak as I am right now."

Ah. "Got you, thanks for the reminder, man." I waited for him to get into his coffin before I walked outside and took a deep breath. I looked at the door and sighed. "You still smell like ass, man. Now it's death and ass."

All I heard was, "Fuck you!"

Maebe and the others, all the members of the party currently with us, waited twenty feet away. Maebe stepped closer to me, concern in her eyes. "How is he?"

"Not good, but we have a plan." Muu and James looked resolute, the Druids uncertain as to what they could do, but we had to try it.

"Time to see if we can lure some powerful beast here to get him a transfusion." Maebe frowned at me. "What's up?"

"Could he not just drink from me?" The hurt and worry she felt pulsed through our connection.

"He would never put you or the baby in danger, Mae." James took the words right out of my mouth.

"So we lure the beast here and what, we make it eat the—you clever bastards." Muu crossed his arms. "You're going to what, supercharge the beast's blood with the plant and water mixture and then he drinks the blood?"

"Since when did you become so brilliant?" Maebe eyed Muu as if he had just grown a second head.

"Maebe, I've always been this brilliant," Muu drawled with a grin on his face, rolling his eyes at her. "It's just hard to realize said brilliance when all people expect from you is badass violence and raw animal sex appeal."

"Is he always like this?" The elder Kirin stared at the dragon-kin in disbelief.

CHAPTER THIRTEEN

If this worked, we would have seriously been underutilizing Maebe's power the entire time she had been with us for petty shit like pride and leveling up.

Her grin grew across her face as she winked at me. My eyes widened as her hands raised, blue and black energy coalescing and swirling across her skin like gloves, before she slammed her hands to the ground before her with a primal growl.

We waited for a few moments, but nothing happened. The rest of us all frowned at each other, then at her just before Muu opened his mouth but she shushed him with a smirk.

Black and white snowflakes fell over us, slowly at first, then faster and heavier; a dense sensation of magical power coated each one. Maebe closed her eyes and her brow knit together in focus as her chest rose and fell steadily.

"I can feel all of you, the Kirin, Kayda, and the raptors." Her voice grew soft for a second before she frowned. "Some kind of hares along the side of the mountain. The house that Denny and his beloved share. There are several larger creatures slumbering under the snow that my magic will take a little more time to penetrate to."

"How long do you need?" James crossed his arms uncomfortably. The magic looked like it was bothering him.

Maebe's eyes clenched a little more, her fingers swirling just before she moved her wrists the same way. Her eyes flew open. "Something felt me. It's not as large as that wyvern, but it knows that I am here and it is coming."

"How far off is it? It can't possibly get here that fast." Kyr frowned at Maebe who looked more than a little sure of herself.

"It's coming, and it leaps higher than Muu."

Muu puffed out his chest and pulled out his spear. "Time to see who's got more vertical!"

"What kind of creature is it?" Wind whipped around us and swirled the snow Maebe had created into the air, stealing my voice.

A figure plummeted from the sky, bringing darkness and snow down with it as it crashed into the warm area, cold air billowing from it in waves. An ape-like creature with glistening and icy-blue fur and glowing blue eyes bared large teeth at us as massive fists cracked against the ground. Shards of ice crackled where its fists met, then exploded as it roared a challenge toward Maebe.

Maebe grinned wildly, stepped forward three steps, and roared in return, her voice reverberating around us. Kirin falling back behind us with some of the younger ones circling toward the front of their kind to fight if needed.

The beast sat up straighter and stared at Maebe hard before huffing at her. Like it was trying to say something. The sun fell quicker and quicker, but the fading light gave me an idea. I pulled out a single coin, light reflecting off it and catching the beast's attention.

"If that's what I think it is, you have one shot before it goes straight for her," James whispered vehemently. "Let's get to it."

I whistled and it flinched toward me, so I did the only thing I could think to do—I cast Hollow Step and moved through Maebe's shadow into the beast's and slapped the Trickster's Coin against its foot.

The beast roared when its shadow burst from the ground in bars that bound it in place, shaking and foaming at the mouth. My shadow magic joined the coin's, thickening the bars slowly as I dropped the ingredients on the ground.

Pounding footsteps behind me drew my attention as James grabbed the two items. "I'm on it!" He hopped up and tossed the plant into the beast's mouth then poured the liquid into it, having to punch the stuff down its throat to get it to swallow them.

Seconds later, it began to convulse and foam at the mouth like I was sure I had and like Muu had started to.

"It's time, Yoh!" The ape's eyes closed slightly, then slammed open as the shadowy bars burst, hundreds of my mana going with it.

A furred fist rocketed into my gut as I prepared for the attack and knocked me backward ass over teakettle into Kyr and Greer who fell with me. Muu roared and shot forward with his spear at the ready, James getting up from an attack I had missed.

He wiped blood from his mouth and snarled as he grabbed the leg closest to him and started to clamber up it.

Greer shoved me from behind, my health replenishing slightly at his touch, putting me back to 70%. It had been a hell of a sucker punch, and the frost still coating my body meant he liked the cold.

Kyr just grinned and surged around me, electrical energy swirling around his fists as Rai joined him.

Suddenly, a shadow appeared above the ape and latched onto its back, a roar of surprise escaping its throat.

It was Yoh having his snack. "Get that thing to sit still, he's too weak to take a beating!"

Shadows shot from the ground and lassoed the beast's arms and legs, pulling them tightly against his body as James and Muu went for the knees. The beast fell with a cry and knelt in the snow that its arrival had brought with it.

Greedy sucking sounds and angry feral growls escaped the

injured vampire as he drank his fill. Glowing blue orbs ebbed and grew heavy lidded as Yohsuke's orange eyes grew brighter. His skin took on a healthier cast and still he drank more and more.

Blood drained down into the beast's fur and onto the man behind him. We stood there for what could have been an eternity while the stench of vampire grew stronger and stronger until I had to fight back the urge to gag.

Finally, Yohsuke lifted his face away from the beast's throat, face plastered and caked with blood and grinned. "That's better."

"What, he doesn't have to suffer like the rest of us?" Muu snarled and kicked the beast in the ribs, the bones breaking. It was on its last legs. "End it, Yoh. We shouldn't play with our food."

He shrugged and grabbed the neck before taking it toward him with both hands. A sickeningly-wet popping, crunch reached my ears and I didn't have to see the health bar to know it no longer drew breath.

I watched my brother over the corpse, already fading from view. "You sure you're okay?"

"Other than feeling like I'm going to need to take a giant shit, I feel better than ever." He laughed at himself and lifted his shirt so that we could all watch as Orlow'thes' blood retracted slowly and the grossness around it receded. "I guess you all had to deal with more?"

"Way more, and let me tell you, it was some bullshit, my friend." James grinned and pulled Yoh into a bear hug. Muu joined them and I just chuckled as I watched them all begin fighting because Yoh didn't care for hugging all that much.

"Thank you for helping there, guys." The Druids nodded and I smiled at Maebe. "You too, my love."

"Can we come out now?" Odany's voice echoed across the field to us from one of the houses. I turned and saw her looking out the window with Vrawn shaking her head in exasperation.

"Yes!" Yoh called back, already trying to wipe his face clear of the blood on him.

"Now that we know that they are okay, should we move on?" Sendak's voice broke my reverie and made me think. "Seeing as though your friend will only be able to travel freely at night?"

Maebe echoed his sentiment. "It would be the safest bet, and some of us do work better in cover of darkness."

"It probably would be better, but Kayda is still recovering, right?" I shivered as I remembered her pained cries and fevered movements. Bea had opted to stay with her, Kaius as well, while Sendak stayed to heal us. "I can't leave her again. I think we should wait."

"Could she not simply follow us where we're going?" Sendak's rebuttal made me more than a little angry, but I could see where he was coming from so I couldn't just blow a gasket on him and call it at that either.

"She probably could, but now that you have Kaius, isn't it odd being away from him?" At the raptor's name, Sendak frowned heavily in thought. "That's only the bond of a few days. I raised Bea from birth. I raised *Kayda* from birth—our bonds and love for each other are immense. It's not a matter of if she can do something like that, but if I'll allow it. She's sick and she needs me. If anything, you guys can move on and we can follow *you*."

"I think he's right." Kyr scratched his head and looked us both over. "We have an advantage in the night with a vampire among us, moving on would be to our benefit."

"Then take Muu, James, and Yohsuke with the three of you, and go," Maebe answered flippantly with a dismissive motion. "So eager to throw away an opportunity to learn from your mentor for advantages against the daylight? Zeke has the ability to create items that would keep him safe from such things, but if you feel all of you have learned enough from him, go and see what you can do."

Oh, sweetheart, that's low. They could have gone on. She glanced at me and winked and I rolled my eyes at her. She knew it and didn't care.

"I suppose there is more we could learn," Sendak said politely with a deferential nod my way.

I turned to the Kirin and smiled. "Is it okay if we spend the night here?"

The eldest Kirin clomped forward and bowed his head. "Yes, Beloved of the Storm, you are welcome in the inner sanctum."

He walked next to me as we walked toward the abandoned homes. One or two of the younger Kirin played close to Sendak, zapping him and cantering away laughing as he howled after them.

Once we arrived at the largest building, the Druids all bowed their heads and stepped inside to prepare food with Yoh joining them. He wanted to cook some more and compare recipes with Greer.

I left the others. "I'm going to go be with Kayda for a bit, you guys check on each other and be safe."

They watched me walk away, but it wasn't long before two sets of footsteps began to follow mine. I knew who it was without even looking, I could smell Vrawn and Maebe together behind me and smiled. "Yes, ladies?"

"We cannot simply allow you to go and visit our favorite bird alone, can we?" The smile in her tone made me turn.

Vrawn grabbed me around my waist and pulled me closer to them both. "I have missed you both so much and now I have you both here. I do not wish to spend time away from you if I can help it."

"And what of Odany?" I raised a brow at her as I tried to look back for the little girl.

"She's strong enough now that her wind elementals would tear almost anything up before it got to her." She kissed the top of my head near my fox ear affectionately. She'd never done that before. "Besides, she's enamored with Muu at present, and the young Kirins love playing with her. Their parents are never too far off anyway."

She squeezed me tightly, making me grunt, and we kept walking toward the outside of the sanctum to Kayda. I could hear her cries through the blizzard outside thanks to my further heightened senses, but that was just me. I hoped. Twenty Kirin lay in the snow around the dome of ice where the giant bird's shadow writhed.

Maebe opened an entrance for us with a wave of her hands and we came into a frigid environment on a completely different level than outside the dome. As soon as we entered, the electrical energy around her snapped and flexed, searching for something to get to ground through. I pulled that energy toward me using my aspected mana, and pushed it toward the earth, the snow below us melting and turning to ice almost instantaneously.

"Hi baby," I cooed to her softly, my hands flattening over her feathers as calmly as I could, her temperature biting at my skin and will. I ignored it and kept touching her and muttering to her softly. Her breathing and crying out soon began to swell, then fell, her pulse lowering.

To ensure she was going to truly be okay, I pressed electrical energy into her body as Maebe patted one of her large clawed talons and passed along icy mana.

Her breathing steadied further and finally she looked to be getting comfortable, but it wasn't over. The worst may have passed from my perspective, but she would need to recover still. Better that we let her rest until fully recovered.

Bea and some of the Kirin opted to stay by her side, not even I could convince the raptor not to. The Kirin assured me they would keep her warm so that she would be okay and I decided to trust them. It was Thor who offered to stay closest to her, using his body to provide warmth. I appreciated that greatly.

Maebe, Vrawn, and I walked back to the house to find dinner waiting for us as the others sparred. I offered advice to

Greer as he fought in aspected forms, able to change them quickly as it was. It was alarming how quickly they all learned.

Hell, Kyr and Rai were nigh inseparable now, and the way he used his Lightning magic to crush Sendak was borderline impressive.

The frustrated Druid brushed himself off and one of the older Kirin children cantered over to check on him, their large muzzle brushing his arm lightly.

"I'm alright, thank you," he muttered and offered his hand to the creature who bumped it up along their head and mane as if to make him pet it. "Oh, you're a forceful one, aren't you, little lady?"

Rai and Kyr stepped closer to them, I didn't know quite why, but when they did, the filly stepped forward and lowered her head menacingly at them.

I looked directly at Maebe and muttered, "I swear to the gods that if he bonds with a Kirin of all animals, I'm fucking done."

She shook her head and I turned to see a look of shock on Sendak's face before he called over, "She wants to be my companion, what do I do?"

"God *fucking fuck!*" I growled and threw my hands in the air, Maebe laughing at my frustration.

"You have a Storm Roc for a companion, why can he not have a Kirin?" Her laughter did nothing to hide her curiosity and I found myself sighing.

"They're just so fucking cool, man." I flipped him off playfully and responded, "Just make sure it's okay with her parents."

"Kirin are their own creatures, if the child has decided to follow the Druid, she has decided her path," the eldest Kirin answered readily and spooked me. "My apologies for startling you, Druid."

"No, no, heightened senses are only useful if you make a habit of never ignoring them." I smiled at him, and he nodded to me. I turned to look at the group of Druids as they stood together. "There's really nothing more I can teach all of you other than just mental stuff and maybe a little advice here and there. When you stop letting others dictate what you can and cannot do, for bullshit reasons, you grow."

I stood and walked over to them. "All of you are so much better off than when you started. And you've seen a little of what it's like to be a true warrior of Mother Nature, none of that fake shit—the real. You serve her, and her ambitions, and the planet. You can't deny yourself a part of your heritage and power because it's inconvenient or a faux pas in someone else's book. You know what I'm trying to say?"

"Stop letting the assholes speak for everyone and rise up to make a difference." Greer shocked us all and I looked pointedly over at Muu who tried and failed at looking innocent.

"Essentially." I nodded, fighting a rueful smile. "Just don't let people walk all over you. You aren't second class citizens. And if they think you are? Leave. You don't deserve that. With the power you have, you could take your people and make your own city."

"You could bring them here," James said suddenly, the rest of us looking at him in alarm. "Yeah, think about it. People are afraid to come here, and you can already teleport to the stone to get in—bring your people here and prosper."

"What about the beasts?" Sendak protested. "We have been accosted by them at almost every turn."

"What about them?" Kyr sneered, which was odd. "We took care of the majority of them easily. And with more of our people free to pursue their own power and way of fighting, we can train a new generation of Druids. Or fighters. Or mages. We could become so much more than we have been allowed to be for decades, Sendak. Can you imagine?"

"No, he cannot." Greer sighed to himself, running his hand through his hand, his fingers brushing his pointed ears. "He's scared, and that is expected. I am too. This is much more than we thought of when we offered to assist Zeke in this. Are we ready for this?"

"I think you are." Maebe stepped forward and looked at all

three of them. "Already you have proven yourself to be capable. You can train your people, and ensure they are cared for. It is hard to take them and put them in a newer environment to make them safer, when in truth there is danger around every curve of the stone or behind every tree. It will be difficult, but not impossible."

She thought for a moment, then amended, "Though it might be easier if you were to let Denny know. He could be a valuable member of this new society."

"It'll require a lot of work, long hours, and probably some ungrateful people barking your way, but if it's what you want, do it." I stared at each of them for a moment before a chill ran down my spine and my fur stood on end.

I am here, and I wish for them to be away from their oppressors. Mother Nature's voice, weakened and raspy, whispered through my mind. *Tell them of my love. Tell them that I will watch over them. Tell them.*

"Yes ma'am." I smiled and each of the Druids frowned at me like I had just turned green. "Mother Nature says she wants you to do it so that you're away from your oppressors."

"You're lying." Sendak looked as though he was ready to attack me for what I just said.

"I swear to you here and now, on my title as King of the Unseelie Fae, that what I just said to you is true, and that Mother Nature said that she loves you and she will watch over you." I dismissed the notification of my word being given off hand and watched as he read it. His face went slack as he dropped to his knees quietly, his hand covering his mouth as he just stared off into nothing.

"It's true, she spoke to you." Kyr spoke as Greer watched and both of them just stared at me.

"Yeah, what we do is kind of important so there's not much guesswork between the two of us." I had to admit their wonder was a little embarrassing and as more and more people grew to be in awe of us, it was more and more irksome. "She speaks to me, and me to her. It's because we're close that she trusts me. You can get there too, trust her and yourselves."

"Let's go get some sleep, we should rest while we can." Yohsuke surprised me with his concern, but it was the fact that he motioned me toward him with a jerk of his head that made me wary.

Not that I didn't trust him, it was just odd.

The other Druids left together, discussing logistics and what they would need. Odany slept already in her own room and both Maebe and Vrawn eyed me knowingly before going off too.

"What's up, buddy?"

"I'm definitely going to need something to keep the sunlight off me tomorrow." He looked nervously at the sky. I would have said something but his eyes glowed orange before he spoke again. "That cocktail did a lot for me, but it completely wore down any humanity I had left. If the sunlight touches my skin without something to cover me or buffer it, I'll die."

"How can you tell?" My heart hammered in my chest and I worried for my brother.

He put his face in his hands, then looked up at me and muttered, "I just know. Will you help me?"

"Don't you ever ask me something stupid like that again— of course I'll help you." I clapped him on the shoulder, the cold emanating from him familiar, and different. He was right. Something was different now. "Do you have anything I could use to make a ring or something for you?"

"All my gear got washed in that shit. I have some stuff that I happened across but nothing that could be of great use to you, I don't think."

I thought about it and wondered if I could just bullshit something, like a weapon for him that would cover the user in darkness? No.

I sighed and walked away, looking into my inventory for anything that might help him and found nothing. What could I do?

Finally I had to bite back my pride and turn to the Kirin for aid. I found the elder Kirin and approached him slowly, he looked tired and close to sleep.

One of the younger Kirin intercepted me. "Dad will be asleep soon. What do you need, Druid?"

I eyed the little thing, his mane barely a half foot long, and quietly related my request, "I was wondering if adventurers or people came here with gear that you all collected? Like rings or armor or something?"

He gouged the ground with his forehooves and thought for a moment before motioning that I follow him with a toss of his head. We walked for ten minutes in near silence toward a small lake in the rear of the grotto.

"This is where we put things that find their way up the mountain." He stepped closer to the water, then backed away with a flash of fear in his gaze. "This water hurts us if we go too far in and everything sinks to the bottom here."

"Is it acid or something?" I blinked at him and he did the same in return, clearing not knowing what I meant. "Does it burn your skin?"

"Oh, no. It just shocks us back." He tossed his little mane and motioned to his markings with his horn. "We are lightning creatures. Submerging in water can hurt us if we aren't careful or have perfect control over our powers."

"I see. Well, thank you." I gave him a friendly pat on his shoulder, static greeting my skin. I ignored it. He likely couldn't control it.

I cast Water Lung on myself and considered taking my clothes off, but left them on just in case. I hopped into the warm water and sure enough, began to slowly sink down into it as if pulled by a current.

I allowed it to pull me as I surveyed the floor of the lake, nothing sticking out to me right away. The flow and intensity of the water changed suddenly and sucked me around and around. Finally I saw where it was taking me and my heart fluttered crazily.

The water swirled toward a deep hole in the lake floor where the underwater current became a whirlpool then swept into the darkness below. Who knew what could be down there, but better that I find out if I could.

My friends needed gear and if this would lead me to it, I would follow this current to the depths themselves. *No need to get the others involved, I can bamf out here with Teleport if needed.*

The darkness closed around me as I slipped into the hole below me and waited for the darkness to pass. Casting my mind into the shadows here was easier for me now. I was so used to it that it felt almost second nature. I couldn't exactly *see* but I could feel things. Fish swimming nearby who moved like they knew I was there, though some of them moved like serpents, long and sinewy.

Normally, I hated snakes, but I had the feeling that these could be some sort of variety of eels, based on how they felt to the darkness.

I cast about for something, anything that could be a potential threat before figuring I would be safe. I didn't want to boil the water I was in, so I decided to make a simple spell to help with the darkness, and to revamp an old one. I mixed light magic with Winter's Blade, a heavy focus on radiance and refracting light so that one could see and also do light damage on top of ice damage.

Winter's Light Blade – Caster summons a blade of frost and light to attack their foes either up close or at range. Cost: 20 MP. Range: 75 feet. Cool down: 5 seconds.

I snorted at the minor cost because it had cost me at least ten times that to make the spell. I cast it after closing my eyes, letting the light flood the area before I opened them again.

Sure enough, more than fifteen eels eyed me angrily. "What do you intrude for?" one of them called to me, making me pause.

Oh, right. I was still under the effect of Nature's Voice. I shook my head, unused to animals speaking to me first.

"I came here to see the items that the Kirin throw in here." I motioned to the now-glittering pile on the floor of the large underwater cavern. "I meant to grab a few useful items, then be on my way with no trouble to any of you."

"You trouble already, scare small fish away." One of the larger eels snapped their teeth angrily in my direction, eyes half-lidded.

"We protect home, lightning horses make offerings so they drink our waters without retaliation." The original speaker hissed, then swam a little closer to me. "What you offer?"

I rolled my eyes, then smiled, there had been enough fighting here already. "I'm a Druid who works closely with Mother Nature. All I want to do is take some things and leave. I don't want to fight you, so what if I let you know that soon there may be people coming to live with the lightning horses? These people might feed you tasty morsels if you help me."

I made careful emphasis on the fact that this was not definite, since my titles would bind me to see it through. "I could put in a kind word for you."

"What *you* give, Druid?" The large one moved closer than the other one had and stared me directly in the eyes, tilting its head to do so. "What you give *now*?"

"I could *eat* all of you," I offered sweetly, most of them ranging from three to six feet in length which easily dwarfed the eels on Earth, if I remembered right. "But I doubt you want that. Remember, an angry Druid is a hungry Druid."

I moved to swim down below them, but an even larger one burst from the pile of miscellaneous materials and surged toward me like it would gobble me up.

So I did what all of you likely wanted me to do from the get-go—I shifted into my own serpentine form that I had collected from the deep ocean, opened my mouth and bit its head clean off. There was a small zap of electrical current, and then I shifted back because I couldn't breathe right. No salt in the water, I'd guessed.

"Now, I didn't want to have to eat *any* of you, but if you

want to play stupid games, I have stupid prizes to give out." I flashed my teeth, the blood in the water making me want to retch. "You stay out of my way, I can still offer a good word. Any more tricks like this? I'll eat all of you. Understand?"

They all fled, the trails of bubbles they left in the water almost comical if not for the crimson clouding around the sinking corpse. I reached down and grabbed it, flinging it away from what I sought out and sunk toward my prize.

Armor and weapons littered the ground here. "Hubris." I willed the weapon into the water before me and I could almost sense its distaste.

This water defiles my wooden body, master.

"Since when has that ever stopped you obeying my will?" I raised an eyebrow at it, but the scepter's thoughts stilled and it floated down toward the pile. "I need gear and materials to make something for Yoh. Anything else of use is now mine too."

Very well, master. But there is something here I wish to possess.

"What is that?" An object floated from the pile below us, a crystalline skull with teeth made of pure gemstones of varying size and type. Two long incisors made of platinum and capped with ruby caught my attention just before the skull stopped directly before the scepter.

It will replace my current gemstone and make me stronger.

I blinked at him and watched as his own gemstone quivered and vibrated as the skull did. The water around them displaced slightly, then more until a bubble of air split the area around them and the two converged. Finally, a ringing peel of gems touching and a brief, blinding flash of light shocked me.

I blinked away the spots in my vision, then turned my gaze to the scepter, the empty sockets of the skull staring at me.

The jaw moved, glittering in the light from my spell as Hubris spoke in my mind. *Yes, this is much more preferable. I sense other objects of power, and those that will accept your enchanting with ease. Shall I gather them for you?*

"Please." I glanced toward the pile more from my own discomfort than to see what the scepter pulled toward us.

Armor, clothes, some small weapons, and even materials floated up. Each of them I put into my inventory as they came with little need to check them right that moment. I took one ring and pocketed it for what I had in mind, and continued to put things away as I could. Finally, a large piece of obsidian floated toward me, and I smiled. I knew what I would do with that.

We spent a few more minutes taking from the pile before Hubris returned to his pocket dimension and I surged through the current with a little help from the water around me. Using water-aspected mana allowed me to control the flow of the current long enough for me to bust through and avoid the worst of it.

The water splashed away from me as I broke the surface, instantly letting Water Lung fade. I coughed up the phlegmy residue that it formed around my lungs in a couple of quick, hacking heaves, then exited the water.

The young Kirin watched me in wonder and I smiled at him. "Thanks for the help!"

He tossed his tiny mane, then bolted away, likely to tell his friends what he had done.

I found the home Maebe had claimed, close to the others but private, and walked inside.

I found them sitting at a small table with bowls before them and rapt expressions. They said nary a word, but offered me a bowl of what they had. Smelled like a hearty beef stew of sorts, with earthy vegetables and a salty kick. I devoured mine hungrily and eyed my wife and girlfriend.

Was that what she was? Was she our concubine? Our mistress? There was no hiding her from each other.

"She can be what she wishes, so long as we call her ours," Maebe said, eyeing me, then she looked at a very confused Vrawn and tapped her ring. "Benefits of this item. He was wondering how we should refer to you."

"I like 'ours.'" She smiled and rubbed my shoulder affectionately. "I take it you have something in mind to assist Yohsuke?"

"I have an idea, but I'm not sure if it will work." I frowned, then looked up at Maebe. "The glamour you use. Would there be a way to project one to make it look *exactly* like a person, but also make it so that light can't pass through?"

"That is the purpose of some glamours, using shadow and finesse to hide flaws, then accentuate and highlight your best features." She tapped the table. "It seems it might be difficult to not allow light to touch the subject of such a glamour at all. Why not do what was done before? With a cloak?"

"I have one for him, but I worry with this recent ramping up in his vampirism, it may not be the most effective way of keeping him safe." I laid the ring on the table, it was pure bone and looked like it was a finger itself, though hollow and jointed to move with the finger inside it. "If we double tap it, the glamour and bending light that way, he will likely be able to stay alive and in the fight."

"Double tap?" Vrawn tilted her head to the side.

"I believe it a colloquialism for making sure something is dead, or in this case truly taken care of?" I stared at her slack jawed and in shock. "I heard this from both Muu and Bokaj at some points when they muttered, 'Yeah, double tap that bitch.' I found their attempts to explain highly amusing."

I snorted and shook my head. "Sounds like them."

"If this is something you believe in doing, then I will assist you." Maebe lifted the bone ring to display it in front of herself. "I will not lie and state that I know how it will best be done, but I will do my best. You have my assistance."

I nodded my thanks to her and closed my eyes. "Hubris, you got anything that could assist us in this?"

I know several runes that will strengthen illusions and others that will intensify a spell, but I do not have anything that will do exactly as you wish.

"We can strengthen the glamour and intensify my will to

keep light from hitting what the glamour covers." I frowned at the thought and nodded. "Does that make sense?"

It does. The runes are complicated, but will fit. You may make your own engraving beforehand.

I blinked and focused my mana, looping it to make a basic outline of a human body, and pressed it to the inside of it. Then did the same again but a little larger around the previous figure. Like a shell.

Hubris ran me through making the runes; it was hard but not impossible. Time consuming as it was, it would be worth it when my brother could stand with us in the sunlight again.

Hubris showed itself to us all before the true enchanting was done. Maebe and Vrawn both gasped at the change, questions flew, and I explained as I could as my mana recovered.

Maebe grabbed the scepter with me and we channeled our mana and intent into the spells. She focused on the glamour, I focused on creating the barrier and refracting the light away from the glamour. It was hard.

Almost too hard. By the time we finished, I was soaked all over again from sweat and my head throbbed wildly.

Ghost Shell

User casts a continuous glamour barrier around themselves for up to 8 hours before needing to either recharge, or consume all the user's mana. This barrier will negate sunlight entering, but will allow the user to be seen as if they were not wearing it.

Ring enchanted by master enchanter Zekiel Erebos.

My enchanting increased to level 54, making me smile. Though the lack of information on who created it was weird.

Good work, master. Hubris vanished and I was okay with that. I could wait a little while before working on Yoh's cloak.

I sighed and Maebe stared at the work we had done appreciatively. "If this is the caliber that Xiphyre and his children could produce, there will be little need to fear the Seelie."

"I hope that they do. I have faith in Xiphyre and his abilities." I grinned at her reassuringly and she smiled back, her eyes tight with worry. "You're worried."

"I am a queen, wife, and a budding mother." She stared at me as if I had been intentionally thick. "Of course I am worried. It is my honor to worry for our people. As much as it is for me to protect them."

"I understand." I put my hand on hers. "It really chaps my ass that I can't help you rule them without Samir's say so."

"He rules his realm with impunity," Maebe stated matter of factly. "But he may not always feel so inclined; we must simply give him good reason to feel you aren't a threat to the creatures there." She smiled mischievously. "Or that you are the right *kind* of threat."

I chuckled. Fae laws and traditions were interesting to say the least. Their power games and constant vying for status were stuff of legend even on Earth, and Maebe weathered it all with grace and poise.

"We can hope." I turned and looked over at Vrawn, her delight at being with us both written all over her smiling face. "What of Vrawn?"

"She is not as strange as you and our friends, she will be fine." Maebe reached for the larger woman's hand and clasped it lovingly. "We all will, no matter what."

Sitting with them both like this was lovely. Just being together and happy in the moment. But thoughts of rescuing the others, or at least finding them, filled my heart with dread and I turned quickly back to my work.

I enchanted for another hour or so, not really keeping track of time before exhaustion. Finally I crawled up into the large bed with Vrawn and Maebe to crash and fall asleep for a while.

CHAPTER FOURTEEN

We woke up and ate breakfast with Yohsuke. I gave him his new gear and promised him that we would get more once we were able to visit the city again. Specifically Anisamara and her shop.

"That's cool, so long as I can go out into the sun safely." Yoh shrugged and shoveled more food onto everyone's plates.

We ate happily for a bit before I heard hooves moving in our direction quickly. "The Kirin are coming and fast."

We left our food on the plates Yoh had found in the house and walked outside. The Kirin stood in a large circle and tossed their heads restlessly, the sky darkening swiftly overhead as storm clouds gathered.

A large figure dropped from the clouds and I recognized Kayda. She landed and the ground shuddered under her sudden growth. She had to be thirty feet tall now, at least and all of that bulk bore down on me. Her beak slapped my head backward and her chest and wings smothered me, the static of her touch clinging to my fur.

Our connection opened wide and all I heard was, *Father! Father, I've missed you so much!*

"I missed you too, baby." I ran my hands through her feathers and her fervent cuddling lessened slightly.

"Tweety got bigger," Muu observed dryly from a slightly greater distance and Kayda turned on him faster than lightning. "No!"

She had him on the ground where she pecked and buffeted him with her wings lovingly.

We all laughed at the commotion and the Kirin just looked happy that she felt better.

"Druid," the eldest Kirin called out to me and I frowned. It had to have been more than twenty-four hours since I cast Nature's Voice, right? "If you are ready, we can take you to the next stone."

I glanced at the others, all of them looking as if they were ready. "Thank you, elder, for your hospitality and your help. We truly appreciate you."

"Our honor is to assist you and the Storm." He tossed his mane and turned north before looking back at us. "Please, allow me to lead you. It is not far."

The Kirin closed ranks around us, Thor cantering closer to me to nudge me along playfully, then bolting forward so the other young ones would follow him.

Our procession walked to the edge of the grotto, stone walls rising high above us protectively. The clouds above us still swirled and as soon as we stopped moving, lightning struck the cliff side. Three more times, rapid fire, arcing electricity struck the stone, creating a rain of rubble and cloud of dust.

Once it cleared, the transport stone stood in stark contrast to the dark stone around it.

"We, the Kirin guardians of this transport stone, give you our blessing to move on to the next isle." The elder reared up onto his hind legs and came down. "The next portion of islands is especially dangerous as it is not fully protected by a barrier and beasts run rampant there. Please be careful."

"Thank you all." Yohsuke stepped closer to the Kirin and

patted some of them. They shied away at first, but let him touch them before touching his shoulders with their long faces.

Vrawn, Maebe, Odany, the Druids, Muu, James, Kayda, the raptors, and I touched the monolith and blinked as the environment changed once again.

This one looked more like the jungle on the continent itself, the heat not as unbearable as it was below, but the trees and fauna here were wild colors. Oranges and yellows all over.

"What kindergartener did they let color here?" Muu grumbled as he eyed our surroundings.

"This is the area of the sacred grounds," Greer muttered quietly with reverence in his voice. "If the old texts are correct, there will be a shrine and temple in this jungle that we will need to go to in order to perform the ceremony."

"How does that go?" Yohsuke stepped forward and stared the other Druids in the eyes. They looked uncomfortable and Greer scratched his head. "What?"

"Is it the geas?" Maebe stared at them intently, but Greer shook his head.

"It's more that… we would have to show you. Talking about it is expressly forbidden. To talk about the process would kill us, not just make us uncomfortable or ill."

Both Kyr and Sendak agreed with nods and I sighed heavily before saying, "Lead the way, then."

"We don't know exactly where to go." Sendak chuckled. "We are as new here as you lot are."

"Well, we need to find it, so let's find it." Yoh looked at me, he stared at his hand and smiled, then looked back up at me. "I know there are beasts here, but we need eyes in the sky. Could you and Kayda check things out?"

Kayda shrunk down into her smaller form just before I shifted into my owl shape and hopped into the air. We flew straight into the sky, the blue hues making me smile inwardly. It was nice to fly again.

I see something, Father. I banked left and caught sight of what she meant a heartbeat before something massive and red launched itself into the sky with a thunderous screech.

Crimson! My wings froze at the sheer size of him, and I dropped from the sky with Kayda on my heels. I shifted mid drop and called out, "Incoming!"

The gigantic bird swung toward me, claws outstretched, but I shifted into my fox form and continued to drop when a gust of air burst below me and pushed me up a bit. I landed on the ground much easier than I would have without and tore off toward the tree line, the others hot on my tails.

I shifted back into fox-man form and kept running, slowing down for some of our slower compatriots to catch up to me. Once they did, I cast Radial Refraction around us and we moved as swiftly as possible, keeping low and watching for Crimson's return.

We ran for half an hour; nothing made it seem like he was coming until the barest shadow flickered into my peripheral vision and a cold sense of dread washed over me.

A cruel screech shattered the silence around us and not even my own heartbeat broke through the racket. Trees before us splintered and crashed aside, completely obliterated by the avian beast's landing before us, his blood red wings spreading wide.

"We have to fight!" Muu snarled before his stride opened up. "I'll take to the sky; you guys go for his stomach."

"What are you talking about?" Kyr's panicked voice carried toward the bird and Crimson's eyes darted to where we moved. Muu squatted down then launched himself into the air, shattering my spell and leaving the rest of us visible to the gigantic beast.

Crimson's eyes flooded red and his head tilted back before a jet of flame that seared the very air around it shot at us. Ice burst from the ground, Kayda and Maebe both surging forward to stop the brunt of the blow. The ice and heat mixing so fast created a thick fog of steam that exploded around us.

Yohsuke's voice rang out around us, "Use the fog to get

close, then go for vital spots!" I felt movement near my right side before a whisper came to my ear, "Zeke, you have anything big enough to contend with him?"

"Not right now, other than my dragon form, and its instincts may take over if I don't have absolute control and my companions to help me." I dodged a feather that streamed through the fog and slammed into the ground like a sword. "With how big and strong this thing is, we can't afford for any of them to be distracted like that, even with Maebe, Bea, and Kayda to back me."

"Then we better figure it out, or that thing is going to get Muu."

The screeching whistle of Muu's spear piercing the air began to build on the breeze and even with my heightened senses I knew he wasn't too close. But that didn't mean he wouldn't be dropping soon. Or that Crimson would stay still for the attack to work either.

Kayda! Beat the shit out of him with ice, baby. I could feel her affirmation and began to run forward. *Bea, I need you to help me clear my mind during this fight, so I need you to hang back.*

Yes! Her barking in the distance comforted me deeply as she no longer questioned not fighting or doing what she wanted to.

Maebe called, "I can tell you wish to do something ill advised, Zeke—be safe."

Our ring on my finger thrummed with concern and pride from my beloved wife. Clenching my fist, I used Predator's Call, then surged forward as fast as I could.

The gigantic bird just stared at me and scree'd back, wings raising and eyes that stabbed toward me.

My body grew with my will and expanded as I shifted into my red dragon form. All it would do for me was keep the flames from doing as much damage if I took the blast for my friends, and that was enough.

If I could keep Crimson on the ground, we had a chance.

The two of us clashed, one of his claws in both of mine,

and his strength was immense. It was all I could do to hold on when the dragons came to try to claim me.

Finally! they growled in unison, then lunged toward me inside my mind. Bea's mind touched mine like a ray of sunshine in the darkness and their pressure backed down a little, but just a bit.

Ice bombarded the bird's head and chest as Maebe and Kayda soared overhead. Crimson's gaze followed them until I bit toward his chest plumage.

A sharp pain erupted between my shoulder blades. Crimson's beak came away covered in my blood and took 50% of my HP with it.

Feral Rage boiled inside my blood and the dragons' voices were lost completely as my rage screamed forward. My scales felt coarse, like they had grown on my body, my fangs and claws thickened and lengthened.

Draconic Rage – the being experiencing this rage grows larger and more beastly by the minute at the sacrifice of mana and intelligence for a short time.

Mana drained. Blood flow quickened. All I wanted was vengeance. I lunged forward, the claw in my hands forgotten, my tail slapped the beast's chest as magic erupted all around us.

My claws raked against his legs as I launched myself upward the same time a catastrophic weight crushed down. I heard laughter, then cast it aside as I bit and tore at feathers and flesh.

Sensing something inside the beast that I *needed* to get to. Legs buckled around me as the bird tried to gore me from the side, flames licked at my back and wind at my tail almost drew my attention.

Several dull impacts and labored breathing of something running through the bird's undercarriage, dark skinned and lashing out with all their limbs irritated me. Ignoring whatever it was, I continued my search.

Cold burst around my scales and I bit harder in retaliation for the disturbance, whipping my head back and forth wildly until a little piece of flesh separated and I could push my nose in. Blood caked my nostrils, but I was happy about it. I was closer now.

A small gray thing came near my hole, magic and a festering scent of death exuding from it. My interest made me glance at it, but it hopped onto my shoulder then off with a weapon slicing into the flesh beside my hole and slid away. My entrance grew larger still and I dove in as far as I could, navigating muscle and ligament alike to try to find my prize.

A rumbling cry of pain and outrage echoed within, ringing my bell and making me recoil a bit, but I kept going.

Hunger ate at me, my insides grumbling with need.

The ground shook wildly beneath my feet and something cried out under me, beating on my scales insistently.

Father... Voices I recognized whipped through my mind insistently. My body lifted and suddenly I could see again.

A large creature lumbered over me, pinkish-purple fur and long arms pushing Crimson away from us.

"That's Jinx!" someone roared and suddenly my body lifted up, two figures beneath me heaving.

I looked down and found a large green creature grabbing my claws and lifting with all her might. I couldn't see the creature behind the green one, but they were strong. I reared my neck back, the heat in my chest growing and beginning to surge down my throat when a set of scaled, green arms wrapped around my jaws before I could spew my hatred at them.

I struggled, whipping my head back and forth before that same black scaled creature jumped at my head and suddenly things went dark.

———

I came to consciousness with a start and found that we had moved.

"Finally awake, you rampaging bastard?" Yohsuke's voice rang in my ear before his face floated into view. "No more dragon form until you know you can handle it, and until we all know that there won't be something that can do that much damage in a single hit. You going into a rage just then was bad."

"I get that." I rubbed my head, then adjusted my jaw with a resounding *pop* that made Yoh cringe. "It's one of the few abilities I have when I'm shapeshifted and it comes on and takes control. It's rough for sure. Who rang my damned bell?"

"That'd be me." James held a hand up and grinned at me. "Muu kept you from roasting Vrawn and Maebe, but you would have drawn Jinx's attention to us while he was preoccupied with Crimson. Couldn't have that."

"Fair, but why would Jinx attack Crimson instead of us?" I glanced over to the Druids who looked contemplative. "If you don't know, maybe you have theories?"

Greer rubbed his face with his hands and finally sat up to speak. "I think maybe it was time for them to duke it out again. Whether it was because Crimson had made such a huge raucous mess, or that he had entered into Jinx's territory. Either way, we weren't even on that huge sloth's list of concerns—and you were a dragon. Those things are ridiculously big and powerful and Crimson will only be coming back stronger."

"Then we need to hurry." I sat up from where I had been laying, Maebe and Vrawn walking toward us. "My loves, I'm so sorry for almost roasting you. Are you okay?"

Vrawn grinned. "Perfectly fine. Now I can say I have fought a dragon and come out alive."

I rolled my eyes and Maebe laughed out loud at that, her outburst making us all pause before she shook her head. "We both can tell our children what a dragon their father was. They'll never believe us."

The whole group laughed softly, then when we stilled, Kyr clapped me on the shoulder and nodded behind me. "We are here, by the way."

I turned and found a temple entrance that reminded me of the entry to a Hindi temple. There were layers to the building that went up into the sky like stairs, each floor smaller than the one below it. We all stood and made our way inside, checking for any beasts that may have been hiding from the larger ones outside, or in wait for a meal. There was nothing.

The interior was sort of decrepit, but wasn't destroyed or anything. Just musty and a little dark.

"Where do we go?" Muu looked around enthusiastically but grew steadily more confused as he found nothing.

"*We* go to the top of the steps." Sendak pointed straight up to a small hole more than three hundred feet above us. "You all will need to stay here. Anyone but a Druid will be attacked by the beasts we call to us."

"What will happen up there?" Yoh frowned at us all, looking to me specifically. "You going to fight it and make it your bitch or something?"

The others looked uncomfortable, so I answered, "The object is to unite with the beast and become one entity. It will make us stronger. More one with nature or something like that. We either do it by forcing the creature to submit to our will, or by beating its ass—though that last one could get ugly."

"Be careful and come back to us." Vrawn grabbed my shoulder and pulled me closer to her and Maebe. "If you do not, I will kick your ass."

My ears flattened against my skull in shock. "Threats now?" I turned to Maebe and grinned. "She really does love me."

Maebe chuckled and kissed me on the cheek, just before Vrawn kissed my forehead. "I'll be back to get real kisses from you both. So wait for me."

"I don't like you being a dumbass on your own," Muu grumped and crossed his arms.

"Fuck you, dude." I rolled my eyes at him playfully.

He nodded his head toward Greer. "I was talking to him." Muu grinned at me. "You can fuck off. I'm on pretty boy's side."

I snorted and Greer blushed furiously, ducking his head

close to me as I stepped closer so he could whisper, "Does he truly think I'm pretty?"

"You really never know with him." I winked and shifted into my owl form before taking off toward the hole above us.

It took a couple minutes to get up the middle of the building, but once all four of us had arrived, we shifted back and took in the sights. The trees surrounding the temple from all sides grew tall and broad, their leaves almost massive closer to the top.

Tiles depicting a story of some sort decorated the temple where we stood, but their images looked dull and beaten up. Likely from time or exposure, but either way reading it was just not to be.

"Zeke, pay attention as one of us will go first." Kyr patted my back and stepped forward to a fountain of water that grew out of the ground at his approach.

He looked at the others, his heart rate beginning to speed up as he pulled deep breaths into his body. He dipped both hands into the basin of the fountain and cupped water to lift into the air.

"I offer myself to the Mother, may her will be exalted and her blessings be upon me in this time of confusion." He let the water fall down over his head, his body jolting at the contact. "I cleanse this mortal body given by the gods so that I might be pure for what is to come."

He cupped another bit of water to his lips, stopping just before his mouth. "I imbibe this holy water so that my voice may call to the beast with whom I share a piece of myself. Half of my whole. The beast who recognizes me as his counter."

He drank the water in his hands easily, then turned and walked to the side of the roof. He pulled one more deep breath into his lungs, then bellowed a wordless cry into the air. He shouted so hard that his fists clenched and I could feel the fur on my body begin to rise as chills covered me.

After the cry finished, Kyr having to stop for air after having fallen to his knees, a cry returned. A long, bellowing roar from somewhere off in the distance that took my attention south.

Trees fell and broke away, missile-like sounds of shattering debris and wood being flung all over rang out around us as something massive ran toward us through the forest. Each of these trees stood almost more than three-fourths of the way up the side of the temple, so this thing was huge.

I looked down the hole, dropping to my knees to shout, "There's going to be a lot of yelling and beastie things going on outside. Stay cool unless you get the high sign. And that'll be me yelling 'fuck.' Got it? 'Kay, love you."

I hopped onto my feet and turned just in time to watch the single largest Tyrannosaurus-rex-lookin' thing I had ever seen in my life. This thing's black-and-green scaled body had sharp blades that looked like metal sticking out of its back and the top of its head like they were horns and its eyes glimmered with green energy.

"The hell *is* that thing?" I didn't have to wait for an answer as it jumped and *stepped off the fucking air.* "Gust raptor?"

"Gale Rex," Greer whispered reverently. I could see his body quivering but the massive beast had eyes only for Kyr.

The two of them stared intently at each other for a bit, then Kyr stepped forward and touched it on the nose before closing his eyes.

They stood like that for two minutes before I turned toward Greer and motioned to the scene. "Isn't there supposed to be some kind of massive brawl? That thing looks like it could fuck up Jinx. What's going on?"

"They *are* having some kind of contest." He made a motion for me to sit with him and Sendak quietly waiting. "The winner takes all. Either way they become one, but the winner is who will be the final form one takes. Either Kyr will gain the abilities, strength, and shape of the Gale Rex, or the Gale Rex will become as intelligent as Kyr and be able to manipulate magic like Irgdarn."

"What would happen if someone were to get Crimson or

Jinx?" They blinked at me and I shrugged. "I've gotten some weird shit before, and it honestly wouldn't surprise me if I ended up with one of them."

They stared at me for a moment, Sendak grunting and pulling his leg out from under his other before sighing. "We do not know. Creatures so powerful may not have living counters to them. If one *were* to be blessed with being the other half to their whole, it would likely take considerable willpower to get them to see you as an equal, let alone to be subservient to you."

"Is that the goal?" I raised a furry eyebrow at them. Kyr grunted and made a face before calming again. "Making them bend to your will?"

"The more harmonious the joining is, the more powerful you can become. That being said, it is almost a partnership akin to what you and your familiars have." I frowned at him and he motioned with his hand at the scene before us. "If they were to see each other as equal, then the Gale Rex would feel that Kyr is his true counter and their power would grow exponentially. But if Kyr were to completely crush the Rex, the beast could withhold its power and hide things from him that would make him weaker."

"Can you repair that bond?" I glanced to Sendak and Greer; both shrugged uncertainly.

The scent of ozone flooded the air and electricity began to crackle around Kyr like he was some kind of powerful anime character.

His breathing quickened and finally he opened his eyes, both of them fixating on the Rex's before it sighed and dissolved into nothing but wind and buffeted Kyr this way and that. He stood his ground and raised his arms, roaring his victory out into the world and another set of chills ran down my back and spine.

Sendak stood next, his nervousness leaving him as he performed the ritual and screamed to the heavens. We listened, awaiting the return call for what seemed like forever. Finally, an echoing cry from the east side of the forest made us all jump.

This one came even faster than the Gale Rex had but no trees were harmed in the making of this ritual. No sir.

Not until King Goddamn Kong stood towering over the elven man, his fur the same green, grass-like fur as Frederick's. This was a Terran Gorilla.

They stared and finally they reached for each other, their hands touching as they closed their eyes.

While Sendak worked, I turned to Kyr, "Well, how do you feel?"

"Whole." Kyr smiled and summoned Rai. The little elemental sparked and clapped with energy quietly. "I feel like my connection to everything is so much *deeper* than it ever has been. And I just know that if I were to try to turn into a Gale Rex right now, I could. And that form will be hugely powerful."

I nodded. "That's awesome, man."

He smiled at me and began to meditate while we waited.

Eventually I grew bored and looked to Greer. "So, why don't you and I go ahead and do ours?"

"Because if one of us is taken over, there will likely be a fight. If all of us are vulnerable like Sendak is now, we would die."

Ah. "Well, alright then." I sighed and went back to watching just in time for both elf and beast to open their eyes and the grassy gorilla leaned forward to hug the Druid before it and dissolved as the Rex had.

"Congratulations, Sendak." I smiled at him and he nodded quickly. "What's wrong?"

"He didn't fight me at all." He seemed perturbed. "He just wanted to talk and ask me questions until he seemed satisfied and then we were done. It was so... *easy.*"

The disgust in his voice made me frown. "That a bad thing?"

He kicked the ground and skidded his bare foot across it angrily. "It either means that the Druids of the council lied to us and have been doing this in secret, or that the risks may not be as they were. Either way, to know there is a taint to this ritual at all like this is… is… *maddening!*"

Greer stepped forward and pulled the other Druid into a fierce hug. "It will be alright, Sendak. We will make this right, I promise you."

"Zeke, why don't you go next? There is much we have to discuss." Kyr suggested somberly from where he sat. He patted the stones and motioned for the other two men to join him. "You can do this."

I nodded and stepped out of my boots, even going so far as to take my armor and shirt off. I stepped in front of the water, crystalline and clear, then dipped my hands into it before going through the motions.

Now for the ritual words. "I offer myself to the Mother, may her will be exalted and her blessings be upon me in this time of confusion." I let the water fall down over me, having known it would be cold as it hit my head and body. "I cleanse this mortal body given by the gods so that I might be pure for what is to come."

I dipped my hands back in for more water to bring to my mouth. "I imbibe this holy water so that my voice may call to the beast with whom I share a piece of myself. Half of my whole. The beast who recognizes me as his counter."

As soon as the water was inside me, a thrilling sense of calm washed over me, like a meditative trance. It was like nirvana. I walked to the edge of the roof, summoned everything I had, and let it flow out of my mouth. Predator's Call activated as if on its own and I heard multiple gasps behind me as the roar carried. My lungs were powerful and my roar lasted longer than both men before me.

Finally, the air in my body fully expelled, and I had to take several deep breaths to recover myself. I waited for ten minutes before finally a resounding roar echoed around us and a creature dropped from the sky.

A wyvern, significantly larger than the one that we had fought before, fierce black eyes watching me intently, flapped no more than thirty feet away, great horns cresting the back of his angular head like a crown, more spikes on his wings that looked almost hollow and some on his knees that protruded forward in a downward curve.

It landed with a clacking of claws against stone and a low growl. It folded its wings in on itself as it eyed me.

My hand rose of its own volition as the wyvern's head dipped toward me. As soon as we made contact, I blinked and we were standing in the middle of a snowstorm more violent than anything I had ever witnessed before. Even going to see the high elves through their magical blizzard had looked tame compared to this.

Who are you? a deep, growling tone echoed through my mind.

This was a dream location, right? That would mean that I could control this too, right? Be able to find where this thing was.

I gathered my will and raised my right hand above my head and pulled the snow down and away from me to the left. The snow dropped, and my mana with it by about 300 MP, leaving the wyvern visible at last.

"Apparently, I'm your other half." I trod closer to him, his curious gaze making him tilt his head. "Who are you?"

Ruler of the frost and peaks of the mountains in these lands, I am Cieth. No one dares fight me in my element, not even Crimson. Irgdarn and his ilk leave me alone. The beast growled and snapped his teeth, the snow beginning to swirl around his feet. *You never named yourself.*

"Forgive me, Cieth. I am King Zekiel Erebos of the Unseelie Court within the Fae realm. Druid, loved by the elements and Mother Nature herself. I am her Primal Warrior." I bowed my head respectfully but kept my gaze on him. "I seek the power to destroy the enemies of this world so that peace may once again reign supreme."

Peace is laughable. Cieth shuffled his wings and the snow swirled less. *Beasts know only the battle for survival and how to take for ourselves. When we felt the blow Orlow'thes took, it enraged us further and showed that if he was not safe to do as he pleases, neither are we. You wish power?*

I stood straighter as the question seemed to be an invitation of some sort. "Yes. Enough to strike out at those who don't deserve to be here creating the messes they are. Enough to protect those who I hold dear."

His teeth flashed, maw opening wide. *Come and take it then!*

The corners of my mouth tugged up in a grin and I launched myself forward as a jet of cold raced toward me. I used my elemental siphoning ring to take part of the hit, filling it to the brim and using it to throw a fireball at the beast.

The snow lifted and formed a snowy wall to block the flames, but I used the opening to shift into my dragon form. But rather than shifting, my body remained the same and two presences joined us.

The red and green dragons lumbered through the snow, their bulky bodies slow at first, but the red loosed a burst of flame that melted the snow around them. "Ah. So here we are at last in the fore of your mind. Free to do as we please."

The green grinned and looked toward me. "I wonder, if we kill you while you do this, will we be able to take over your body?"

"And gain the power of this lesser reptile?" the red finished.

You have got to be fucking kidding me, I growled at myself. "Listen, you two fuckheads don't get to control my body again. Ever. *I* am in control here."

The dragon sent a burst of flame toward me and I dodged it easily, the green moving to stand closer to where I had landed so it could whisper, "Are you though?"

I will not be called lesser by mere dragons. And I will not allow you to be taken from me, Druid.

"You wanna work together, then duke it out after?" I suggested politely.

Agreed. Ice and tempestuous wind battered the dragons around us just before I cast Falfyre. The holy flame sword grasped in my right hand, I lunged at the green dragon with a roar, Cieth going for the red dragon.

Roars and earth-shattering cracks echoed behind me, but I focused on my enemy. The green speared his tail at my head, but I ducked and lashed out with my blade. The seared scent of dragon tail cloyed the air and his snarl of rage drew my attention.

A clawed leg kicked the ground before me and I stabbed into it, using the hilt of my sword to launch off of like a diving board onto his back.

"Stop being so cowardly!" the dragon roared.

"Bitch, I ain't ran from you since ever—you just hate losing." I spent the mana to summon my sword back to me, really only a few points, and stabbed it into his back and ran for it up the spine.

Quaking pain roiled through the dragon beneath me, and before I could go for the coup de grace and slice his head off, his tail whipped into my body and threw me toward the other two fighters.

I landed on Cieth's wings and plopped painfully onto the ground, no more than 5% of my health lost at that point.

Get up, Druid, this thing is stronger than it appears.

"Very well." I faded into his shadow and stepped out of the shadows beneath the dragon and stabbed upward with Falfyre as hard as I could.

The dragon reared up and I faded out of the shadows once more, glancing at the green dragon and picking his shadow as my destination. I popped out of the shadows, coming eye to eye with the green dragon whose mouth opened and a film of green poison spewed out into my face. I held my breath and willed Falfyre to come to me, reaching up into the smoke-like poison to grasp for it. A heartbeat later it was there and I shoved it into the dragon's mouth and willed it to explode as I fell back into the shadows and came out by Cieth's legs.

I turned in time to catch a muted *pop* as the dragon's head exploded from the holy and fire energy bursting.

Good work, the wyvern growled and pushed the red dragon back, the dragon's feet fighting for purchase.

I focused, pulling the shadows around us together, pumping water and wind mana into them to make freezing shadows like Maebe might, and thrust them into the dragon's stomach. Cieth yanked the dragon down onto the spikes further, the red crying out in pain and frustration.

The wyvern's jaws clamped around the base of the red dragon's skull just as I summoned Falfyre once more and shoved it straight through the creature's eye into its brain. I swirled it a bit and willed the heat to intensify before pulling it out and leaving the body there.

I growled deeply, spitting some blood out of my mouth and saying, "Hopefully they remember this next time they want to try to take me over."

You admit weakness in front of a foe? Cieth stared down at me with what looked like contempt in his eyes.

"I speak candidly to an ally, and if you think it a weakness, you're welcome to the same brutal end they got." I grinned up at him and his reptilian face contorted into a frown. "You sure you want to fight me? We made a decent team there. I can tell that you're intelligent and cunning. Ruthless. I can be too, as evidenced by their deaths."

This was brutal? Cieth chuckled and his eyes lowered to look into mine. *I know of a way to truly see whether you are worthy.*

"Yeah, and?"

Close your eyes and hold out your hand.

I sighed and sent my consciousness into the shadows below me. My powers had gotten significantly better than they had ever been since I started working with Maebe again. I closed my eyes physically and opened them within the shadows, watching the beast from below.

He quirked his head to the side, opened his jaws, and slowly crept forward until his maw was opened around my head. Hot, fetid breath flowing over my fur, my mouth contorted and nose crinkled at the smell.

I stayed still but ready. A low growl vibrated my chest as I muttered, "You try to bite, I kill you."

Don't trust me? Cieth pondered innocently before replacing his mouth around my head.

Blood ran as one of his fangs nicked my temple just as a trio of pointed shadows pierced the scales under his throat, angled so they would reach his brain with a flex of my will.

A warm, wet tongue lapped up the blood flowing from my wound, then the mouth was gone.

Cieth closed his eyes and thought for a while, then grinned. *My, you* can *be brutal. And those mates of yours as well. If fighting you will mean that I have to die, I think it best we work together. I could get used to having a partner worthy of my time.*

I opened my eyes and tilted my head. "Partners?"

Cieth dipped his head and growled, *Partners.*

His broad head ducked down and touched mine and when I opened my eyes, I was standing watching out over the side of the temple, Cieth flowing into me like a cold wind.

Inexplicably, my mind and body were at ease. Soothed by his presence. I could feel him there in my mind, like having someone watching over your shoulder, but it was one of the most comforting things I'd ever felt.

I will not always be awake like this, but I will be here. Watching. Waiting. Do not prove my acceptance misinformed.

I nodded to myself and turned to find the others staring at me. "What?"

"The shadows bent around you like living things." Kyr gulped and blinked. "There was so much happening with that."

"Things got a little scaly in there." My lip quirked at the attempted joke and nodded to Greer. "You're up, buddy." I clapped him on the shoulder and gave him a reassuring smile and watched as he walked toward the water taking deep breaths.

He performed the ritual expertly and stepped out to the side of the roof before screaming until he coughed from it. His elven features screwed up in discomfort as he waited.

Finally a low, almost-mournful call returned slow and steady. Something massive moved through the trees from where we had been just a little while before and we watched in fascinated horror as Jinx slowly worked his way up the side of the temple to stare at Greer.

Fresh blood dripped from the giant pink sloth's muzzle, bloody claws latched onto the roof easily and they eyed each other steadily. Greer's hand rose and Jinx butt his head against it.

We waited for a moment, Greer's breathing quickening, his heart hammering in his chest. Sweat built on his brow, then soaked his shirt as he grunted and groaned.

"Come on, Greer, you quick-learning bastard, you can do this!" I seethed quietly.

I went through my notifications quickly, all of them telling me that I was stronger now than I had been before and that I could take Cieth's form at will.

I could sift through the specifics later, right now Greer fought for his life and he needed us. Finally, eyes opened and Jinx took a deep breath as the elf faded to ash and swirled into the sloth's open mouth. His eyes glowed a deep maroon.

Frustration and guilt tore through me but the only thing I could think to do was scream, "*Fuck!*"

CHAPTER FIFTEEN

The three of us charged the giant beast. I speared it with shadows and punched as hard as I could with my right hand, lightning rocketing by me at the same time as wind ripped past on my left.

A quickly growing sound of shouting came from behind us but I didn't give a shit.

Greer was gone—I had lost a new friend and I wanted this damned thing to *pay*.

The lightning blasted an eye and it closed as the sloth swung over our heads. I ducked and took my Ursolon form, stabbing my claws into the injured eye and pushed with all my weight until I felt it give and a clawed fist came at me.

I shifted into my fox form and dropped beneath the attack before shifting into Belgar form and crashing into his damned head for all I was worth.

Massive green arms grasped me and pulled me backward bodily, as heavy as I was, then something gray and green rammed into the beast, knocking it from the side of the temple. I shifted back, looking at the gorilla, tears streaming from his eyes.

He beat his chest and hopped off the side of the temple after Jinx before Kyr shifted and followed in bird form.

Muu landed next to me, and I pointed wordlessly to Jinx and the other two Druids.

"Kill him, got it." Muu snarled and jumped straight into the air again.

I looked down and saw the others filtering out of the temple and bellowed, "Kill Jinx! He took Greer!"

They all converged on the place where the sloth lay struggling with both Sendak and Kyr as Muu shot through the air past me and into the beast's exposed chest. I shifted into my owl form and soared straight up into the air, a hundred feet above him, shifted into fox form, then my carnivorous whale form, dropping with all my weight aimed right at his body.

He stood and fought now, the others picking away at him slowly, Muu taking the hate from the beast as he could with his enmity-generating rambling.

"Look out!" Vrawn shouted just seconds before I slammed into Jinx's back. A sharp cracking beneath me and within me, I grunted and tried to turn my massive bulk to bite at him, but Jinx rolled me off and I shifted, bolting out of the way in time to avoid getting hit.

Sendak stood in front of me and shifted back, healed me for 25% of my health, and then shifted once more to keep fighting.

I had the broken bone notification under my health bar, my left arm dangled dangerously, and every step shaved another point of my HP away.

Vrawn sprinted closer to me, her hands grabbing my wounded arm to yank it straight. "Heal it!"

I cast Heal on myself and growled as the bones seemed to be knitting themselves back together. Once the notification was gone, I shifted once more, this time calling to Cieth.

Power flooded my being and I stood so much taller now. I hopped onto Jinx's shoulders, grasped at his long arms and yanked him skyward.

This is ill advised, Zekiel. Warmth flooded through me as his consciousness melded with mine. *If you want to lift him and drop him, you need to freeze him first!*

Our wings worked to lift us skyward as we leaned our head toward Jinx and spewed sleet-like ice at his face. His intelligent eyes widened and his clawed hand shot over to our hip, goring us.

The grass grew swiftly down below us and rose to grab at the sloth's legs, one of them finding purchase long enough to keep us from ascending.

Cieth and I roared our frustration to the world just as the grass caught fire and Muu landed on the Jinx's shoulder. "I think I know what you're planning and I'm into it! Let's go! I'll keep his arms away as long as I can."

Birds flew up to us, harrying the sloth as we climbed further into the sky. Muu stabbed and fired whatever he could, occasionally the claws would almost get him but he would stab into the sloth's ears and scream loudly which seemed to discombobulate the beast.

Here is a good height. He may try to catch the temple—oh. Cieth's voice caught in surprise. *Your mate has a plan.*

We glanced down in time to see that the area was covered in ice and shadow so thick it would be hard to miss and the spikes rose like the deadliest trap.

We grinned, growling as we angled our wings. *We aren't dropping him, Cieth.*

Understanding hit him and his roaring laughter echoed through our heads as we folded our wings and pushed ourselves down to deliver our payload personally.

Arms attempted to grab us, but we shook them away and snarled loudly. *Accept your end!*

As soon as we came within a dozen yards of the trap, we flung Jinx with everything we had in us, spikes goring him as he cried out loudly in agony. It was too late to save ourselves from the dive and pull up; we leaned into it and I shifted into my fox-man form to cast Hollow Step.

I shot into the shadows and out of my desired shadow right next to it at the same velocity and back into the sky. I growled and cast Lightning Storm at the bastard, pushing every bit of mana I could into the blast. Kayda joined me and lightning rained down from her where she flew.

Part of his body disintegrated from the hit; I had poured more than 1,500 MP into the spell as I began to fall. I shifted into my eagle form and landed on the ground as my friends blasted the dying creature with magic and whatever ranged attacks they had at their disposal. Muu had opted to lift a broken tree roughly as wide as my shoulders and hucked it at him like a javelin, his muscles straining with the motion.

Finally, Jinx's health bar was gone and all of us breathed a sigh of relief. We couldn't get Greer back, but his death had been avenged.

I walked over to Sendak and Kyr who stood together in silence and pulled them into a rough group hug. "I'm so sorry, you guys."

"We knew there was a chance, we just didn't believe it." Kyr sniffed a bit, dragging the back of his hand across his cheeks and nose angrily. "Who could ever hope to match this monster?"

"You guys will someday." I smiled reassuringly at them, Kayda landed next to us, and the raptors sprinted over to smell us and check that we were okay.

I patted both my familiars and they nuzzled closer as I turned back to the others. "What will you do now?"

"We should get back and prepare our people for what is to come." Sendak finished petting Kaius as his Kirin companion trotted forward. "Logistically speaking, it will be a nightmare to get everything done without the humans trying to stop us. We will need to move carefully."

"What about you?" Kyr crossed his arms as if to hug himself. "What will all of you do?"

"I think we will need to gear up, then keep hunting down

our friends." I sighed and scratched my head frustratedly. "I just wish we had some sort of way to locate them."

"There's an old woman, some kind of priestess, in our city who can scry on people. Maybe she could teach one of you how to do the spell?" Sendak offered quietly. "Honestly, with how powerful you all were, I thought you would have access to some kind of spell like that already."

I snorted. "Yeah, that'd be pretty damned convenient."

They both chuckled and finally the others joined us. I was turned so fast that my head spun until Vrawn caught my chin. "Shift."

"Yes ma'am." I shifted into my human form and she kissed me so fiercely that I felt dizzy after.

Maebe pulled me bodily from the woman and did the same until my head swam even more before declaring, "We have to get all the loot."

Yohsuke mocked sniffling and dabbing his eyes. "They grow up so fast."

We opened the chest Jinx's corpse left behind and pulled out fur, bones, four of his claws, moss, a book of something that looked like spells, and finally what looked like a broken sword hilt that Yohsuke immediately gushed over.

"That's an adapter!" He snatched it out of my hand and fed mana into it. The magic blade and immediately became a large, curved longsword. "Oh shit, dude. This thing has five forms! Check it!"

He blinked and the weapon grew in size until it was the same size as a certain buster sword we all knew and loved. He swung it with ease and I was more than a little irked at that. Then it shifted into a battle axe and my jaw dropped. Then it became a spear and finally a bow.

He pulled the string taut and as he released it, an astral arrow launched into a nearby tree, making Sendak flinch and jump out of the way. "Ah!"

"Sorry!" Yohsuke sheepishly put the weapon away. "Still cool as shit though, man."

"Yeah, it is. Damn buster sword? Fuck." Muu grunted to himself and muttered a bit before sighing and looking around. "May as well spend the night here. If we try to make the trip to the city now, we may not make it and I'm pretty whooped after that fight."

"That does make sense." Yohsuke agreed and pointed to the temple. "Let's camp inside for the night. I'll cook us up some stuff."

"Zeke?" Maebe called softly and waved me over toward her as the others went back into the building.

"Yes, my love?"

She pulled me close and lowered her voice, "What was that thing you became?"

Your mate is observant, Cieth growled happily in my mind.

"That was Cieth, and he is a wyvern." A sharp pain flared up in the back of my neck. "Ah!"

I am no 'wyvern,' fool, the beast hissed angrily. *I am an Ice Airy. We are stronger, faster, larger, and better than mere wyverns.*

"Sorry, he's an Ice Airy, apparently they're better than normal wyverns." I shrugged as she frowned. "It's what he said."

"He's inside you?" Her eyes widened slightly as she stared at me with new curiosity.

I frowned, searching for the right words. "Yes and no? We were two halves of the same whole, as far as nature was concerned. Now that we've been united, we're stronger and better than we ever were alone."

"I see. And he speaks to you?" I nodded at her and she nodded to herself.

"Was there anything else you wanted to know?"

"No, dear. I wanted to see if you had anything else you need to do or enchant for the journey ahead." I frowned and then perked up. "You do?"

"Yes I do." I pulled out the large piece of obsidian and grinned. "I'm going to make somewhere for my babies to be safe and away if we need them to be."

"That's a good idea. Also, I can feel that you've become stronger." She squeezed my bicep and winked at me cutely. "Make sure to spend your stat points."

"Yes ma'am." I kissed her until she was breathless before touching her cheek lovingly and winking at her. She grinned and patted my backside as I walked away.

I settled inside the temple to go over my leveling up and stat changes.

Level up!

Looks like I had gotten to level 44.

Better look at my stats to see where I should put things, I grumbled to myself. Jinx must have been powerful to help us jump that high.

Name: Zekiel Erebos
Race: Kitsune (Celestial)
Level: 44
Strength: 57
Dexterity: 52
Constitution: 50
Intelligence: 95
Wisdom: 50
Charisma: 19
Unspent Attribute Points: 10

Oh, that was nice. Five points went into Intelligence right away, putting me to a hundred. The other five I split, with three points to Strength and then two to Dexterity.

Those are not truly your stats, Druid. Check again with my power at your command.

"Uh, okay?"

Name: Zekiel Erebos
Race: Kitsune (Celestial/Beast-Bonded)
Level: 44
Strength: 67

Dexterity: 66
Constitution: 55
Intelligence: 100
Wisdom: 55
Charisma: 22
Unspent Attribute Points: 0

"Woah! How does that work?" I kept staring at my status as he explained.

Where you lack, I give. Cieth's growling voice echoed through my mind. *For instance, your stats are all lower than mine save for intelligence. I cannot take from you for it, but the difference in our stats is yours now.*

"Very well, thank you." I could almost feel him nod and then he slumbered.

I shrugged before I summoned Hubris. "Time to get to work, friend." It stayed quiet but I could feel that was more out of eagerness to hear what I had planned. "I want to make a necklace similar to the one I had previously, but that can hold more than just one creature."

I can help with that, master. But it will cost you another bout of information. Three questions.

I raised an eyebrow at it, but left it at that and waited for the questions.

Who brought you here?

"The gods did," I answered easily. It was true and common knowledge to a lot of people.

I see. And where from?

"Didn't you ask that already?" I frowned at him but I felt a sort of mental shake from the scepter.

Earth, I know, but where *is that?*

"The Milky Way galaxy." Then I thought about it for a second. "Swear to me you will not lie, on all your power and knowledge, about my question and I'll let you ask another question of me."

The skull appeared before my face and the empty sockets

stared into mine. *I swear by all my power and knowledge that I will not lie to you when I answer this question.*

"Do you work for, with, or have any involvement with any of my enemies, such as the Seelie, Children of Brindolla, human mages, or War?" My suspicion made my fur stand on end and I fought to shield my thoughts from the weapon.

The scepter was silent for a moment before answering, *Yes, but only in that whatever involvement you have with them, I will have by relation to you. Otherwise, I know none of these entities. I will ask my third question now.*

I breathed a sigh of relief and sagged where I sat. "Sure, Hubris, go ahead."

Why do you only enchant pre-made items?

"Is this a trick question? Because the things I can make are very limited." I shrugged and frowned at it. "It's all I can really work with, isn't it?"

No, it is not, Hubris corrected me gently. *With your powers, you could make almost anything you wanted. See that obsidian hunk in your hands? You were just thinking of how to attach it to a necklace or something. With your earth magic, you could manipulate it to make one out of itself. You could also make something to attach it to easily.*

Not to mention, so much more.

"What do you mean?" I frowned even further and visions flashed through my mind.

Golems walking and fighting for me, weapons of glorious make and power wielded by my friends.

You could make so much, yet you limit yourself.

I looked down at my right arm and sighed. "Only because I know what my own deficiencies can cost me. And others too. I won't put them at risk because I want to bite more than I can chew."

As you wish, master, but please, allow yourself some small experimentation. You could make a fine necklace out of that obsidian. Or a bracer that will render the same desired effect you wish to have.

"Thank you, Hubris." I lifted the item, then focused on it.

The sort of spell the scepter had in mind flooded into my mind and making it was easy.

I cast Manipulate Stone and molded the obsidian into a collar of sorts, flat bars with stone that fed copper into to make links out of. I didn't stop until I could fully fit it comfortably around the base of my neck and had enough for a two inch by four inch plate that sat in the front.

Using Hubris, I easily engraved runes for stasis, comfort, rejuvenation, holding, and release in the back.

You will need to refill your shield ring for this. Or get assistance.

I nodded and called, "Yohsuke! C'mere."

He stood next to me instantly. "Sup?"

"I need you to help me with a mana deficiency." He shrugged and nodded before I pulled out two platinum pieces and a small piece of bone we'd taken from Jinx's loot chest.

Hubris came out once more. "Aw man, I love the fucking skull."

He grabbed the scepter with me and we focused on sending mana into the necklace. My intent and will sharper than they likely had ever been as we worked. I dropped the two components in and finished enchanting it, Yohsuke having to use his racial ability to recover his spent mana.

Even with more than a thousand mana at my disposal without a ring, it took everything we had and more, but it was done and with a twist.

Collector's Collar

Holds up to three willing creatures within, in perfect stasis that will even heal some wounds. Will work up to five feet away.

While no one knows what goes on while we sleep, this collar sees that only one thing happens—you stay as long as necessary in perfect comfort. For an hour, days, or eons, your stay is but the blink of an eye.

"Oh, that's wild." I grinned and called Bea and Kayda to me. "Ladies, we have a new collar."

Hate it. Bea immediately growled at it, baring her fangs at it. *Never liked it.*

I snorted at her reaction and she actually hissed at me. "Hey, hey. Chill. It's just for the times when we're in populated places where people want to kill us, and for times we need to move fast, like teleporting. Okay? Oh, if you're hurt too. It heals you. Want to try it?"

No, Bea growled. Kayda pecked it once and was just gone. I assumed she was inside, until Bea looked closely at the collar and tilted her head. *Pretty.*

She touched it with her snout and popped away. I took the collar off and stared in shock. There were tiny images of them both on the front, like tiny chibi versions of them.

"So cute," I breathed with a pained look. I summoned them both back before me.

No! Want back! Bea barked angrily at me, her tail lashing the air behind her and touched the collar again only to pop away.

I looked at Kayda and her bird-like laugh. *It is comfortable inside there. I like it.*

"I'm happy to know that you appreciate my work, love." She nuzzled me with her beak before crossing back into the collar again.

I smiled contentedly for a moment before joining the rest of the group and nodding to the chef. "Dinner ready, brother?"

"I just got done helping you create that damned collar, you expect me to cook *and* clean up your messes?" He raised an eyebrow as I nodded immaturely and grinned at him. "Listen, motherfucker, I swear, I'll kick your dog-ass out to the dog house. Mutt, comin' over to *my* cooking fire, asking about food and shit…"

He broke off into angry muttering that began to turn almost homicidal when he turned toward me and flipped me the bird. "And I don't give a shit if Maebe is here—I'll whoop your ass, Fido."

We all laughed and he broke into a halfhearted smile. Kyr

and Sendak looked a bit sullen, but they still chuckled as they waited to eat like us. It would likely be a time before they would truly feel okay.

The two of them alone taking their people, protecting them, and trying to get them to be okay in a completely new environment? It was going to be hard, to say the least.

"Kyr, Sendak, might I make an offer to you both as former subjects of the Fae?" I spoke at last, an idea having finally formed in my head.

"What is it, Zeke?" Sendak asked tiredly, his eyes beginning to grow splotchy from tears over his loss.

"I want to offer you help from the Unseelie Court." Maebe stilled next to me, her entire being just *stopping* so that all her attention could be directed at this conversation.

"Nothing comes without cost for the courts, King Zeke." Kyr sounded rough too, his tail hung low and I ached for them both in their loss.

"No, I know that." I took a deep breath and let it out. "What I offer you is experience and guidance from a trusted ally, as well as support in protecting yourselves when you need it. With exception, of course, for when the court needs the military might."

"And what will this cost us?" Sendak asked testily, his voice rising as he spoke again. "Do you mean to take us back into the fold when we had been left to our own devices for too long? When the *humans* kept us weak?"

I blinked at him in confusion, and I saw James and Muu rising from their seats, but I waved them away. I knew he was hurting.

"No." He frowned at me and glanced at Kyr, the Kitsune watching me carefully. "I want to make sure that Greer losing his life wasn't in vain, and that your people have a chance to be stronger than he ever was so that this doesn't happen ever again. If the Druids are stronger, then they can be one with the beasts and truly make this world a better place."

I stared at him, Cieth watching from inside me, as I pushed on. "The humans kept you weak out of fear. The Unseelie would see you grow strong again, as is right. As is *your* right. Mother Nature wanted you to bring your people here, to this place among the Floating Isles so that you could be free of their tyranny for the first time in so long—and I want to give you a chance."

"What makes you think we need your help, or even want it?" The elf's anger seemed to have passed slightly, leaving him petulant and petty. "You never came to help before."

"I wasn't here until just now, buddy." I grinned at him and it threw him a little. "All we want in return is mutual aid and supplies. Give us some beast materials every once in a while, maybe every third chest or so, and we will help you with your people until such a time as you need nothing else from us. Then, we can renegotiate the terms of an alliance with the Unseelie Court. You get your people to safety, we get an ally and supplies, and then we help you *keep* those people safe while you train them to be better Druids."

"It seems too good to be true." Kyr sighed heavily, shaking his head then staring me straight in the eye. "Almost like you want this to go in our favor."

"He does," Maebe interjected softly, taking both our attention. I stared at her and she fixed me with a knowing smile. "Your negotiation tactics need work, my love. You are giving them *far* more than they realize, and it would put *us* at a bit of a loss here."

"How so?" Sendak jumped on that morsel of information and sat forward a bit.

"It would mean that as soon as the deal was struck, I would be duty bound to send people to assist you in not only getting your people from the city to your new home, but the means with which to lead them." She turned her gaze to me. "To include lessons on ruling structures, politicking, leadership, underling selection, manipulation tactics, advice on judgements —all of it."

"Ah, so only one chest in three isn't all that great on the supplies things, is it?" I scratched my head. "Sorry, boys, I'll have to rethink my offer."

"Two of every five," Sendak offered quickly, his eyes wide. Kyr flinched, but didn't object.

Maebe mulled it over, her face a mask of pure boredom for a moment before she turned her gaze at me and I took the cue. "Two of five chests, access to Anisamara for the supplies to be made into weapons or gear for our people, and a bonus of one chest for every day we have to assist you in any matter of significant aid. The latter to be decided *within reason*, by Queen Maebe."

Kyr held up a hand to hush Sendak. "Only if you have whatever enchanters you will be using for the Fae help to enchant our weapons and gear for a significant discount. I am talking dirt cheap."

Thinking of how we would have apprentice enchanters soon made me smile; this would be an excellent chance for them to work with materials that would be of the highest grade.

"We can amend that into the deal." I stared at both Sendak and Kyr. "What do you boys think? Oh! And let's not forget that Queen Maebe also reserves the right to end the contract— as do you—if anyone feels that they are being taken advantage of. Also, she may be required to send a proxy and ambassador to live among you as she cannot always be here at your beck and call."

"Allow us to discuss this?" Kyr spoke softly, I nodded and they headed outside to speak.

"Excellently done, my love," Maebe purred as she grasped my hand. "Sending a proxy, an ambassador, *and* a nulling clause? Those are strokes of a masterful penning. I didn't know that you would take my gentle guidance and use it so."

"Well, all I did was try to benefit us both." I shrugged and kissed her hand.

"What you did was more than an untrained king could be expected to do," Maebe corrected me. "And you thought of our future with Anisamara. She likely would have done the work anyway had I asked, but now she will definitely do it because she will be paid. Not to mention the enchanting? Well done indeed."

"He's learning." Vrawn chuckled and winked at me when I threw her a feigned hurt look. "That look doesn't work on me, Zeke. I'm happy that you are trying to do better, and from the way it sounds, working more as a king too."

"Yes, I am proud of that fact." Maebe kissed my cheek and smiled at me.

"They could be deciding against the deal as we all sit there," Muu pointed out tiredly. "What's the point in celebration?"

"Because Zeke is learning to think of more than just his mission and his duty to you all and thinking of his people too," Maebe answered him evenly. "Not that he has not before, but the fact that he found and attempted to obtain a potentially powerful—*malleable*—ally means that he is learning to aid me as a true king would. This deal means little to me, as I could always send Fae here to raid for materials. But having them here to do it for us would be beneficial to us as they know the area and how to fight these beasts."

"Dude, your wife is cold *blooded*." James shook his head and sighed.

"I am not, James." Maebe seemed concerned. "I have power over the cold but I am *not* cold blooded."

We laughed again, waiting for more than half an hour before the two Druids returned and held out a hand each. "We agree to your terms, King Zeke."

I reached out and pulled Kyr into a hug with the proffered hand and clapped him on the back. Then did the same to Sendak. "This is going to be a beautiful partnership, you guys. Simply beautiful. Mae, if you wouldn't mind the contract dealings?"

"As soon as they agreed to the terms, the contract was sealed. All you must do is ask for a copy to be shown to you in your status screen, and it will appear for your browsing at any time." Her voice held notes of pride and pleasure that made me grin even more.

I done good.

CHAPTER SIXTEEN

We woke the next morning chipper and alert to the smell of cooking food and birds chirping all about us.

I stretched out between Maebe and Vrawn, all of us grabbing food together in relative quiet as the sun rose.

"How are we getting back again?" James stretched and began to sit and meditate.

"Zeke will Teleport us," Maebe said, her voice sure as she turned to me. "Your intelligence is at what, one hundred now? If I recall, you can move that number divided by five?"

"Twenty people is what I can move with me when I teleport now."

"That sounds awesome." Muu grinned, and then frowned. "I just remembered that I hate teleporting."

"It happens to the best of us, just deal with it," Kyr growled as he finished his plate of food. "When we get back to the city, you and I will need to take human form to get to the priestess, as she is human and thus in the human section of the city."

I nodded and shifted, their eyes falling on me in shock. "Oh, your human form isn't any better."

I looked down and realized that I was still covered in the celestial markings of my race. "That's fair."

"I can cast a simple glamour over him if I come with you," Maebe volunteered and stepped closer to us.

"I will stay and guard the others while you go on this miniature adventure." Vrawn grabbed Muu by the back of the neck and he yelped like a puppy. "I will protect them."

"We don't need protecting in our own city." We all turned to stare expectantly at Sendak, who stood by the door to the temple with his arms crossed. "Well, it *was* our city. Who knows how well the humans will take this?"

"Come on, kids, let's get you home then." I motioned for everyone to gather around as I stood and adjusted my back. I was going to hate having to go back to my old body—if I did. I still hadn't decided on that.

Once everyone was around us, I pulled the Teleportation map up in my mind and chose the outskirts of the city where we might be able to sneak in. Luckily, I had the perfect spot to do so. Anisamara's lair.

The ground left our feet, then came back a heartbeat later.

That's right, baby! Daddy's finally getting used to teleporting. Woo!

I heard someone gasp and something sharp tore into my hip, then turned to find Anisamara grunting and shoving a dagger into my ribcage. "Ouch?"

She snarled, "What did I tell you about coming unannounced!"

"Don't?" I shrugged and stepped away, casting Heal on myself to close the wound.

"I would so appreciate you *not* stabbing my hus—" Maebe froze, the air around her chilled and the light in the cavernous shop dimmed significantly. "Seelie."

The hair on my body stood on end and I whispered, "Milnolian, Tan'rbleth come to me now."

Ice crystalized in the air nearest Maebe and Yve slunk from

it in her sabertooth form, her eyes sweeping the area as Servant leapt from my shadow.

"He summons the ancient Fae creatures so easily?" Anisamara whispered in shock, making me turn to her with a glare. "I heard nothing."

"Of course you didn't, and if I find out that you summoned my friends Yve and Servant, I'll consider it a death wish. I swear that on my power." Her breath caught in her chest, my malevolence sliding out of me as I said it and turned back to Yve and Servant. "You two are on high alert."

Yve growled low, "Seelie stench pervades this place." Her gaze flicked to Anisamara as she inhaled. "You. Young one. Tell me the last time you dealt with them."

"Hours ago, your ancientness." Anisamara bowed her head. "They came seeking the king and queen, but I told them that they were not here."

"And is that all?" Servant paced around her, his shadowy body so close to brushing up against her. His sister joined him, both of them circling her like sharks in chum-blooded water.

"No, but I swore I would speak nothing of it." She looked supremely nervous now, carefully moving back toward the wall.

Low growls emanated from both of them, their teeth flashing in the growing darkness, but I had another idea. "That leaves us a loophole. Servant, Yve, to me."

Both Fae moved to my side as Maebe stepped closer to me, several sets of eyes watching us from the darkness—reinforcements.

"You can't speak about what you said to them?" She nodded. "So that leaves us open to interpretation. We're going to say things that you could have said to them and you're going to either nod or shake your head to confirm or deny."

She stilled, her eyes flicking side to side in front of her face, then she looked up at me in hope and nodded excitedly.

"Did you tell them of our goals here?" Maebe's voice was carefully devoid of emotion as she spoke. Anisamara nodded once. "Did you tell them of whom we searched?"

She shook her head, and a weight fell from my shoulders. "Did you tell them of your people's plight?" A nod. Fuck. "Did they offer to help you?"

She shook her head, which surprised me, but Maebe gasped. "Did you tell them that we were interested in helping you? Was it alluded to at all?"

She frowned, opening her mouth as if to speak, but remembered that she couldn't so she shrugged.

"Fuck!" Maebe snarled viciously, the shadows in the room lengthening away from her in a circle.

"There it is!" Muu smiled and everyone turned to glare at him. "And there is that. What's so bad?"

"They could start rampaging through this city and claim to be the Unseelie!" Maebe turned to the watching eyes and snarled, "Find them! Kill all of the Seelie you find, and make sure you do it so that they cannot ever be found again!"

"Servant." The black and gray tiger eyed me as I spoke his name. "You and Yve are needed with us. I need you to guard my friends. Yve, you're with me."

"My king, I would prefer to be by your side." Servant aired his grievance politely but I heard the edge of uncertainty in his voice.

"I know, bud—but Yve would have fun playing with her food and my friends." The larger Fae simply licked her paw as we spoke about her as if she couldn't care less about what was said. "I trust you with their lives, and I think you know that I'm not lying."

He didn't even have to scent the air like he normally did, he just nodded and padded closer to the group. "All of you will stay close to me, and if you move too far from me, I will let you die."

I rolled my eyes, knowing that he wouldn't, but turned to Kyr and motioned him forward. "We need to go. Now."

My skin itched fiercely as Maebe's intent and will washed over me. The starry constellations all over my skin disappeared with her glamour covering me as we prepared to leave. "Yve, stealth mode."

"I like this bossy side of you, my king." She purred and rubbed up against my hip only to yowl as a green hand grasped the back of her neck and lifted her like a kitten.

Vrawn grimaced and pulled the great cat closer to her so she could stare in Yve's eyes, "Touch what is mine flirtatiously again and I will wear you."

Harsh, barking laughter rang out from behind me and I caught both Servant and Muu almost doubled over in delight at the scene.

I rolled my eyes. "It's okay, Vrawn, I have all the women in my life that I can handle." I kissed her and rubbed her cheek with my thumb. "Do me a favor and put the kitty down?"

"I am not a kitty! *Oof.*" Yve growled and it sounded like a panther attacking but I grabbed her and shoved her toward the exit. "This is not over, green thing!"

"It is for now, goddamnit, let's go!" I kicked after her tail and she scooted out of the way as we moved. I stopped and turned back, dumping all the materials I had onto the ground and staring at Anisamara. "I need these made into weapons, James, Muu, Yoh—you all know what kinds of weapons and gear we need for the others too. Let's get geared up and get this shit over with."

We piled into the tunnel from the cavern and moved swiftly into the room beyond where we found the large Kitsune man waiting for us with his sword drawn. He stopped and breathed a sigh of relief. "They charged in here and almost killed me to get to her. I am sorry, my Queen."

"It is alright, just tell us which way they went." He pointed outside, then shook his head.

"I think they remain nearby, someone screamed not seconds ago." He ran his hand through his fur.

"That may be a Seelie dying," Maebe growled in satisfaction. She touched his arm and posited, "If anyone comes in here who is not us, or is Seelie, slay them."

He nodded and set the rug by his feet over top of the entrance to the tunnel before we left.

Kyr, his human form a little forgettable, led us toward the human side of the city through throngs of people who seemed to be keen to something going on.

Up ahead of us, a copper scent wafted toward me and a crumbled wall with blood splattered all over it greeted us as we passed it. There was no body, but the claw marks on the stone were massive and people looked ready to panic. Some of them even whispered about a being of pure shadow screeching from a nearby wall to attack a man and pull him screaming and bleeding into the void.

I found myself oddly satisfied that our people had been so adept at rooting them out so quickly, I just hoped they kept up the good work.

"What are Kitsune such as you doing here?" I heard a strangely familiar voice call out to our left. Maebe, Kyr, and I turned to find one of the quintuplets standing with his arms folded across his chest with a sneer of distaste. "Filth sneaking through the streets while attacks are being perpetrated against normal humans seems suspicious to me."

Well, Zeke, you did say that you would punch one of the little bastards the next time you saw them—no time like the present. I grinned to myself and stepped into Kyr's shadow, popping out of the other Druid's shadow to slap the taste out of his mouth. His head bounced off the wall and I sighed heavily as he crumpled, muttering, "At least I keep my pimp hand strong."

I dragged him into the alley behind him and left him there before rejoining the others, throwing a nasty look toward a little boy who watched and tugged at his mother's sleeve so that she would stop.

We moved swiftly through side alleys and streets until we stood in the shadow of a massive building with pillars in front of it that would have given the Greek Parthenon a run for its money. The white, pearlescent stone almost hurt my eyes as I gazed up at it. "Zeke!"

Kyr's urgent whisper grabbed my attention. Loud banging

and shouting came from the inside of the temple. "Something is wrong."

"Let's go then." I took a running start and jumped the steps in a bound, barging into the temple with Yve and Maebe hot on my tails.

Bodies covered the ground, a couple of them some of the creatures that Maebe had summoned slowly crumbling where they lay, bitten and torn in half, their blood splattered on the walls and floors as humans groaned and lay on their sides injured and dying.

"The fuck happened here?" I hissed to myself before a shriek drew my attention toward the back of the temple.

A large being, something I thought only existed in the myths and legends of my world, lumbered out of a back room, nearly having to fold itself in half to do so, holding a woman by her hair and her waist as if she were a doll waiting to be broken in half for its play.

A goddamn wendigo. A boney, almost-tree-like body capped with a buffalo skull for a head with hateful, leering green eyes floating in the empty sockets.

It screeched at us and threw the woman to the side to charge at Maebe and I. "Kyr, get to her and keep her safe!"

Yve bolted between the wendigo and I, spitting and yowling loudly, "Come get your beating, fel creature!"

"That is their king's right hand, Zeke, he is powerful—be careful!" Maebe warned as she began to circle it and flank it.

"I get that, babe." The humans all caught my attention and I shook my head. "Yve, get the humans out of here while we distract it."

Her fur raised slightly. "This is the thing that killed me in my previous life—my vengeance will not be denied!"

I lowered my voice and whispered, "If you will not listen to me, Tan'rbleth, I will send you away and deny you more than that. Obey my will, and you will have time to help us kill it!"

Her snarled rage sent chills down my spine and she slashed at the creature on her way past it to get to a human woman, her body shifting to stand tall and elven. "Get up, you mewling thing!"

I summoned my will and sent a Winter's Blade swirling through the air at it, the spell melting before it got there. "Very well then."

I pulled Nether Bolt from my inventory and cast Aspect of the Ursolon. As my body grew and swelled to strengthen my muscles, the Wendigo and I clashed, claws tearing into my shoulder as my great axe slashed the creature's boney stomach and rib cage.

The wendigo's claws grew and the body began to change, but Maebe's ice and shadows slammed into it, barely moving it. Was it just immune to magic?

I cracked my neck and bore down on it, my fists crashing into anything I could reach as more muscle and sinew began to grow over the boney body. I push-kicked it away from me before it could attack, but it seemed more interested in whatever it was doing at the time.

I reached into my inventory and found the items I had from Jaken, Bokaj, and Balmur, throwing them to Kyr. "Have her use those to find my friends, we have his attention."

"Fine!" he called back and began to speak to the woman in a low voice as I focused on the wendigo.

"Mae, what the hell can hurt this thing?" I didn't have time to hear her answer as a foot planted itself in my chest and rocketed me backward into a wall, my head smacking against the bricks. Thankfully, I didn't pass out, but my bell was rung and I lost 18% of my HP in that one attack.

A tall man stood where the wendigo had, his features fair and beautiful even, flaming red hair billowing from the top of his head as his ears peeked out of the sides of his head. He watched us with blazing blue eyes and grinned, his otherworldly voice almost echoing around us, "So nice to finally see you again, Queen Maebe. I hope this message finds you well. Is King Zeke here? Forgive me, this is merely a recorded message of sorts for whichever of you my beloved minion finds first, though I do hope I have both of you in attendance."

He rubbed his hands and for a recording he did a damned fine job staring me in the eyes as he grinned wider. "This would normally be an act of war, but since this isn't the Fae realm, Samir's decree cannot reach us. But since I am ever the cautious king, I have taken the time to disavow and exile my wendigo friend and allowed him to carry a message for old times' sake. I digress, as soon as this damnable decree is over, Maebe, the Seelie and the Unseelie will clash like never before, and we will finally see who the deserving rulers of the realm are. All the Fae will belong to me, as is right since we Seelie are the more beautiful and true."

"Is this guy seriously drawing a target on his chest like this?" I lifted myself to my feet and shook myself out.

"Yes he is, but I doubt he means for us to make it out of this alive." She spat and stepped forward. "Oberron, I know you can hear me, you bastard. The Unseelie will never bow to you."

The area around us felt suddenly warm and a summer breeze filtered into the temple. A now-familiar voice whispering, "I expected nothing less. Kill them, wendigo."

The flesh on the wendigo sloughed off it in a single go as it roared wordlessly at us. I let my spell fade and dashed forward in time to join Yve in a charge against it, a fist clenched at my side. As soon as she leapt onto its chest, I blasted the pelvis with my right hand and sent both of them careening through the air.

"Maebe, I have an idea on what may kill this thing, but it's a gamble," I whispered toher, seeing her turn her head my way as she pulled her star-covered Morningstar sword from her inventory with a savage fury I didn't recognize at first. "I'm going to drop him in the ocean and hope that Orlow'thes' toxin is still in it."

"That is a gamble, but if it works, it works," she whispered back. "What do you need me to do?"

"If you have silver, it may slow it down a tiny bit so that Cieth and I can grab it and fly it out." She scowled and finally reached into her inventory and pulled out a spike that looked to me like silver. "I like how prepared you are."

"You really do not, and I will tell you why I carry this someday." She moved forward and threw the spike as hard as she could, pinning the wendigo to the wall behind it as it threw Yve off it. It screeched and clawed at the metal spike, but each touch burned its hands wildly to the point that it couldn't grip.

"Ready, Cieth?" I felt the wyvern in me stir and look at the wendigo with spiteful hatred. "Let's get to work."

Happily, his sudden snarling pleasure at the idea of killing this thing confused me, but I'd take it.

We shifted and surged forward with our claws opened wide. Yve clambered onto my back as Maebe grabbed onto our leg to continue subduing the creature with her sword while we burst through the temple doorway.

Our wings pumped and we took on altitude steadily, birds flocking behind us, *Druids coming after us.*

Let them come and see what they should never have given up! His inward smile at my retort made me grin in return as we continued out over the water to deliver our payload.

Over the water, we let go, but the crafty creature clutched carefully to our talons and no amount of shaking would get it to let go. Yve scrambled down my shoulder and onto the bastard as we looked down. Massive claws grew from her fingertips. "For killing me once, I will have my *revenge!*"

She slashed three times in quick succession and they both plummeted toward the water, clawing at each other wildly. I shifted and grabbed Maebe. "Yve, dismissed!"

She screamed, "No! I want to watch him die!" Then she disappeared and I summoned her again just above us.

"Get us out of here, catch us, do something!" I felt clawed feet grasp me, my fall stopping as I kept hold of Maebe and watched as the wendigo fell into the water. Maebe and I reached out together and willed the water below us to freeze in a globe.

"We will bring it back to the others and kill it together," Maebe advised softly. "You could all use the experience."

I watched in awe as her shadow rose from ours on the water, thickening into an ink splotch on the ocean that swallowed the orb easily.

Yve turned and took us back to the temple, landing with us and returning to her sabertooth form quietly, patiently waiting as we did what we had to do. Honestly, I wanted to see how she was doing, but pressing matters and all that.

"She's found them!" Kyr rushed over to us, panting and waving for us to follow him into the building once more.

We found the woman sitting in the room that she had been carried out of, her dark brown hair mussed and her lip bloodied; she looked frightened to see us. "Don't worry, we will kill the creature soon. It can't hurt you anymore. Can you tell me where our friends are?"

She nodded and held her hand out, touching my arm. A sensation of warmth drifted toward me and it seemed so inviting.

Relaxing, I allowed the warmth to pervade my mind and images began to flow into me. A cove under the water where Bokaj strummed his guitar for a bevy of beautiful mermaids as Balmur rolled his eyes and returned to penning things in his spellbook that he looked to be coping from something else.

A shift in area made me nauseous, but the scene before me made me even more so.

Jaken stood alone with the great serpent guardian Orlow'thes' giant head in front of him, the serpent watching him cautiously as my paladin friend spoke softly with his hands out to his side.

"Where are these places?" My eyes unclouded and the priestess frowned to herself before glancing from the door to me before tapping my head.

Agony ripped through my body as the memories and sensations of these places forged themselves inside me. I *knew* where these places were like I had been there a hundred times before.

"That is the extent of what I can do for you, there is no more—please leave before more danger befalls us because of your presence." Her voice was soft but firm as she ordered us away, as I turned, I felt a hand on my wrist, turned and saw that she had tears in her eyes. "Thank you."

I nodded once and made sure the time on Teleport was up before turning to Mae, then stopped, suddenly very aware of something.

This temple was fucking massive—and well kept. I turned to glare at her. "You're going to start preaching that your god wants to love *all* sentient creatures; human, Fae, dwarf, elf, Kitsune—I don't give a shit what it is, he loves them and wants them treated with dignity and respect."

She froze and stared at me in silent shock, so I reached down and shook her. "I want your word that you will, or the creatures out there killing people are going to turn on this fucking church so fast your head will spin off those pretty little shoulders of yours." She still said nothing so I roared in her face, "Swear it to me now!"

"I swear I'll preach equality for all races!" she screamed and began to cry in great heaving sobs.

I got a notification from it and let her go before turning back to Maebe. "Mae, I need for you to order a shield, a bow, and some daggers, or handaxes like Balmur originally had."

"Anisamara has those orders, as well as the items you gave her before we left. I take it that you are going to get them?" I nodded and kissed her. "I will return to the others. Be safe."

"I will." I cast Teleport to get to Balmur and Bokaj.

CHAPTER SEVENTEEN

I appeared in front of a large pool of water where Bokaj sat singing a lovely melody, his fingers deftly strumming notes on his guitar strings.

"I hate to interrupt your concert, Bokaj, but we have shit to do." I cleared my throat as twenty mermaids, all of them beautiful in their own right, turned and began to sing in unison at me. I shrugged, thanks to being immune like my friends, and Bokaj sprinted to me. His arms closed around my shoulders and tightened in a rough grip. "Hey buddy."

"We thought that we had lost you guys," Bokaj whispered as I patted his back, Tmont's bleary-eyed head popping out of his hood, seeing me and popping back into the hood. "After the mermaids finished treating us for the toxin, we had no idea what to do, but here you are."

"We know that things are hard, but we haven't been idle." I pulled away from him and looked to where Balmur still worked diligently. "What's with him?"

Bokaj just shrugged. "He found that they had a whole bunch of treasure and stuff from the world above us, and has spent any time we aren't hunting and trying to get stronger working with his spellbook."

"And for good reason!" Balmur smirked as he thumped the book with the back of his hand. "I just figured out a way to wipe a cooldown from one person and give it to another." His hand lifted, eyes glowing purple as he stared at me, and his fingers worked through a complicated set of movements before something in me shifted and Bokaj listed to the side before righting himself.

"Oh, that is so sucky, but cool," he groaned as he rubbed his head.

"How often can you use that?" He held up two fingers, then put one of them down dramatically. "Fucking wizards, man. Say goodbye, guys. We have a paladin to rescue."

"Hold on!" Bokaj skittered across the wet floor and bent down to the ladies. "Thank you all for your instructions and training. I feel like I sing now better than ever before, and all the hunting techniques you taught us are amazing."

One of the mermaids stood, her tail giving way to legs that made the cartoon wolf in me drool despite the wonders I already knew and I looked away quickly, her voice sure as she teased, "That wasn't all we taught you, and you know it. If you need to fight in the sea again, call us and we will come."

I caught his nod before the mermaid kissed him passionately and I blinked and whistled a soft tune to myself. Balmur bustled around the other side of the room, pulling things into a small bag that he held on his hip with a grin on his face and finally he came back to me.

"You better have that spell ready to rock, buddy," I warned him and he whipped his book out of the small holster he now had for it on his other hip. "Nice gear."

"These mermaids are incredible crafters, man," was all he would say as Bokaj finally joined us. "Ready? Cool. Let's go interrupt a guardian's meal."

"I'm sorry, what?" Bokaj yelped as I touched their shoulders and cast Teleport once more to get to Jaken.

My bones ached, ears popping as the familiar pulling sensation paused longer than we were used to, and finally we bounced out to the other side of the void with the scent of rot and sickness all around us. Orlow'thes' body coiled around, wounds in various stages of healing as Jaken spoke to him in a strangely soothing voice.

"Don't worry, once my friends arrive, we can heal you up good as new!" He patted the creature's head, a low growl shaking the cavernous place easily even though it hadn't sounded like a threat. That same familiar sensation came over me and then it was Balmur's turn to list to the side.

"We're here, but it's good to see that you can make friends anywhere, buddy."

He turned and sprinted to us, knocking all three of us onto the ground with his excitement and bulky body. "You guys made it, finally!" He stood and yanked me to my feet. "Come on, Orlow needs us."

His body glowed golden and healing energy washed over the guardian's massive body, but the creature just hissed loudly and turned to stare at us.

"Druids, tell him to stop wasting his magic." The mouth barely moved, but the guardian's whispered plea still shocked me. I still had yet to cast Nature's Voice since the last time I had, but I understood him perfectly. "All he does is delay the inevitable."

"Zeke, come on, you gotta help me." Jaken shoved my arm in uncharacteristic irritation. "He needs our help if we're going to be able to stand up to Baranzil."

"I will not face that creature again in this life, I will choose another to champion my cause." Orlow'thes turned his gaze from me to Jaken. "His kindness is not for naught. I will live on after I pass."

"Jake, bud." I grabbed his shoulder, but he shook me off.

"No!" He bashed his fist against the armor he barely wore, it was eaten and rusting even as we watched. "No! He needs our help. I'm so sick of other people having to pay with their lives because we can't get our shit together! He's a guardian! A natural badass! He *has* to live, Zeke."

"He said he has a champion in mind to carry on his fight, and I think you know who that is." Jaken's eyes watered as he scowled at the great beast. "He's going to live on even after his body fades here."

"Another will take his place," Balmur whispered. We all turned to see him staring at a wall, his hand casting a coin into the air and stopping it so that it would glow with unnatural light. Glyphs of some kind littered the wall but he seemed to be reading them perfectly. "After the guardian fades and their body is no more, their experiences and memories will grow inside the body of a new guardian."

"We are the Mother's perfect creations in cooperation with the gods, my sisters, brother and I." Orlow'thes lifted his massive head, one of his long whiskers brushing against Jaken as he stared sullenly. "As a creation of the gods, I can bestow my strength to those who have earned it. I would like for you to earn it. Take my strength and end this threat to this world. Like the beasts above, I will leave behind treasure. If I can, I will leave behind something useful to my champion."

"He wants us to kill him," I muttered and sighed.

Jaken's fist clenched so tight that it was hard to watch him suffering, but finally he breathed through it. "If he's going to come back, then fine. I fucking hate it," he growled and turned his head toward me so that I could look him in the eyes. "I swear I will play the goddamn pacifist in any game I can after all this shit. Fuck, man. Let's get this over with."

"Okay, how would you like to do this?" I stepped close to him, but Orlow'thes shook his massive head.

"All of you will be needed. I would share my strength as far as I can." Finally he laid down his head and closed his eyes. "Do not keep me waiting long."

I nodded and turned to the others. "We're going to come back with the others so we can do this right. Let's go."

Jaken touched the guardian's side once more, then turned

and joined the three of us with his jaw set. "Time to get the ball rolling then."

I cast the spell and we appeared just inside Anisamara's home, Dir'ish coming to his feet with a sword bared and ready to slash, but I grasped the blade and squeezed. "The lady already stabbed me once today and I don't want a repeat performance."

"I understand. Please, go on in."

He shook hands with the others as we passed through the home and into the tunnel below. We had things to prepare. Good and bad.

I spent three hours poring over enchantments for everyone's gear, making sure things were just right. I even made sure that Maebe and Vrawn had armor and accessories to boot. It hurt, and the headache I had whooped my ass like no other, but it was worth it.

I have to admit, master, this is wonderful progress and quite the cunning bit of planning.

"Everything they have on is resistant to water damage, and lightning damage." I grinned. "That way, we can fry that motherfucker where he stands." I thought better of that and amended, "Swims."

I will assist you in frying him. I smiled at the fact that Hubris was trying so hard to be a little more hip.

"We ready to go see Orlow'thes?" The party nodded and I looked over at Kyr and Greer. "If you guys wanna hold off on getting your people out of here, I get it. What we're about to do may really send the beasts over the edge. It may not be safe to travel in their territories for a while, but it may calm them down too."

"We will do what we can," Kyr assured us as he stepped forward, glancing at Jaken, Bokaj, and Balmur. "It's nice to meet you all."

They nodded to him, grim visaged and trying to be ready for whatever lay ahead. We all clasped arms as I readied my spell and finally we were off.

Orlow'thes stood as we appeared, Maebe's breath catching as the magnificent, injured guardian rose to his full height. "I do not mean to go easily. I will not attack you, but I will need to see that you are capable of fighting on in my stead."

"Then, if you would allow us to prepare a little more?" I asked and he leaned back giving us a little more room. "Maebe?"

"We mean to bring an enemy of the Unseelie into this place, a wendigo. Magic does not work well, but silver harms it." My fur rose on end as everyone else in the group chuckled evilly as their gazes turned to me as I let Kayda and Bea out of the collar to help us. Tmont purred next to Bokaj's side and eyed the wendigo hungrily.

I groaned, hating the images they likely all had of the various times that silver had ruined me with my lycanthropy.

We all spread out, me taking my lucky coin into my hand and getting ready as a globule of shadow pooled into the center of the cavern and the ice holding the wendigo burst forth from it.

The green, flaming eyes burned hot and the ice around it finally began to melt. "Wait until it's fully out and then we can get to work," Yoh muttered as the rest of us took calming breaths.

Once it was free, the echoing ethereal howling began as it screamed at us, then buckled as the flames in its eyes began to dim. "It worked! The toxin is in it now!"

I threw the coin at it and it froze once more as the shadows beneath it rose and grasped it to hold it still.

Yohsuke and James led the charge as the two fastest, though Balmur chanted a spell of sorts of his own, his hand flickering with odd green light. As Yoh's astral blade slashed and James's foot cracked it in the jaw, the green energy coalesced and rocketed forward and splashed over the wendigo, corroding it as it screamed without moving its mouth.

Arrows clattered against the bone, but he dared not send in Tmont as spells flew. I took Nether Bolt and activated Charge, slamming into the creature and chopping its leg as both Muu and Jaken joined me.

Lightning flashed above our heads and crashed into the wendigo just before Bea jumped onto its back to claw and bite at it, ripping her head back and forth.

Jaken's sword slashed as Muu's hammer crashed and the beast fell, dying as silver punctured it. The fires in the creature's eyes faded and finally it fell as the shadows no longer had anything to hold.

I will take from this beast as well please, master, Hubris whispered to me softly. *There is great magic to it that I feel would benefit us both.*

This is twice in a few days. Why has this never happened before?

The items that we had found before were inferior and as you grow—I grow. Your power is much more than it had been, and now that we find the necessary materials, I can evolve as I was meant to.

"Take your payment, Hubris." I waved to the pile of bones as the scepter appeared, the horns from the wendigo rose and attached themselves to the skull, giving it an almost demon-like quality, as one of the bones in the pile shot into the wood portion of the scepter, the item rippling with power as wood became bone with runes of green fire shimmering within it.

"An interesting piece of equipment you hold for a Druid." Orlow'thes' head lowered toward me. "I sense much about it, yet I have no memory of ever having met it. It seems... familiar."

I shrugged and checked my notifications. The wendigo had nearly given me enough experience to level up again. That was considerable, considering all of us having taken part.

"It is time." Orlow'thes growled low. "All of you, come at me. Show me my sacrifice will be worthy."

I turned to the others, nodding once and grasping Hubris by the newly-made bone, Maebe, Balmur, Bokaj, Jaken, and Yohsuke joining me to place their hands on the shaft of the weapon as I focused on what I wished to attack with.

Hubris' eyes lit up with radiant energy as it soaked in every bit of mana it could as I cast Falfyre. The weapon started off normal sized at first, but grew until it was the size of an SUV by the time we finished channeling mana into it. Yohsuke grimaced at the proximity to the holy weapon, but grit his teeth and carried on, Jaken shielding him as best as he could with his body. This was an idea we had to fight the general, hoping he was still too stupid to know that we could improve.

Orlow'thes reared and electricity crackled around his body. "Come! Let us see what you are made of!"

We roared together and I sent the sword forward as the opening salvo took place. Muu's spear crashed down on top of the guardian's exposed head, making it roar in agony as his hammer connected with the butt of the previous weapon and nailed it into the flesh.

While Orlow'thes was distracted by the flighty fighter tap dancing on his head, James focused his ki blades on the chest between the guardian's arms. As the flesh and scales of his underbelly split, my sword slid home and struck deeply.

Orlow'thes screamed one, long last bellow as the blow struck home and he fell to his side, his toxic blood leaking onto the ground. As it pooled closer to us, his clawed hand swept out and created a trench of sorts to keep it away from us.

"Good." He grunted and laid down. "Thank you for ending my suffering."

His clawed hand reached out. "Paladin, step forward." Jaken, stricken but understanding, stepped forward and allowed the water dragon to gaze upon him. "As guardian of your peers, I bequeath to you my title, and with it may the scales tip in your favor."

As the last rasping breath left the great guardian Orlow'thes, his breath tousled the paladin's hair, a halo of black forming above his head. Jaken fell to a knee and read something in front of his face, tears streaming from his eyes. I stepped closer to him as the guardian's body faded and disregarded several notifications so that I could get to him.

"You alright? Something wrong?" I tried to keep my voice even, but he just turned to me and gave me a sad smile.

"He gave me his title." He pointed to his new halo. "When he's reborn, he will no longer be divine until he dies again, and even then, he will only have a fifty percent chance to come back."

"So he really did give his everything to this," I whispered more to myself than him and he stood next to me.

"We gotta get these fuckers, man." He looked me in the eyes, determination mounting in his gaze. He lifted his hand and squeezed my arm with more strength than he likely meant to. "They have to pay for every life they took."

"They will," I grasped him back and pulled him into a hug. "We're going to make sure of it."

LEVEL UP!

I checked and my jaw dropped as I realized what had happened. It was the sort of Hail Mary play that we needed, but it was almost too much. Orlow'thes' sacrifice had netted me eleven levels, getting me up to level 55.

I glanced at the others and they had the same shocked looks on their faces. As dumbfounded as we looked, it was only a drop in the bucket compared to how fast Baranzil had leveled up. And there was no telling if he was stronger or not since the last time we had fought him.

I frowned and began the process of sussing out how I would split up my stat points since I had fifty-five free ones to use. I opted to put twenty-five into Intelligence, ten into Constitution, Dexterity, and Strength. The normal changes ensued, my muscles growing denser and my body a little lighter as my MP bar grew larger. I felt healthier and it made me smile.

I turned to Kayda and Bea. "This is likely crunch time, and I trust you to pick your own stats to make sure that you're the best you can be in the coming fight. If you need help, let me know."

They both looked to each other before they stepped close and began to rub against my face affectionately, silently just being there for me as I patted them back lovingly.

I watched as Bea and Kayda distributed their own stats.

The majority for both going into dexterity. For Bea?—no surprise there. Though the four points to Strength and Constitution, and two each to Intelligence and Wisdom, did surprise me for her normally impulsive nature. I had to admit, the pride swelling in my chest at seeing her mature made me puff up a bit.

Kayda put more into Strength than anything else, nine points dropping in easily, with six to Constitution and four to Dexterity. For levels twenty seven and thirty five, their stats looked good.

Father, worry about yourself, Kayda ordered sagely, her wing shoving me away.

Grinning, I checked the rest of my notifications.

Congratulations!

For taking part in the killing of a guardian, you have earned your seventh and final tail available at your current age. Your next tail will be available in two hundred years.

"Well, that's horseshit," I grumped to myself but read on.

This tail bestows the trickster's ultimate gift, Switch. Switch allows you to pick a target you can see and magically switch places with them. You can use this a number of times equal to your wisdom divided by ten rounded down daily. (5 times per day.)

That would tactically be fucking awesome. I would have to save that for something that would be really deadly... *Or to trick our opponent into a false sense of security!*

I would keep that close to the chest until everyone else had finished leveling up, though it sucked that there was nothing else that we got for cresting fifty. *Oh well, shit happens, bud.*

I leaned back until I felt a tug on my rump and turned to find Maebe standing with Vrawn and the shadows tugging my tails. She motioned me toward her with a nod and I popped over to her. "What's up?"

"How do we mean to find Baranzil?" she asked me quietly as the other finished leveling up.

"I couldn't tell you. We could try to coax him out of hiding, but the ocean isn't my wheelhouse."

"It's mine, now." Jaken grunted, his halo still floating above his head. "Orlow'thes passed that knowledge on to me before he faded. We can either go to him, or call him to the shore here."

"How do you know he will come?" Bokaj groaned and stretched as he stood up from where he sat. "What if he power levels the way that he had before?"

"What if grasshoppers had machine guns?" I blurted angrily, the others looking at me like a dick had grown out of my head.

"I'm sorry, I'm the stupid one here, not you." Muu crossed his arms over his chest. "You want to explain that?"

"It means that it doesn't fucking matter, because even if it does happen, we will still do our fucking best." I shook my head, still remembering the defeat we suffered. "Yeah, he got stronger last time because we got fucking cocky. Not this time. This time, we turn shit on his head. We can plan and plot, and call him to us so that he's out of his element. We're going to have to work harder than we ever have, but we can do this. We have no choice but to."

"Zeke's right." Yohsuke sighed. "We have a fuck ton of friends and allies here, and it's to the point where these mother-fuckers don't even care if there are Brindollans in the way. They just want to kill us. Honestly, we stand more of a chance now that we're ready and know what to expect. Let's consolidate and see what we're working with now. I'm sitting at more than one thousand, three hundred mana and a hundred dex. You all?"

"Fuck it, why don't we all just show off our stat pages?" James shrugged and opened his for the rest of us to see.

Name: James Bautista
Race: Dragon Elf (Partial incubation)
Level: 54
Strength: 50
Dexterity: 100

Constitution: 76
Intelligence: 20
Wisdom: 100
Charisma: 12
Unspent Attribute Points: 0

"Damn, bro." Yohsuke whistled to himself. "That's a lot of ki to be throwing around. Decent build over all. Here's me."

Name: Yohsuke
Race: Abomination Elf (Vampire Lord)
Level: 55
Strength: 19
Dexterity: 100
Constitution: 65
Intelligence: 133
Wisdom: 60
Charisma: 13
Unspent Attribute Points: 0

Jesus, he has more mana than me? I shook my head and grinned, leave it to Yoh.

Bokaj was next with a huge grin.

Name: Bokaj
Race: Ice Elf
Level: 55
Strength: 18
Dexterity: 105
Constitution: 85
Intelligence: 35
Wisdom: 20
Charisma: 100
Unspent Attribute Points: 0

"Charisma don't have to be a dump stat, boys." We all

chuckled with him and some of the tension in us fled a bit as Balmur shared his stats.

Name: Balmur
Race: Azer Dwarf
Level: 55
Strength: 40
Dexterity: 100
Constitution: 60
Intelligence: 109
Wisdom: 40
Charisma: 16
Unspent Attribute Points: 0

"Looks like studying's paid off for you, huh, Balmur?" He grinned and winked at me as I threw my hat into the ring.

Name: Zekiel Erebos
Race: Kitsune (Celestial/Beast-Bonded)
Level: 55
Strength: 77
Dexterity: 76
Constitution: 65
Intelligence: 125
Wisdom: 55
Charisma: 22
Unspent Attribute Points: 0

The others nodded. "Those are good all-around stats, Z." Yoh punched my shoulder lightly and I just shrugged.

We looked to Muu and Jaken, Muu offering the proverbial floor to the other man first with a wave of his hand.

Name: Jaken Warmecht
Race: Fae-Orc (Guardian)
Level: 56

Strength: 97
Dexterity: 34
Constitution: 120
Intelligence: 16
Wisdom: 119
Charisma: 19
Unspent Attribute Points: 0

"Holy shit!" James gasped as he stared at the screen. "More than a thousand HP? Tank-zilla over here!"

Muu just grinned at all of us as we turned expectant gazes at him. He flicked his wrist with a flourish and his stats populated before us.

Name: Muu Ankiman
Race: Dragon Beast-kin
Level: 53
Strength: 100
Dexterity: 100
Constitution: 110
Intelligence: 20
Wisdom: 19
Charisma: 19
Unspent Attribute Points: 0

"Jesus Christ!" I muttered with feeling. I'd have to level a dozen more times to have the level of stats he was sporting.

"Yeah, I'll fucking murderize all of you magic bitches." He grinned just before Maebe stepped closer and threw the poor bastard twenty feet into the air. "Ahhhh!"

"Ah, he is so aerodynamic now, see how he flies?" Maebe's laughter at her own joke made the rest of us burst out laughing as Muu landed in a heap fourteen feet away from the rest of us.

"So what were we planning to do?" James asked as he gasped for air. "We can't just fight on the sea, can we? We would need a ship, and that is not going to happen with the humans experiencing a mass exodus of the people who do the menial jobs in their city."

"No, it won't." I smiled to myself as a plan began to formulate in my mind. "But there's a coast south of here we can try that will allow for a much more interesting land battle."

"Land battle?" Yohsuke sneered and shook his head. "There's no way he's going to come on land to fight with us."

"Not willingly, no," I allowed, then my smile grew as I winked at him and activated Switch.

He blinked at me, suddenly very aware of why I was grinning at him. "You bastard."

"I know. Four more times I can do that—*today.*" The rest of the group grinned at me and I nodded. "Five times daily. We have a means and a way for this to happen, but we need to be prepared. I know we can do this; we just have some work to do before we call him to us."

I motioned everyone to me, Jaken looting the chest that Orlow'thes had left for him with a somber but dedicated set to his face. I clapped him on the shoulder and stared him in the eyes. "We'll get ours. And we will make damn sure he pays for what he did to Orlow'thes."

Jaken growled, his tusks flashing in the dim light. "All of War's minions and generals will pay. Let's go and set this thing up."

I was about to cast Teleport when Jaken broke away from us with a smirk and sprinted toward where the gouge in the stone was, taking a large bowl and dipping into what was left of the toxic blood that remained inside it.

He held it up, some of the contents sloshing over the lip of the bowl and onto his forearm. "Dude, you'll be out for like a day and a half from having to clear that toxin from your system," Muu groaned loudly.

"No, I'm immune since I'm a guardian." Jaken's grin turned malicious. "But that fuckstick won't be."

He came back and we teleported to the scene of our trap.

It was time to get a little payback.

CHAPTER EIGHTEEN

"You're sure this will work?" Bokaj asked uncertainly as he scoped out where he would be firing from.

"Yup." I grunted as I put the finishing touches on my own portion of his work. "You and Balmur ready with those mobile ballistae that Anisamara made for us yesterday?"

He nodded and patted them. Those had taken her a day to make and the materials had been costly. We were running low on money at long last but it was a small price to pay for getting rid of this fucker.

Bokaj wore his new armor, a leather jerkin with wyvern scales sewn onto it that looked like a vest, matching pants and boots made from the hide of that mist crawling thing we'd fought before the Floating Isles.

Balmur appeared close to us, heaving the last of the bone bolts that they would be firing at Baranzil from here thanks to the ballista. Both were enchanted to throw their payloads faster the farther and higher up they were compared to the target, plus some other little bonuses.

All of this had been from the stuff I'd gotten from the Kirin pool, the guardian loot, and stuff that Bokassa and Balmur had managed to gather from their hunts with the mermaids.

Balmur wore a robe made of Jinx's fur, trimmed with black and scales sewn on the inside for added protection, leather pants made from the wyvern materials we had gotten, and boots made from the chameleon-like beast James had killed to save Muu.

"And I will be making sure we have cover here as well, thanks to the items we enchanted." Balmur smiled at me and tapped the stake he held as he slammed it home into the ground. "This is going to be a lot of moving parts, you sure we can handle this?"

"Yeah, I know we can." I gave them both a nod as I turned and jumped off the cliffside to shift and fly down to our trap area where the others would lie in wait.

Maebe and Vrawn couldn't have been any more opposite each other. Maebe wore black metallic-looking bone mail, shoulders covered by two small skulls painted red and purple that had glowing gems in the sockets. She moved quietly and carried a rather large axe that made me smile. She had wanted to give it to me, but liked it so much she had decided to use it.

Vrawn wore leather dyed black and purple to match her Queen, and carried both Arc Cutter and a new sword called Whisper. Which was funny considering it was a greatsword made from the jawbone of the wyvern that we had killed, serrated with the blade-like teeth that were still in it, the gums having been replaced by metal and sharpened as well. It was enchanted to be nearly impossible to lift by anyone who wasn't Vrawn, or chosen by the sword, and she could swing it almost as easily as she did Arc Cutter.

I also added lightning damage to it because I wanted her to have a matching set.

Muu wore sky-blue metal-like bone armor with more spikes and scales on it that were raised and sharpened but just enough not to hurt him. Not that it would matter with his amount of health, and the level of defensive buffing I had put onto it to make him a literal tank. Plus, he got some awesome boots that he was excited to try out.

"Gravity boots!" He cackled manically as he hopped around in them. "They may take all my mana to use, but I cannot *wait* to use them!"

I rolled my eyes and turned my gaze to Yohsuke and James where they sat getting ready. Yohsuke had a set of leather and fur armor on under a short cloak, all of it colored blood red and enchanted to provide both protection and increased damage to his vampiric abilities.

James had nearly no armor on, his pants having been padded to help somewhat but that was all he could have. No, this time he sported updated tattoos along his body thanks to Maebe's tattooing Fae. I could never remember the guy's name; he was so bland and forgettable.

He had used the elemental essences that we had along with several bits of blood and powdered bone to give the winged bastard some serious buffs. Even going so far as to tattoo lines on his wings that were meant to do something that only James knew of and he wasn't going to share.

His other tattoos looked like cartoon drawings of the creatures from which the elements had been collected. It was hard to look at, but they seemed to add to his power and defense a lot.

That left us with ol' Jaken after that, and his new plate mail was amazing and much of what I had always hoped to see him in.

It was called Leviathan's Scales, and I had barely had to touch it as the armor itself had come powerful already. It was highly resistant to water damage, and the wearer could swim like the water dragon had been able to in life. I had added more water damage resistance, as well as adding a gem to it that would recharge a small defensive shield like it had on the Pussy Willow. It wouldn't do much if Jaken wasn't attacked by water, or in the water first, but it was a little added insurance and we needed that right now.

The armor looked like Orlow'thes' scales, dark and forbidding with a slightly lighter underbelly, but the scales there were harder than diamond so the fact that they had been penetrated at all was surprising and a tad daunting.

His sword, much like Vrawn's, was made from the jawbone of a beast, but the enchantment was a lot more dynamic since both he and Balmur had been able to help me fuel and create it. The holy weapon would smite the absolute tits off anything it touched with radiant lighting and fire. I was surprised that the two elements had come to work so well together, but we would take it.

I nodded to him as I passed, he lifted a hand in a mock salute and I rolled my eyes at him.

Carefully, I stepped out onto the empty ground in front of us. We had cleared the area swiftly using the trees to what we hoped was greater effect than they had above ground. There were multiple traps here, and we had to hope that the sudden shifting would be enough.

I took a deep, steadying breath and let it go before tapping Jaken on the shoulder to let him know. "It's time."

Jaken stepped forward and began to radiate red energy like a cloud around his body. The sky above us darkened as the wind whipped furiously over the waves. He turned his gaze back to me, their glowing red irises looking more beastly than his own. He nodded once and turned back to the waves that crashed into the beach hundreds of feet from us and opened his mouth.

A long, mournful bellow that started off soft burst from his mouth, then rose in both bass and pitch, becoming more of a roar than a howl. The wind stilled and the clouds above us darkened further before there were answering bellows behind us, the beasts of the continent supporting their new guardian in issuing his challenge.

The call went unanswered for a moment more before the red cloud of violently swirling energy cloying the air around the paladin thickened and formed into chains, his desire for retribution and revenge forming and shaping them, their ends becoming sickles before shooting into the ocean at a frightening speed.

We had only to wait another half an hour as the storm around us continued to brew and threatened to boil over. The creatures of the land and sea venturing closer to see what was going on, only to be greeted with the perfect image of the Mother's Fury and the gods' wrath standing beside each other —waiting.

Deeper than even I expected, Jaken snarled and the chains of his enmity stopped flowing forward and pulled taut, his voice straining as he grasped them and *pulled*. "Get your evil ass up here and pay up!"

As he pulled, the chains piled behind him and the waters before us boiled and roiled as if on fire. After another two minutes, our quarry had arrived.

Baranzil broke the surface of the water and began to laugh. "You think you can handle me? Ha! I'm stronger than even your puny guardians now!"

"Go, Jaken. Get out of the way," I spat and he ran off to the back where the others waited in the shadows.

"Think you can get away?" Water gathered around the General's mouth, his kraken body grotesque and malformed, even more so than the last time we had fought. I lifted off of the ground just in time for his blast of water to miss me and hit Jaken squarely in the back, my eagle wings working overtime as I flew up.

I knew that Muu had seen the attack and my lift off because Kayda reached out, *Now, Father!*

I shifted into my fox-man form and used Switch on Baranzil.

Suddenly I was surrounded by water and his gargantuan bulk appeared hundreds of feet in the air, tentacles and arms flailing ineffectively as he plummeted.

A blur from above made me smile, even as I stood on the water and sprinted toward the shoreline. Muu slammed into Baranzil's open head and they plummeted even faster as his gravity boots made them fall like sixty tons of shit from a rocket. Muu's savage cry almost drowned out the fear in the bastard's voice but we weren't done with him by a long shot.

He crashed into the hardened and sharpened tree spears below, enchanted for strength and coated with Muu's venom and from my vorpal viper forms to make him as sick as we could possibly make him before the rune traps that Balmur made activated upon contact. The explosions rocked us all, the blast leaving bloodied stumps behind as the General reeled from the blows.

Bolts peppered his upper body, their guardian-toxin-laced payloads electrocuting him and bringing him below half health with another six blasting him with incendiary rounds that melted and covered him in iron.

Vrawn, Muu, James, and Yohsuke surrounded him and ran from the trees that still stood after the blasts. There weren't many of them left, but the General's tentacles whipped out and defended his body from the main attack as the casters and Bokaj began their assault.

But Bokaj didn't fire any more arrows this time as Tmont sprang onto one of the tentacles that came for him, batting it aside so he could work.

His voice carried for what had to be miles, gently at first, then turning harsh as the answering calls from the water behind me took on a lulling beat like a supporting choir. The mermaids had come, and they summoned the beasts of the land and ocean with them.

Raiko wolves launched themselves from the northern portion of the land, the trees not hindering their movements. Or their massive leader's stride. The elephant-like beast that I had seen fighting before blasting a note of challenge from its long trunk and charging the kraken, tusks flashing in the crackling lightning above us.

Kayda's vengeance dropped on Baranzil, her lightning crashing into the metal melted on his side, blasting more of his health away.

My mouth opened and a fervent howl of absolute rage rushed out of me, adrenaline pulsing through my veins as I cast Aspect of the Storm and felt my fur stand on end. The elephant and winged raiko wolf struck the same time I stomped my feet in front of the kraken and grinned savagely as I grasped Hubris. I charged Lightening Storm for twenty seconds, dumping my absolute most into it, but what made me grin this savagely was the fact that Balmur and Maebe had their own plans.

I released the spell and the blast of lighting energy poured out of me and into a funnel of ice and magic, taking the energy and channeling it into a thinner, more powerful line like a laser beam.

Blood splattered against me as a tentacle tried to ward the shot off, but my attack sawed through it like a knife through butter. More red life fell away. A larger portion leaving built the surprise that Baranzil now had more tentacles, and lifted the elephant off the ground the same time that a new tentacle crashed into me, sending me flying toward the water.

Something stopped my flight and healing energy put me back up to 90%. "Don't go flying on my account, friend."

I turned to find Kyr and Sendak standing together behind me, their grins as savage as mine had been before my charge.

Kyr lifted his arm and electricity crackled through the air and a massive lightning elemental burst from the sand, glass forming where it stood. "We came here to help you, like we promised."

"Grateful," I grunted at him as the elemental spun away from me and toward the general in the distance.

I had no mana and that left me with little I could do other than attack with Magus Bane to get some more.

I lifted the great axe from my inventory and kissed it. "Nothing quite like an old-fashioned ass whoopin' eh?"

I still had my aspect active, so moving into combat range was insanely easy and swift, my axe clacking against the scaled limbs that swatted at everything. More swinging and my mana began to replenish faster as my attack speed quickened, Bokaj's song changing tune.

"Mighty limbs might dance and swing
But there's not a damned thing in the ring,
That can stand your might as I play and sing
Rise from the ground and make those attacks sting!"

His words rang out through me and I found that Vrawn, Muu, and James glowed blue with me. Our attacks were faster, we could almost guess where the return attacks would come from, and it was all I could do to keep from laughing in pure joy as every single time I swung my axe, I seemed to be growing stronger and so did they.

Bea and her brother Kaius ran circles around Baranzil, his attempts to attack them thwarted by their sheer speed and ability to walk on the air itself with little effort. When Bea's tail whipped out behind her and blood rushed from a line thirty feet from her, I knew I had done the right thing letting her pick her own stats.

Tmont bounded over and pounced on one of the raiko wolves who tried to attack us, then bounced over a tentacle and slashed at Baranzil with all her might.

Muu and James grabbed and pulled me out of the way when a tentacle almost impaled me. "Thanks!"

"Be our springboard!" Muu grabbed me into his arms like I was a sack of potatoes, shifting into my fox form in time for him to jump straight up with his other arm wrapped around James. Fifty, seventy, ninety feet into the air, his momentum faltered. He dropped me and I shifted into my Belgar form, his feet planting on my back and kicking down as hard as they could, which sent me plummeting toward Baranzil. I shifted twice and then flew toward the thing as an eagle before shifting and pulling out Magus Bane to attack.

I activated Charge, Cleave, and Epicenter as soon as I was close enough to actually hit the open spot on his head. The kraken cried out in pain, then pulled the elephant toward his fat-ass mouth and I instantly knew what he planned was bad.

Fuck it, I growled to myself, then out loud, shouted, "Pie time!"

"No!" Maebe bellowed back, but it was already too late. The elephant crashed down on top of the general's head in time for me to appear in the loosened grasp and cast Lightning Storm again, the energy shooting him right in the mouth.

He struggled, trying to grab me as Maebe soared over his limbs and grabbed me by the scruff of my neck, yanking me out of the way when he tried to bite me. "What did I say?"

I didn't have time for her fury to get to me, the elephant rolled off his head and Muu slammed down harder than before as Jaken, angel wings unfurled, unleashed a flurry of slashes and strikes from his weapon and closed fist that were almost blinding.

His sword flashed painfully, each strike leaving a line of radiant energy as his fury built. "You're done here, Baranzil, and not even the Hells will take you when we're done!"

"Mae, grab him with ice, I'll get him with shadows." Her sullen gaze found mine and I raised my voice. "*Now!*"

The temperature dropped to sub-zero levels in less than a heartbeat and ice crackled into place around the general's limbs as my shadows pooled around his lower body; I felt two more sets of wills with my own and the shadows thickened considerably.

"Lady Radiance, and Her armies on high, hear my cry," Jaken called loudly as he struck, his tempo increasing. "Make me your divine hammer and crush this evil that is within my sight, bestow me your gift—Divine Smite!"

His halo burned with bright light and his sword blazed, crackling with both flaming and electrical energy in equal parts, but it was the white light that flooded his eyes and golden energy coursing from Jaken's body down his arms that froze us.

He lifted his blade and it turned into a massive hammer of golden energy that he brought down with a cry of absolute fury, the light bending slightly as he brought his rage and vengeance down on the evil fuck.

I would swear even in the city miles and miles away, they would have been able to see the fallout of the celestial beat down that took place, as a radiant cloud of purifying white light in the shape of a mushroom cloud burst overhead. The explosion released a shockwave that shook the very foundation of the rocks and earth beneath us and made anyone who stood fall to their knees or asses from the sheer awesome strength of it.

As the radiant radiation cleared and the debris and raining blood stopped falling over our heads, I noticed that both the elephant and the winged raiko no longer moved.

Their bodies faded next to the crater that the general left behind. No longer living and his gear left for us, we took stock of what had happened as Jaken fell to the ground, unconscious.

It seemed that a portion of the ice had been broken and Baranzil had been able to attack the paladin, his armor saving him from the worst of it, but the bastard had once again penetrated the water guardian's scales.

I hit Jaken with every healing spell I had, Sendak and Kyr joining me as they could, limping closer to us. Jaken's body lifted from the ground as Maebe lifted him from below with her shadows, his eyes opening slowly.

Yohsuke sighed with relief, falling onto his ass exhausted just like the rest of us. "Thank God. What kind of shitty group lets their healer die?" He glanced over at Maebe. "Choice work with the shadows that saved me from that nuke, Majesty."

She smiled and nodded once to him before looking over to Jaken. "Are you alright?"

Jaken smiled for the first time I had seen in a while, a true, relaxed smile. "A shittier one than what we have, buddy. I'm not going down that easily."

"Yeah, he's the guy in the relationship," Muu added and the rest of us groaned as Maebe and Vrawn looked at him in confusion. He just shook his head and fell over with a grin on his face.

"What do we do now?" James raised his voice over the low groans and several of us looked at each other. "We still don't know where the other general is, right? Other than she's somewhere here on this continent?"

"That's the way it had seemed to me in that dream, and with the ship coming this way, all the demon supplies being delivered to this continent." I scratched my head as Balmur and Bokaj jogged over toward us, Bokaj waving to the mermaids as they retreated into the waves and surf.

"Should we check on the folks back home?" Yohsuke's voice sounded almost groggy as he spoke; he looked wiped. "I need to sleep, like, so much in my coffin. I'mma nail that bitch shut."

"Yeah, I can always do that I suppose, I do have the means to create a spell like that." I sighed at the thought of another spell being added to my already vast repertoire.

"I can do that, Z," Balmur said, pulling his spellbook from the holster on his hip, flipping it open. "Give me a minute, and I can create a long-range message spell. Oh! And I have our ride home. I learned an awesome new spell, kind of like a modified version of Teleport."

He sat down with his book and a quill and began to pour over a spell that he had written down already. I guessed I'd have to just be patient if I wanted to avoid the work, and after that fight? I happily would.

We sat in silence for a moment, the chests from the beasts ready for Jaken to open any time he was ready and the gear that we hoped the general left behind in his crater.

"You can be so misguided at times." Maebe's abrupt interruption of my reverie made me tilt my head her way. "Switching places with that beast like that, you could have been devoured, and then where would we be?"

"I would have been inside that fucker, blasting him like the heartburn we all know I would be." I grunted and shook myself out. "You know better than I do what would have happened if he had eaten that beast. He would have healed, or even grown stronger—I couldn't let that happen. Not so close to him dying."

"Zeke did the right thing, my love," Vrawn added on my behalf.

"You need not defend him to me, Vrawn," Maebe warned the other woman testily, her eyes narrowed dangerously.

"I shouldn't need to, as what he did was brave—stupid—but brave." She smiled at me, her tusks flashing as she did so. "What more could we tell our children if he had died than that he did his best to protect his friends and loved ones the best way he knew how? We could not do so if he had been too afraid to act and the worst came to be."

"Are a warrior's instincts so important to you, Vrawn, that the father of our children put himself in harm's way needlessly when others could do something about it?" Maebe rose from where she had knelt before and only came up to the larger woman's navel as she stared up.

"Bravery is everything to my kind," Vrawn insisted and nodded to Maebe. "You complain about him putting himself in danger 'needlessly' when you and I fight alongside him despite our conditions. Tell me, Maebe, is that truly what is wrong?"

"I am stronger than I have ever been!" Maebe retorted bitterly.

"You're avoiding the question, my love," I whispered and she stiffened.

"I know that you would miss him should anything happen to him—I would as well." Vrawn put a hand on Maebe's shoulder before kneeling in front of her. "If you wish him to survive, like he wishes for us to survive, we need to be prepared. It is you and I who risk the most. It is we who hold him back in this trying time."

Maebe sniffed, and I watched as a single tear rolled down her cheek as Vrawn pulled her closer to her chest in a fierce hug. Maebe muttering, "I do not wish to hold anyone back. All I want is my family."

I stood and walked over to them both, pulling both women against my chest in a tight hug. "I'm not going to die in a fight here, ladies. I will do everything in my power to protect the people I love. You both, and my brothers. All the people on this planet. I'll fight for all of you. Then we can have our family."

A twinge of sadness and guilt ate at me, my breath caught and I had to fight against my own morose thoughts. Instead, I had to focus on the here and now. I had to keep fighting to protect everyone. Here and at home.

"Guys!" Balmur's voice rang out like a bell that drew all our attention. We turned as one to the Azer dwarf. "She's not here."

"What?" Yohsuke sat up, his fangs flashing in the light.

"What she said!" Muu spat and hopped onto his feet. "What the fuck's that supposed to mean?"

"She's. Not. Fucking. *Here!*" Balmur said slowly. "I just spoke to Fainnir and he's said that there's something going on in Lindyberg. Something big. The people are acting weird and they're preparing for war."

"Well they were getting ready to fight the folks from Zephyth, weren't they?" Jaken rubbed his head.

"No, dude, they weren't," Balmur answered and my heart nearly stopped. "Their first fight was a draw, the governess in Lindyberg summoned demons. A horde of them, and the one who is leading them is her, but she's so different now that he swears she's possessed."

"Looks like we found out who is summoning demons against Archemillian's wishes." Bokaj harrumphed then looked at the rest of us. "Well… what do we do, guys?"

Yohsuke, Jaken, and the others looked to me for some reason, Vrawn and Maebe looking up, waiting for me to say something.

I shook my head and frowned before muttering, "Looks like we're going to have to go into the fray."

End Book Six

Wait. What? Hell no. Come on, big guy—the story just started getting good and I swear to every god that is listening, if you give me that badass line and end the book there, I will stop telling you these stories.

No man, these folks have lives they need to get to. Stuff to do. You really think they want to read this next bit?

Bitch, I know they do! Muu, tell him.

I swear to God, if you don't finish this, I will cry.

Okay?

And blow my nose on your eulogy.

Oh.

Seriously, boss, we want this to go on. Right, guys?

Yup. Uh, huh. Sure, sounds good to me.

Fine, fine. But this is it. Think you guys can handle that?

...No? Who the hell could handle that shit? Just keep typing, big guy—we got this shit.

Very well.

CHAPTER NINETEEN

"Alright, Jaken, you get that gear over there out of those chests and let's see what kind of loot that asshat dropped for us, if any." We began to move and see about our tasks as Kyr and Sendak came over to speak to Maebe.

"Yo, Zeke!" Jaken called and motioned me over into the crater. "Come here."

I rolled my eyes and popped over the side of the crater, sliding down to the center of it where he stood and motioned me toward a great axe. The haft of it was a little longer than I was used to, but it was massive and I could tell how heavy it was right away.

Kraxen
+24 to attack and damage, +26 water damage.
Sticky fingers, will return to you when thrown.
Rulers of the sea hardly ever have to worry about their prey knowing where they are, they just have to understand their time as lunch has yet to come.

I grinned and hefted the weapon. It wasn't too much of an awkward weight, but it would take some effort to throw if I had a mind to. "You sure you want me to take this?"

Jaken shook his head. "Dude, who else is going to use that monstrosity if not you?"

"That's fair. He drop anything else?" I glanced around and he shook his head again. "Alright. Well, get that gear in the chests and let's go see Anisamara before we leave, to repair our gear and get the best she has to offer. If we're going to fight the bitch over there and a horde of demons, we need the best that we can get."

He nodded and went off as I remembered to call out to Balmur, "Message Anisamara to let her know that we're going to be on our way and that she shouldn't stab me."

"Already did first thing, man." Balmur chuckled to himself and grinned. "We also got those ballistae as well, those will likely help, right?"

"Yeah, man, we can get some holy damage going on 'em." He nodded and walked off as I turned to the others.

They stood, ready but weary, beaten up and exhausted. "We won't go into a battle right away, but we need to go sooner rather than later. And we should make sure that Sunrise is okay too."

"How are we going to fight that many demons?" James sounded worried for once and I could see that he was a little frightened, his face tight and pinched.

"The same way we did in the Hells, fool." Yohsuke snorted. "Viciously and without remorse when they die. We can do this thing and, if you haven't noticed, I leveled up again from that fight. A few times. I reckon we all did. We're stronger than them and we won't quit. So let's stop being scared and get pissed off."

I nodded at him and offered him a fist, bumping his against it before turning to see to my own thoughts and fears. Then remembering. "Yohsuke, go check in with Archemillian and tell him we found out who is responsible. If he wants to send backup, we will take it. I think we're probably going to have to go in guns blazing and balls deep for this one. It ain't gonna be easy."

"Pft, when is it ever?" He rolled his eyes and walked off, shadows seeping into the tree line and covering him in a dome.

"I can summon the Fae to us," Maebe advised as she stepped closer to me, Vrawn joining her. "We can have many of them here in no time at all if we use that item to thin the veil."

"That would leave us overextended, and we need to honor our deal to Kyr and Sendak here. As much as I would love to have the numbers to stand up against these assholes, I can't risk that." I growled as I thought on it some more, but stopped and shrugged, at a loss.

Maebe nodded once and remained silent and contemplative for a moment, then grinned. "I am going to go speak to someone for a moment, I will return."

I went to say something but she was off and away before I could. I shook my head and turned to my own business, there was nothing I could do until the group was ready to go, so I figured I'd go through my notifications.

Oh yeah, I'd leveled up six more times, but that didn't make sense. How had we gotten that much experience from him? "Yoh! You get a lot of experience from that guy?"

"Him?" He pointed to the crater and shrugged. "Yeah, but we also killed the other two beasts and at least twenty-five smaller wolves that were caught in the crossfire. Plus, he was level, like, eighty-six or something?"

"Seriously?" He rolled his eyes at me and I just growled at him. "Stop being a dick."

"Since when have I ever?" He flipped me off and chuckled as he walked away while humming a tune to himself. "By the way, I'll pass word from the demon shithead here before we leave."

My breath burst from me in a massive sigh. "You keep weird company, Zeke." My mouth twitched up in a smile and I turned my sights to my stats and notifications.

I added three and four to my Strength and Dexterity to put me at eighty each. Then ten to both Constitution and Intelligence, and the final three points I spent in Charisma to round it to twenty-five.

I felt prettier, and I also knew that I would be a little more potent in my casting and fighting. Let's hope it would be enough to face the horde of demons waiting for us.

Congratulations!

Abilities Unlocked!

As of level 60, you have gained Perfect Shift. This ability allows you to shift from any form you currently reside in to another of your choosing, animal or natural.

"Oh, that's going to be useful as fuck," I muttered to myself before a boisterous bout of laughter reached my ear.

"I caught up?" Muu shouted loudly, his delight evident. He looked James square in the face. "I caught up to you and I'm stronger than you? Ha!"

He started dancing. His large, thick tail waving behind him as he shook his ass made me snort and Vrawn just chuckled next to me.

I glanced over at her and touched her shoulder. "Thanks for defending me, and giving reason to my thoughts. Honestly, I reacted without really even thinking about it."

"I know." She brushed her hand over my head and easily pulled me close. "Warriors react more on instinct in combat than they realize. While she is a warrior queen of sorts, Mae has a way of still judging her actions as they come, or outplanning people as time goes on. Must be a Fae thing."

I snorted and she laughed with me, the sun glistening off her smile and the mirth in her eyes making them sparkle just right. It hit me that I was close to accomplishing more than I had ever done in my life, and I owed part of that to this woman next me. "I love you."

She smiled wider and pressed her large forehead against mine. "I love you as well."

"Cut the soap opera shit and let's get a move on. We got bogeys coming in from the north, and it looks like there are lots of them," Yohsuke called, the rest of us scrambling to our feet.

We all moved closer together, Maebe the last one to join us as the birds, various water-affiliated avian creatures of differing types, started to circle above us and call to each other. I cast Teleport as Maebe touched James' shoulder and we all landed in Anisamara's shop.

For once I was glad we had warned her ahead of time, since she had a rather wicked-looking scythe in her hands, but it was the dozens of glowing eyes in the darkness that bothered me.

"Maebe, are those ones ours?" I didn't dare look away from them as several misshapen creatures stepped from the shadows to stand still beside Anisamara.

"Yes, I called them all here to assist Kyr and Sendak in getting their people out." Maebe stepped closer to me and lifted a hand. "Kyr and Sendak will be giving orders to you shortly. You are to assist them however is needed, and defend them in a manner befitting of the Unseelie Court. Do not fail me."

They all lowered their heads and turned to regard the other two Druids standing off to my right. Sendak was the first to speak. "For now, we have already started the rumors that the Fae will be coming to guide our people out. If one of you could go out and find the elderly and infirm, bring them here so that we might take them. Ten or so at a time, please."

One of the shadowed creatures stepped back into the inky darkness and disappeared.

"Alright, y'all," Yohsuke began, holding his hands up to get our attention. "Archemillian, the bitch that he fuckin' is, can't send us anything to help, because demons aren't allowed to interfere with demons on other planes of existence, so he's out. He did, however, give us an extension on the whole sending an evil Balmur to try to kill ours, so there is that. He also let slip that if we can kill the summoners, the demons will be released and return to their natural homes, or they can be sent home like Nicolas did with Maebe."

I nodded and looked over at Balmur, who shook his head.

"I'm not that strong yet, but if the Braves are there, I will let him know so that we can use that avenue to fight back."

"Good to know, bud." I patted him on the shoulder. "Anisamara, I know that it might be a little outside your purview, but we need repairs and to give you some mats to make more weapons and shit for us. I'm talking the works. Hell, accessories too. That cool?"

"You mentioned demons?" I nodded and she smiled savagely. "I hate demons. Give me a few hours."

"Good to go." I turned back to the group. "You heard the lady. I'll enchant what I can. If you need to sleep and rest, by all means do it, but be sure you allocate your points before you do. We want to be the fuck out of here by tomorrow morning at the latest to get to the other continent as soon as possible."

"Zeke?" Balmur tapped my shoulder and I glanced at him. "That won't be necessary. That spell I told you about? It's called Gate. It allows me to go places I've been before. It takes a shit ton of MP, but I can manage it and get us to Sunrise easily."

"Fuckin' A, I love wizards," I grumbled as I grinned at him. "You'll be our Uber then. Cool? You need anything for it? Components or the like?"

"A wand, but that's easily made, I think, if Anisamara can handle that?" She looked at him as if he had just challenged her for the rights to her shop and he lifted his hands up. "She can handle it just fine, it seems."

"Cool, good shit." I grinned some more and sighed, finally as exhausted as I felt. Maebe and Vrawn had gone off together to speak amongst themselves and I just fucked off to a corner of the room and laid on the ground for a light nap.

CHAPTER TWENTY

I woke up a few hours later, better rested than I had been, to all of my friends snoozing and Maebe sitting vigil next to both Vrawn and I.

"Hello, my love," I whispered to her so that I wouldn't wake Vrawn.

"Hello, Zeke." She placed a hand on my chest and smiled down at me. "Did you rest well, my King?"

"Well enough, how about you?" She shook her head and frowned into the darkness across the cavernous room. "Not at all?"

"No," she whispered back. "I have much weighing on my mind and heart, and there is little time to dwell on it."

"What's on your heart?"

"I want you to return to your world." She turned to look at me and I could see there was true hurt and uncertainty behind her gaze.

"We both do," Vrawn agreed tiredly and kissed my shoulder.

"Why is this coming on now?" I sat up and stared at them

both in disbelief. "I've just been thinking of that myself, what's going on? Why do you feel the need to reiterate?"

"Your child on Earth will grow without you, and will be able to live a life of nothing but wondering where his father was." Vrawn yawned and sat up with us. "I did not know my family and I have wondered my entire life if I did something wrong to deserve that. No child should have that happen to them. You deserve to be a part of his life as he deserves to be part of yours."

"But what about our children? Both of them." I ground my teeth at having to have this same conversation yet again. "Both of *you*."

"We will have each other, and I have decided that I will also perform the blood rite on Vrawn once she has her child." Maebe sat a little straighter and blinked at me. "I will not risk her child, and I will not risk her. Once she is blooded, she will be immortal as I am."

"What about the chance that the blooding kills her?" My heart raced and I looked between them both trying to find some semblance of calm but nothing came.

"I am aware of what could happen, but I would face it so that I do not have to allow our children to see me wither and die before… certain events in their lives." Vrawn cupped my cheek and I leaned into her caress cautiously before I even thought of trying to say anything.

"We have thought of everything that we can," Maebe offered softly, her hand reaching for mine. "We can only offer you that they will hear stories of you as often as we can allow them to, and they will know of your sacrifice for them."

"I wonder if someday I could come back here." Where I sat was suddenly too hot as Maebe and Vrawn shared a look of concern for me. I took the queen's hand to squeeze it lightly. "I think I need to think on some stuff before I decide anything. But you make a sound argument."

I let go and stood moving to the table to start enchanting anything I could get my hands on. There was armor for Jaken that he bought on his own that I was going to need to enchant to withstand demon attacks. Some gear and whatnot.

Using Hubris, it was easy to make his armor a radiant equivalent to a walking anti-demon time bomb. Anything that got too close to him that could be harmed by holy damage would be taking damage over time and it wouldn't be pretty for them. That meant that we would need to keep Yohsuke away from him, but he could heal himself with blood, so I wasn't too terribly worried about him.

I also gave him some rings that added to his healing distances and even gave him a ring of mana storing to keep more heals and damage flowing. He would be a crux for our assault on the city. Hell, I had even been able to make the ring myself, which I was rather proud of.

Once I was finished, I noted that I was halfway to grand-master level in enchanting. *Wonder what it would be like to reach grandmaster enchanting?* I looked around, wondering if I would ever see this place again. Brindolla. Maebe. Vrawn. Kayda and Bea.

All my friends here.

You can't let this get you down, Zeke. Seriously, I growled at myself mentally. *Butch up, and handle your shit. At the very least, you'll leave a legacy behind for your kids. They can love and live happy lives because of the shit you'll be doing.*

Staring at the others for a moment, turning to see Maebe and Vrawn comforting each other with soft words, made me think more. *Maybe you can request that Radiance pull you back here once your boy is old enough? Or when you pass? Who knows. All that matters is that they're safe and there's hope for them.*

"Get up, you lazy bastards, it's time to get a move on." The others sat up, ready to fight but realized it was just me. "We have places to be, demons to kill, and a world to save."

They grumbled and growled but moved about well enough to get on their feet and start gathering themselves and their gear.

"We're going to need backup we can trust, but we need the

full story." I glanced over to Balmur who yawned and nodded. "Think you could get word to one of the Braves for me?"

"Yeah, let's get to Sunrise first." He opened his book and stood waiting beside the wall to the cavern.

"Thanks for all your hard work, Anisamara, it was lovely to make your acquaintance even with the stabbing." I grinned at the woman and she just frowned at me in return.

I stepped closer to the Azer dwarf and he began muttering a spell and making large motions with a bone wand in his hand. He tapped the wall three times, then a large, blackened doorway with spirals of reds, greens, yellows, and blues swirled before us.

"Go!" Balmur barked and I was the first one through with the others moving behind me.

When the swirling ceased, I found that I stood outside of Dillon's tavern in Sunrise. The village looked a little different from our time away, but not too terribly much.

There were new buildings closer to the tavern than before, and definitely more dawn elves than before too. Some of them stared at us as we piled through the spell and more than a few of them backed away even as I smiled and waved toward them.

"By the gods, is that you, Zeke?" Willem's voice rang out left of where I stood, and I turned to find the old Paladin wearing tarnished mail and a sword on his hip. "It is, thank the gods, you are just in time."

"What's going on?" He grabbed me by the shoulders and pulled me into a tight hug.

"Demons in the forest, they've been harassing the bears who patrol the area and attacking our hunters." His eyes widened as the others found their way through. "Thank Lady Radiance Herself you all have returned. Please, help us slay these demons."

A feral snarl escaped from me before I could reign myself in and I spun on my heel to walk away.

I summoned my will and called to Yve and Servant. Both came, though Yve actually resisted me at first. Once they appeared before me, I leveled my gaze at her. "You had your revenge, Yve. I don't know why you resisted my call, but we have shit to do. Can I trust you?"

She glowered at me before bowing her head. "I am only upset I did not get to give the killing blow. I trust that he is dead and gone?"

"He is." Servant nodded before she could look at him and their attention was mine wholly. "Demons are in the forest. I want you to find and kill them. *All of them.* And keep my people safe. That includes the bears as well. Go!"

Both of them turned and bounded over the fence protecting the village, savage snarls and hellish cries filtering into the darkened sky immediately.

"That answers that question," Bokaj muttered and took out his bow. "How close are they and what are we killing?"

"Demons harassing the bears and villagers." My voice held notes of rage that I hadn't felt since my wolf hadn't been contained. "They've sent scouts to root out our home to keep us distracted while they build their forces."

"Then we will need to retaliate in kind," Maebe spat, her own anger rising over mine through our connection. She spoke a few words and shadows around us thickened.

"We need to call our allies to us and fast." I turned to Balmur, "I need you to get both the Mugfist Clan and King Telfino, let them know what's going on, and we will see about getting them to the battle grounds as swiftly as possible. I want their best people and I want them ready to go as soon as we can get them to the front lines."

"Dude, cool it with the king-level ordering." Yohsuke grunted as one of the others smacked him. "No, he's not going to put them all in danger." He looked at me and motioned to the others. "You, me, and them are all immune to the general's influence. If the others get involved, they can be used against us and that puts us all in danger."

"So we just have them fight at a safer distance." I frowned at him and he just shrugged. "The army hasn't been turned, have they?"

"No," Balmur answered, listening to something then opening his eyes. "Manly just told me that the demons are fighting with some of the citizens among their ranks, but the army is moving of its own volition and holding the line. But without casters, they're sitting ducks to the demons' attacks."

"So then maybe she's doing something different," James offered after a moment, his hands moving back and forth as he thought. "What's their goal?"

"To create as much mayhem and chaos as possible so that it distracts the gods," Willem answered readily. "Once they are distracted, their attention will turn from the fight above and let War and his legions in to take over."

"And who better to call to the gods than mortals at war with demons," Vrawn reasoned and looked to Yohsuke. "She won't allow them to be taken over by her influence so that they will call to their various gods."

"So then there is a way." Muu clapped his hands together. "We have to get them help, Yoh. Zeke has the right idea. They need healers and the best fighters we can manage. All of the help we can get, and while the demons are distracted, we have a way to get into the middle of the city to get to her."

Finally, Yohsuke nodded and gave me the "Sorry, man," look before I shook my head. No apologies, we just had to get this shit going.

While Balmur worked, we moved on to get ready for the fight. Rowland and Vilmas worked to give the village enchanted means by which to defend itself, so I added my prowess to theirs as Jaken helped the smiths.

We created spikes for the fence and arrowheads that would pierce their flesh and kill them with holy damage while swords and pikes would kill by hand.

We worked for what felt like hours, resting every once in a while to replenish mana and eat.

"The dwarves are ready, Zeke." Balmur rushed into the

smithy and grabbed me. "I need to know if we're going to the battlefield or not."

"Yes, we will. If I get you to them, will you be able to get them to the plains around the area?" He nodded, then I turned to Jaken. "Let the others know we're getting our allies to the battlefield." He nodded before I reached out and tapped Balmur's shoulder and cast Teleport.

We popped out of it at the runed doorway to the city of Djurn Forge, finding six of the Ironnose guards waiting to usher us inside. "C'mon, lads!"

The traditional greetings set aside, we rushed in to find more than two hundred dwarves waiting with more piling into the area.

"Mugfist!" One of the first dwarves to see us bellowed and the entire city echoed with cries from the clan as they greeted us.

Farnik and Gerty sprinted over to us with their weapons on their hips and armor ready, grim and ready expressions firmly set upon their faces. Farnik was the first to reach us, his beard a bit more than a finger's length now. "Lads, we heard a wee bit about the tiff topside, an' figure we should join in. Ye donnae mind sharin', do ye?"

"Not at all." I pulled the smaller man into a fierce hug. "You don't mind fighting demons, do you?"

"Lad, we'd have faced the entirety o' the Hells for one o' our own—ye really think we would allow the demon hordes to threaten our whole *world*?" Gerty snorted and pulled Balmur close to give him a peck on the cheek. "Ye look a wee bit thin, lad. Ye eatin' proper?"

"Yes ma'am, just working out differently." The Azer dwarf grinned at her and winked. She chuckled and smacked his shoulder with her fist.

"We got every clan member we have here, an' a few volunteers seekin' the glory fightin' with heroes may bring," Farnik explained, then motioned to a platform. "Get up there an' brief 'em, let 'em all know what for."

Balmur and I hopped up onto it and the dwarves raised their voices in unison, sending chills down my spine.

"You start us off, Zeke?" Balmur clapped me on the back and stepped back, leaving me standing before hundreds of dwarves by myself. "Thanks."

I rolled my eyes and took a few breaths to steady my nerves before projecting my voice and calling, "Brothers and sisters! You stand ready to march into battle against demons summoned by a horrid creature who seeks nothing more than the annihilation of this planet. She seeks to end you, your families, and every other creature on this planets' walk along the Way."

I watched as the faces of those close to me turned downright murderous, clenching teeth and tugging at their beards; these dwarves looked ready to fucking *kill* someone.

"But we won't let that happen!" I roared and raised my fist into the air. The dwarves snarled and raised their weapons with hoots and hollers that threatened to make the earth around us quake.

"Dwarves of Djurn Forge, you stand ready to defend this planet, and keep true to the tenets of the Way—will you fight with us?" Their call in return was louder still and I watched in delight as the earth behind them raised and Fainnir stood on Grav's shoulder to scream too. "We need you to hold the line while we get the casters there, then rest up for our portion of the assault."

They all looked ready to fight right then and there, making me grin.

"Balmur, you're up." I shoved the dwarven wizard forward and he just grunted and stumbled.

"I'm going to cast a spell to get you all to the battlefield. Then we're going to get you some help from more casters." He motioned to the doorway off to our right. "Once you're through, keep moving! And by Fainne's beard, don't you *dare* die!"

The dwarves roared loudly, Farnik shaking his fists with

them in the air before one of the oldest dwarves I had ever seen stepped forward. He raised a mace before yelling, "The hammer falls!"

Balmur and I returned, "And rises again!"

The dwarves behind the elder bellowed together, "The path is long and winding, but never are we alone!"

"I'll need your help to cast this, Zeke." He and I rushed to the doorway and I called Hubris into my hand. "It'll only last a few seconds on my own."

Together, we cast Gate for the dwarves to sprint through, our mana draining despite Hubris keeping things even for us. The last dwarves made it through just before both of us collapsed, panting heavily with serious migraines.

It took about five minutes for both of us to recover enough for me to get us to T'agnolian Val. We arrived at the entrance where the guards nearly pincushioned us, but Balmur slapped the arrows away from us.

"Attack first and ask questions later is just annoying," I grumped loudly and the guard's horrified faces were enough for me to know they recognized us. "Yes, that was nearly aggravating, now if you'll excuse us, I need to get to King Telfino. Bye."

I cast Polymorph on Balmur, turning him into a finch before I sprinted off the cliff behind the guards and shifted into my eagle form.

I got there faster than he did, but then again, I was more used to flying than he was.

When I landed in front of the crystalline palace that the high elf king called home, I was delighted to see both him and Questis standing with more than a hundred elves with bows and staves in hand. I returned to my fox-man form and smiled.

"King Telfino, my friend." I pulled him into a hug and he laughed with me as he hugged me back.

"*King* Zeke, it is good to see you again, my friend." He patted my back and eyed me surreptitiously. "I see you have truly been to the other continent."

"I have, and the Mother has plans there, Telfino. I expect

she will make you aware of them as soon as she can." He nodded at me and I motioned to the elves who stood awaiting orders. "These who you're bringing?"

He nodded and smiled. "We have several other budding clerics of the Mother and many Druids, as well as other spell-casters. We are even bringing along archers to help, but are we really fighting demons?"

Balmur and I both nodded and he shook his head in disgust. "Get us there, my friend. And we will fight them for you."

"Thank you." I turned to Balmur who nodded and cast Gate once more. The elves sprinted through it with Telfino pulling up the rear with Questis and Fern on his heels. I touched Balmur once more and stepped through with him, just to see what was on the other side.

It was chaos and blood.

CHAPTER TWENTY-ONE

The stench of sulfur, copper, and shit bled into the air like a noxious perfume as the screams of warriors in battle against the chittering hordes of infernal demons echoed through the air.

Bodies writhed in the distance as the elves joined the fray, their bows snapping arrows across the distance with ease, the projectiles flying through the air to hit some and miss others but the main thing was that battle had been joined and there was little more than chaos before us.

Red and black beings surged forth once more, as the dwarves looked to have begun to add to the fight, their numbers matching the ferocity of the demons and then surpassing it tenfold as their weapons swung and blood splattered the ground and their armor.

I had trained for this while I was in the Marine Corps, the fog of war something all of us learned about but it was something spectacularly different from the dread and nervousness fighting my resolve. The ground slick with blood and bodies as the masses battled for supremacy over an open field was much different from the terrain of Afghanistan and Iraq's urban environments that had been drilled into me during bootcamp.

There was no sand here to dry and clot the blood and hide the guts.

Bile rose in my throat but I swallowed it down, and growled at myself, *Get a fucking grip, devil.*

This is rather more gruesome than I thought it would be, Cieth muttered softly as he surveyed the carnage through me. *Why do you call yourself that?*

Retching beside me brought me to my senses and made ignoring Cieth's question acceptable as I found Balmur doubled over vomiting. At first, I thought it was due to the carnage below, but then I realized that he was also still terrified of the demons in the distance. His shaking and fear confirmed it as he fought to stand.

"Don't worry, bud, we're going to send these dicks back to where they came from." I patted his back and his fist rocketed toward my stomach. I stepped back as it grazed me, knowing he hadn't meant to lash out. "Balmur, it's okay. You'll be okay."

He stood, his eyes blood red. "Stop telling me that it will be okay!" Spittle flew from his mouth as he screamed at me. "It won't be alright until every last goddamned demon is dead!"

"And we're going to make that happen!" I barked, his attention all over the place as I spoke. "We need to rest up and plan right now!"

I stepped closer to him and his eyes zeroed back in on me. "Gate us back to the others, buddy. We can come back and get them all as soon as Teleport cools down if we have to."

He growled low, his hands twitching toward his weapons as he watched the movement and fighting in the distance. It looked to be much smaller than it had, the forces from the castle closing ranks to defend and make sure nothing got in. Fighting at night didn't look like it was a thing here.

They probably want the fighters to see what they're facing and what is happening to up the fear and everything. We might have until morning.

"Come on, Balmur, we need the others—let's go back."

He panted for a few more seconds before I raised a wall of

shadows behind me. His gaze not finding anything, he turned back to me. "Gate, right?"

"Yeah, back to Sunrise." He lifted his hand and went through the motions before I tapped his hand with Hubris and lent him the mana for the spell.

I shoved him through when he tried to push me and we ended up tumbling together as I shoved the shadows away from him before he could shadow step away from me.

We rolled and fought, his fist pummeling me as we appeared next to the tavern. "Let me go! I have to go back and fight them; I have to kill them!"

"Fuck, Balmur! We're all going to go together, you shitty prick, now stop hitting me before I slap the shit out of you!" He socked me right in my jaw as two ridiculously large hands grabbed us both and tore us away from each other.

"What the hell is going on here?" Muu grunted and yanked us both around to shake some sense into us as he looked back and forth. "We have demons to fuck up and you're going to pick a fight with each other?"

"His PTSD is acting up and he's lashing out. I was trying to keep him from doing something we might all regret," I spat as the dragon-kin set me down and I rubbed my lip. The bastard sure could punch, fuck.

Music started to play nearby and I noticed that Bokaj had walked in and seen what happened. "Hey Balmur, it's cool, broski. We're gonna get ours. Just chill."

The dwarf's fury faded slowly, his attempts to swing at Muu and clamber onto his arm ceding to an almost stupor-like state. Finally, he came back to himself. He blinked at the world around him as if seeing it for the first time. "Wha?"

"You're good now?" I raised a brow at him and he frowned. "Good. Let's get some more rest—the fighting looked to be a lot more calm than it had been from what they reported—eat and get ready."

They nodded, Balmur back on the ground at last before we

turned and went back into the tavern to enjoy a meal together as a family. A dysfunctional, mishmashed, and ridiculous family.

We ate in relative silence, all of us trying to come to terms with what we were about to go into, but none of us seemed to be ready to leave.

"It is done, my King." Servant's voice made me flinch and throw my cup into the air, the others instantly laughing at my distress.

I turned to look at him and Yve, both of them covered in gore and looking very pleased with themselves. "Thank you both."

"We would like to follow you into battle, my King and Queen." Yve bowed her head and lowered the front half of her big-cat body in a sort of animal-like curtsy. "I wish to atone for my... disruptive behavior before."

I glanced at Maebe and she nodded, my frown turning into a smile as I realized what that gave me. "Fine. You can accompany us, but your post is with the Queen and Vrawn."

"Zeke—" Maebe began but I held up a hand and shot her a look.

"You made your wishes known, and now I am making mine known." I turned from the suddenly sullen Unseelie and eyed the two Fae before me. "You will protect them both with your lives and kill anyone and anything that threatens them. My orders are absolute."

They both bowed low and answered, "As my King wishes."

Their unity in this made my skin crawl, but it was enough for me. I glanced at the others, toying with their food, sipping drinks but barely tasting them.

"For months, this has been the only home we've known." They raised their eyes to meet mine as I turned to each of them in turn. "We have fought, sweat, bled, and some of us have even died for these people. They have tried to kill us, secluded us, and some have given us their all. Brindolla is a home I never knew that I would want or need so badly as I do now."

Muu nodded his head, carefully avoiding my gaze as I

looked at him. "This place is so much more than anything I have ever experienced and I cannot think of anyone I would rather share it with. No matter what happens in this coming fight, I want you to know that I love you all. My brothers in arms, my brothers in spirit and blood. Thank you for being you, and thank you for being here."

I raised my cup in a toast. "To Storm Company."

The others raised their glasses, James and Yoh smiling softly, Balmur, Bokaj, Muu, and Vrawn quietly contemplating, but they raised their eyes to meet mine. Maebe raised her glass and stared at all of us. "To Storm Company and friendship."

We all grunted, "Here here." Then drank together.

Yohsuke stood, looking at each of us before smiling. "Get some rest, you sappy fucks. We attack at dawn."

We all went to our respective rooms, Vrawn and Maebe joining me for one last night together that we spent telling and showing each other just how much we meant to one another.

It was the saddest and most heartwarming thing I had ever experienced in my life, but because of them, I knew what it meant to find true love.

CHAPTER TWENTY-TWO

We woke to each other, I kissed both Vrawn and Maebe before walking out of my room and into the dining area to find Muu and Ampharia sitting together.

"Ampharia, what are you doing here?" She looked up at me and frowned before smiling in a way that was all too familiar. "Oh no."

I whipped around and grabbed a tiny being which had launched itself at my back, screeching, "Mommy!" at the top of their lungs.

I blinked in surprise at the tiny, child-like red dragon-kin who stared at me lovingly. "I brought your child, Zeke. I also came to... speak with Muu last night. It seemed that all of you were much too busy to come and visit me, so I decided to take the initiative."

I turned my gaze to Muu and he started whistling noncha-lantly, so I just shook my head and turned to the little thing in my arms. "I'm not your mommy, little one, we've been over this."

"Mommy!" She huffed and her tail lashed at my ankles as both Maebe and Vrawn laughed. She turned her head, fighting to look at both women until finally I had to set her on the floor. Her nostrils flared as she looked at them, then pointed. "Nestmates!"

"Oh for fu—they're my *actual* kids!" I tried to reason with her but she just launched herself at the two of them with arms open. Her horned head bobbing as she sprinted toward them.

Maebe held a hand out and she skidded to a halt, her tail swishing back and forth, smacking tables and chairs. "What, mommy mate?"

Vrawn's eyes widened in surprise and it was my turn to laugh as Maebe tried to get the little dragon in dragon-kin form to understand. "You must be cautious when you touch us, little dear, or you could hurt your nestmates."

"Traitor!" I loosed in a halfhearted snarl her way that only made her smile more.

"I be caush…" She seemed to have trouble with the word and I had to fight my paternal instincts to correct her as she decided on, "Conscious? Yeah, conscious of them."

I snorted and she glared at me as the little creature touched both of their stomachs, muttering, "Strong bellies."

The others joined us soon after for a snack and we had to say our goodbyes, Ampharia staring at Muu longingly before turning her attention on me.

"You must leave something behind for her to cling to when she misses you." The little dragon-kin girl held tightly to my leg as she spoke, her eyes squeezed tight.

I frowned and filtered through my inventory, finally deciding on one of the first things I had ever made. I pulled the great dagger out of my inventory and pulled her away from my leg. "Here, little one, this is for you, from me."

She took the dagger, still in the sheath, and held it to her chest.

"You'll keep that for me, okay?"

She stared at it for a second before nodding and returned to hugging me. I hugged her back, the misguided little thing, then scooted her toward Ampharia who grabbed her shoulder and pulled her close.

I turned to the others and nodded before we headed outside and found Willem waiting for us with Rowland, Vilmas, and Thogan standing together behind him.

"Ye didnae think we would be lettin' ye leave to fight these beasties on yer own, did ye?" Rowland smirked at us with his hammer in his hands at the ready. "Not sharin' in a fight be dangerously close to losin' yer Way, lads an' lasses."

Thogan nodded sagely. "All o' ye damned well be kin to me, 'specially me Queen." He bowed his head respectfully. "I'll be returnin' to yer service so's I can protect ye like I did yer mam."

Maebe shook her head and smiled at the craggily skinned dwarf. "I accept, on the condition that you protect your clan and kill as many demons as you can."

Thogan lifted his axe and grinned at the other two dwarves with him. "See? Told ye she would be for it. Come on, time to fight."

Vrawn stepped over to Vilmas and stared down at the other woman before holding out her hand. "We will protect each other, yes?"

"I'd not have it any other way, you puke-skinned beef cake." Vrawn laughed at the insult and pulled Vilmas close to her side before nodding to us.

"Let's go whoop some ass!" Yohsuke snarled as each hand in the area clasped. I smiled at his fervor and cast Teleport to take us to the battlefield.

———

We landed and all hell broke loose, both of Maebe's Fae protectors launching themselves at two large demons that lumbered toward us immediately. Their savagery reached new heights as they took the first down, Yve ripping off the arm holding a serrated blade and then shifted into her elven form to use the blade as if it were her own.

The blade slashed the other demon and cut it through the midsection as Servant slammed into it and tore, his jaws growing larger by the moment.

Cieth broke his silence to murmur, *I like these ones.*

I snorted and turned my attention to our surroundings. The Zephythians fought bravely, their banners waving proudly in the daylight as the sun rose, but it was the cacophony of screams and explosions just due west of us near the dwarven lines that drew my attention.

"That way, we need to help the dwarves before we go in to take out the summoners." Yohsuke beat me to the punch and I was already moving as he finished.

My feet pounded the slick earth beneath me, then I shook myself out and jumped as high as I could, taking Cieth's wyvern form, my massive tail slamming into several of the smaller demons and sending them careening into the air with screams and shrieks. I circled back and Muu, James, and Yohsuke hopped onto my back. Bokaj stuck with Balmur, grabbing my legs, and Maebe lifted the rest of the group with her shadows as we soared overhead.

We traveled swiftly, a battalion of soldiers from Zephyth cheering as we passed them, and Bokaj used silver-tipped arrows to pin down enemy forces while ground troops moved in for the kill. Tmont, Bea, and Kayda worked their way through the area below, cutting a bloody swath through the demons as they followed us.

I roared and breathed ice down on the demons below us, their bodies freezing as my mana drained slightly. James kicked a flying imp as it tried to attack me, and Yohsuke threw Star Bursts down into crowds of closely-gathered foes to great effect. Muu bounced off my back and jumped along beside us, stabbing and stamping and cackling as he blooded his weapon before hopping back onto my shoulders.

A familiar trundling porcine figure caught my attention and I found Humphrey's partner in crime a moment later, covered in blood with her bow in hand.

We landed and the only reason she didn't put an arrow in me was because Muu called, "Short stuff! How you bee—*oof.*"

He fell off my back with a metallic *ding* as an arrow fell out of the corner of my eye. "Now what did I tell you about callin' me names, ya idjit?"

"Ouch," was all that came from him as the others clambered off my back so I could shift.

"Zeke, that was you?" She hollered in surprise. "Well, I'll be, y'all really did head on over there, didn't you? How was the huntin'?"

"It was good—where are the other Braves, Manly?" I answered politely but she shrugged.

"I reckon they're 'round here somewhere. Bonnie got real worked up the last time we fought some demons, so I'd wager she's closer to the thick o' things, havin' her fun." She took a small rag and wiped some of the sulfurous gore off her cheek and forehead, but all that did was smear it a bit more. "Y'all fixin' to storm the city?"

"You know us." Yohsuke grunted as Jaken stepped too close and his skin started to blister a bit. He grunted and tried to smile at the woman. "You wanna come and party with us on the way in?"

Manly held a hand to her chest in surprise, glancing at Humphrey. "Why, Humphrey, I reckon we just got asked to the ball by one o' the sourest cusses this side the Lightning Mountains."

Muu coughed loudly and Yohsuke rolled his eyes. "You want to come and help us get in or not?"

Manly's grin spread across her face. "Why I do declare, sugar, I won't even charge y'all for this dance." She hopped onto her mount's back and stood in his saddle. "Go'n, Humphrey, *git.*"

The massive beast beneath her reared, bellowing an oink that made me almost freeze before he charged toward the city with reckless abandon, head low and tusks pointed to kill anything in front of him and his target.

"God damn, she's so cute!" Muu gushed as he glanced at me. "Ready to send in the cavalry?"

I nodded and summoned both Bea and Kayda with a mental call. "Bea, give Muu a lift. Kayda, make it rain, baby."

"Good thing I packed a fuckin' umbrella." Yohsuke rolled his eyes and pulled out a cloth that I enchanted for him for this very reason. He whispered the command word, "Yogurt," and the cloth floated from his hand up above his head like a ten-foot squared umbrella just for him.

The enemies under it wouldn't benefit from the cover because they'd be getting dead as fuck via his astral blade and crazy vampire skills.

As we jogged across the field behind Manly, we truly got to behold the brutal strength and resolve of the dwarves. They had laid waste to the demons before them and even though some of them looked to be actively resting, there were others still swinging their axes.

As they moved on, the high elves reached us, their casters cutting a swath through the demon forces and Telfino's magic burst over the injured dwarves like a tidal wave of healing energy that saw to the resurgence of their will to fight on.

One such dwarf, surprisingly, the old timer that I had seen, stood and cracked his back loudly before bellowing and leaping on one of the largest demons with his mace raised and beard flying in the wind.

"Y'all bring these ones here?" Manly called back and I just grinned at her. She rolled her eyes and shook her head. "Y'all never did keep normal company."

"Pot calling the kettle black?" James retorted and Manly lifted her bow to lash out at a demon that had gotten past one of the elven warriors and their astral blades.

We closed on the wall now, the rubble of it being augmented by larger and more mean-looking demons, their bodies swollen and muscled enough to make even Vrawn look tiny.

"I got these ones," Jaken barked back at us so we would slow down. "Muu, you and James take my flanks. Casters to the rear, but Bokaj, I want you singing."

"Bring the jukebox!" Bokaj hollered as he whipped out his guitar and began to strum a tune that picked up swiftly.

Jaken's armor pulsed white and gold as he closed the distance between himself and the four large demons that had noticed him. He lifted his sword and the shield that I had enchanted for him that Thogan and Rowland had whipped up over the time we had been away.

The shield looked like a fox's head but the mouth was open and from the outside, you could just barely see the ruby within that would spew holy flames like a dragon.

"Devious design, by the way." Maebe smiled and cracked her neck, turning her attention to me. "It is time for us to part ways, my love."

The discussion last night hadn't been pretty, but it had been crucial—Maebe and Vrawn being close to the action against the general left the rest of us vulnerable to them being used against us.

They would stay outside the city, deal with the demon casters and keep Telfino safe while we worked on the enemy from within. Not to mention, Maebe had also offered to be a catapult of sorts for us.

"I love you both," I shouted over the agonized screams of the demons falling to Jaken and the others. They nodded at me, no more need for words in that moment. "Light 'em up, baby."

Maebe's perfect white teeth flashed at me as massive pillars of ice with shadows writhing inside appeared overhead and dropped into the city. Soldiers behind us called out in dismay, then joy as they realized the magic was on our side.

"Zeke, we're through!" Yohsuke's voice turned my head and followed the others into Lindyberg.

CHAPTER TWENTY-THREE

Thanks to Jaken's demon decimating armor and Kayda's holy and healing rain, the demon denizens of the city stood next to no chance against our assault. We conserved our mana as much as we possibly could, casting the occasional healing spell here and there for those on our side who had managed to make it inside the wall.

The city was ruined. Blood and gore the only decorations among the now-destroyed shops and homes that had the fel creatures falling out of them and into them as the fighting grew worse.

Maebe's destructive volley had crushed dozens of demons, and the impact had exploded the ice with force enough that shards of frozen water pierced stone. Anything struck by that looked like a frozen pincushion and the creatures strong, or far enough away, to have lived died courtesy of our animal companions and small spell fire.

"Fuck, that armor is powerful," Yohsuke grunted as he fell back to heal himself once more by touching one of the human puppets and draining the life from him with just his hand. "Did you have to make it so strong?"

"Pulling out all the stops, remember?" I raised a brow at him and cast Winter's Blade at a group of five impish creatures skulking in an alleyway over a dead body that they probably ambushed.

The force from the explosion burst the first victim's head, the icy shrapnel tearing the wings off the others so that Muu could step in and stab them with an efficiency and cold-blooded ease I hadn't seen coming. Tmont saw something hiding in the shadows and jumped, a small figure crying out in fear and pain as she savagely pulled an imp from the darkness and stabbed it with Lady Finger still attached to her tail.

"Thanks, Puss." Muu grinned at her and the massive cat just panted before nodding once.

We fought on.

Demons would come and try to ambush us, and we would kill them as swiftly and efficiently as we could. The rain made it a lot harder on them, their bodies sizzling as we came upon them. They stood and were brutally knocked down and aside. So many times I would pick one up and toss them over to Muu and Jaken to be impaled and cut in half then move on.

We had finally become the well-oiled killing machines the gods had wanted us to be. Had tipped the scales in our favor to be.

We were damn near unstoppable.

We continued fighting and murdering demons for more than half an hour before finally reaching the castle, and I was suddenly so glad that I hadn't just teleported us in.

The walls had broken apart, stones floating and slowly swirling in some kind of purple vortex that sucked the light into it, the rain not even getting to it.

Inside on the same podium stood Belltree, her eyes pure white as she smiled at us. She looked haggard and worn, exhausted even, but still she stood with her hands raised. A small figure that I recognized as Tarron Dillingsley was tied up in the corner of the room. But he was no longer the guy in command.

"Twenty gold says that's not a good fucking sign," Balmur spat vehemently. "We need to interrupt whatever that is."

"Yeah, but where are her guards?" Jaken looked around, his head swiveling slowly.

"Don't worry about them, let's get her!" I snarled and started forward as a massive impact threw all of us back.

"Now who brings the shitty consequences?" Muu groaned as we all stood back up twenty feet away, a massive demonic being draped from head to toe in black and red armor that reminded me of Melvaren holding a glaive out at the ready with a shield in its left hand.

"Oh, that thing is fucking huge," Bokaj whispered more to himself than the rest of us, Tmont yowling in agreement.

Jaken's wings burst from his back and his halo returned in full force, his voice taking on an almost-androgynous tone. "She's summoning War to this world, you must stop her now! He's slipping through, and we have other forces now turning toward us that we have to fend off. Hurry!"

"Radiance?" My gaze flicked to him, her voice coming from his body threw me off, but that meant we had to get in there and had little to no time to fuck with this guy.

"You all heard the boss, let's go," Jaken whispered as he returned to himself and brandished his sword.

Demons poured from portals that opened around us, Hubris surprising me. *That is the same demon guardian that protected her last time. It is much stronger now and can summon others. You must kill it or get it away from her.*

"We have to kill that one!" I shouted as I cast Falfyre and brought it to my hand. "Let's go, now!"

Muu, Jaken, and James launched themselves forward. Jaken on the main baddy with the armor and the other two at the portals to attempt stemming the tide of infernal bodies as Bokaj started to play rapidly.

Balmur, Yohsuke, and I stood in the rear and started blasting with minor spells, but my focus was getting to that bitch. I whispered to Hubris, "See that this spell reaches her, okay?"

I felt the mental nod from the scepter and sent Falfyre shooting forward straight at the giant demon in front of Jaken. It sliced at the creature's leg, then spun and careened toward Belltree in the back where the spell disappeared, my connection to it shot.

"Ah-ah!" She grinned at me evilly as she wagged a finger. "My lord comes and I am to greet him myself. No one must interfere."

Fuck, I turned my mind back to the fight and sighed as I noticed the armored demon healing as the other demons began to fall near it.

"Yoh, get in my collar real fast, I'm using a holy spell I have stored." I called out to the others as he filtered into it, "Get behind Jaken, now!"

The others rushed forward as I used the stored spell in the ring I had made for this raid to cast Solar Flare at the armored demon and his growing horde.

The burst of holy flames seared the air around us, burning the flesh of the demons it touched and melted the armor of the larger brute, making it scream, "Graaahhhh!"

I sucked it up and held my hand out, casting the same spell again as I grabbed Balmur. "Can you use Gate to get us in there with her?"

"I think so." His panicked breathing quickened as he glanced around Jaken's shield. "Yeah, yeah, give me a second."

He paced through the motions of the spell, the words falling from his lips swiftly but well-practiced and the spell opened ten feet behind us.

I grabbed Jaken and the others and started to haul them toward it, their steps uncertain until they saw it, then we broke into a run. Balmur was right beside me, but stopped as something cruelly-barbed burst from his chest. His head mechanically tilted down to look at the tip of the glaive piercing through his chest, blood bubbling out of his mouth as his lips moved.

"No!" I could hear the shout in the other room now with Belltree, time slowing down.

Balmur looked up at me with determined resignation in his gaze as he lifted a booted foot and kicked my shoulder, shoving me into the Gate before it closed.

His resignation gave way to a cruel smile as he opened his spellbook and touched his bloodied hand to the runes on the last page. His gaze softened as he mouthed, *Sorry, guys.* An arcane storm of green and red burst from him and time sped up again.

I flew through the Gate and watched in horror with my friends as Balmur and the beastly demon vanished in a spray of gore and magic, leaving little more than a crater behind where they had been.

"Damn," Belltree muttered intensely, but turned to eye us as the portals summoning the demons closed. "Seems there won't be the retinue I had hoped for when my master arrives, so I shall have to settle for delivering your heads to him."

The general pulled a sword from the ether around her and stepped toward us with it raised. She barely lifted her foot for a second step when arrows rained down on her head, the blade weaving in and out as she fought desperately to keep from being shot, but that wasn't all.

Yohsuke and James shot forward, screaming wordlessly, both firing off spells and ki like madmen. Some attacks hit her and made her falter, letting an arrow in to hit her shoulder. Others simply bounced away from her off some kind of force field or barrier.

Tears stung my eyes as I found myself stepping forward, casting Aspect of the Beast.

My fur formed scales and my back ached as wings burst from it. Cieth's mind melded with mine, Kayda and Bea fighting nearby paused as they felt his presence. *We fight!*

They drew near us, their visions and sensations shut down as the wyvern tugged them closer.

I was stronger and faster now; pulling Kraxen out and

bellowing a challenge at the bitch, I heaved it as hard as I could at her. A tentacle wrapped around my wrist from the haft as the weapon flew from my grasp, blade whirling and closing on her.

She grabbed it and I grinned as I cast Hollow Step and came out of her shadow, grasping the weapon against her body as my brothers beat their vengeance into her flesh.

Her health squalered and fell below half just before the void-like astral swirls darkened immensely. She grinned, mouth bloody and spat at us, "My time here is done, War is nigh!"

Electricity surged from the darkness in the room and struck her body, flinging us away violently, closing the small area off with more astral clouding as Bea and Kayda turned the corner to get to us.

We were on our own here, and weakened as we were, we had no choice but to get back up.

Bokaj still seethed, his rage almost getting the best of him, Jaken's golden energy hitting all of us except for Yoh, who pulled a vial of blood from his inventory and downed it. His HP replenished a bit and seemed to be regenerating faster as he climbed to his feet.

I got to my own feet shakily, trying to look for Belltree or the gnomish pain in our ass, but instead we found a short, squat figure that reminded me of a dwarf. His skin was plain, but slightly wrinkled all over with a bald head. Odd looking eyes, that seemed misshapen for his face.

"Was anyone else expecting like a certain big, purple guy from the movies?" Muu grunted as he stood and limped forward. "Because I am woefully underwhelmed by whatever this is."

A deep voice rolled through my mind. "Leave it to mortals to make short jokes."

"Leave it to whatever you are to be short," Muu retorted and crossed his arms. "What are you, another general?"

The being turned to look at us, the same voice speaking, "No. I am War. I am timeless and all consuming. I am inevitable and I am right. I am justice." He looked down and scowled at his hands, shrunken and malformed like the rest of him. "It seems that she was not able to fully pierce the veil and distract them for my whole self to come through. No matter."

"Well, you look like the K-Mart Thanos, ball-sack lookin' ass." James wipes some blood from his chin and glanced at us. "We gonna fuck this guy up or not?"

"He looks fucked up already, like is he squinting or are his eyes just too small? Did she fuck up the summoning or what?" Yohsuke sneered, his wink making me think for a moment. Then it dawned on me—they were stalling so our mana would recover. "Out here with a fucked up body claiming, 'I am justice.' This fool looks like a dum—"

Thunder cracked and the man suddenly stood in front of us with an arrow grasped between his fingers, glaring at each of us. "I find it vexing that none of my generals could finish you. So I will do so myself, even in this weakened state. Then I will come for your planet."

"Your mother," I snarled and punched him straight in the face with my metallic fist as I cast Winter's Blade straight at his chin. The ice broke as soon as it hit his face and a small chunk of his health fell away.

"He bleeds!" The words were no sooner out of my mouth than Cieth yanked control away from me and leaned back, wind whipping close to my cheek as he lashed back out.

Arrows snapped from Bokaj's bow toward him and War just slapped them out of the air like they flew through molasses. Tmont leapt onto his back and raked him with her claws just before a spear slammed into his stomach, barely penetrating, but Muu's abilities continued to prick at him. His spear thrust and stabbed a hundred times before he went to thrust one last time and disappeared as the bastard tried to punch him.

This attack had more power and created a vacuum of sorts as it soared by. Muu appeared next to me and stabbed with both hands before taking out his hammer and clobbering War in the back of the head, just missing Tmont as she scrabbled over his shoulder and out of his reach.

"Coal!" I roared and something within me broke as a massive black and red wolf the size of a truck fell on War. Coal grabbed his arm and lifted him, throwing the lumpy figure away from us.

War collided with the wall and looked like he had felt little of that, his scowl turning to joy as he crossed the distance between him and the massive wolf. "Coal, no!"

The wolf collided with him and the two fought as we tried to get close, but War lifted him and threw him like he was a puppy. Coal flew and hit the wall, a snapping sound making me lose my damned mind.

"Motherfucker!" I lunged forward and slammed my metal fist into his face and made it a blade before it nicked his skin slightly.

The being's health fell again, his arm whipping back and his elbow closing in on us as I ducked, taking Muu with me and kicking away from him.

I used my magic, creating chains of pure shadow that grasped at his ankles but War didn't seem to care. Content to try to swat the nuisances that we were, his hands remained open and he tried again to slap one of us.

Shadows grasped at his fist just as Jaken rushed him with his shield held out, slamming into his head where a burst of holy fire boiled over War.

His health bar continued to drop slowly, point by precious point as each of us did our best.

Yohsuke and James harried him from his flanks and rear, the astral blade doing slightly more damage than the more physical attacks from Jaken and Muu.

"Must you fight so fruitlessly against the end?" War sighed and elbowed Jaken in his shield and sent the paladin flying into whatever weird wall was there. His health plummeted to less than half and I hit him with Heal and Void's Respite to get him back on his feet.

"Magic hurts him most!" Muu grunted and grabbed his hammer in both hands. "I hate that I can't do more for this."

"You dying would be plenty, or joining me," War offered, his hands raised as if in offer. "I could use talented people like yourself to join me in my conquest."

"Bitch, please. You couldn't afford me." Muu rolled his eyes and bounded forward to attack, catching a fist directly in his stomach for it.

The attack made him cough up blood, his health falling dangerously despite his high Constitution and defense. His ring healed him for a bit but his main healing came from Jaken.

Tmont hopped in front of an attack that was meant for Bokaj, flying away and into a wall painfully to lay there wheezing. Bokaj screamed, "T!"

He yelled as loudly as he could and fired elemental arrows at War, the spells having some minute effects but little else.

I put Kraxen away and pulled out Hubris and Magus Bane. *Hubris, we need to end this quickly if we can. Any ideas?*

I dodged an attack thanks to Cieth's agile mental reflexes and skittered to the side.

This room is eighty feet by ninety-five feet long, and in another plane of existence shut off from the world of Brindolla, but not.

I cast a Lightning Bolt at him and the electricity only minutely affected him, chasing my friends around. *Okay, and?*

If you can make a sort of dimensional bomb, you could open a rift and get us all back onto Brindolla.

What's the worst case? I ducked another blow and skittered away.

You would explode the space and all of you would be sucked into an unknown void, dying slowly due to asphyxiation and doomed to float for eternity?

"Oh, that doesn't seem so bad." I rolled my eyes and slammed the bladed portion of Magus Bane into War's foot, some of my mana recovering. "How we gonna do it?"

Take your Bagged Avarice and throw it at the wall closest to him.

I didn't hesitate as he had just become cornered in the far side of the room, likely trying to keep us all in front of him.

"Pie!" I bellowed and rushed forward, the others recognizing my favorite safe word and backing away swiftly, Yohsuke falling over James trying to get clear.

I took out the bag and threw it between his legs and struck the back wall, a deafening crash like hundreds of windows shattering splintering my sensitive ears as the corner of the room cascaded away and the void sucked him out. I fell after him and landed twenty feet below on solid ground with him groaning nearby on his back.

"They're here!" a familiar voice called out and I glanced up in time to see Nick sprinting toward us with the rest of the Braves in tow.

The other members of Storm Company gathered behind me, someone bodily lifting me off the ground and putting me onto my feet.

Maebe, Vrawn, Kayda, and Bea came close to us, staring hard at War as he tried to stand but began to look ill. I saw some of the demons skulking in the area, but they looked ravaged and broken.

"Is that who I think it could be?" Maebe whispered to me and I nodded, her eyes widening.

Yohsuke snarled loudly, "He's weakened, guys—hit him with every spell you got!"

"No!" War snapped back, rising to a knee. "I will not fall here! My ambition is too great!"

He lifted his hands skyward and the clouds darkened once more, lightning crackling above us before streaking down to the ground. Kayda and I both reached out for it, the electricity becoming hers more than mine, her ice magic melding with it before she sent it careening into him. Fire and arrows rained down on him, ki blasts and blades sliced and slammed as ice and shadow began to carve into the malformed creature's body, pain and rage consuming him as we fought with all of our hatred and remorse for having lost one of ours.

All the turmoil and suffering we had endured because of War's careless crusade against the universes and galaxies of countless other worlds had dared come here.

He came here to end it, and ended up being the one conquered.

His body started to disintegrate as he seethed, "I am not done. I will return to take you all!"

He reached up and crashed his fist down toward the ground before Jaken and Muu stood together before the blow, Jaken's nearly-ruined shield held out with Muu assisting him in bracing it. The blow shattered the shield but they held firm, Yohsuke braving the contact with Jaken long enough to use the Shield Bracelet I had made for him to block the blow.

James flitted closer and flung the vampire bodily away as arrows pierced the slowly failing form of War.

"Come back, and we'll bite your ass again!" I called back, sending Falfyre into his chest and willing the blade to burn as hot as it could go.

His body burned, the hatred on his half-gone face as clear as the sun in the sky. When he was gone, I could feel again.

It was over. It was finally over. But at what cost?

Balmur was gone.

We had failed him, and we had no way of knowing what was going to happen.

Jaken stood in the middle of the crater and raised his hands, his body glowing golden for a heartbeat before he turned and a rent opened in the air.

Rather than an angel, or a being made of pure light, a frail, tired-looking woman stepped through. Her smile was pure, graying hair cascading down her shoulder over the platinum armor she wore that was dinged up and slightly bloody in places.

As soon as Jaken saw her, he fell to his knees before her. "Lady Radiance."

All of the mortals within earshot fell to their knees, Maebe standing close to me and the others with her eyes glued to the other woman.

"My faithful servant, rise, for your duty is fulfilled." She turned her attention to the rest of the people in the area, her gaze stopping at each of us. "It is time for you to return to your little moon, Paladin Jaken."

She turned to look at us all. "We had our moments there. When he slipped through in part due to your gods trying to find you, we worried that he would be too much for us. Not for all of you though. Thank you Jaken, Bokaj, Yohsuke, James, Muu, and Zeke. Your sacrifices, blood, sweat and tears were worth it. You've saved this planet."

"What about Balmur?" Bokaj whispered as he stepped forward, the loss of his best friend once again tearing at his heart. "Where's Balmur? Is he okay?"

"He will think this nothing more than a dream, but he will awaken at home in his bed thanks to your efforts here." Bokaj fell to his knees with a massive sigh of relief, his tears shed unabashed. "I wish that I could offer you all more, but I fear that my power wanes and I must send you all home before your gods decide to come and take you by force."

"What?" I looked at her as if she were crazy. "Our gods?"

"Many of them, yes, and all of them much angrier than we." Radiance smiled sadly. "I can allow you a few moments more, but that is it."

"Wait, I can't stay?" Muu rushed forward to get her attention. "I love it here. I would happily stay here for the rest of my life; gods be damned."

"We are not powerful enough to stop them from taking you back, Muu." Radiance touched his face and his shoulders slumped slowly. "Please, as grateful as I am, I cannot risk that fight. None of us can."

He nodded wordlessly and turned to walk back toward us. Two sets of hands touched my shoulders as I watched, Maebe and Vrawn pulling me back to my own predicament.

I shifted into my human form, Vrawn kissing me once, then hugging me. "I love you, Zeke."

"I love you too, Vrawn." I touched her cheek and wiped away a tear as it fell.

Maebe floated up, levitating so that she could meet me eye to eye before muttering, "I will see you again, my love."

Her word notification surprised me, but there wasn't time to ask her what she meant.

"I love you, Queen Maebe." She kissed me twice and pulled my hands to her stomach, then Vrawn's. "Tell my children I love them, and that they should grow to be as strong as their mothers."

I could tell there was so much more they wanted to say; there was more I wanted to say and I knew there was little time. I took out my inventory and gave it all over to Maebe. "Give our children what you think is best suited to them as a gift from their father. Please love each other and take care of each other, and do not fall to the Seelie."

"We will see to them, and they will rue the day they *ever* threatened our family," Maebe swore, another notification making me blink. I smiled, comforted but still distressed that I couldn't help them.

I turned to Kayda and Bea, both of them having been connected to me the entire time I was saying goodbye to the girls, came close to me.

Kayda leaned down and touched her head to mine. *I love you, Father. I will miss you terribly.*

I'll miss you too, you big crazy bird. I hugged her massive head and kissed her beak. *You take care of Maebe, Vrawn, and Bea okay?*

I will take care of her. Bea stared at me as she clacked closer to me. *We didn't get to fight much, but I hope to fight with you again, Father. Live well. I will watch over them all.*

She licked my entire face, making me laugh as I choked up a bit. *Thanks, baby. I love you too.*

"Look after them?" Maebe and Vrawn nodded, holding each other as I backed away, stepping closer to my friends,

Radiance holding out her hands as a wild wind danced around us. "I'll come back to you somehow. No matter how it happens, I'll make it work. You'll see."

There was a slight pause as the others began to crowd closer to our position. Both Maebe and Vrawn nodded as tears fell down their faces and I sighed, knowing I was the cause once more.

"Y'all take care, hear?" Manly called out loudly, the other Braves waving. Thogan and Rowland sprinted closer as Vilmas brought up the rear, wordlessly crying out as a vortex surrounded us.

I looked at each of the friends that we had made in this whole wide wild world and my heart broke because despite the victory we shared, it seemed we were losing.

The wind whirled faster and enveloped us all. I couldn't see them, but I could feel their proximity. "Thank you all for coming here and being a part of all this. I don't know where I would have been without any of you."

Jaken clapped me on the shoulder, calling, "Wouldn't dream of being anywhere else, brother."

———

My breathing changing woke me from the soundest sleep I'd probably had in years, sunlight filtering into my room around the thick blanket I used to keep the sun out. I stumbled out of my room into the small hallway to the closet and the bathroom and into the living room on my left.

I blinked around blearily at everything. Deciding to turn my console on, I hopped online and saw that some of my friends were in a party chat. I plugged in my headset and groggily asked, "Did you all have a weird dream too?"

"Yeah, man," Evan grunted. "Yeah, it was really weird. That's the last time I play before bed for a minute."

"Mine was fun," Jake chimed in chipperly. "Luna seems like she's in a good mood today too."

I found myself smiling, at least the kid was happy, right? Speaking of. "I'll see you guys later—I'm going to see my son."

I logged off, got dressed, suddenly much more comfortable in the dark than I had ever been in my life, and shoved myself out the door to see my kiddo. It was time for us to spend some time together.

EPILOGUE

Shadows ebbed and flowed in the room like tidal waves as her breathing quickened and calmed. The queen focused herself on her breathing as the midwife bid her to, but the pain was almost as unbearable as losing her husband to the gods.

"My love, you're thinking of it again." Vrawn's achingly cool voice caressed her shot nerves and eased her mind. Her large hand found the queen's and Maebe's heart beat slower already even as another painful contraction came.

The door to the room opened and the ancient brownie stomped in whistling a tune, the melody almost in time for Maebe's contractions now.

"Why are you here, Brogden?" Maebe's voice sounded more like a hiss than her normal tone.

"I am here to see that you deliver safely, among other things that you needn't worry yourself over, Majesty." His grin too wide for his face, another bout of pain cramped Maebe's innards.

Vrawn's gentle squeeze became a slowly growing pressure as she grunted and looked at her lover in shock. She wasn't supposed to be due for another month.

"Fetch another bed, midwife!" Brogden chuckled and snapped his fingers as the elven woman sprinted from the room.

Power built in waves as the brownie worked his magic, lulling both the women into an almost-comforted state when the midwife returned with servants carrying a bed that they set up next to the queen's.

More power thrummed through the room, for hours the brownie whistled his lullaby-like tune and the time for birthing came.

Gritting their teeth, both women began to push for everything they were worth, their cries echoing through the halls of the pristine glacial palace of the Unseelie. The flames of the torches in the room guttered and the icy walls glistened before the flames failed entirely.

A heartbeat later they returned, but with them stood seven figures, one of fire, water, wind, earth, darkness, light, and lightning.

"What are they doing here?" Vrawn roared, trying to stand as Brogden waved a hand and her blanket wrapped around her chest to hold her down.

The flame answered, "We have come to witness the birth of your child, respect to be paid to those who have given everything to see that we return to the world and that magic is safe."

The water stepped forward. "That *we* are safe."

The other elementals agreed with nods, though the water and darkness stepped close to stand over Maebe, the shadows whispering, "Hello, beloved."

Maebe tried to smile, but the movement was disturbed by discomfort that twisted her greeting into a howl of pain.

Moments later, two screaming babes lay in their mothers' arms, tears of bitter joy falling from their eyes.

"My queen, what will the prince's name be?" Brogden asked softly. His beady eyes watching her as all the Unseelie in the room would.

"His name will be Azlo, until he ascends the throne." Her announcement meant that every breath in the room could be released, the fear of not hearing her decree gone. She turned to Vrawn. "And what of your daughter, the princess?"

Vrawn looked surprised but then shrugged. "I had so many names that I had thought of to ask Zeke, but I never had the chance to. I guess I'll just have to do it on my own."

"He liked the name Nadïr," Maebe offered softly, her hand reaching for the other woman's.

"Nadïr?" She smiled down at the bundle in her arms. "I like that. I will call her Nadïr."

"And when Nadïr is five, she will be my apprentice." Brogden cackled delightedly as the shadows in the room deepened.

"You will *not* have the princess or the prince!" Maebe roared.

"It is what I am *owed*, your majesty," Brogden corrected, pulling the contract onto a screen for her to look at. "I saved your life in exchange for any apprentice I choose. I choose her. She will be stronger than I ever could have been."

Maebe tilted her head back, her eyes closed. Zeke could not have known what he was doing and that was her fault. But like him, she had foolishly assumed that the child would be one of the humans to have been brought over, or the new births to take place since their arrival.

For the ten-thousandth time since they had returned to their own planet, Maebe looked to the sky above her and wondered if her stars were the same as his.

"We will meet again, my love," she whispered to the void. "We *will* be a family."

Her gaze fell to her son and took in his beautiful blue eyes, like his father's. Azlo. Her smile widened as she wondered what it would be like for him to grow under her reign. It would be hard, but he would likely be a wonderful ruler.

She would be sure that these children were the best. She kissed Vrawn softly as she held the other woman and contemplated how his schooling would begin.

There was nothing to keep them from becoming who they would, and they would hear tell of their father's glories, and triumphs.

And so she began, "It all started with a whisper on the wind, someone calling my name…"

AUTHOR'S NOTE

Hey guys, thank you all for being here for this amazing journey, and what a trip it has been. Thank you for loving these characters as I have, and as I continue to do.

Though it seems that Storm Company's time in Brindolla has come to an end, there are still many adventures to come. And with the birth of a new generation comes new problems.

I hope that all of you will be as excited as I am to begin the walk once more with two new characters, my children Azlo and Nadïr as they find their way in life, however that may go.

Thank you, and we love you. From all of us on Brindolla, you are loved, you are welcome.

You are family.

Zeke.

———

Wow. Thank all of you who made it so far into this series. Thank you for being here for the rises and falls. The triumphs, the hardships, and all the craziness.

Most of all—thank you for caring.

To those of you who may or may not know, our beloved paladin fell before this series was ever even more than a half-baked dream from a guy who just missed his friends. And this was always my way of trying to keep him around. As you likely know, the people who knew him, miss him terribly. And now that you know him, I'm sure you do too.

I know. It sucks. But with this, it's my sincerest hope that he can be remembered, and that the people who meet him will be as pleased by him as we always were.

Jake, buddy, we miss you.

To those of you still reeling from that ending, I want to be the first to let you know that this is far from the end.

There will be much more for this world to come in the near future, and I am so excited to share with you the new characters of the next story, siblings Azlo and Nadïr. What their lives will be like is still very much up in the air, but I cannot wait to explore their tale.

But that isn't all that it is, and don't count Zeke out of the fight just yet, because he ain't one to give up, and he's going to get back to his family somehow.

Thank you again, and with all my heart—I cannot wait for you all to join me again in Brindolla.

Lovingly,

Chris.

ABOUT CHRISTOPHER JOHNS

Christopher Johns is a former photojournalist for the United States Marine Corps with published works telling hundreds of other peoples' stories through word, photo, and even video.

But throughout that time, his editors and superiors had always said that his love of reading fantasy and about worlds of fantastic beauty and horrible power bled into his work. That meant he should write a book.

Well, ta-da!

Chris has been an avid devourer of fantasy and science fiction for more than twenty years and looks forward to sharing that love with his son, his loving fiancée and almost anyone he could ever hope to meet.

Connect with Chris:
Twitter.com/jonsyjohns
Facebook.com/AxeDruidAuthor
Patreon.com/StormCompanyandBeyond

ABOUT MOUNTAINDALE PRESS

Dakota and Danielle Krout, a husband and wife team, strive to create as well as publish excellent fantasy and science fiction novels. Self-publishing *The Divine Dungeon: Dungeon Born* in 2016 transformed their careers from Dakota's military and programming background and Danielle's Ph.D. in pharmacology to President and CEO, respectively, of a small press. Their goal is to share their success with other authors and provide captivating fiction to readers with the purpose of solidifying Mountaindale Press as the place 'Where Fantasy Transforms Reality.'

Connect with Mountaindale Press:
MountaindalePress.com
Facebook.com/MountaindalePress
Twitter.com/_Mountaindale
Instagram.com/MountaindalePress

MOUNTAINDALE PRESS TITLES

GameLit and LitRPG

The Completionist Chronicles,
The Divine Dungeon, and
Full Murderhobo by Dakota Krout

King's League by Jason Anspach and J.N. Chaney

A Touch of Power by Jay Boyce

Red Mage by Xander Boyce

Space Seasons by Dawn Chapman

Ether Collapse and
Ether Flows by Ryan DeBruyn

Bloodgames by Christian J. Gilliland

Wolfman Warlock by James Hunter and Dakota Krout

Axe Druid and
Mephisto's Magic Online by Christopher Johns

Skeleton in Space by Andries Louws

Chronicles of Ethan by John L. Monk

Pixel Dust by David Petrie

Henchman by Carl Stubblefield

Artorian's Archives by Dennis Vanderkerken and Dakota Krout

APPENDIX

THE GOOD

Zekiel Erebos (Zee-key-uhl Air-uh-bows) – Marine who loves gaming as a civilian with his buddies who are still in. Class: Druid. Race: Kitsune, has a tail. Seven, actually. But who's counting?

Yohsuke (Yo-s'kay) – Zeke's best bud/brother from the Marine Corps. Overlord, yeah, you read that right. Class: Spell blade. Race: Abomination (halfbreed drow and high elf) (Vampire lord to boot, lucky shithead)

Jaken Warmecht (Jay-ken) – Zeke's friend who typically needs help catching up in the games the group plays together. Class: Paladin of Radiance. Race: Fae-Orc. (Guardian there for a while too.)

Bokaj (Bow-ka-jh) – A friend from the gym who loves video games and is in a pretty wicked band! Class: Ranger. Race: Ice Elf.

Tmont (Tee-M-on-t) – A panther with a taste for tails who happens to not just be a walking bag of assholes but is also Bokaj's pet. Mainly that first one, though.

Balmur (Ball-mer) – Bokaj's best friend, and another good buddy of Zeke's who loves to game! Class: Rogue. Race: Azer Dwarf (Fire dwarf) HIS BEARD IS A FLAME!

James Bautista (Really?) – Another Marine that Yohsuke and Zeke know and game with often. Class: Monk. Race: Dragon Elf partially incubated.

Muu Ankiman (Moo Ahn-key-men) – Dragon beast-kin with green scales and Zeke's roommate on Earth. Liiiiittle crazy, but he's okay. Class: Fighter. Race: Dragon-kin (it's shorter!)

Kayda (Kay-duh) – A pretty little bird with a shitty past, and hopefully, a bright future. Recently turned into a Storm Roc. Very protective of a certain flame wolf.

Coal – A flame wolf that Zeke was taking care of for a bit on behalf of the Primordial Flame Elemental. He has a good temperament, a little heated at times, but he's a cool pup.

Sir Willem Dillon – Owner of the tavern in Sunrise Village (the starter town) and Paladin of Radiance. The first guy the group meets and doesn't try to kill. (Or do they? MUAHAHAHA— No, really, do they?) Jaken's trainer.

Dinnia (Dih-nee-uh) – An elven Druid who takes pity on poor Zeke and brings him into Mother Nature's good graces. Zeke's trainer.

Sharo (Shah-row) – Another panther who assists his partner in crime Dinnia in training her student. Not a walking bag of assholes.

Kyra – Queen of the bears and good friend of Dinnia's. We like her.

Marin (Mare-in) – We, uh… we don't talk about her. 10 out of 10, though. Kickass dire bear.

Rowland – Blacksmith in Sunrise, who decides he likes the travelers, especially the one with the tail—no bias.

Maebe (May-buh—soft buh—if she hears you talking shit, I'm not responsible, yeah?) – Unseelie Queen of Winter and Darkness, who somehow gets thrown into the mix. Also, Zeke's girlfriend. I know, right?

Thogan (Tho-gun) – Champion of the Unseelie Fae, and a rather clingy dwarf with a rough complexion.

Titania – Queen of the Seelie Fae, who has a predisposition of being a raging bitch to anyone and everyone she doesn't like. Like outsiders.

Craglim (Crag-limb) – Rowland's cousin. Racist piece of shit—but he's a good fighter.

Zhavron (Zah-vrun) – Orc fighter with a sordid past. Muu's trainer in all things fighting. A little intense at times.

Pharazulla (Far-uh-zu-la) – A bard of some renown, though a bit of a stuck-up asshole.

Vrawn – A lovely orcish woman with a soft spot for our local Druid. She's built like a busty, brick shit house.

Sam – Mayor of Sunrise village. A fair man whose bear-kin wife and half bear-kin children believe in him wholeheartedly. Prefers to hunt for the village rather than govern.

The villagers of Sunrise – Great people who recently went through a lot of bullshit. Go easy on 'em, yeah?

Set – A decent little Fae-orc kid, duped into hunting a Belgar.

Ampharia (Am-far-ee-uh) – An elder green dragon friend of Mother Nature's who comes to Muu with her blessing and teaches him how to fight dragons.

Natholdi, Granite, and son (Nath-ol-dee) – A good, humble dwarven family that both Muu and Zeke love dearly. Newest additions to the Light Hand Clan.

Farnik Mugfist (Far-nick) – Leader of the Mugfist clan and good friend to the party. Loves a good cup of mead and song.

Shellica Light Hand (Shell-ih-cuh) – Leader of the Light Hand Clan and a Grand Master Enchanter. Crazy as shit with a diabolical wit. Zeke's trainer, unfortunately.

Silvannas (Sill-vahn-us) – Queen of the High Elves on the prime plane of existence. Sort of a role model to Maebe.

Questis (Quest-ihs) – A high elf Druid enchanter who has a soft spot for kitties and bait. Pretty awesome guy. Seriously loves cats, though.

Fern (Like the plant) – A sabertooth cat that has a serious god complex. Loves to be fed and worshipped. Gives his Druid Questis hell all the time.

Telfino (Tell-fee-no) – Son of Queen Silvannas, and inheritor of the throne. He's a good kid with a seriously strong class.

Manly Warbottom – A rascal bounty hunter halfling with a weird motley crew of badasses. Good lady, likes money. A lot.

Braves of the Thorn – Manly's peeps and party, consisting of

Dawn, Nick, Nic, Bonnie, and Manly's best buddy Humphrey. Quality people.

Milnolian (Mill-Gnoll-Ian) – Goes by Servant, but he's a loyal servant of Maebe's who she passed to Zeke as a gift.

Eiran'a (Ee-rahn-ah) – Maebe's momma and a highly skilled ice mage. She doesn't really care for the loving protagonist, but hey —beggars and choosers, am I right?

Westwind Royalty – The royal family of Zephyth, good people with a lovely daughter. Aboye (A-boy-Eh), the king, and Chareen (Shareen) his wife.

Villeroa Westwind (Vill-er-oah) – Princess and water mage, with her elemental friend.

Zygnal (Zig-nahl) – Water Elemental assigned to protect and help train Villeroa.

Jafrik (Ya-frick) – A Drow boy chosen by the Primordial Light Elemental to become the first of a new race, the dawn elves.

Greer – A lovely elven Druid who learned how to be a Primal Warrior thanks to training with Zeke.

Kyr – A Kitsune Druid who turned out to be the Lightning Elemental Champion. Go figure, right?

Sendak – A bit of a wet blanket at times, but a very pragmatic Druid.

Orlow'thes (Or-low-thehs) – One of the four guardians of the oceans and the world of Brindolla, this draconic beast of a thing kicked some serious ass and deserves a place in all our hearts.

THE BAD

War – Galactic conqueror who probably suffers from only child syndrome. Probably needs a hug, or he will keep trying to take over the universe.

Minions of War – Not the lovable minions everyone loves. You know, not the yellow ones, or that fish from that one Will Ferrell animated movie. These guys seek to undermine the strength of the gods by eroding the world around them slowly. And serve the other assholes in this list.

The Generals – A number of War's better warriors capable of taking out the strongest people on the planet—and together they did. Dick move.

Rowan – I'm not gonna say much about this guy—read the book, then you'll know what a dickbag he is. Haha, was—sonofabitch is dead now.

Pastella (Pahs-tell-uh) – Crazy elven woman with a taste for torture and violence.

Tarron Dillingsley (Tair-run Dill-night-slee) – Gnomish enchanter who—let's face it shall we?—sucks as a teacher for various reasons and lest we forget, the asshole in charge of the Children of Brindolla.

Children of Brindolla – A group of misguided citizens who believe they are the only ones who can truly save their world. They found themselves on the receiving end of an ass-kicking—but was that all of them?

Decay – A greater Fiend who held his own against the party and Maebe. Fell due to a brilliant plan and a little bit of finesse.

Okay, the plan was half-cocked, and the finesse resulted in some bullshit—happy now?

Spiders – Just a bunch of overgrown pests that needed an ass-kicking. Nightmare fuel FOREVER.

Lothir (Low-theer) – Big ol' wannabe snake goddess who has a village of elves, orcs, and Fae-orcs under her command and demands sacrifices to restore and keep her beauty. All of that means that she's cuckoo for Cocoa Puffs.

Melvaren (Mel-vah-ren) – General who took claim over Balmur and tortured him in the Hells for his entire tenure there. We killed the shit out of him. But not before he whipped our asses. Still dead though.

Archemillian (Ark-em-illion) – The demon who Yohsuke summoned and gets his warlock powers from. Has a huge hard-on for souls, but he helped us this once. Didn't mean he was a fucking good guy, though.

Riktolth (Rick-talth) – The great black dragon who killed a mother red in a bid to die in combat. Yeah, you guessed it. We kicked his ass.

Governess Belltree – The lady leader of Lindyberg with a serious distaste for magic. Like genocide level crazy.

Lilith – Drow queen and crazy manipulative, also a spider lady —creepy as hell.

Vampire Lord – Vampires, right? Yeah, she was on some serious minion shit, but had beef with her sister that saw her die.

Xaenth (Shane-th) – Drow guide and a general dickhead.

Irgdarn (Earg-darn) – A massive asshat that we didn't even get to meet.

Jinx – Giant pink sloth that killed a friend of ours, so he had to die badly.

Crimson – A big ass birdie with a lot of anger issues.
Belltree General – You know, we never even got to know her real name.

War – This poor schmuck got *roasted*, and then you know. You read the book.

AND THE UGLY

Insane Wolves – Think crazy wolves, but you know, crazier and angrier for some reason. Due to proximity to a minion of War, the minds of these animals have eroded to nothing but the drive to kill and eat anything that is not them, or another wolf.

Undead creatures – As you can imagine, due to proximity to a minion of War, these poor bastards rose from the dead in order to protect their alien masters. Even the stronger versions are worthy of a small bit of sympathy—they sure as hell didn't get any, but they were worthy of it.

Bone Dragon – I mean, pretty self-explanatory, right? It's a bone dragon! No skin, no muscle—all bleached bones and hate for the living.

General of War (Blight) – The asshole who did some truly terrible things, sent us on a supposedly one-way trip to the Fae Realm, and got his ASS kicked. Yeah. That guy.

Ursolon – Think of a giant, striped bear with an anger management issue the size of North Dakota. Yeah. Now go fight one.

Werewolves – The heroes in some tales—but not this one. Oh no. These guys suck, big time! Hairy, needy pieces of crap.

Alpha Werewolf – The jerk in charge of the other jerks above. Bigger, badder, stronger, and usually way more cunning and ruthless.

The Wild Hunt – A flock of assholes (read: demons) who patrol the realm of the Fae and take out anything they believe doesn't belong there.

Order of the Prime – A bunch of human wizards bent on controlling the elements and restoring mankind to their rightful place as rulers. Some real xenophobic asshats, these ones.

Spiders – Oh, I mentioned these already? Because there were a lot of them. With fangs. And all the feet. Seriously, I need to book an appointment for therapy now.

Belgar – A rhino-like Fae creature with a surprising sense of honor and code that it lives by. Big as shit, and it will run anyone in its way through.

Dofilnarr (Dough-fill-nar) – A Fae creature thought to have been hunted to extinction that takes the forms and abilities of creatures it touches while in its base state. Highly vulnerable to Fae Iron.

Vampire bats – Ugly bastards that looked like man-bats that did a number on the party.

Hulking vampires – Vampires on steroids that would make Dr. Banner feel normal.

Dungeon baddies – Doing what they were designed to do, right?

And other random jerks too unimportant for now to mention— they know who they are. Bunch of assholes.

Made in the USA
Columbia, SC
23 December 2020